EVEN MONEY

Dick Francis has written forty-two novels, a volume of short stories (*Field of 13*), his autobiography (*The Sport of Queens*) and the biography of Lester Piggott. He is rightly acclaimed as one of the greatest thriller writers in the world.

He has received many awards, amongst them the prestigious Crime Writers' Association's Cartier Diamond Dagger for his outstanding contribution to the genre. The Mystery Writers of America have given him three Edgar Allen Poe awards for best novel of the year, and in 1996 made him a Grand Master for a lifetime's achievement. He was awarded a CBE in the Queen's Birthday Honours List in 2000.

Felix Francis is the younger of Dick's two sons. Having spent seventeen years teaching A-level Physics, he took on the role of managing his father's affairs in 1991. Over the last forty years, Felix has assisted with the research of many of the Dick Francis novels, not least *Twice Shy*, which drew on Felix's experiences both as a Physics teacher and a marksman, *Shattered* and *Under Orders*. With the publication of *Dead Heat* Felix took on a more significant role in the writing, which has continued brilliantly with the top ten bestseller *Silks* – *Even Money* is the third novel of this father-and-son collaboration.

EVEN MONEY

DICK FRANCIS

and

FELIX FRANCIS

MICHAEL JOSEPH
an imprint of
PENGUIN BOOKS

MICHAEL JOSEPH

Published by the Penguin Group

Penguin Books Ltd, 80 Strand, London WC2R ORL, England

Penguin Group (USA) Inc., 375 Hudson Street, New York, New York 10014, USA

Penguin Group (Canada), 90 Eglinton Avenue East, Suite 700, Toronto, Ontario, Canada M4P 2Y3
(a division of Pearson Penguin Canada Inc.)

Penguin Ireland, 25 St Stephen's Green, Dublin 2, Ireland (a division of Penguin Books Ltd)

Penguin Group (Australia), 250 Camberwell Road, Camberwell, Victoria 3124, Australia
(a division of Pearson Australia Group Pty Ltd)

Penguin Books India Pvt Ltd, 11 Community Centre, Panchsheel Park, New Delhi – 110 017, India

Penguin Group (NZ), 67 Apollo Drive, Rosedale, North Shore 0632, New Zealand
(a division of Pearson New Zealand Ltd)

Penguin Books (South Africa) (Pty) Ltd, 24 Sturdee Avenue,
Rosebank, Johannesburg 2196, South Africa

Penguin Books Ltd, Registered Offices: 80 Strand, London WC2R ORL, England

www.penguin.com

First published 2009

1

Set in 11.5/16 pt PostScript Adobe Sabon
Typeset by Rowland Phototypesetting Ltd, Bury St Edmunds, Suffolk
Printed in Great Britain by Clays Ltd, St Ives plc

A CIP catalogue record for this book is available from the British Library

ISBN: 978-0-718-15472-1

www.greenpenguin.co.uk

For our grandsons and sons

MATTHEW
on his marriage to Anna

and

WILLIAM
on passing out from
The Royal Military Academy, Sandhurst

so proud of them both

with thanks to

NICK BENNETT
bookmaker's assistant

MALCOLM PALMER
Coral Bookmakers

and

The Hanging Rock Racing Club
Victoria, Australia

Bookmaker's odds as used on British racecourses

	Odds	Fractional odds	Winnings to £1 stake	
	one hundred-to-one	100/1	£100.00	very long
	fifty-to-one	50/1	£50.00	
	thirty-three-to-one	33/1	£33.00	
	twenty-to-one	20/1	£20.00	long
	fifteen-to-one	15/1	£15.00	(high price)
	twelve-to-one	12/1	£12.00	
	ten-to-one	10/1	£10.00	
	nine-to-one	9/1	£9.00	
	seventeen-to-two	17/2	£8.50	
	eight-to-one	8/1	£8.00	
Odds	fifteen-to-two	15/2	£7.50	
	seven-to-one	7/1	£7.00	
	thirteen-to-two	13/2	£6.50	
against	six-to-one	6/1	£6.00	
	eleven-to-two	11/2	£5.50	
	five-to-one	5/1	£5.00	
	nine-to-two	9/2	£4.50	medium
	four-to-one	4/1	£4.00	
	seven-to-two	7/2	£3.50	
	one hundred-to-thirty	100/30	£3.33	
	three-to-one	3/1	£3.00	
	eleven-to-four	11/4	£2.75	
	five-to-two	5/2	£2.50	
	nine-to-four	9/4	£2.25	

Odds	Fractional odds	Winnings to £1 stake	
eighty-five-to-forty	85/40	£2.12	
two-to-one	2/1	£2.00	
fifteen-to-eight	15/8	£1.88	
Odds seven-to-four	7/4	£1.75	
thirteen-to-eight	13/8	£1.63	
against six-to-four	6/4	£1.50	
eleven-to-eight	11/8	£1.38	short
five-to-four	5/4	£1.25	(low price)
six-to-five	6/5	£1.20	
eleven-to-ten	11/10	£1.10	
EVEN MONEY	1/1	£1.00	
eleven-to-ten on	10/11	£0.91	
six-to-five on	5/6	£0.83	
five-to-four on	4/5	£0.80	
eleven-to-eight on	8/11	£0.73	
six-to-four on	4/6	£0.67	**very short**
thirteen-to-eight on	8/13	£0.62	
Odds seven-to-four on	4/7	£0.57	
fifteen-to-eight on	8/15	£0.53	
on two-to-one on	1/2	£0.50	
nine-to-four on	4/9	£0.44	
five-to-two on	2/5	£0.40	
three-to-one on	1/3	£0.33	**very, very short**
four-to-one on	1/4	£0.25	
five-to-one on	1/5	£0.20	
ten-to-one on	1/10	£0.10	**ultra short**

CHAPTER 1

I sank deeper into depression as the Royal Ascot crowd enthusi-astically cheered home another short-priced winning favourite. To be fair, it wasn't clinical depression – I knew all about that – but it was pretty demoralizing, just the same.

I asked myself yet again what I was doing here. I had never really enjoyed coming to Ascot, especially for these five days in June. It was usually much too hot to be wearing morning dress, or else it rained, and I would get soaked. I preferred the informality of my usual haunts, the smaller steeplechase tracks of the Midlands. But my grandfather, who had started the family business, had always used the fact that we stood at the Royal meeting as one of our major marketing tools. He claimed that it gave us some form of respectability, something he had always craved.

We were bookmakers. Pariahs of the racing world. Disliked by all, and positively hated by many, including large numbers of those whose very livelihood depended on gambling. I had discovered over the years that my clients were never my friends. Whereas city investors might develop a close relationship with their stockbrokers, punters never wanted to be seen socializing with their bookies. Most of my regulars didn't even know my name, nor did they want to. I suppose that was fair. I didn't know most of their names either. We were simply participants in transactions where each of us was trying to bankrupt the other. I suppose it was a situation not really likely to engender mutual respect.

'Score on seven,' said a tall top-hatted young man thrusting a banknote towards me. I glanced up at our board to check the odds we were offering on horse number seven.

'Twenty pounds on number seven at eleven-to-two,' I said, taking his note and adding it to the wad of others in my left hand.

A small printer in front of me whirred and disgorged a ticket that I handed to the man. He snatched it from me and moved quickly away into the throng as if he didn't want to be seen fraternizing with the enemy. His place in front of me was taken by a short portly gentleman whose multicoloured waistcoat was fighting a losing battle against his expansive stomach. He was one of my regular Royal Ascot customers. I knew him only as AJ, but I had no idea what the AJ stood for.

'Hundred on Silverstone to win,' he wheezed at me, holding out some folded twenty-pound notes in his chubby fingers.

'Hundred on two at even money,' I said taking his cash and checking the amount. Another betting slip appeared out of the small printer as if by magic and I passed it over. 'Good luck, AJ,' I said to him, not really meaning it.

'Huh?' he said, somewhat surprised by my comment.

'Good luck,' I repeated.

'Thanks,' he wheezed, and departed.

In the good old days, when bookmaking was an art rather than a science, every transaction was written down in 'the book' by an assistant. Nowadays, as in most things, it was on a computer that everything was recorded. The same computer that printed the betting slips.

It kept a running tally of all the bets that we had taken, and also constantly updated our profit or liability for every possible outcome of the race. Gone were the days when it was down to the gut reaction of the bookmaker to decide when and by how much to change the prices we displayed on our fancy electronic board. Now the computer decided. Bookmaking was no longer by instinct, it was by fractions.

When I had started working for my grandfather I had been his 'runner'. It had been my job to take cash from his hand and use it to back a horse with other bookmakers – a horse on which he had taken some large bets – in order to spread his risk. If the horse was beaten, he didn't make so much but, conversely, if it won, he didn't lose so much either. Now even that was done by computer, betting and laying horses on the internet exchanges, even during the actual running of the race. Somehow, the romance and the fun had disappeared.

Just as mobile phones have caused the demise of the tic-tac men, computer gambling was now killing off any bookmakers with personality who were prepared to back their hunches. And I wasn't at all sure if it was good for the punters, or for racing.

'Twenty pounds, horse two,' said another man taking the plunge.

'Twenty on two at evens,' I repeated, not so much for the man in front of me, more for Luca Mandini, my assistant, to enter the bet on his computer.

Luca was my magician, my internet whizz-kid with a razor-sharp mathematical brain who stood right behind me. His fingers tapped his keyboard and the betting slip duly appeared from the printer.

Without Luca I was sure I would have given up by now, forced out by the relentless bully-boy tactics of the big book-making firms who did all they could to squeeze the profit out of the small independents. It was the same in the grocery trade, where the big supermarkets used their muscle to force the small shops to close. They didn't necessarily do it on purpose; they just did it in their never-ending drive for bottom-line figures to satisfy the expectations of some faceless group of shareholders. I was the sole shareholder in my business, and I felt the pain.

I lived in daily fear that Luca would be enticed away from me by some other outfit, maybe one of those big firms who, it seemed, would stop at nothing to put the likes of me out of business in their greedy quest to capture a larger share of the betting market.

I took the slip from the printer and handed it to the man standing patiently in front of me.

'Are you Teddy Talbot?' he asked.

'Who wants to know?' I asked him back while looking beyond for my next customer.

'I know your grandfather,' said the man, ignoring my question.

My grandfather's name had indeed been Teddy Talbot, and it was his name that was still prominently displayed above our prices board next to me. The slogan actually read TRUST TEDDY TALBOT, as if the extra word might somehow encourage punters to bet with us rather than the next man.

'My grandfather's dead,' I said, still looking beyond him and hoping that he would move away. He was disrupting my business.

'Oh,' he said. 'When did he die?'

I looked down at him from my lofty position on a foot-high metal platform. He was grey haired, in his late fifties or early sixties and wearing a cream linen suit over a light blue shirt that was open at the neck. I envied the coolness of his attire. 'Look,' I said, 'I'm busy. If you want to talk come back later – after the last. Now please move aside.'

'Oh,' he said again. 'Sorry.'

He moved away, but only a short distance, from where he stood and watched me. I found it quite disconcerting.

'Weighed in,' announced someone over the public address system.

A lady in a straw hat came up and held out a slip to me. I took it from her. TRUST TEDDY TALBOT was printed across the top, as it was on all our betting slips. It was a winning ticket from the previous race, the first of rather too many. Nowadays, the potential win amount had to be printed on the slip so I scanned the details and paid her out for her win, tearing the slip in half and placing the bits into a hopper to my left. The transaction was wordless – no communication was necessary.

A line of winning-ticket holders was forming in front of me.

Betsy, Luca's girlfriend, came and stood on my left. She paid out the winners while I took some of their winnings back as new bets on the next race. Luca scanned his screen and adjusted the prices on our board according to the bets I took and also the bets and lays he made on the internet gambling exchanges via his computer behind me. It was like a balancing act, comparing potential gains against potential losses, always trying to keep both possibilities within acceptable ranges.

It was my surname on our board and I was the handler of the punters' cash but, in truth, it was Luca with his computer who was the real bookmaker, betting on-line and setting our board prices to always try and keep our predicted return greater than one hundred per cent as indicated on his screen. Anything over a hundred per cent was called the overround and represented profit, less than a hundred indicated loss. Our aim was to keep the overround at about nine per cent, but all the mathematics relied on us taking bets in the correct proportions for our odds, something we tried to ensure by continually adjusting our prices. However, the punters didn't always cooperate with our plans, so Luca tried his best to compensate by betting and laying on the internet.

The computer was both our best friend and our worst enemy. We liked to think that it was our slave, doing the jobs we gave it more efficiently than we could have done them ourselves. But, in reality, the computer was the master, and we were its slaves. The analysis and figures on its screen controlled our decisions without question. Technology, rather than insight, was now the idol we worshipped.

And so our day progressed. I became hotter and hotter, both over and under the collar as the sun broke through the veil of cloud, while heavily backed short-priced winners continued to make it a great day for the punters while pushing down our percentage return into the red.

I didn't need to wear my stifling morning suit as our pitch wasn't actually in the Royal Enclosure. But we were close to the enclosure rail, in a prime position, and many of my clients wore the coveted name badges of those admitted to the inner sanctum. Besides, my grandfather had always worn formal dress at this meeting and, since my eighteenth birthday, he had insisted that I did so too. At least he hadn't decreed that we should have top hats as well.

I had never, in fact, applied to be admitted to the Royal Enclosure because there were no bookmaker pitches on that side of the fence. I did sometimes wonder if being a bookmaker would somehow disqualify one from admittance, like being a divorcee had once done.

Another favourite won the fifth race to huge cheers from the packed grandstands. I sighed audibly.

'It's not so bad,' said Luca in my ear. 'I had most of that covered.'

'Good,' I said over my shoulder.

The string of short-priced winners had forced us to try and limit our losses by adjusting down the offered prices on our board. Unlike in a shop, punters went in search of the highest prices as that represented a better return for their bets, provided, of course, they won. So lower prices meant that we didn't do as much business. Even our regular clients tended to go elsewhere chasing the fractionally better odds offered by others – there was absolutely no loyalty amongst punters.

The man in the linen suit still stood about five yards away and watched.

'Hold the fort,' I said to Betsy. 'I need a pee.'

'Will do,' she said.

I walked across to the man.

'What exactly do you want?' I demanded.

'Nothing,' he said defensively. 'I was just watching.'

'Why?' I demanded again.

'No reason,' he said.

'Then why don't you go and watch someone else instead?' I said forcefully.

'I'm not doing any harm,' he almost wailed.

'Maybe not, but I don't like it,' I said. 'So go away. Now.'

I walked past him and into the grandstand in search of the Gents.

When I returned, he'd gone.

'Thanks,' I said to Betsy as I again stood up on the platform.

'Come on,' I shouted at the small crowd in front of me. 'Who wants a wager?' I glanced up at the board. 'Eleven-to-four the field.'

There were a few takers but business was slow. As every race seemed to be a losing one from our point of view, it was probably just as well. At this rate, the more business we did, the more we lost.

However, there was some respite when the last race of the day was won by a twenty-to-one rank outsider, the favourite having been boxed in against the rails until it was too late.

'That saved our bacon,' said Luca with a broad grin.

'Saved your job, you mean,' I said, smiling back at him.

'In your dreams,' he replied.

In my nightmares, more like.

'So what's the total?' I asked him.

In the good old days it was easy to tell how we had done simply by the size of the wad of banknotes in my pocket, but these days we also had to consider our credit-card balance with the internet exchanges.

'Down fifteen hundred and sixty-two,' he said with certainty, consulting his machine.

'Could be worse,' I said, but I couldn't actually remember a previous first-day Tuesday at Royal Ascot when we had lost money.

'Sure could,' he said. 'If the favourite had won the last we would have been off another grand more, at least.'

I raised my eyebrows at him and he grinned. 'I didn't manage to take as much of the favourite as I wanted on the exchanges. Damn internet link went down.'

'Just us or everyone?' I asked seriously.

'Dunno,' he said intrigued. 'I'll find out.'

Luca and I started to pack up our equipment as Betsy paid out the occasional winning ticket. Most of the racegoers were streaming for the exits to try to beat the traffic jams and, no doubt, there would be more winning tickets from the last race handed in the following day.

We kept a record on our computer of all the bets taken, both winning and losing, and it never ceased to amaze me how many of the winning tickets were never cashed. Presumably some were lost, and perhaps some inebriated punters didn't realize they were winners, but almost every day there were two or three winning bets that were never claimed. Sleepers, they were called, and they were like a cash bonus for us. But it was one we could never completely rely on. Our tickets didn't have an expiry date on them and, only the day before, I'd had to cash a sleeper from the Royal Ascot meeting of the previous year. Maybe it had been hiding for twelve months in the deep recesses of someone's morning-coat pocket, or tucked into the hatband of a topper, waiting quietly to be discovered and paid out.

The crowd had mostly dispersed to the car parks by the time Luca, Betsy and I had packed up the majority of our gear and loaded it onto our little wheeled trolley that ingeniously doubled up as a base for our computer during the racing. The betting ring was deserted save for the other bookmakers who, like us, were packing up amongst the detritus of a day's gambling: discarded newspapers, torn-up betting slips, crumpled coffee cups and half-eaten sandwiches.

'Do you fancy a beer?' Luca asked as I pulled one of the elastic straps over our equipment.

'I'd love one,' I said looking up at him. 'But I can't. I have to go and see Sophie.'

He nodded at me knowingly. 'Some other time, then. Betsy and I are going to go and have one if that's all right with you. We're taking the train into town later to go to the party in the park.'

'Right,' I said. 'You go on. I'll pack up the rest of the stuff.'

'Can you manage?' he asked.

He knew I could. I did it all the time. But this little exchange was his way of not taking it completely for granted.

I smiled at him. 'No problem,' I said waving a dismissing hand at them. 'Go on. I'll see you both in the morning. Usual time.'

'OK,' said Luca. 'Thanks.'

Luca and Betsy went off together, leaving me standing alone next to the tarpaulin-covered equipment trolley. I watched them go, Betsy hand in hand beside her young man. At one point they stopped and embraced before disappearing out of my sight into the grandstand. Just another happy couple on their way, I assumed, to the bandstand bar, where there was usually an impromptu drinking party after each day's racing.

I sighed.

I supposed I must have been that happy once. But it had been a long time ago. What, I wondered, had happened to all the happy times? Had they deserted me for ever?

I wiped my brow with the sleeve of my jacket and thought about how I would absolutely adore a nice cooling beer. I wanted to change my mind and go to find the other two, but I knew that it would end up being more trouble than it was worth. It always was.

I sighed again and stacked the last few of our equipment boxes onto the trolley, then fixed the rest of the elastic cords across the green tarpaulin. I took hold of the handle and released the brakes from the wheels. As I had told Luca, I could just about manage it alone, although it was always easier with two, especially up the concrete slope towards the tunnel through the grandstand. I tugged hard on the handle.

'Do you want a hand with that?' a voice shouted from behind me.

I stopped pulling and turned round. It was the man in the cream linen suit. He was about fifteen yards away leaning up against the metal fence between the betting ring and the Royal Enclosure. I hadn't noticed him as we'd packed up and I wondered how long he'd been there watching me.

'Who's offering?' I called back to him.

'I knew your grandfather,' he said again while walking over to me.

'You said,' I replied.

But lots of people knew my grandfather and nearly all of them hadn't liked him. He had been a typically belligerent bookie who had treated both his customers and his fellow bookmakers with almost the same degree of contempt that they clearly held for him. He had been what many might have called 'a character' on the racecourse, standing out in all weathers at an age when most men would be content to put their feet up in retirement. Yes, indeed, lots of people had known my grandfather, but he'd had precious few friends, if any.

'When did he die?' asked the man, taking hold of one side of the handle.

We pulled the trolley together in silence up the slope to the grandstand and stopped on the flat of the concourse. I turned and looked at my helper. His grey hair was accentuated by the deeply tanned skin of his face. I reckoned it wasn't an English summer tan.

'Seven years ago,' I said.

'What did he die from?' he asked. I could detect a slight accent in his voice but I couldn't quite place it.

'Nothing, really,' I said. 'Just old age.' And bloody mindedness, I thought. It was as if he had decided that he'd had his allocated stretch in this world and it was time to go to the next. He had returned from Cheltenham races and had seemingly switched off inside on the Friday, and then he had expired on the Sunday evening. The post-mortem pathologist couldn't say why he'd died. All his bits had apparently been working quite well and his brain had been sharp. I was sure he had simply willed himself to death.

'But he wasn't very old,' said the man.

'Seventy-eight,' I said. 'And two days.'

'That's not old,' said the man, 'not these days.'

'It was old enough for him,' I said.

The man looked at me quizzically.

'My grandfather decided that his time was up so he lay down and died.'

'You're kidding?' he said.

'Nope,' I said. 'Absolutely serious.'

'Silly old bugger,' he said, almost under his breath.

'Exactly how well did you know my grandfather?' I asked him.

'I'm his son,' he said.

I stared at him with an open mouth.

'So you must be my uncle,' I said.

'No,' he said, staring back. 'I'm your father.'

CHAPTER 2

'But you can't be my father,' I said, nonplussed.

'I can,' he said with certainty, 'and I am.'

'My father's dead,' I said.

'How do you know?' he asked. 'Did you see him die?'

'No,' I said. 'I just . . . know. My parents died in a car crash.'

'Is that what your grandfather told you?'

My legs felt detached from my body. I was thirty-seven years old and I had believed for as long as I could remember that I was fatherless. And motherless too. An orphan. I had been raised by my grandparents who had told me that both my parents had died when I was a baby. Why would they lie?

'But I've seen a photo,' I said.

'Of what?' he asked.

'Of my parents,' I said.

'So you recognize me then?'

'No,' I said. But the photo was very small and at least thirty-seven years old, so would I actually recognize him now?

'Look,' he said. 'Is there anywhere we could go and sit down?'

*

In the end I did have that beer.

We sat at a table near the bar overlooking the pre-parade ring while the man in the cream linen suit told me who I was.

I wasn't sure what to believe. I couldn't understand why my grandparents would have lied to me but, equally, why would this stranger suddenly appear and lie to me now? It made no sense.

'Your mother and I were in a road accident,' he told me. He looked down. 'And then she died.' He paused for a long time as if wondering whether to carry on.

I sat there in silence looking at him. I didn't feel any real emotion, just confusion.

'Why?' I asked.

'Why what?' he said.

'Why have you come here today to tell me this?' I began to feel angry that he had chosen to disrupt my life in this way. 'Why didn't you stay away?' I raised my voice at him. 'Why didn't you stay away as you have done for the past thirty-seven years?'

'Because I wanted to see you,' he said. 'You are my son.'

'No, I'm not,' I shouted at him.

There were a few others enjoying a quick drink before making their way home, and they were looking in our direction.

'You are,' he said quietly, 'whether you like it or not.'

'But how can you be so sure?' I was clutching at imaginary straws.

'Edward, don't be stupid,' he said, picking at his fingers.

It was the first time he had used my name and it sounded odd. I had been christened Edward, but I'd been known as Ned all my life. Not even my grandfather had called me Edward, except, that was, when he was cross with me or I had done something naughty as a child.

'What's your name?' I asked him.

'Peter,' he said. 'Peter James Talbot.'

My father's name was indeed Peter James Talbot. It said so in green ink on both my birth certificate and his. I knew by heart every element of those documents. Over the years the handwritten details on those papers had somehow been the only tangible link to my parents, that and the small creased and fading photograph that I still carried with me everywhere.

I removed my wallet from my pocket and passed the photo over to him.

'Blackpool,' he said with confidence, studying the image. 'This was taken in Blackpool. We were there for the illuminations in November. Tricia, your mother, was about three months pregnant. With you.'

I took the photo back and looked again closely at the young man standing next to a dark green Ford Cortina, as I had done hundreds of times before. I glanced up at the man in front of me and then back down at the picture. I couldn't say for sure that they were the same person but, equally, I couldn't say they weren't.

'It is me, I assure you,' he said. 'That was my first car. I was nineteen when that picture was taken.'

'How old was my mother?' I asked.

'Seventeen, I think,' he said. 'Yes, she must have been just seventeen. I tried to teach her to drive on that trip.'

'You started young.'

'Yes . . . well.' He seemed embarrassed. 'You weren't actually planned, as such. More of a surprise.'

'Oh, thanks,' I replied somewhat sarcastically. 'Were you married?' I asked.

'Not when that picture was taken, no.'

'How about when I was born?' I wasn't sure that I wanted to know.

'Oh yes,' he said with certainty. 'We were by then.'

Strangely, I was relieved that I was legitimate and not a bastard. But did it really matter? Yes, I decided, it did. It meant that there had been commitment between my parents, maybe even love. They cared, or at least, they had then.

'Why did you leave?' I asked him. It was the big question.

He didn't answer immediately but sat quite still, looking at me.

'Shame, I suppose,' he said eventually. 'After your mother died, I couldn't cope with having a baby and no wife. So I ran away.'

'Where to?' I asked.

'Australia,' he said. 'Eventually. First I signed onto a Liberian-registered cargo ship in Liverpool docks. I went all over the world for a while. I got off one day in Melbourne and just stayed there.'

'So why come back now?'

'It seemed like a good idea,' he said.

It wasn't.

'What did you expect?' I asked. 'Did you think I would just welcome you with open arms after all this time? I thought you were dead.' I looked him. 'I think it might be better for me if you were.'

He looked back at me with doleful eyes. Perhaps I had been a bit hard.

'Well,' I said, 'it would definitely have been better if you hadn't come back.'

'But I wanted to see you,' he said.

'Why?' I demanded loudly. 'You haven't wanted to for the last thirty-seven years.'

'Thirty-six,' he said.

I threw my hands up in frustration. 'That's even worse,' I said. 'It means you deserted me when I was a year old. How could a father do that?' I was getting angry again. So far my own life had not been blessed with children, but it was not from a lack of longing.

'I'm sorry,' he said.

I wasn't sure it was enough.

'So what made you want to see me now?' I said. 'You can't just have decided suddenly after all this time.' He sat there in front of me in silence. 'You didn't even know that your own father was dead. And what about your mother? You haven't asked me about her.'

'It was only you I wanted to see,' he said.

'But why now?' I asked him again.

'I've been thinking about it for some time,' he said.

'Don't try and tell me you had a fit of conscience after all these years,' I scoffed at him with an ironic laugh.

'Edward,' he said somewhat sternly, 'it doesn't befit you to be so caustic.'

The laughter died in my throat. 'You have no right to tell me how to behave,' I replied with equal sternness. 'You forfeited that right when you walked away.' He looked down like a scalded cat. 'So what do you want?' I asked him. 'I've got no money.'

His head came up again quickly. 'I don't want your money,' he said.

'What, then?' I asked. 'Don't expect me to give you any love.'

'Are you happy?' he asked suddenly.

'Deliriously,' I lied. 'I leap out of bed each morning with joy in my heart, delighting at the miracle of a new day.'

'Are you married?' he asked.

'Yes,' I said, giving no more details. 'Are you?'

'No,' he replied. 'Not any more. But I have been. Twice – three times if you count your mother.'

I thought I probably would count my mother.

'Widowed twice and divorced once,' he said with a wry smile. 'In that order.'

'Children?' I asked. 'Other than me.'

'Two,' he said. 'Both girls.'

I had sisters. Half-sisters, anyway.

'How old are they?'

'Both in their twenties now, late twenties, I suppose. I haven't seen them for, oh, fifteen years.'

'You seem to have made a habit of deserting your children.'

'Yes,' he said wistfully. 'It appears I have.'

'Why didn't you leave me alone, and go and find *them*?'

'But I know where they are,' he said. 'They won't see me, not the other way round. They blame me for their mother's death.'

'Did she die in a car crash too?' I said with a touch of cruelty in my voice.

'No,' he said slowly. 'Maureen killed herself.' He paused and I sat still, watching him. 'I was made bankrupt and she swallowed enough tablets to kill a horse. I came home from the court to find bailiffs sitting in the driveway and my wife lying dead in the house.'

His life was like a soap-opera, I thought. Disaster and sorrow had been a constant companion.

'Why were you made bankrupt?' I asked.

'Gambling debts,' he said.

'Gambling debts!' I was astounded. 'And you the son of a bookmaker.'

'It was being a bookie that got me into trouble,' he said. 'Obviously I hadn't learned enough standing at my father's side. I was a bad bookie.'

'I thought gambling debts couldn't be enforced in a court.'

'Maybe not technically, but I had borrowed against everything and I couldn't afford the repayments. Lost the lot. Every single thing, including the girls, who went off to live with their aunt. I never saw them again.'

'Are you still bankrupt?' I asked.

'Oh no,' he said. 'That was years ago. I've been doing fine recently.'

'As what?' I said.

'Business,' he said unhelpfully. 'My business.'

One of the bar staff in a white shirt and black trousers came over to us.

'Sorry, we're closing,' he said. 'Can you drink up, please?'

I looked at my watch. It was well past six o'clock already. I stood up and drank down the last of my beer.

'Can we go somewhere to continue talking?' my father asked.

I thought about Sophie. I had promised I would go and see her straight after the races.

'I have to go to my wife,' I said.

'Can't she wait?' he implored. 'Call her. Or I could come with you.'

'No,' I said, rather too quickly.

'Why not?' he persisted. 'She's my daughter-in-law.'

'No,' I said decisively. 'I need time to get used to this first.'

'OK,' he said. 'But call her and say you've been held up and will be home later.'

I thought again about Sophie, my wife. She wasn't at home. She would be sitting in front of the television in her room watching the news as she always did at six o'clock. I knew she would be there because she wasn't allowed not to be.

Sophie's room was locked, from the outside.

Sophie Talbot had been sectioned under the Mental Health Act 1983 and detained for the past five months in secure accommodation. It wasn't actually a prison, it was a hospital, a low-risk mental hospital, but it was a prison to her. And this wasn't the first time. In all, my wife had spent more than half the previous ten years in one mental institution or another. And, in spite of their care and treatment, her condition had progressively deteriorated. What the future held was anyone's guess.

'How about a pub somewhere?' my father said, interrupting my thoughts.

I needed to be at the hospital by nine at the latest. I looked at my watch.

'I have about an hour, maximum,' I said. 'Then I'll have to go.'

'Fine,' he said.

'Do you have a car?' I asked him.

'No,' he said. 'Came on the train from Waterloo.'

'Where are you staying?' I asked.

'Some seedy little hotel in Sussex Gardens,' he said. 'Guest house, really. Near Paddington station.'

'Right,' I said, deciding. 'I'll drive you somewhere for a drink then I'll drop you at the railway station in Maidenhead and you can get the train back to London.'

'Great,' he said, smiling.

'Come on, then.'

Together we pulled the trolley out through the racecourse main gate and across the busy road.

'What sort of business are you in now?' I asked him as we hauled our load through the deep gravel at the entrance to the car park.

'This and that,' he said.

'Bookmaking?' I persisted.

'Sometimes,' he said. 'But mostly not.'

He seemed determined to be vague and evasive.

'Is it legal?' I asked.

'Sometimes,' he repeated.

'But mostly not?' I asked, echoing his previous answer.

He just smiled at me and pulled harder on the trolley.

'Are you going to go back to Australia?' I asked, changing the subject.

'Expect so,' he said. 'But I'm just lying low for a while.'

'Why?' I asked.

He just smiled again. Perhaps it's better, I thought, if I don't know why.

I had parked my car, my trusty twelve-year-old Volvo 940 estate, at the back of car park number two, behind the owners' and trainers' area. As always, I'd had to pay for my parking. The racecourses gave bookmakers nothing.

Bookmakers' pitches had once been held on a basis of seniority and long-standing, as they still were in Ireland. However, in Britain, pitch positions had been offered for sale and, once bought, remained the property of the bookie, to keep or sell on if he wished. Whoever owned number one had the first choice of where to stand in the betting ring, number two had second choice, and so on. My number was eight, bought by my grandfather about twenty years ago for a king's ransom. I stood not quite at the best position, but good enough.

A bookmaker's badge fee, paid by me to the racecourse to be allowed to stand on any day at the races, was set at five times the public-entry cost. So if a racegoer paid forty pounds each day to get into the betting ring, as they did at Royal Ascot, then the badge fee was set at two hundred. Plus, of course, the regular entrance cost for Betsy and Luca to get in. On any day at the Royal meeting I was many hundreds out of pocket before I even took my first bet.

There were controversial plans for the old system to be thrown out in 2012 and for pitches to be auctioned by each racecourse to the highest bidder. The bookmakers objected to what they saw as the stealing of their property, and they believed that the racecourses were greedy, while everyone else thought the reverse was true.

The downtrodden bookie, the man that all and sundry love to hate. 'You never see a poor bookie,' people always say with a degree of loathing. That's because poor bookies rapidly go out of business. You never see a poor lawyer either. But, there again, all and sundry love to hate them too.

'How long are you staying?' I asked my father.

'A while,' he replied unhelpfully.

If he was going to be like this, I thought, then there was no purpose in going to a pub to talk. And I could use the time to go and spend longer with Sophie.

'Look,' I said. 'Perhaps it's better if you go straight back to London now. There's little point in going for a drink if you are going to ignore all my questions.'

'I want to talk about the past, not the future,' he said.

'Well, I don't.'

We were still pulling the trolley towards my car, passing through a gap in the hedge to the back of car park two when I heard running footsteps behind us. I turned my head and caught a glimpse of someone coming straight at me. In one continuous move he ran straight up onto the tarpaulin-covered trolley and kicked me square in the face.

Shit, I thought as I fell to the ground, I'm being robbed.

Didn't this idiot know that it had been a dreadful day for the bookies? There was precious little left to steal. He would have done better to rob me on my way into the course this morning when I'd had a few grand of readies in my pockets.

I was down on all fours with my head hanging between my shoulders. I could feel on my face the warmth of fresh blood and I could see it running in a bright red rivulet from my chin to the earth beneath, where it was soaking into the grass.

I was half expecting another blow to my head or even a boot in my guts. My arms didn't seem to be working too well but I managed to manoeuvre my right hand into my deep trouser pocket where I had put the envelope containing the small wad of remaining banknotes. Experience had taught me that it was better to give up the money early rather than to lie there taking a beating only to have the cash taken later anyway.

I pulled the envelope out of my pocket and threw it on the grass.

'That's all I have.' I could taste the saltiness of the blood in my mouth as I spoke.

I rolled over onto my side. I didn't really want to see my attacker's face. Experience had also taught me that a positive identification usually leads to a further kicking. However, I needn't have worried. The young man, and I was sure from his strength and agility that he was a young man, was wearing a scarf around his face and the hood of his dark grey sweatshirt was pulled up over his head. Identification would have been impossible even if he had been facing towards me. Instead he was facing half away, standing in front of my father.

'Here,' I shouted at him. 'Take it and leave us be.'

He turned his head slightly towards me then turned back to face my father.

'Where's the money?' he hissed at him.

'There,' I said pointing at the envelope.

The man ignored me.

'Go to hell,' my father said to him, lashing out with his foot and catching the man in the groin.

'You bastard,' hissed the man with anger.

The man appeared to punch my father twice rapidly in the stomach.

'Where's the bloody money?' hissed our attacker once again.

This time my father said nothing. He merely sat down heavily on the ground with his back up against the hedge.

'Leave him be,' I shouted at the hooded figure. 'It's there,' I said, once again pointing at the white envelope on the grass. The man simply ignored me again and turned back to my father, so I screamed at the top of my voice, 'Help! Help! Help!'

Car park two was mostly deserted but there were still some after-racing parties taking place in the owners' and trainers' area. Heads turned our way and three or four brave souls took a few steps in our direction. No doubt, I thought ironically, they would probably come and help with the beating if they knew the victim was a bookmaker.

The man took one look over his shoulder at the approaching group and was off, running between the few remaining cars

24

before disappearing over the wooden fence on the far side of the car park. I sat on the grass and watched him go. He never once looked back.

The envelope of money still sat on the grass next to me. Not much of a thief, I mused. I leaned over, picked up the envelope and thrust it back into the deep recess of my pocket. I struggled to my feet, cursing at the green grass stains that had appeared on the knees of my trousers.

Three of the waistcoated revellers, still clutching their champagne glasses, had arrived.

'Are you all right?' asked one. 'That's quite a cut on your face.'

I could still feel the blood, now running down my neck.

'I think I'll be fine,' I said. 'Thanks to you. We were mugged but he didn't get away with anything.' I took a couple of steps over to my father. 'Are you OK . . . Dad?' I asked him. The sound of the word, Dad, was strange to my ears.

He looked up at me with frightened eyes.

'What is it?' I asked urgently, taking another couple of steps towards him.

He was clutching his abdomen and now he moved his hand away. The cream linen jacket was rapidly turning bright red. My father hadn't been punched in the stomach by the young man, he'd been stabbed.

The ambulance took an age to arrive. I tried to dial 999 on my mobile phone but, in my panic, my fingers felt more like sausages and kept pressing the wrong keys. Eventually one of the champagne revellers took the phone from my hand and made the call while I knelt down on the grass next to my father.

The blood had spread alarmingly right across his abdomen and his face had turned ashen grey.

'Lay him down,' someone said. 'Put his head lower than his heart.'

Quite a crowd had drifted over from the various car park parties. Somehow it seemed absurd for people to be standing round sipping champagne while my father was fighting for breath at their feet.

'It's OK,' I said to my father. 'Help is on the way.'

He nodded very slightly and then tried to say something.

'Keep still,' I instructed. 'Save your energy.' But he continued to try and speak.

'Be very careful.' He said it softly but quite distinctly.

'Of what?' I replied.

'Of everyone,' he said in a whisper.

He coughed and blood appeared on his lips.

'Where is that damn ambulance?' I shouted at no one in particular.

But it was the police who arrived first. Two officers appeared on foot. They were probably more used to dealing with race-day traffic than a violent stabbing in broad daylight and one of them was immediately on his personal radio calling for reinforcements. The other one knelt down next to me and tended to my father by placing his large traffic-stopping right hand on the wound and pushing down.

My father groaned.

'Sorry, mate,' said the policeman. 'Pressure is the best thing.'

Eventually the ambulance arrived with the driver apologizing for the time taken. 'Going against the race traffic,' he explained. 'Jams everywhere and half the roads made one way – the wrong way.'

26

My father was rapidly assessed and given oxygen through a face mask, and intravenous fluids via a needle in his forearm. He was lifted carefully onto a stretcher and loaded into the vehicle, the pressure on his stomach being maintained throughout.

I tried to climb in with him but was stopped by one of the policemen.

'You wait here with us, sir,' he said.

'But that's my father,' I said.

'We will get you to the hospital shortly,' he said. 'It looks like you need a stitch or two in that head anyway.'

The paramedics closed the ambulance doors and bore my father away just as the police back-up arrived in two blue-flashing cars.

I spent much of the evening in a hospital, but not the one where I had planned to be.

I knew my father had been alive when they had placed him in the ambulance at the racecourse, I'd heard him coughing, and according to one of the nurses he'd still been alive when he'd arrived at the hospital. But he didn't make it to the operating theatre. The combination of massive shock and drowning in his own blood had killed him in the accident and emergency department reception area. So sorry, they said, there was nothing they could have done.

I sat on a grey-plastic-and-tubular-steel chair in a curtained-off cubicle next to the body of my dead parent, a parent I hadn't known existed until three hours previously, and wondered how the world could be so cruel.

I was numb. I had grieved for my father when I was about

eight, when I was just old enough to begin to realize what I was missing. I could still remember it clearly. I had seen my school friends with their young mums and dads and, for the first time, had realized that my aged grandparents were different. I could remember the tears I had shed longing for my parents to be alive and with me.

I had wanted so much for my father to be there and to be like the other dads, shouting encouragement from the touch-line during my school football games, carrying me high on his shoulders when we won, consoling and wiping away the tears when we lost.

I had amused my team mates with made-up stories about how my father had died bravely saving me from drowning, or from enemies, or from monsters. Now I discovered that even the story I had been told, and had believed unquestioningly, had itself been a lie.

I looked at the figure lying silently on his back in front of me, covered by a crisp white sheet. I folded the sheet down to his chest so I could see his face. He looked as if he was just asleep, peaceful, with his eyes closed, as if he could be wakened by my touch. I placed my hand on his shoulder. His flesh was already cooling and there would be no awakening here ever again. I stroked his suntanned forehead for the first and last time in my life and considered what might have been.

I should be angry with him, I thought. Angry for going away and leaving me all those years ago. Angry that he had then taken so long to come back. Angry that I'd had sisters for nearly thirty years whom I'd never met. And angry that he'd come back at all and added complications to my already complex existence.

But I have always believed that anger is an emotion that needs to be expressed, to be vocalized with passion towards someone who can respond, or be hurt. Somehow, directing anger towards my dead father's corpse seemed pointless and wasteful of my energy.

I would save my anger, I decided, for the young man who had so abruptly taken away any chance I might have had to make up for time lost in the past. I grieved not so much for the death of my father but for the loss of the opportunity that had come so close.

I stood up and pulled the sheet back over his face.

A man in a light brown suit came into the secluded cubicle behind me.

'Mr Talbot?' he asked.

'Yes,' I said, turning round.

'I'm Detective Sergeant Murray,' he said, showing me his warrant card. 'Thames Valley Police.' He paused, looking down at the inert form beneath the sheet. 'I'm very sorry about your father,' he said, 'but we really need to ask you some questions.'

'Yes, of course,' I said. 'Shall we go and find somewhere more suitable?'

He seemed relieved. 'Yes, good idea.'

One of the nurses showed the two of us into a small room provided for families – grieving families no doubt – and a second plain-clothes policeman came in to join us. We sat down on more of the grey-plastic-and-tubular-steel chairs.

'This is DC Walton,' said Sergeant Murray, introducing his colleague. 'Now, what can you tell us about the incident in the car park at Ascot?'

'I'd call it more than just an incident,' I said. 'I was attacked and my father was fatally stabbed.'

'We will have to wait for the post mortem to determine the actual cause of death, sir,' said the sergeant rather formally.

'But I saw my father being stabbed,' I said.

'So you did see your attacker?' he asked.

'Yes,' I said. 'But I don't know that I'd recognize him again. His face was covered. All I could see were his eyes, and that was only for a split second.'

'But you are sure it was a man?' he asked.

'Oh yes,' I said. 'He had a man's shape.'

'And what shape was that?'

'Thin, lithe and agile,' I said. 'He ran at me and came straight up onto my equipment trolley and kicked me in the face.' I instinctively put my hand up to the now-stitched cut in my left eyebrow.

'Was he white or black?' he asked.

'White, I think,' I said slowly, going over again in my mind the whole episode. 'Yes, he was white,' I said with some certainty. 'He had white hands.'

'Are you sure he wasn't wearing light-coloured gloves?' the sergeant asked.

I hadn't thought about gloves. 'No,' I said. 'I'm not sure, but I still think he was white. His eyes were those of a white man.' I remembered that I'd thought at the time that they were shifty-looking eyes, rather too close together for the shape of his face.

'Can you describe what he was wearing?' he asked.

'Blue denim jeans and a charcoal-grey hoodie, with a black scarf over the lower part of his face,' I said. 'And black boots, like army boots with deep-cut soles, I saw one of those rather too close up.' The constable wrote it all down in his notebook.

'Tall or short?' the sergeant asked.

'Neither, really,' I said. 'About the same as my father.'

'Tell us about your father,' he said, changing direction. 'Can you think why anyone would want him dead?'

'Want my father dead?' I repeated. 'But surely this was just a robbery that went wrong?'

'Why do you think that?' he asked.

'I just assumed it was,' I said. 'It certainly wouldn't be the first time a bookmaker has been robbed in a racecourse car park. Not even the first time for me.'

Both policemen raised their eyebrows a notch, in unison.

'About five years ago,' I said. 'At Newbury. I was walking back to my car in the dark after racing in late November. There was a gang of them on that occasion, not just one like today.'

I could still recall the pain of the ribs they had broken with their boots when I refused to hand over my heavy load of cash after a particularly bad day for the punters. I could also remember the indifference of the Newbury police to the robbing of a bookmaker. One of them had even gone as far as to say that it was my own fault for carrying so much money in my pocket. As far as I could tell, no serious attempt had been made by them to catch the perpetrators.

'Bookies get robbed all the time,' I said. 'Some people will try anything to get their money back.'

'But you say you weren't robbed on this occasion,' said the sergeant.

'No,' I admitted, feeling for the envelope of cash that was still safely in my trouser pocket. 'But I simply imagined the thief was disturbed to find he had an audience, so he took off.'

'Now, about your father,' he said. 'What was his full name?'

'Peter James Talbot,' I said. The constable wrote it down.

'And his address?' he asked.

'I'm not sure of his full address,' I said, 'but I believe he lived in Melbourne, Australia.'

'Then can you tell us, Mr Talbot,' the detective sergeant said, 'why the man who you claim was your father had a credit card and a driving licence in his jacket, both in the name of Alan Charles Grady?'

CHAPTER 3

'Are you telling us that you didn't know your father existed?' the chief inspector asked.

'Well . . .' I said slowly. 'Yes and no.'

'Which?' he demanded.

'Yes, obviously I knew that he existed thirty-seven years ago, but no, I didn't know until today that he still existed.' It was confusing. After all, he didn't now exist, not as a living being, anyway.

I was again with Detective Sergeant Murray and DC Walton but we had transferred as a group from Wexham Park hospital to Windsor police station, swapping the grieving families room for a stark police interview room with no windows. The chairs at each place, I noticed, could have come from the same manufacturer's batch.

We had been joined by Detective Chief Inspector Llewellyn, who did not extend the nicety of expressing sympathy for my dead father. I decided I didn't like him very much, and he clearly had no good feelings towards me either.

'A bookmaker, eh?' he'd said by way of introduction, curling his lip. He, like many, clearly believed that all bookmakers were villains unless proved otherwise, and even then there'd be some doubt remaining.

'Are you absolutely certain that this man was your father?' He stabbed his finger at the driving licence that sat on the table in front of me, its black-and-white photograph clearly being that of the man I had left lying dead under a sheet at the hospital.

'No,' I said looking up at the chief inspector, 'I can't say I am absolutely certain. But I still think he was. It was not so much what he looked like or what he said, but his mannerisms and demeanour that convinced me. He picked at his fingers in the same way I watched my grandfather do a million times, and there was something about his lolloping walk that is somehow reminiscent of my own.'

'Then why is this licence in the name of someone called Alan Grady?' he asked.

'I have no idea,' I said. 'Is it genuine?'

'We're checking,' he said.

'Well, I still believe the man in that photograph is my father.'

The chief inspector clearly didn't share my confidence. 'The DNA will tell us for sure one way or another,' he said. I had been asked for, and had given, a sample of my DNA at the hospital. 'And you say he's lived in Australia for the past thirty years or so?'

'That's what he told me, yes,' I replied.

'And you believed him?'

'Yes.'

'Why?'

'Why not?' I said. 'Why would he lie to me?'

'Mr Talbot,' he said, 'in my experience, people lie all the

34

time.' He leaned forward and looked at me closely. 'And I think you might be lying to me right now.'

'Think away,' I said. 'But I'm not.'

'We'll see,' said the chief inspector, standing up abruptly and walking out of the room.

'Chief Inspector Llewellyn has left the room,' said the sergeant for the benefit of the audio recording machine that sat on the table to my left.

'Can I go now?' I asked.

'Mr Talbot,' said the sergeant. 'You can leave any time you like. You are not under arrest.'

Maybe not, I thought, but I had been questioned under caution.

'Then I would like to go home,' I said. 'I have to be back at Ascot racecourse at ten thirty in the morning.'

'Interview terminated,' said the sergeant glancing up at the clock on the wall, 'at twenty-two forty-five.' He pushed the STOP button on the front of the recorder.

'Have you spoken to any of the other people who were there in the car park?' I asked him as we walked along the corridor.

'We continue to make enquiries,' he answered unhelpfully.

'Please can I have a photocopy of that driving licence?' I asked him.

'What for?' he said.

'The photograph. The only one I have of my father was taken before I was born. I would like to have another.'

'Er,' said the sergeant, looking round at Constable Walton. 'I'm not sure that I can.'

'Please,' I said in my most charming manner.

Constable Walton shrugged his shoulders.

35

'OK,' said the sergeant. 'But don't tell the chief inspector.'

I wouldn't, I assured him. I wouldn't have told the chief inspector if his flies had been undone.

Sergeant Murray disappeared for a moment and returned with a blown-up copy of the licence, which I gratefully folded and placed in my trouser pocket alongside the envelope of cash.

'Thank you,' I said.

'Yeah,' he said wistfully. 'Lost my dad too, about three months ago.'

'Sorry,' I said.

'Thanks,' he replied. 'Cancer.'

He walked me to the door of the police station, where we shook hands warmly, the comradeship of those with recently deceased fathers.

'Now, how do I get home?' I said, turning my morning-coat collar up against the chill of an English June night.

'Where's your car?' he asked.

'In the car park at Ascot, I expect. That's where I left it.' With, I hoped, all our equipment still safely in the boot. The uniformed boys had helped me load everything in there before insisting they drove me to the hospital. 'You might have a concussion from that kick,' they had said. 'Better safe than sorry.'

So here I was in Windsor town centre at eleven o'clock at night with no transport, and I knew there was no chance of getting a hotel room anywhere near Ascot during the Royal meeting.

'Where's home?' asked the sergeant.

'Kenilworth,' I said, 'in Warwickshire.'

'Outside our patch,' said Sergeant Murray.

'Does that mean you won't send me home in a police car?' I asked him.

'Er,' he seemed to be undecided. 'I suppose it does. You'll have to get a taxi.'

'Do you have any idea how much a taxi to Kenilworth would cost?' I asked in exasperation. 'Especially at this time of night.'

'I could arrange a lift to Ascot to get your car,' he said.

'It'll probably be locked in the car park,' I said. 'Or towed away.'

'Sorry, sir,' he said rather formally. 'Nothing else I can do.'

'Don't you have a spare cell I could use?' I asked.

'We can't go offering cells as hotel rooms, now can we?' he said sarcastically.

'Why not?' I said. 'If I was drunk and disorderly you'd put me in a cell to sleep it off.'

'But you're not,' he said.

'I could be,' I said, grinning at him. 'It'd be cheaper than taking a taxi to Kenilworth.' And back again tomorrow, I thought. Much cheaper, even allowing for a fine, and more comfortable than sleeping in my car.

'I'll see,' he said. 'Wait here.'

He disappeared into the police station for a few minutes.

'OK,' he said. 'On compassionate grounds only. I've had to say that you are distraught over the death of your father and in no state to be allowed to go home. And for God's sake don't tell Chief Inspector Llewellyn. He thinks you're up to your neck in something dodgy.'

'Well, he'll know where to find me, then.'

*

I didn't sleep very well but, in fairness, it was mostly due to having a thumping headache rather than the starkness of my surroundings. Understandably, my night's accommodation hadn't been designed with comfort in mind, but the kindly night-custody sergeant had provided me with a second blue-plastic-covered mattress from an empty cell next door. It had helped to make the hardness of the concrete sleeping platform almost bearable.

'We're not very busy tonight,' he'd explained. 'Just a couple of drunk drivers from the races. Bit too much of the champers, silly buggers.' He rolled his eyes. 'Friday and Saturday nights are our busy times. We sometimes need camp beds and two or more in a cell.'

I was luckier than the two other residents as I slept with the light off and the door slightly ajar. Even though my cell had its own basic en suite facilities in the corner, I was invited in the morning to make use of the more salubrious staff wash-room down the corridor, where I found a shower, shampoo and a disposable razor.

I looked at myself in the washroom mirror. It wasn't a pretty sight. My left eyebrow was swollen and turning a nice shade of deep purple, while my white shirt was decidedly pink around the collar where the previous evening I had unsuccessfully tried to wash out the blood that had run down my neck. It would have to do, I thought. No one really cares how their bookmaker dresses. The pinkish shirt would go well with the green-stained knees of my trousers.

Breakfast was also provided by my hosts.

'We are required to feed the drunks before their court appearances so I ordered you a breakfast too,' said the custody sergeant.

'Thanks,' I said taking the offered tray of cornflakes and toast with a mug of sweet white tea. 'Don't have a copy of the *Racing Post* as well, do you?'

'Don't push your luck, Mr Talbot,' he said with a grin.

My opinion of the police had risen a few rungs; except, that was, for Chief Inspector Llewellyn. But, fortunately for me, there was no sign of him as I took my leave of their hospitality and rode in a taxi back to the racecourse.

I walked into the still-closed car park two at ten minutes to eight to find my old Volvo was exactly where I had left it the previous evening. It stood all alone on the grass, not very far from the gap in the hedge where there was now a white tent surrounded by blue-and-white POLICE DO NOT CROSS tape. A bored-looking constable stood guard on one side of the tent while a three-man television crew were setting up close by on the other, no doubt for a live broadcast for breakfast news.

I didn't volunteer to them that I was the star witness to the crime. Instead I went over to my car, started the engine for warmth and used the cigarette lighter socket to charge up my mobile phone.

I then used it to call Luca.

'Sorry,' I said to him. 'I can't pick you and Betsy up today. Can you make it here by train?'

'No problem,' he said sleepily. 'See you later.' He hung up.

I sat in the driver's seat of my car and took stock of the situation.

The previous afternoon I had discovered that I hadn't been an orphan all those years, only to be violently orphaned for real a little under an hour later. Or had I? Had the man in the linen suit really been my father? I had told Chief Inspector Llewellyn that I believed so, but did I still believe it in the cold light of a new day? Did I really have two Australian sisters? If so, shouldn't someone tell them that their father had been murdered? Would they care? Did they know about me? And were their names Talbot or Grady? Or something else entirely?

I pulled the copy of the driving licence from my pocket and looked at the black-and-white photograph of my father. He had looked straight into the camera and it seemed that his eyes were staring into my soul. Alan Charles Grady, the licence read, of 312 Macpherson Street, Carlton North, Victoria 3054. I wondered what his home was like. There was so much I didn't know.

I also wondered, as I had done for much of my sleepless night, if the sergeant had been right and the purpose for the attack had been specifically to do my father harm rather than to rob me. I realized that I still thought of him as my father, so that, at least, answered one of my questions. But why would anyone do him harm, let alone murder him?

'Where is the money?' the murderer had hissed at him. I had thought at the time that he meant the money from the bookmaking. But did he? Was there some other money that my father had had? Or owed? The police had shown me the total contents of his pockets. Other than the driving licence and the credit cards with the name Grady on them, there had been a return ticket from Waterloo to Ascot, a packet of boiled sweets, the TRUST TEDDY TALBOT betting slip I had given him myself, and about thirty pounds in cash. Surely that wasn't enough to kill for?

'Be very careful,' my father had said to me as he lay dying on the grass where the white tent now stood. 'Be very careful of everyone.'

But who in particular, I pondered. I glanced around me as if there might have been somebody creeping up on me. But I was still alone in the car park, save for the police guard at the tent and the TV crew, who were now packing up their equipment, the broadcast over.

I called Sophie. Rather I tried to, but she wouldn't answer her phone. She was cross with me. She had told me so at great length when I had telephoned her from Wexham Park hospital to say I wasn't coming to see her. I had thought about what I should say and had decided not to mention the sudden appearance of a living father in my life followed by his equally sudden permanent removal. Stress caused by unexpected situations did nothing for her condition and could bring on a severe bout of depression. Currently she was improving and I was hopeful that she would soon be coming home, until the next attack.

Sophie rode a rollercoaster life with great peaks of mania followed by deep troughs of despair, every cycle seemingly taking her higher and lower than ever before. Between the extremities there were generally periods of calm rational behaviour. These were the good times when we were able to lead a fairly normal married life. Sadly they were becoming rarer, and shorter.

'Have you been drinking again?' she'd asked accusingly.

I wasn't an alcoholic. In fact quite the reverse: I had never drunk to excess, except perhaps an excess of Diet Coke. But Sophie, in her irrational mind, believed absolutely that I lived for alcohol. However, her obsession was probably good for my health as I now rarely touched the stuff. It made for a quieter life.

I'd had a single beer four hours previously but I had still promised her that I hadn't touched a drop. She wouldn't be convinced.

'You're always drinking,' she had gone on at full volume down the line. 'You won't come and see me because you're drunk. Admit it.'

At that point I had come close to telling her that my father had been murdered and I couldn't come to see her because I was being interviewed by the police. But then she may have become convinced that I was a murderer and that might have sent her back over the edge of the chasm out of which she was slowly climbing. Better to be thought of as a drunk than a killer.

'I'm sorry,' I'd said, admitting nothing. 'I'll come and see you tomorrow.'

'I may not be here tomorrow,' she had replied more calmly. It was her way of telling me once again that, one day, she intended to commit suicide. Just a little reminder to me that she believed she was in control of the situation. It was a game we had been playing for at least the past ten years. I had no doubts that she had convinced herself it was true. However, after all this time, I was not so certain. The only occasions I thought she might actually do it were during some of her manic phases when she would imagine she had superhuman powers. One day there might be no one around to prevent her leaping from a window when she was convinced she could fly. It wouldn't be a true suicide, more like an accident or misadventure.

I, meanwhile, was completely fed up with this half existence. In my darker moments, I had sometimes wondered if suicide would be the only means of escape from it for me too.

The second day of Royal Ascot didn't quite have the excitement of the first. Murder in the car park was the talk of the racecourse with conspiracy theories running at full tilt.

'Did you hear that the victim was someone involved in doping?' I heard one man confidently telling another.

'Really?' replied the second. 'Well, you never know what's going on right under your nose, do you?'

For all I knew they might have been right. There was scant factual information being given out by the police. Probably, I thought, because they couldn't be sure of the true identity of the victim, let alone the perpetrator.

Luca and Betsy were surprisingly not at all inquisitive about my rapidly darkening eye. However they were suitably sympathetic, which was more than could be said for my fellow bookmakers, or even my clients.

'Morning, Ned,' said Larry Porter, the bookie on the neighbouring pitch. 'Did yer missus do that?' He was obviously enjoying my discomfort.

'Good morning to you too, Larry,' I replied. 'And no. I walked into a door.'

'Oh yeah,' he said. 'Pull the other one.'

I felt sorry for people who really had walked into a door. No one must ever believe them.

'Actually, I was mugged,' I said.

'We were all mugged yesterday,' he said, laughing expansively at his little joke, 'by the bloody punters.'

'Maybe this punter,' I put my hand to my eye, 'wanted more.'

The smile disappeared from his face. 'Were you robbed, then?' he asked. Robbery of bookmakers was never a laughing matter in our business.

'No,' I said, thinking fast. I didn't really want to say that it might have been murder on the mugger's mind, not robbery. 'Seems he was frightened off.'

'Not by your physique, surely,' said Larry, laughing again.

43

I just smiled at him and let it go. He must have weighed a good eighteen stones with a waist that a sumo wrestler would have been proud of. I, meanwhile, was a lean, mean, fighting-machine in comparison, though truthfully I was somewhat scrawny. I never seemed to have any time to eat, or the incli-nation to cook, in my married, but mostly solitary, lifestyle.

Thankfully, neither Luca, Betsy, Larry nor anyone else seemed to connect the murder in the car park with my black eye, and the novelty of it slowly wore off as the afternoon's sport progressed.

'Was it just us or was the internet down for everyone?' I asked Luca during a lull after the third race.

'What?' he said, busy with his keyboard.

'Yesterday. For the last,' I said. 'Was it just us or everyone?'

'Oh,' he said. 'It seems the whole system was down for nearly five minutes. And you know what else was funny?'

'What?' I asked.

'The phones were off, too.'

'Which phones?' I asked.

'Mobiles,' he said. 'All of them. Every network. Nothing.'

'But that's impossible,' I said.

'I know,' he said. 'But it happened. Everyone I spoke to said their phone wouldn't work for about five minutes. No signal, they said. The boys from the big outfits were going nuts.'

By 'the big outfits' Luca meant the four or five large com-panies that ran strings of betting shops across the country. Each company had a man or two at the races who would bet for them with the on-course bookmakers to affect the starting prices.

The odds offered by on-course bookmakers often change before the race starts. If a horse is heavily backed they will shorten its odds and offer better prices on the other horses to compensate. The official starting price, or SP, is an approximate average of the prices offered on the bookmakers' boards on the racecourse just as the race starts.

Big winning bets in high-street betting shops are nearly always paid on the official SP so, if someone loads money on a horse in their local betting shop, the company arranges for money to be bet on that horse with the racecourse bookmakers so that the odds on their boards drop and consequently the starting price will be shorter.

For example, if a betting shop has taken a hundred thousand pounds' worth of bets on a horse priced at ten-to-one, they stand to lose a million pounds if it wins. So the company will simply have its staff on the racecourse bet cash on that horse with the bookmakers, who will then shorten its odds. If the starting price drops to, say five-to-one and it wins, the betting shop will only have to pay out half what it would otherwise have done.

If both the internet and the telephones were not working for the five minutes before the race then the betting shop companies would have had no way of getting the messages to their staff to make the bets and change the starting prices.

'Any word on anyone being caught out?' I asked Luca.

'No, nothing,' he said. 'Quiet as a whisper.'

A customer thrust a twenty-pound note at me and I gratefully relieved him of it in exchange for a slip from the printer.

'Either someone doesn't want to admit it,' I said, 'or it was just a simple accidental glitch in the systems.'

Word usually went round pretty quickly if a big company believed they had been 'done'. They typically moaned about it ad nauseam and refused to pay out. Gambling wins, as well as losses, were notoriously difficult to pursue through the courts.

The big boys believed that it was their God-given right to control the starting prices and if someone managed to get one over on them, it was unfair. Most others believed that what was really unfair was how the major bookmaking chains could change the on-course prices so easily, often with only a very few of the many thousands of pounds that was bet across the counters in their high street shops.

I shrugged my shoulders and took a bet off another customer. Luca pushed the keys on his computer and out popped the ticket from the printer.

'At least our computer and printer didn't go off as well,' I said to him over my shoulder.

'Well they wouldn't,' he said confidently. 'Unless the battery went flat.'

Our system, like every other bookmaker's, was powered by a twelve-volt car battery hidden away under the platforms we stood on. The batteries were provided freshly charged each day by the racecourse technology company, which also provided the internet access – for a fee, of course. The same battery also powered the red light-emitting-diodes that showed the horses' names and prices on our board. If the battery went flat we would soon know about it. Our lights would go out first.

The lights stayed on and we recouped most of our losses from the previous day as favourites were beaten in each of the first five races. I was beginning even to enjoy the day when Chief Inspector Llewellyn pitched up in front of me with DC Walton in tow.

'Making a bet, Chief Inspector?' I asked with a smile, looking down at him from my lofty position.

He didn't appear amused. 'We need to talk,' he said. 'Now.'

'Can't it wait?' I said. 'I'm busy.'

'No,' he said crossly. 'I need to ask you some more questions, now.' He emphasized the final word so sharply that Betsy looked questioningly at me.

I smiled at her. 'Can you hold the fort for five minutes?'

'Sure, no problem,' she said.

I stepped down and moved away with the policemen to a quieter spot on the grass.

'Now, what's so bloody urgent?' I said, deciding not to go on the defensive. 'I've got a business to manage.'

'And I've got a murder investigation to run,' he replied unapologetically. 'May I remind you, Mr Talbot, that you remain under caution and that anything you say will be recorded.'

'Where's your machine, then?' I asked.

'DC Walton will write down what is said.'

DC Walton was already writing.

'If you prefer,' he said, knowing I wouldn't, 'you can accompany us to the police station and be formally interviewed there.'

'Here is fine,' I said.

'I thought so,' he said almost smugly. 'Now, Mr Talbot, have you anything to add to your account of the incident in the car park last evening that resulted in the death of a man.'

'No,' I said. 'I don't.'

'And you still believe that the man killed was your father?' he asked.

'Yes,' I said. 'I do.'

'It seems you may be right,' he said slowly. 'The DNA analysis appears to suggest that you and the deceased were closely related. It's by no means a hundred per cent certain, but it would be more than enough to settle a paternity case.'

So at least my father had been truthful about that.

47

'However,' he said, 'the DNA results have thrown up something else.' He paused for effect. 'Your father was still wanted for murder, from thirty-six years ago.'

'What?' I said, unable to properly take it in. 'Are you sure?'

'Completely sure,' he said. 'The DNA match is one hundred per cent.'

'But who did he murder?' I asked, almost as if in a trance.

'Patricia Jane Talbot. His wife.'

My mother.

CHAPTER 4

Sophie was still cross when I went to see her but at least she was speaking to me, albeit with thinly disguised anger.

It was after eight by the time I made it to the hospital near Hemel Hempstead.

'I thought you weren't coming again,' she said with a degree of accusation.

'I said I would come,' I said, smiling at her and trying to lighten the atmosphere. 'And here I am, my darling.'

'What have you done to your eye?' she demanded.

'Silly, really,' I said. 'I caught it on the corner of the kitchen cupboard, you know, the one by the fridge.' We had both done it before, often, though neither of us had actually cut ourselves in the process.

'Were you drunk?' she asked.

'No,' I said. 'I was not. I was making tea. To be precise, I was getting the milk out.'

I leaned down to give her a kiss and she made a point of smelling my breath. Finding no trace of the demon drink, she relaxed somewhat and even smiled at me.

'You should be more careful,' she said.

'I'll try,' I replied, smiling back at her.

'Have you had a good day?' she asked.

'Yes,' I said. 'Particularly good. All six favourites lost and we recouped the entire amount of yesterday's losses, and then some.' I decided against mentioning anything about my visit from a detective chief inspector of police, or the discovery that my father had murdered my mother.

'Good,' she said, sounding genuinely pleased.

We sat together in armchairs in front of the television in what might have been a normal domestic situation if not for the multi-adjustable hospital bed in the corner of the room and the white-smock-uniformed male nurse who brought us in a tray of coffee, together with Sophie's medication.

'Good evening, Mr Talbot,' the nurse said to me. 'Glad you could make it tonight.' He smiled. 'Your wife was so disappointed yesterday, as were we all.'

He gave the impression that I was being officially told off, which I probably was. Sophie's treatment relied heavily on having a steady routine with no surprises.

'Good evening, Jason,' I said to the nurse, smiling back and resisting the temptation to make excuses. Now was neither the time, nor the place.

'My, what have you done to yourself?' he said, looking at my face.

'Head-butted our kitchen cabinet,' I said.

Jason raised his eyebrows in a questioning *Oh, yes, pull the other one* fashion.

'We do it all the time,' said Sophie, coming to my aid. 'We ought to get that cupboard moved.'

Jason relaxed and seemed satisfied that my black eye was accidental.

'The guest suite is available if you want to stay,' he said with a smile, his admonishment for yesterday's absence clearly over.

'Thank you,' I said, 'but I can't. I need to go home and change.' I also decided against explaining that I had worn exactly the same clothes for two days running, and why. 'But I can stay for a while longer.'

Sophie and I watched the television news together before I departed into the night and the road to Kenilworth, and home.

Our house was a 1950s-built three-bedroom semi-detached in what was still called Station Road, although the railway station to which it referred had closed down in the 1960s. The previous owners had transformed the postage-stamp-sized front garden into an off-road parking space and I gratefully pulled my Volvo into it at ten minutes to midnight.

As usual, the house was cold and lonely. Even on a mid-summer's day it rarely could be described as warm and cosy. It was as if, somehow, the very bricks and mortar were aware of the daily sadness and despair experienced by the occupants within.

Sophie and I had moved here from a rented one-bedroom over-shop flat soon after our wedding. Her parents hadn't approved of the union. They were God-fearing Methodists who believed that bookmakers were agents of the Devil. So it felt as if we were both orphans, but we didn't care. We were in love and we only needed each other.

The house in Station Road was the first home we had owned and we knew it would be a struggle. The mortgage company loan had been to their utmost limit and, at first, Sophie had worked in the evenings behind the bar at the local pub in order to help meet the repayments. I had toiled six days a week on the Midland racecourses and, quite quickly, we were able to pay down the mortgage to a more manageable level where we could spend more time together at home.

I had always wanted children and I soon made mental plans to turn the smallest bedroom into a nursery. Perhaps it was the pain of having endured a largely abandoned and unhappy childhood that had made me so keen to nurture the next generation. Not that my grandparents hadn't been loving and caring. They had. But they had also been somewhat distant and secretive. Now I knew why.

'How could God have taken Mummy and Daddy to Heaven?' I had constantly asked my grandmother, who, of course, had no answer to give me. Now I discovered that it had been my father, not God, who had been responsible for my mother's death and he himself, far from going to Heaven, had gone to Australia. The car crash story had simply been as convenient as it was untrue.

In spite of her longing for a child, Sophie's illness had soon put our family plans on hold.

All had seemed fine until, one night, I woke to find her side of our bed empty. It was half past three in the morning and I could hear her somewhere downstairs, singing loudly, so I went to investigate.

She was in the kitchen and had clearly been there for quite a while. Every shelf and cupboard had been emptied, their contents stacked on both the kitchen table and on the floor, and she had been cleaning.

She had seen me come into the room but had carried on singing even louder than before. She simply couldn't stop. And so it had gone on all night and into the following day. I couldn't reason with her. Eventually, in desperation and fear, I had called the doctor.

This manic state had lasted for nearly a week with her spending much of the time in bed, asleep and heavily sedated. When awake she had hardly stopped talking or singing, and she was greatly irritated to be interrupted.

And then, almost as quickly, she had dived into a deep depression, refusing to eat and blaming herself for all the ills of the world. It was irrational and obsessive behaviour but she believed it absolutely. Sedatives were exchanged for anti-depressants and for a while we didn't seem to know whether she was going up or down.

Mental illness can be very frightening, and I was utterly terrified. Physical disease usually manifests itself with visible symptoms: a rash, a fever, or a swelling. And there is nearly always some pain or discomfort to which the patient can point and describe.

However, a sickness of the mind, and its function, has no such easy-to-understand physical indicators. Sufferers appear just as they did before the disorder hit and often, as in Sophie's case, have no comprehension that they are ill. To them, their behaviour appears quite normal and logical. It is everyone else who's mad for even suggesting they need psychiatric help in the first place.

The plans for a family that I had initially placed on hold had, by now, been well and truly switched off. The little bedroom, that had long ago become my office and storeroom, would, it seemed, never contain a cot and teddy bears, at least not while Sophie and I owned the house.

It was not just that Sophie was too often ill to look after a child, it was also the risk that a pregnancy would cause an upset to her hormones that could tip her over entirely into a void from which she would never recover. Post-natal depression can severely debilitate even the sanest of mothers, so what might it do to Sophie? And, even though a professor of psychiatry had told us it wasn't likely, there was some evidence to suggest that manic-depression could be a hereditary condition. I was wary of creating a manic-depressive child. For ten years I had witnessed the destruction from within of a bubbly, lively and fun-loving young woman. I didn't relish the thought of the same thing happening to my children.

I supposed I still loved Sophie, although after five months of medically enforced separation I was sometimes unsure. It was true that, during those months, there had occasionally been some good moments, but they had been rare, and mostly we existed in limbo, our lives on pause, waiting for someone to push the play button if things improved.

We had definitely been dealt a bum hand in life. Sophie's parents, typically and loudly, had blamed me for their daughter's illness while I silently blamed them back for rejecting her over her choice of husband. The doctors wouldn't say for sure if that had been a factor in her illness, but it certainly hadn't helped.

Alice, Sophie's younger sister, constantly said I was a saint to stick by her all these years. But what else could I do? It wasn't her fault she was ill. What sort of husband would desert his wife in her time of need? 'In sickness and in health,' we had vowed, 'until death us do part.' Perhaps, I thought, death would indeed be the only way out of this nightmare.

I shook myself out of these morbid thoughts, let myself into the house, and went straight to bed.

Thursday at Royal Ascot is Gold Cup Day. It is also known as Ladies Day when the female of the species preens herself in her best couture under an extravagant hat she wouldn't be seen dead in at any other time or place.

This particular Thursday the sun had decided to play the game and it was shining brightly out of a clear blue sky. The champagne flowed and seafood lunches were being consumed by the trawler-load. All was set for a spectacular day of racing. Even I, a cynical bookie, was looking forward to it all with hope and expectation for another bunch of long-priced winners.

'Didn't walk into another door, then?' asked Larry Porter as he set up his pitch next to ours.

'No,' I replied. 'No doors in the car park last night.'

He grinned at me. 'And all that cash yesterday.' He rubbed his hands. 'Fancy trying to rob you on Tuesday when you're broke, then let you off yesterday with bulging pockets. Bloody mad.'

'Yes,' I said quietly, wondering once again if it really had been an attempted robbery in the first place.

'Let's hope we have bulging pockets again today,' Larry said, still smiling.

'Yes,' I said again, my mind still elsewhere.

Larry Porter and I could not be properly described as friends. In truth, I didn't have any friends amongst my fellow book-makers. We were competitors. Many punters believed that there was an ongoing war between them and the bookies but, in fact, the really nasty war was between the bookmakers them-selves. Not only did we fight for the custom of the general public, we fought hardest and dirtiest amongst ourselves, bet-ting and laying horses, doing our utmost to get one over on our neighbours. There was very little love lost between us and, whereas Larry had been genuinely concerned that I had been mugged in the car park, it was more because he saw a danger to himself than out of compassion for any injury or loss that I had sustained.

Many in the racing industry, both privately and publicly, called all bookmakers 'the enemy'. They accused us of taking money out of racing. But we were only making a living, just like them. They, too, bought their fancy cars and enjoyed their foreign holidays, and what was that if it wasn't 'taking money out of racing'? The big firms, although no friends of mine, spent millions of their profits on race sponsorship, and we all paid extra tax on gambling profits on top of the 'levy', a sum that was also taken from bookmakers' profits and put back into racing via the Horserace Betting Levy Board.

The betting levy provided more than half the country's total race prize money, as well as contributing to the cost of the dope testing, the patrol cameras, and the photo-finish systems. Plenty of the trainers hated all bookmakers with a passion, but they still bet with them, and they couldn't seem to see that the future of racing, and consequently their own futures, relied totally on the public continuing to gamble on the horses.

'Larry,' I said, 'did your internet go down just before the last race on Tuesday?'

'I believe it did,' he said. 'But it happens all the time. You know that.'

'Yes,' I said. 'But did you know that all the mobile phones went off at the same time?'

'Did they indeed?' he said. 'Anyone hit?'

'Not that I know of,' I replied.

'I'll bet there was quite a queue at the phone box on the high street,' he said with a laugh. There was a public telephone just outside the racecourse, one of the few remaining, now that everyone seemed to have a mobile.

'Yeah,' I said, joining in with his amusement. 'I bet you're right.'

Business was brisk in the run-up to the first race. As always when there was a really big crowd, many punters liked to place all their bets for the whole day before the first so that they didn't have to relinquish their viewing spots between races. Acquiring seats in the Royal Enclosure viewing area on the fourth floor of the grandstand was as difficult as getting straight answers from politicians about their expenses.

Once secured they were not given up lightly.

Consequently we were taking bets for all races, able to quote our odds thanks to the prices offered on the internet gambling sites where bets would have been made all morning. Again it was the computer running the show with us humans at its beck and call.

'What did that copper want yesterday afternoon?' Betsy asked me.

'Just a few more questions about getting mugged on Tuesday,' I replied matter-of-factly. Even though I had initially asked Betsy to take over for just a few minutes, I had actually left her and Luca for the whole of the last race. They had also had to pack up all our equipment on their own while I had spoken with Chief Inspector Llewellyn for well over an hour. But it was not often that a man discovers that his mother was murdered by his father.

I thought back to what the chief inspector had told me.

'Your mother was strangled,' he'd said. It had turned me icy cold on one of the hottest days of the year.

'But how do you know that my father was responsible?' I'd asked him.

'Well,' he'd said, 'it seems it was suspected as much when he suddenly disappeared at the same time. According to the records, some people thought he must have killed himself as well, though no body was ever found, of course. But the DNA match has proved it.'

'How?' I asked, although I was dreading the answer.

'Your mother apparently scratched her attacker and his skin was found under her fingernails. At the time of the murder, DNA testing wasn't available, but the evidence samples were kept. During a cold-case review about five years ago a DNA profile of the killer was produced and added to the national DNA database. As we have now discovered, it matches your father exactly.' He had said it in a very deadpan manner, unaware of the torment such knowledge was creating in my head.

In less than a single twenty-four-hour period I had first met my father and realized that I was not the orphan I'd thought I had been for the past thirty-seven years, had watched helplessly while my new-found parent was fatally stabbed, and finally, I had discovered that he'd been nothing more than a callous murderer, the killer of my mother. It wasn't my father's life that was the soap-opera, it was mine.

'Do they have any idea who did it?' asked Betsy, suddenly bringing me back from my daydreaming.

'Did what?' I asked.

'The mugging, stupid.'

'Oh,' I said. 'No, I don't think so. They didn't say so, anyway.'

'Probably some kids,' she said. She was little more than a kid herself. 'Larking about.'

I didn't think that murder was exactly larking about, but I

decided not to say so. Family secrets were best kept that way, secret.

The afternoon seemed to slip by without me really noticing. Luca had to keep reminding me to pay attention to our customers.

'For God's sake, Ned,' he shouted in my ear. 'Get the bloody things right.' He exchanged yet another inaccurate ticket. 'What's wrong with you today?'

'Nothing,' I replied. But I felt lousy and my mind was elsewhere.

'Could have fooled me,' he said. 'You never normally make mistakes.'

I did, but I was usually more expert at covering them up.

'Sophie's not good,' I said. It was the easy excuse. Luca knew all about Sophie's condition. I may have wanted to keep it a secret, even from him, but that had been impossible over the years. Too often I had been forced to take days off work in order to be with her. Luca Mandini was a licensed bookmaker in his own right and he'd often covered for me, first with a friend and, more recently, with Betsy, who could hardly conceal her excitement when she knew I would be away.

'Sorry,' Luca said. He never asked for details. He seemed almost embarrassed. 'Bloody hell,' he suddenly shouted.

'What is it?' I asked, alarmed.

'Internet's gone down again,' he said stabbing his keyboard with his finger.

I looked at my watch. A little less than five minutes to go before the Gold Cup was due to start.

'How about the phones?' I asked him, turning round.

He was already pushing the buttons on his mobile.

'Nothing,' he said, looking up at me. 'No signal. Same as before.'

I turned and looked round the betting ring at the other book-makers, especially those to my right along the Royal Enclosure rail. Outwardly there appeared to be no sense of alarm. Business was being carried on as usual. I could see a few of the boys from the big outfits pushing buttons on their phones with no success. One or two of them dashed away to seek other forms of communication with their head offices, and the man from the Press Association who was responsible for setting the start-ing prices had come down from his place in the stand to look at the bookies' boards. No internet connection also meant he didn't get the necessary information directly to his computer screen.

'Two monkeys, six horse,' said a punter in front of me.

A 'monkey' was betting slang for five hundred pounds, two monkeys was a thousand, or a grand. It was a fair-sized bet and bigger than most but, over the year, we took lots of bets of a thousand pounds or more, so it was not that unusual. However, I took a careful look at my customer. Was it a coincidence, I wondered, that our biggest bet of the day was laid just seconds after the internet and the phones went off?

There was nothing about the man that made me think that he was up to no good. He was a regular racegoer with a white shirt open at the neck and fawn chinos. I didn't recognize him as one of the regular boys from the big outfits, but I would know him again, I made sure of that.

I glanced up at our board as I relieved him of the bundle of fifty-pound notes he held out to me. Horse number six, Lifejacket, was quoted at four-to-one.

'Four thousand-to-one thousand on horse six,' I said over my shoulder. 'OK with you, Luca?'

There was a pause while Luca consulted with his digital mate. 'We'll take it at seven-to-two,' he said slowly.

'Seven-to-two,' I said to the man in the white shirt and chinos.

'OK,' he said. He didn't seem to mind the change in odds.

'A grand at seven-to-two, horse number six,' I said.

Luca pushed the computer keys and the ticket popped out of the printer. I gave it to the man who moved on to Larry Porter and appeared to make another bet there.

'A grand on six at fours,' shouted Luca. He was laying the bet with Norman Joyner, another bookmaker whose pitch was in the line behind us, and he was trying to do so at a better price than we had just offered to the man in the white shirt. But Norman was wise to his attempt.

'Hundred-to-thirty,' Norman called back. The price offered on horse number six was rapidly on its way down.

'OK,' said Luca. 'I'll take it.'

There was no money passed, no ticket issued. Norman Joyner was a regular on the Midland tracks where we did most of our business and, while none of us may have actually been friends, one bookmaker's word to another was still his bond.

'Internet still down?' I asked over my shoulder.

'Yup,' said Luca.

There was beginning to be a touch of panic in the ring. Technicians from the company that provided the internet links were running round in circles, seemingly not knowing where to look for a solution. Frowns on the faces of those from the betting office chains reflected their concern that something was afoot.

'Fifty pounds on Brent Crude,' said a voice in front of me.

I looked down. 'Hi, AJ,' I said, noticing the fancy blue-and-yellow striped waistcoat he was wearing. 'Sorry, what did you say?'

'Fifty on Brent Crude,' AJ repeated.

'Fifty pounds to win number one,' I said over my shoulder, glancing at our prices board, 'at fifteen-to-eight.' There was considerable surprise in the tone of my voice.

The ticket appeared and I passed it over.

'They're off,' said the race commentator over the public-address system, announcing the start of the race.

'It's back,' said Luca. 'Now is that a coincidence or what?'

'Phones too?' I asked.

'Yup.' He repeatedly pushed the buttons.

No coincidence, surely.

Lifejacket, horse number six, finished third in a close race with the second horse, both of them ten lengths behind the winner, number one, Brent Crude, the favourite, who was returned at the surprisingly long odds of fifteen-to-eight, or nearly two-to-one. Brent Crude had been the real class horse in the race with every newspaper and TV pundit singing his praises. He had been expected to start at evens at best, and quite likely at odds-on.

'I reckon there's been a bit of manipulating of the starting price going on here,' said Luca with a huge grin. 'Serves them right.'

'Who?' said Betsy.

'The big-chain bastards,' I said to her.

Luca nodded, laughing. 'I think someone has been playing them at their own game.'

'What do you mean?' asked Betsy.

'Someone has managed to stop the big companies from contacting their staff on the racecourse to make bets with us.'

'So?' she said, clearly none the wiser.

'So someone has been placing largish bets on several horses,' I said, 'to shorten their odds, which would, in turn, lengthen the price on the favourite.'

'I still don't get it,' said Betsy.

'Suppose,' I said, 'that really large bets were being placed in the betting shops on Brent Crude, all of them at the official starting price, then the shops wouldn't have been able to contact their staff to get them to bet on him on the course and shorten his price.'

'It must have driven them bonkers in the shops to see the starting price lengthen,' said Luca, 'just when they wanted it to shorten. All their big bets would have been at the starting price whether they were part of the scam or not.'

'Isn't that illegal?' asked Betsy.

'Probably,' I said. 'But the big companies are forever controlling the starting prices. I think they just got a taste of their own medicine.'

'It's almost certainly illegal to interrupt communications,' said Luca. 'But I think it's brilliant.'

'But how can they do that?' asked Betsy.

'What?' I said.

'Disrupt all the phones.'

'I know it can be done,' Luca said. 'I saw it on a television programme. They used an electronic jammer. The police can do it too. I know that. When there was a bomb scare at Aintree one year, they shut down all the phone systems, left everyone completely stranded. Perhaps this was the same thing, but I doubt it. We would be evacuating the racecourse by now.'

63

'How did the prices change in the last few minutes before the off?' I asked him.

He consulted his micro-processing friend.

'Lifejacket came right in from four-to-one to two-to-one,' he said. 'Five other horses tightened as the race approached but Brent Crude drifted all the way from even money to fifteen-to-eight. He was very nearly not even the favourite.'

'That's a lot,' I said.

'Yeah,' said Luca, 'but there was a whisper in the ring that he was sweating badly in the paddock. Colic was even mentioned.'

I knew, I'd heard the talk. 'Was it true?' I said.

'Dunno,' he said, grinning again. 'I doubt it.'

CHAPTER 5

There was an unusual feeling of bonhomie amongst the bookies in the ring as we waited to see who had been taken to the cleaners. Except, that was, for the on-course teams from the big outfits, who had been as much in the dark as the rest of us and who would, no doubt, carry the blame for something over which they had had no control.

Rumours abounded, most of which were false, but by the end of the day there was pretty strong evidence that all the big boys had been hit to some extent. That was, if they ever paid out. Bookmakers in general, and the betting shop chains in particular, didn't like losing and were quick to refuse to honour bets. They seemed to believe that fixing the starting prices was their right and privilege, and theirs alone.

From our own point of view, it hadn't made a whole lot of difference. I had taken two large bets of a thousand pounds each, with quite a few smaller ones following as punters chased the big money. Three-quarters of that had been laid by Luca with other bookies as their prices had tumbled, and he had laid a little more on the internet during the actual running of the race. Both the horses that had been heavily backed with us had lost, of course, while we had taken only a very few last-minute wagers on the favourite on which we'd had to pay out, including that fifty pounds to win from AJ. Most of the bets with us on Brent Crude had been taken earlier in the day when his price had been even money, not fifteen-to-eight. Unlike the betting shops, we always paid out at the price offered at the time of the bet and not on the starting price. A satisfactory result all round, I thought. And a bloody nose to the bullies, to boot. Now, that was a real bonus.

Luca, Betsy and I were still in good spirits as we packed up for the day after the last. There had been no repeat of the earlier excitement but the betting ring was still buzzing.

'A great day for the little man,' said Larry Porter.

'They'll cry foul, you know,' said Norman Joyner from behind me.

'Probably,' Larry agreed. 'But it'll make them uncomfortable, and it's fun while it lasts.'

'They might want to change the system,' I said.

'Not a chance,' Norman said. 'The current system lets them do whatever they like with the odds. Except today, of course. They will probably now demand more security for their communications.'

'Give them carrier pigeons,' I said, laughing.

'Then the fixers will have shotguns to shoot them down,' said Larry. 'Where's there a will, they'll find a way.'

In the First World War, British soldiers were mentioned in despatches for shooting down the enemy's carrier pigeons. Reliable communications had always been the key to success, one way or the other.

Luca and I hauled the trolley up the slope to the grandstand and then on through to the high street outside. Betsy carried our master, the computer, in its black bag.

'No drinks at the bandstand bar tonight?' I said to them.

'No,' said Luca. 'We're going straight from here to a birthday party.'

'Not either of yours?' I said in alarm, thinking I had missed it.

'No,' he said smiling. 'Betsy's in March and mine was last week.'

So I had missed it. 'Sorry,' I said.

'No problem,' he said. 'Wouldn't know when yours was either.'

No, I thought. It wasn't something I advertised. Not for any good reason, but because my private life was just that.

'Millie, my kid sister, she's twenty-one today,' said Betsy. 'Big family party tonight.'

'I hope you have fun,' I said. 'Wish Millie a happy twenty-first from me.'

'Thanks,' she said warmly. 'I will.'

I thought about my own kid sisters in Australia and wondered if anyone had told them yet that their father was dead.

Luca, Betsy and I made it to the car park, on this occasion unmolested, and we loaded our gear into my capacious Volvo estate. Then they both started to move away.

'Don't you need a lift?' I said to them.

'No, thanks,' said Luca. 'Not tonight. We'll take the train from here to Richmond. That's where the party is.'

'Look,' I said to him. 'I fancy giving it a miss tomorrow. I could do with a day off. What do you think? You're welcome to work with Betsy if you want.'

Even though I paid Luca and Betsy a salary as my assistants, they made easily as much again from sharing the profits, assuming there were some profits. Over the last couple of days we had far more than recouped our losses from Tuesday, and the days at Royal Ascot were some of our busiest of the year.

'What about the stuff?' he said nodding towards my car. 'We planned to stay at Millie's place tonight. In Wimbledon.'

Luca and Betsy lived somewhere between High Wycombe and Beaconsfield in Buckinghamshire. I had collected them that morning, as I had often done so, from a lay-by just off junction 3 on the M40.

'Isn't your car in the lay-by?' I asked. I had sometimes transferred the gear into his car there.

'No,' said Luca. 'Betsy's mum dropped us off this morning.'

Bugger, I thought. I would either have to come to Ascot again tomorrow or deprive Luca and Betsy of their day.

'OK,' I said with resignation in my voice. 'I'll be here. But I'm fed up with dressing like this. I'll be more casual tomorrow.'

Luca smiled broadly. I knew he loved the exhilaration and energy of the big race days. I constantly reminded myself that I would lose him if I concentrated too much on the smaller tracks and stopped going to Ascot in June, Cheltenham in March, and Aintree in April.

'Great,' said Luca, still grinning. 'And you'd hate to miss another day like today, now wouldn't you?'

'I can't believe there will be another day like today. Not ever,' I said. 'But, no, I wouldn't want to miss it if there were.'

'We must dash,' said Luca. 'See you here tomorrow, then. Usual time?'

'Yes, all right,' I replied. 'Have fun tonight.'

They disappeared off towards the station through the gap in

the hedge from where the police tent had now been removed, the gap in the hedge where my father had been stabbed.

I stood and watched them go. I couldn't remember when I had last been to a birthday party.

Jason, the nurse, hadn't been very happy when I called him to say that I would be late at the hospital. I had a job to do. I had hoped to do it the following day but . . .

I looked again at my watch. It was half past eight.

I'd promised Jason I'd be there in time to watch the ten o'clock news with Sophie. I still hoped I might make it, but things were not going quite as I had planned.

Having left my morning coat, waistcoat and tie in my parked car, I was on foot in Sussex Gardens, in London, looking for a certain seedy hotel or guest house. The problem was not that I couldn't find any, quite the reverse. Everywhere I looked there were seedy little hotels and guest houses. There were so many of them and I hadn't a clue which was the one I wanted.

'Near Paddington station,' my father had said.

I imagined him getting off the Heathrow Express at Paddington with his luggage after the long flight from Australia and pitching up at the first place with a vacancy. So I had started close to the station and worked my way outwards. So far, after an hour and a half, I had drawn a complete blank and I was getting frustrated.

'Do you, or did you, have a guest this week called Talbot?' I asked without much hope in yet another of the little places I had been in. 'Or one called Grady?'

I pulled out the now rather creased copy of the driving licence that Sergeant Murray had made for me. A young woman behind

69

the reception counter looked down at the picture then up at me.

'Who wants know?' she asked in a very eastern European accent 'Are you police?' she added, looking worried.

'No,' I assured her. 'Not police.'

'Who you say you want?'

'Mr Talbot or Mr Grady,' I repeated patiently.

'You need ask Freddie,' she said.

'Where is Freddie?' I asked, looking round at the empty hallway.

'In pub,' she said.

'Which pub?' I asked patiently.

'I not know which pub,' she said crossly. 'This pub, that pub. Always pub.'

This was going nowhere. 'Thank you anyway,' I said politely, and left.

Even if my father had been staying there I wouldn't have known about it. It had been a stupid idea, I realized. I thought that if I found out where he had been staying, and recovered his luggage, I might learn why he had really come back to England. There had to have been more of a reason than simply to see me after a thirty-six-year absence. After all, he had risked getting arrested for murder.

Chief Inspector Llewellyn hadn't asked me if I knew where my father had been staying in England, so I hadn't told him. I wasn't really sure why I hadn't. I was generally a law-abiding citizen who, under normal circumstances, would be most help-ful to the police. But the circumstances hadn't been normal and the chief inspector hadn't been very nice to me. He had point-blank accused me of lying to him, which I hadn't, but, I now realized, I had also not told him the whole truth either.

I was rapidly coming to the conclusion that it was a hopeless task. Over half the hotels and guest houses I had been into either had no proper record of their guests, or they wouldn't tell me even if they had.

Just another couple more, I decided, and then I must leave for Hemel Hempstead.

Many of the properties in Sussex Gardens had been constructed at a time when households regularly had servants. The grand pillared entrances had been for the family's use only, while the servants had access to the house via a steep stairway down from street level to a lower ground floor behind iron railings.

The Royal Sovereign Hotel was one such property, but nowadays its name was rather grander than its appearance. The iron railings were rusting and the white paint was flaking from the stucco pillars set either side of the dimly lit entrance. And the doormat looked as if it had been doing sterling service removing city dirt and dog muck from travellers' shoes for at least half a century.

'Do you, or did you, have a guest this week called Mr Talbot, or Mr Grady?' I asked yet again, placing the driving licence photocopy down on the Royal Sovereign Hotel reception desk and pushing it towards the plump middle-aged woman who stood behind it. She looked down carefully at the photograph.

'Have you come for 'is stuff?' she asked, looking up at me.

'Yes, I have,' I said excitedly, hardly believing my good luck.

'Good,' she said. 'It's cluttering up my office floor. 'E only paid cash in advance for two nights so I've 'ad to move it this morning. I needed 'is room, you see.'

'Yes, I do see,' I said, nodding at her. 'That's fine. Thank you.'

'But we only 'ad 'im 'ere,' she said, looking down at the picture again. 'Not any other one. And 'is name wasn't Talbot

71

or Grady. It was Van something or other. South African 'e said 'e was. But it was definitely 'im.' She put her finger firmly down on the picture.

'Oh, yes,' I said. 'There is only one person but he sometimes uses different names.' She looked at me quizzically. 'One's his real name, and the others are professional names,' I said. She didn't look any the wiser, and I didn't elaborate.

'Where is 'e, then?' she asked, pointing again at the picture.

What should I say?

'He's in hospital,' I said. Technically it was true.

''Ad an accident, did 'e?' she asked.

'Yes, sort of,' I said.

'Looks like you did too,' she said, putting her hand up to her own eye.

My left eyebrow remained swollen and my whole eye was turning a nasty shade of purple with orange streaks. I was getting used to it but it must have been quite a sight for all the hotel and guest house reception staff I had encountered.

'Same accident,' I said, putting my hand up to my face. 'I'm his son.'

'Oh,' she said. 'Right. Back 'ere, then.' She disappeared through a curtain hanging behind her. I placed the photocopy carefully back in my pocket, went round behind the reception desk and followed her through the curtain.

To call it an office was more than a slight exaggeration. It was a windowless alcove about eight foot square with a narrow table on one side piled high with papers, and a cheap yellow secretary's chair that had seen better days, the white stuffing of the seat appearing in clumps through the yellow vinyl covering. Most of the remaining floor space was occupied by mountains of mega-size packs of white toilet paper.

'Got 'em on offer,' the woman said, by way of explanation.

Must have been a good one, I thought. There were enough rolls here for an army on manoeuvres.

'There,' she said, pointing. 'That's 'is stuff. I 'ad to pack up some of 'is things. Wash kit and so on, 'cause, as I said, 'e only paid for two nights.'

There were two bags. One was a black and red rucksack, the other a small black roll-along suitcase with an extendable handle like those favoured by airline stewardesses. I found it strange to think of my father with a rucksack on his back, but things were different in Australia.

'Thank you,' I said to the woman with a smile. 'I'll let you have your floor back.' I picked up the rucksack by its straps and slung it over my shoulder.

'Shouldn't I get a signature or something?' she said.

'On what?' I asked.

She dug around on the desk for a clean piece of paper and ended up with the back of a used envelope.

'Could you just put your name and signature?' she asked, holding out a pen. 'You know. Just so I'm covered. And a phone number as well.'

'Sure,' I said. I took her pen and the envelope. *Van something*, she had said my father was called. I printed my name as Dick Van Dyke and signed the same with a flourish. The number I wrote down could have been anywhere. I made it up. I didn't really want Chief Inspector Llewellyn on my telephone asking questions that would have been difficult for me to answer.

'Thanks,' she said, tucking the envelope back under a pile of stuff on her desk. ''E only paid for two nights,' she repeated yet again. ''Is stuff's been 'ere for nearly three now.'

At last, I worked out her meaning.

73

'Here,' I said, holding out a twenty-pound note. 'This is for your trouble.'

'Thanks,' she said, taking the money rapidly and thrusting it into a pocket in her skirt.

'I'll be off then,' I said, and backed out of the claustrophobic space with the two bags. 'Thanks again.'

'I 'ope 'e gets better soon,' she said. 'Give 'im my best.'

I promised her I would, and then rapidly took my leave. If she had known her erstwhile guest was now dead, she may well not have given me his things. If she'd been aware that he'd been murdered, I was sure she wouldn't have. But she wasn't to know that the Royal Sovereign Hotel had been about the twentieth such place I had been into that evening asking the same question. For all she knew, my father had directed me straight there to collect his belongings.

I turned out of the hotel and moved quickly down Sussex Gardens towards my car that I had parked near Lancaster Gate tube station. I didn't want to give the woman time to change her mind and come after me.

I looked down at my watch. It was five past nine. I would have to get a move on if I was to be at the hospital in time for the television news at ten o'clock.

I was still looking down at my watch when a man came out of the building to my right and bumped straight into the roll-along suitcase I was pulling. 'Sorry,' I said, almost automatically. The man didn't reply but hurried on, paying me no attention whatsoever. I had glanced up at his eyes and I suddenly felt an icy chill down my spine. I realized I had seen those eyes before. They were the shifty close-set eyes that I had seen in car park number two at Ascot on Tuesday afternoon when the man who owned them had twice punched a knife through my father's

74

abdomen and into his lungs. I didn't stop walking. In fact, I speeded up and forced myself not to look back. I prayed he hadn't seen me, or at least he hadn't recognized me with my swollen and blackened eye.

Only after another twenty or so rapid strides did I step into another of the pillared entrance ways and chance a glance back. There was no sign of him. I must have stopped breathing when I first saw him and I now gasped for air, my heart pounding in my chest like a jackhammer.

I peeped around the pillar and saw him come out of one of the hotels and then disappear into the one next door. It looked as if he might be on the same errand that had also brought me to Sussex Gardens.

I noticed with dismay that, if he continued to work his way along the road, the very next place he would go into was the Royal Sovereign Hotel. High time, I decided, to leave the area.

Checking that he was still inside and out of sight, I nipped back out onto the pavement and hurried away, turning right at the next street. It wasn't the most direct route to my car but I was keen to get out of sight of the Royal Sovereign. I could imagine the plump middle-aged woman standing behind her reception desk. *Oh, yes,* she'd say to the man, *'is son's just been 'ere. 'E took the bags. Only a moment ago. 'E's got a nasty black eye. I'm sure you'll catch 'im if you 'urry.*

Not if I could 'elp it, 'e wouldn't.

Surprisingly, I made it back to my Volvo without actually walking into any lamp posts, so preoccupied had I been with looking behind me. I flung my father's bags onto the back seat and quickly climbed into the front. My hands were shaking so much that I couldn't get the key into the ignition. I held tightly to the steering wheel and took several deep breaths and told myself to calm down. This plan seemed to be working well until I saw the man again. He was jogging down the road, and he was coming straight towards me. My heart rate shot up off the scale.

I tried again to get the key in the hole but the damn thing wouldn't go in. I leaned to my right to see better and was still looking down trying to match the key to the lock when I heard the man walk calmly past me and climb into the car parked right behind mine. I slid down further so that he wouldn't see that there was anyone there. From my lowly position I could just about see the top of his car in my wing mirror.

He sat there for what seemed like an age before he finally started his engine and drove away. I began to breathe again. I seriously thought about following him but I was worried that, in my present state, I would quite likely run straight into the back of him when he stopped at traffic lights.

I should be grateful to Luca, I thought, that I hadn't waited until the following day to do my private detective act. My father's bags would, by then, have been long gone. But it would have been much less stressful on my body.

I sat in my car for a good five to ten minutes wondering if I should go and report the encounter directly to Chief Inspector Llewellyn. I had been so eager that the man shouldn't see me as he drove past that I had slipped down to a nearly horizontal position on the seat. Consequently I hadn't even seen the type or colour of the car he drove, let alone the number plate. I wasn't much of a private detective after all, and I would have had little to tell. And I particularly didn't relish having to explain to the chief inspector why I had said nothing to him earlier about any hotel or guest house in Sussex Gardens. In the end, I decided to have a look at the luggage first. I could always call the police then if I wanted to.

My breathing and pulse had at last returned to their normal rates so I started the Volvo and made tracks to Hemel Hempstead and the hospital.

I sat in the sitting room of my house in Kenilworth surrounded by the contents of my father's bags, wondering what it was amongst this lot that his murderer would bother spending an evening looking for.

I had made it to the hospital to watch the second half of the news with Sophie. Jason had given me a stern look as I had arrived and he had tapped his watch. What could I tell him? 'Sorry I'm late; I've been dodging a murderer on the streets of west London.' Fortunately Sophie didn't seem at all perturbed and she gave me a warm kiss on the cheek without even appearing to check if I had been touching the demon drink. She hadn't even objected when I'd made my excuses and left. I'd had things to do.

So here I sat at nearly midnight surrounded by piles of my father's clothes.

There was nothing much else in the bags. His washing kit was minimal, consisting of just a toothbrush and a half-full tube of paste wrapped up in a cheap see-through plastic case with a white zip along the top. He didn't appear to have any regular medications, although there was a half-used pack of painkillers loose in the small suitcase.

He'd obviously had a penchant for blue shirts, of which there were six, all neatly folded but not very well ironed, and he had preferred an electric razor to a wet shave, and boxer shorts to briefs. He'd worn woollen socks, carefully folded into pairs of mostly dark colours, and had clearly favoured large handkerchiefs with white spots on a dark background.

But there was nothing that struck me as remarkable, certainly nothing worth killing for.

'Where is the money?' the man had said to my father in the Ascot car park.

What money? I wondered. There must be something I had missed. I went through everything again, searching through the pockets of the two jackets and even taking the top off his electric razor in case there could somehow be a safe deposit box key hidden in the minute space beneath. Of course, there wasn't.

The only things I found that sparked my interest were his passport, a mobile telephone and some keys. They had all been in one of the side pockets of the rucksack.

Nothing happened when I pushed the buttons of the telephone. Either it was broken or the battery was flat. I searched in vain for a charger, then put the phone to one side. I picked up the keys. There were three of them on a small split-ring. House keys, I thought, and not very exciting without the house.

The passport was more informative. It was an Australian national's passport in the name of Alan Charles Grady, and tucked inside it was a print-out of a British Airways e-ticket receipt and a boarding card, both also in the name of Grady. I noted with interest that he had actually arrived at Heathrow ten days previously. So where had he been staying for the first week of his visit? The lady at the Royal Sovereign Hotel had clearly said that he had only paid cash in advance for two nights, and she'd moved his stuff on Thursday morning. That would mean he'd arrived there on Tuesday, the same day he had come to Ascot to see me, or possibly on the Monday if she hadn't moved his bags straight away. That left at least six nights unaccounted for. Obviously, I'd been wrong in thinking he must have come straight in on the Heathrow Express from the airport and found the first available hotel room. Unless, of course, he had flown elsewhere in the interim. I looked again at the British Airways ticket receipt but the only other flight listed was his return to Melbourne via Hong Kong scheduled for two weeks next Sunday. A return flight he wouldn't now make.

I again pulled the driving licence copy from my pocket and looked at the address: 312 Macpherson Street, Carlton North in the Australian state of Victoria.

Where exactly was Carlton North, I wondered?

I went upstairs to my office, to the nursery that had never been, and logged onto the internet. Google Earth provided a fine close-up view of Carlton North. It was a mostly residential suburb of Melbourne just two or three miles north of the city centre. Macpherson Street, appropriately for the address of a dead man, ran along the northern edge of an enormous cemetery that covered several blocks in each direction. I rubbed the keys from the key ring between my fingers and thumb, and wondered which of the properties on the screen they opened.

I'd never been to Australia and it was difficult to imagine the upside-down world of Melbourne from the pictures on my computer screen. I sat there looking at the images and wondered if my sisters lived in one of those houses packed so close together into squares or rectangles, each such element of the grid separated from its neighbours by relatively wide tree-lined streets.

As far as I was aware, both my parents had been only children and I had consequently grown up with no aunts and uncles, and hence no cousins either. My mother's parents had died before

I was born, at least that is what my paternal grandmother had told me, but I now wondered if I could still take her word for it. Teddy Talbot, my father's father, was certainly dead – as with my father, I had seen his cooling body – but my paternal grandmother was still alive, though nowadays more in body than in mind. She currently lived, if that was the right term, in a residential care home in Warwick. I went to visit her occasionally but age and Alzheimer's had taken their toll and she was no longer the woman who had raised me, and whom I had known for so long. Thankfully, she wasn't unhappy with her lot, she was just mostly lost in a different existence from the rest of us.

In spite of all her troubles, I had always envied Sophie for having had several siblings and masses of cousins. Despite the rift with her parents over her choice of husband, she had remained as close to the rest of her large family as her illness had allowed. I, meanwhile, had no one other than my demented old grandmother who sometimes didn't recognize me any more.

Except that I now knew I did have family after all. I had two half-sisters in Australia. The only problem was that I didn't know their names or where they lived, and they, in turn, would have absolutely no idea that I existed. I couldn't imagine my father had told his new family that he already had a son, the offspring of a wife that he had strangled in England before fleeing by ship to the Antipodes.

I went downstairs again and back into the sitting room.

Once more I sifted through the sad piles of shirts, underwear and handkerchiefs as if I would now find something I had previously missed. But there was nothing.

I looked at the red-and-black canvas rucksack. An airline baggage label with LHR printed across it in large bold capital letters was fastened round one of the straps with the name GRADY printed smaller on it alongside a barcode, but there was no actual indication of where the label had been attached to the strap. Once again I stared into the rucksack as if I might have somehow overlooked something. As before, it appeared to be completely empty but, nevertheless, I tipped the whole thing upside down and gave it a good shake. It was more out of frustration than in any expectation of finding anything.

As I turned it over, back and forth, I could feel something move.

I placed it down on the floor and peered inside once more.

The rucksack had a waterproof liner sewn into the canvas with a drawstring at the top. There was a gap at the back and I slid my hand down between the liner and the canvas. A space about two inches deep across the whole bottom of the rucksack existed between the liner and the base, and here I found the treasure that the man in the Ascot carpark must have sought.

I pulled out three blue-cling-film-covered packages and carefully used a pair of kitchen scissors to open them at one end. Each contained sizable wads of large-denomination bank-notes, two in British pounds and the other in Australian dollars. I counted each pack in turn and did some rough mental arithmetic.

My father had taken lodgings in a cheap seedy one-star hotel in Sussex Gardens with about thirty thousand pounds' worth of cash in his luggage.

And he had died for it.

CHAPTER 6

There were five other items hidden in the space, in addition to the money.

One was a South African passport in the name of Willem Van Buren.

Another was a small polythene bag containing what appeared at first to be ten grains of rice but, on closer examination, were clearly man made. They looked like frosted glass.

Two others were photocopied booklets about six by eight inches with DOCUMENT OF DESCRIPTION printed along the top of the front cover.

And the fifth was a flat black object about six inches long and two wide with some buttons on it. At first I thought it was a television remote control but it didn't appear to have volume and channel buttons, just 0 to 9 plus an 'enter' button. I pushed them all. Nothing happened. I turned it over. There was a battery compartment on the back that, I discovered, was empty so I took the device through to the kitchen and scavenged the battery from the kitchen clock.

I pushed the buttons again and, this time, was rewarded by a small red light that appeared in the top right-hand corner for a moment before going out. Nothing else happened. I pointed the thing at the television and pushed again. Unsurprisingly, nothing happened other than the flash of the little red light.

I didn't know much about electronics in general, or TV remotes in particular, but I did know that they had to be programmed correctly.

I would show the thing to Luca, I thought. He was not only my whizz-kid at using the computer, he also understood what went on under its cover. Luca had even worked as an electronics maintenance man briefly before he transferred to the racecourse, while my own technical ability ran simply to giving something a sharp clout with my hand if it failed to perform as expected.

I put the battery back in the kitchen clock, which I reset to the right time of twenty to one. I had to be back on the road by nine o'clock in the morning.

I suddenly felt very hungry. I hadn't eaten anything since I'd had a bowl of cereal and a slice of toast for breakfast sixteen hours ago. I hadn't had the time.

I looked in the fridge. There wasn't much there. I usually went to the supermarket once a week on a Sunday to get the essentials like milk, bread and those ready-cooked meals I could simply stuff in the microwave. But this last weekend I had somehow forgotten to go. I shook the plastic milk bottle. There was only enough left for a small bowl of cereal and maybe a cup of coffee in the morning. The loaf of bread was down to the last few slices and they looked to have passed their best with green mould spots appearing round the edges.

I found a tin of baked beans in a cupboard and made myself beans on toast, carefully removing a few mouldy bits from the bread before placing it in the toaster.

I spread the bounty from the rucksack's secret compartment out on the kitchen table in front of me and looked at it as I ate.

I picked up the two booklets with the heading DOCUMENT OF DESCRIPTION. I hadn't seen one close-up before but I knew what they were. Horse passports, I believed they were called, and every racehorse had to have one in order to race. They were a detailed record of a horse's marking and hair whorls. A horse presented at a racecourse for a race had to match the one described in its passport to ensure that another horse wasn't running in its place. In the olden days unscrupulous trainers might have presented a 'ringer' that would run as if it were another horse. The ringer was usually much better than the horse that should have been running and hence it would start at much more favourable odds than if its true identity had been known. Many such a deception had raked in the cash before the introduction of detailed horse passports had put a stop to it.

But the two in front of me were photocopies, not the originals, and could never have been passed off as the real thing. I scanned through them but could see nothing out of the ordinary.

Next I picked up the human passport, that of Willem Van Buren from South Africa, and looked at the photograph. It wasn't the same man I had seen in Sussex Gardens, I was sure of that, because the face that looked out at me from the image in the passport was that of my father. Van Buren must have been the name he had used to check into the Royal Sovereign Hotel.

Did I have yet more sisters, or perhaps some brothers, in Cape Town or Johannesburg?

I was also intrigued by the little bag of rice-type grains. I took one of them out of the bag and rolled it between my thumb and index finger. It was, in fact, slightly larger than a grain of rice, being about a centimetre long and about a third of that in diameter. I held it up to the light but I couldn't see through as it was opaque. I shook it by my ear but it made no noise.

Why, I wondered, would anyone bother to hide a few chips of frosted glass? There had to be more to them than the eye, or the ear, could tell.

I took my tomato-sauce-covered knife and recklessly crushed the grain against the table. It actually broke surprisingly easily. I could now see that the grain was not made of solid glass but was a cylinder with what appeared to be a minute electronic circuit housed inside.

I looked carefully at the nine of them still left in the bag. There were definitely no external connections, no terminals to connect to. Again, I would ask Luca. If anyone knew what they were, he would. I scooped the broken bits back into the bag and placed it on the table.

And then, of course, there was the money.

What should I do with it all?

Well, I told myself, I *should* go and give it to Chief Inspector Llewellyn. But how could I? He certainly wouldn't take it very kindly that I hadn't told him about my father's luggage earlier. He might accuse me again of being somehow involved in his murder.

I began to wish I had told him straight away about the seedy hotel in Sussex Gardens. It would have made things much easier, and also I wouldn't have suffered the fright of my life. I still came out in a cold sweat just thinking about what would have happened if the man had recognized me.

What should I do?

I decided to sleep on it, and went to bed.

Friday at Ascot was wet with an Atlantic weather front sweeping in from the west and bringing a ten-degree drop in temperature. Trust me, I thought, to choose this day to switch from my thick and usually over-warm morning coat to a lining-free lightweight blazer. I took shelter under our large yellow TRUST TEDDY TALBOT emblazoned umbrella and shivered in the strengthening breeze.

'Good party?' I asked Luca and Betsy.

They had been uncharacteristically quiet as we had set up our pitch.

'Great,' said Betsy without much conviction.

'Late night?' I asked, enjoying myself.

'Very,' she said.

'Excellent,' I said. 'A good party has to end in a late night.'

'Yes. But we could have done without the gatecrashers,' she said, 'and the police.'

'The police?'

'My aunt called the police,' she said, clearly not pleased.

'But why?' I asked.

'About a hundred uninvited guests turned up at her house,' she said. 'That's where the party was.'

'Yobs, you mean,' said Luca with a degree of bitterness I hadn't witnessed in him before. 'Your stupid sister. Ruined her own party.'

'She didn't ruin it,' Betsy retorted in a pained tone.

86

I was beginning to wish I'd never asked.

'What do you call inviting people to a party on Facebook?' he said. 'Not bloody surprising so many weirdos turned up and trashed the place.'

'And you weren't much help,' Betsy said icily.

'And what exactly do you mean by that?' Luca demanded.

'Look,' I said, interrupting them. 'I'm sorry now I asked. Calm down, both of you. We have work to do.'

They both fell silent but their body language continued to speak louder than words, and the unspoken conversation was far removed from the loving episode I had witnessed on Tuesday as they had walked, hand in hand, on their way to a drink at the bandstand bar.

Oh dear, I thought. It wasn't just the weather that had turned cool.

The afternoon progressed without any of the excitement of the previous day. The incessant rain understandably kept many punters away from the betting ring. They preferred the dry, warm surroundings of the grandstand bars and restaurants, placing bets with the staff from the Tote who would come to them rather than vice versa.

I was allowed by the racecourse to ply my trade as a book-maker, for a sizable fee, of course, but only at my chosen pitch. I couldn't wander the bars and restaurants relieving punters of their cash as they sat at table eating their lunch or drinking their champagne.

There were no outages of the internet service, no disruptions of the mobile phones, no last-minute wild swings in the prices. Everything was as predicable as it was boring. Favourites won three of the six races while a couple of rank outsiders gave us bookies some respite in the others.

All in all, it was a remarkably unremarkable day. Other than the ongoing frosty relations between my staff, the only memorable feature was the number of technical staff from both the internet provider and the mobile phone networks who stood around waiting in vain for their systems to crash. Clearly, somebody's tail had been seriously pulled by the events of yesterday.

'Do you two combatants need a lift home?' I asked as we packed up in deathly silence. Neither of them said a word. 'For God's sake,' I went on. 'Do either of you want on go on living or what?'

It raised a smile on Luca's face. A slight smile that evaporated almost as quickly as it appeared.

'The Teddy Talbot bus leaves for High Wycombe and beyond in five minutes whether you're on it or not,' I said with a degree of exasperation in my tone.

Still nothing.

'Do I assume, then, that we won't be back here tomorrow?' I asked as we made it to the car park unrobbed. Even muggers don't like the rain.

Royal Ascot Saturday had become one of our busiest days of the year.

'I'm game,' said Luca.

I looked expectantly at Betsy.

'OK,' she said grudgingly. 'I'll be here.'

'Good,' I said. 'And can I expect a thawing of the cold war?'

There was no answer from either of them.

I was getting bored with this game.

'OK,' I said. 'New rule number one. No talking – no lift.'

'I'm sorry,' Luca said.

'No problem,' I said.

'Not you, Ned,' he said with irritation. 'I'm sorry to Betsy.' He turned to her.

'Oh . . .' Betsy burst into tears, gasping great gulps of air.

She and Luca dissolved into each other's arms and just stood there hugging each other, getting wet, like a scene from a romantic film.

'Oh, for goodness' sake,' I said. 'You lovebirds had better get in the back seat while I drive.'

I was quite thankful that Luca didn't in fact sit in the back with Betsy but up front next to me. I don't think I could have taken all that lovey-dovey stuff all the way to High Wycombe.

'What do you think that is?' I said to him. I handed over the black plastic object that resembled a television remote that I had put in the door pocket of the Volvo that morning.

He turned the device over and over in his hands. Then he removed the battery compartment cover.

'Here,' I said and passed him a pack of batteries I'd bought on my way to the races.

He slid a battery into the housing and was rewarded by the brief flash of red whenever he pushed any of the buttons, just as I had been.

'The light stays on a few moments longer if you press the "enter" button,' I said. He pressed it, and it did. 'Do you think it's a remote for something?'

'Dunno,' he said, still turning the device over and over. 'It obviously can't be for a television or a radio, there's no volume control. How about a garage door opener or something?'

'But why the numbers?' I said. 'Surely garage door openers just have one button?'

'How about if they need a code?' he said. 'Maybe you need to push 1066 or something and then enter.'

'Yeah, maybe,' I said. 'How about these?' I passed him the small plastic bag containing the unbroken grains, along with the one I had crushed.

He poured the tiny items out of the bag onto his hand then he held the broken one up in between his thumb and forefinger.

'I assume this one was like the others before you stamped on it?'

'I used a knife actually,' I said. 'And yes, it was. They're quite easy to break.'

'They're definitely electronic,' he said.

'Even I can see that,' I replied sarcastically. 'But what are they for? They don't seem to have any connections and I also know that glass doesn't conduct electricity, so how do they work?'

'It's also a bit small to have its own battery,' he said.

'So how does it work?' I asked him.

'If I knew what it did, I'd probably know how it worked.' He continued to study the tiny circuit. 'Passive electronics,' he said very quietly, as if to himself.

'What?' I said.

'Passive electronics,' he repeated.

'And what are they when they're at home?' I said.

He laughed. 'Devices with no gain,' he said. 'They're called passive electronic components or passive devices.'

'So?' I said, none the wiser.

'Transistors provide gain,' he said. 'They can be used as amplifiers to give a signal gain so, for example, it can drive a speaker in a radio. The signal received by the aerial is very, very small so, in simple terms, it has to be amplified by a series of transistors in order to drive the speaker so you can hear the music.'

'The higher the volume, the greater the gain?' I said.

'Just so,' he said. 'But transistors need a power supply. They must either have a battery or be connected to the mains for them to work, so this little sucker can't have transistors.' He held up the tiny electrical circuit from the broken grain.

'Passive electronics,' I said.

'You've got it,' he said, smiling.

'What are you two on about?' asked Betsy suddenly from the back seat.

'This,' said Luca, carefully handing her one of the unbroken grains.

'Oh, I know what that is,' she said, rather condescendingly.

'What?' Luca and I said together.

'It's a chip for dogs,' she said. 'We had one put in our Irish setter last year.'

'What do they do?' I asked over my shoulder.

'They're for identification. They're injected under the skin using a syringe. We had one put in our dog so Mum and Dad could take her to France without having to do that quarantine thing when she came back. She simply got scanned by customs to check she was the right dog with the right vaccinations.'

'Like horses,' I said.

'Eh?' said Luca.

'Horses have them too,' I said. 'To check they are indeed who their owner says they are. All of them have to have chips inserted or they can't run. I read about it in the *Racing Post*, ages ago. I just didn't know what the chips looked like. I don't know why but I somehow expected them to be bigger, rectangular and flat.'

Luca looked again at the tiny electrical circuit.

'It must be a passive arfid circuit,' he said. 'This little coil must be the antenna.'

'I'll take your word for it,' I said. 'What's an arfid when it's at home?'

'A radio frequency identification circuit, R-F-I-D, pronounced arfid,' he said slowly, as if for a child. 'You put a scanner close by that emits a radio wave. The wave is picked up by the little antenna and that provides just enough power for the circuit to transmit back an identification number.'

'Sounds complicated,' I said.

'Not really,' Luca replied. 'They exist all over the place. Those alarm things in shops that go off if you try and take things out without paying, they use RFIDs. They simply have the tag on the items, and the scanners are the vertical things by the doors you have to walk between. Also the tube and buses in London use them in the Oyster cards. You put the card on the scanner and it reads the information to make sure you have enough credit to travel. They're very clever.'

'So I see,' I said.

'Not everyone is keen on them, though,' he went on. 'Some people call them Spychips because they allow a person to be tracked without their knowledge. But I think they'll soon be on everything. You know, instead of barcodes. The supermarkets are already experimenting with them for checkout. You only have to walk past the scanner and everything is automatically checked out without you even having to take it out of the trolley. One day, your credit card will be scanned in the same way and the total amount deducted from your bank account without you having to do anything except push the whole lot out to your car, load up and drive away.'

'Amazing,' I said.

'Yeah. But the trouble is that, theoretically, the same RFIDs could also be used to tell the cops if you broke the speed limit on the way home from the store.'

'Surely not,' I said.

'Oh yes they could,' he said. 'They already use RFIDs in cars to pay road and bridge tolls in lots of places, E-ZPass in New York for one. It's not much more of a step for them to calculate your average speed between two points and issue a ticket if you were going too fast. Big Brother is definitely watching you, and, even if he isn't now, he will be soon.'

'How do you know so much about these RFID things?' I asked.

'Studied them at college and I also read electronics magazines,' he said. 'But I've never seen one this small before.' He held up one of the tiny glass grains.

So why, I thought, had my father had ten of them in his luggage? Perhaps they were something to do with the photocopied horse passports.

'Is the black remote thing a scanner?' I asked.

Luca pointed it at the chip and pushed the enter button. The red light came on briefly and then went off again, just as before.

'It doesn't have any sort of read-out, so I doubt it,' said Luca. 'I'll ask at my electronics club, if you like.'

'Electronics club?' I said.

'Yeah. Mostly teenagers,' he said. 'Making robots or radio-controlled cars and such. Every Friday night in the local youth centre in Wycombe. I help them out most weeks.'

I thought about whether I should give the device to him, or to the police, along with the money.

'OK,' I said. 'Ask at your club if anyone knows what it's for. Take the glass grains as well, in case they're somehow connected.'

'Right,' he replied, smiling. 'We love a challenge. Can we take it apart?'

'I suppose so,' I said. 'But make sure it goes back together again.'

'Right,' he said again. 'I'll take it with me tonight. I'll let you know in the morning if we get anywhere.'

I dropped Luca and Betsy in High Wycombe, and then I went to see my grandmother.

Her room at the nursing home in Warwick was a microcosm of my childhood memories. On the wall over her bed was a nineteenth-century original watercolour of a child feeding chickens that had once hung over the mantelpiece in the family sitting room. Photographs in silver frames stood alongside little porcelain pots and other knick-knacks on her antique chest of drawers as they had always done in my grandparents' bedroom. A framed tapestry of the Queen in her coronation coach shared wall space with a hand-painted plate that I had given them in celebration of their ruby wedding anniversary.

Each item was so familiar to me. It was only my grandmother herself who was unfamiliar. As unfamiliar to me as I sometimes was to her.

'Hello, Nanna,' I said to her, leaning down and kissing her on the forehead.

She briefly looked up at me with confused recognition, and

said nothing. The nurses told me that she could still chat away quite well on some days, but not at all on others, and I personally hadn't heard her speak now for quite a few weeks.

'How are you feeling?' I asked her. 'Have you been watching the racing on the television? And the Queen?'

There was no reply, not a flicker of apparent understanding. Today was clearly not one of her good days.

The decision to place her in a nursing home had been both a difficult and an easy one. I had realized for some time that she had been losing her memory but had simply put it down to old age. Only when I was contacted by the police, who had found her wandering the streets in her pink nightie and slippers, had I taken her to the doctor's. There had been a period of testing and several visits to neurologists before a diagnosis of Alzheimer's had been confirmed. Sophie had abdicated all responsibility in the caring department, which was fair enough as she had her own problems to worry about, so I arranged for a live-in nurse to look after my grandmother in her own house. I was determined that she shouldn't have to live in a care home full of old people who sat in a circle all day staring at the floor.

Then one day, when I went to spend an evening with her, she became very agitated and confused. She didn't seem to know who I was and continually accused me of stealing her wedding ring. It was more distressing for me than it was for her, but it was her live-in nurse who was the most upset.

The poor girl was totally exhausted from the ever-increasing workload, and was at the end of her tether. Between bouts of tears, she had told me what life for my grandmother was really like. Above all she was lonely. Keeping her in her own home had been no real kindness to anyone, and certainly not to her. So the following day I had made arrangements for my grandmother to go into permanent residential care, and had promptly sold her house to pay for it.

That had been two and a half years ago and the money was starting to run out. I hated to think what would happen if she lived much longer.

As usual in the evenings she was sitting in her room with all the lights full on. She didn't like the dark and insisted that the lights be left on both day and night. As it was, on this mid-summer day, the sun was still shining brightly through her west-facing window, but that made no difference to her need for maximum electric light as well.

I sat down on a chair facing her and took her hand in mine. She looked at my face with hollow staring eyes. I stroked her hand and smiled at her. I was beginning to think this had been a waste of my time.

'Nanna,' I said to her slowly, 'I've come to ask you about Peter. Do you remember your son Peter?'

She went on looking at me without giving any sign that she had heard.

'Your son Peter,' I repeated. 'He married a girl called Tricia. Do you remember? They had a little boy called Ned. Do you remember Ned? You looked after him.'

I thought she hadn't registered anything but then she smiled and spoke, softly but clearly. 'Ned,' she said. 'My little Ned.'

Her voice was unchanged and I felt myself welling up with emotion.

'Yes,' I said. 'Your little Ned. Nanna, I'm right here.'

Her eyes focused on my face.

'Ned,' she repeated. I wasn't sure if she was remembering the past or whether she was able to recognize me.

'Nanna,' I said, 'do you remember Peter? Your son Peter?'

'Dead,' she said.

'Do you remember his wife, Tricia?' I asked her gently.

'Dead,' she repeated.

'Yes,' I said. 'But do you know how she died?'

My grandmother just looked at me with a quizzical expression on her face.

Finally she said, 'Secret,' and put one of her long thin fingers to her lips.

'And Peter,' I said. 'Where did Peter go?'

'Dead,' she repeated.

'No,' I said. 'Peter wasn't dead. Tricia was dead. Where is Peter?'

She didn't say anything and her eyes had returned to their distant stare.

Secret, she had said. So she must have known.

I pulled the photocopy of my father's photographs from my pocket and put it on her lap. She looked down at it. I placed the tiny photo of my mother and father at Blackpool there too.

She looked down for some time and I thought at one point that she had drifted off to sleep so I took the pictures and put them back in my pocket.

I stood up to leave but, as I leaned forward to kiss her on her head, she sat up straight.

'Murderer,' she said, quietly but quite distinctly.

'Who was a murderer?' I asked, kneeling down so that my face was close to hers.

'Murderer,' she repeated.

'Yes,' I said. 'But who was a murderer?'

'Murderer,' she said once more.

'Who was murdered?' I asked changing tack. I already knew the answer.

'He murdered Tricia,' she said. She began to cry and I gave her a tissue from the box beside her bed. She wiped her nose and then she turned and looked at me, her eyes momentarily full of recognition and understanding.

'And he murdered her baby.'

CHAPTER 7

'It emits a radio signal,' said Luca in the car on the way to Ascot on Saturday morning. He was holding the black remote-type thing with the buttons. 'You were bloody lucky this wasn't nicked,' he added.

'Why would it be nicked?' I asked him.

'Because the teenagers at the electronics club are a bunch of hooligans,' he said. 'Most of them are only there because the courts make them go. To keep them off the streets on Friday nights. Supposed to be part of their rehabilitation. I ask you. Most of them wouldn't be rehabilitated by a stretch in the army.'

'But what about this?' I said, pointing at the device.

'One of the little horrors had it in his bag,' he said. 'God knows what he thought he would do with it. Just liked the look of it so he lifted it. They are like bloody magpies. If it shines, they'll nick it.'

'You said it emits a radio signal,' I said. 'What sort of signal?'

'Fairly low frequency,' he said. 'But quite powerful. One of the staff at the club was able to set up an oscilloscope to see it.'

'What's an oscilloscope?' I asked.

'Like one of those things in a hospital that shows the heart rate of patients,' he said. 'It displays a trace on a screen.'

'But what's the thing for?' I asked.

'I'm not sure but I think it might be for writing information onto the RFIDs.'

'The glass grains?' I asked.

'Yes,' he said. 'The end slides off.' He showed me. 'And you can fit one of the grains into this hollow.' He pointed at it as I drove. 'When you push the "enter" button, it sends out a signal. I think that must program the RFID with the numbers you punch into it before pushing the "enter" button.'

'Is that really possible?' I said. 'There aren't any connectors.'

'It's easy,' he said. 'Writing to RFIDs occurs all the time. When someone puts their Oyster card near one of those round yellow pads on the tube gates, the card is first scanned to determine the available credit, then the system automatically deducts the fare and rewrites the card with a new balance. Same thing on all the buses. It's done by radio waves. It doesn't need connectors.'

I was slightly disappointed. I had somehow hoped that the device was going to be more exciting than something that was fitted to every bus in London. But why then, I wondered, did my father think it was necessary to hide it in his rucksack?

I yawned. Sleep had not come easily to me after my visit to my grandmother. I had lain awake for hours thinking about what she had said to me, and also how that secret must have burned ferociously in her for so long. What did you do when you found out that your son was a murderer? More to the point for me, what did you do when you found out that your father was one?

I thought back to when I had sat by my father's body in

the hospital after he had died. Was it really just four days previously? It felt like half a lifetime.

I had mourned for what might have been, for the lost years of opportunity. Somehow, even in spite of the knowledge I had gained since, I felt some form of affinity with the man who now lay silently in some mortuary cold storage. But what had he done? Had he really deprived me not only of himself but also of my mother, and a brother or sister as well?

I had tried to telephone Detective Sergeant Murray at Windsor police station but I was told he was either elsewhere or off duty. I had left a message for him to call me but, so far, there had been nothing.

'It's the Wokingham today,' said Luca, rubbing his hands and bringing me back from my daydreaming.

'Sure is,' I said.

The Wokingham Stakes was the fourth race of the day on Royal Ascot Saturday and it was one of the most lucrative races of the whole meeting for us bookmakers. It was also a popular race with the trainers with the number of runners limited only by how many starting stalls could be accommodated across the width of the racecourse.

But it was not only a cash-cow for the bookies, it was fun as well. While it was true that most bets tended to be smaller than for some of the group races, there were plenty of them and it seemed like a happy race with no one placing white-knuckle wagers that they couldn't afford to lose.

Betsy went to sleep in the back and Luca looked through the *Racing Post* as I drove.

'Thirty runners again today,' he said. 'They reckon here that Burton Bank will start favourite at about six- or seven-to-one.'

'Who trains him?' I asked.

'George Wiley,' Luca replied.

'Wiley trains in Cumbria, doesn't he?' I said. 'That's quite a way to come. He must think he's a good prospect. How about the others?'

Luca studied the paper. 'About ten with a realistic chance, I'd say, but the Wokingham is always a bit of a lottery.' He smiled.

'How about the Golden Jubilee?' I asked. The Golden Jubilee Stakes was the big race of the day. Like the Wokingham, it was also run over a straight six furlongs and was for three-year-olds and upwards.

'Eighteen runners this year,' he said. 'Pulpit Reader will probably be favourite but, again, it's anyone's race. Always the same in the sprints.'

We discussed the afternoon's races and runners for a while longer. I thought we would need the unpredictability of the Wokingham and the Golden Jubilee Stakes after the first two races of the day. The Chesham Stakes and the Hardwicke Stakes were both renowned for producing short-priced winners, favouring the punter.

The previous day's rain had swept away eastwards into the North Sea and the sun had returned, bringing out the Saturday crowd that was streaming into the racecourse by the time we had negotiated the traffic jams and parked the car. It looked like being another busy day at the office.

Chief Inspector Llewellyn and Sergeant Murray were waiting for me in the betting ring.

'That was quick,' I said to the sergeant before either of them could say a word.

'What was quick?' he asked.

'Didn't you get my message?' I asked him.

'No,' he replied blankly.

'Oh,' I said. 'I left one for you this morning at Windsor police station.'

'What did it say?' he asked.

'Just to call me,' I said.

'And what exactly did you want to speak to my sergeant about?' the chief inspector asked in his accusing tone.

'Nothing much,' I said. 'Forget it.'

I had wanted to ask Sergeant Murray for more details about my mother's demise, but I wasn't going to ask his boss. I didn't want to give the chief inspector the pleasure of refusing to answer, as I was certain he would.

'We need to ask you some more questions,' he said.

I hoped the questions weren't about bundles of cash in a missing rucksack.

'What about?' I said. 'Can't it wait until after I've finished work?'

'No,' he said with no apology.

'Sorry, Luca,' I said. 'Can you and Betsy set things up?'

'No problem,' Luca said.

The policemen and I wandered down away from the grand-stand to a quieter area.

'Now, Chief Inspector,' I said. 'How can I help you today?'

'Did your father tell you which hotel he was staying at in London?' he said.

'No,' I replied truthfully, 'he did not.'

'We have been unable to find any hotel where someone called Grady or Talbot checked in,' he said.

'He told me that he'd only recently arrived from Australia

but not exactly when. Perhaps he arrived that morning and came straight to Ascot races.'

'No, sir,' said the chief inspector. 'British Airways have confirmed that he arrived from Australia on one of their flights, but that was the previous week.'

'I'm sorry,' I said. 'The first time he contacted me was on the day he died.'

'According to the airline, when he arrived at Heathrow he had a piece of hold luggage with him,' he said. 'We have been unable to trace it. Did he give you anything? A left-luggage receipt for example?'

'No,' I said. 'I'm afraid not. He gave me nothing.'

Why, I wondered, didn't I just tell them I had the luggage? And the money, and the other things. There was something that stopped me doing so. Maybe it was a hope that my father was not, in fact, a murderer as everyone seemed to think, and the only chance I might ever have of finding out was somehow connected with the dubious contents of that rucksack. Or perhaps it was just down to my natural aversion towards policemen in general, and Chief Inspector Llewellyn in particular.

'Do you have any further recollection of the person who attacked you?' he asked.

'Not really,' I said. 'But I am sure he was a white man aged somewhere in his mid- to late thirties wearing a charcoal-grey hoodie and a dark scarf. And he wore army boots.'

'How about his trousers?' the chief inspector asked.

'Blue jeans,' I said.

'A distinctive belt or buckle?' he said.

'Sorry, I didn't see.'

'Any distinguishing marks, scars or so forth?'

'None that I could see,' I said, again truthfully. 'I think he had fairish hair.'

'How could you tell if his hood was up?' asked the chief inspector.

'Thinking back, I believe I could see it under the hood.'

'Long or short?' he said.

'Short,' I said with certainty. 'It stood upright on his head.'

'Mmm,' he said. 'You didn't say that on Tuesday night.'

'I hadn't remembered on Tuesday night,' I said. Or seen it, I thought.

'Could you do an e-fit for us?' he asked.

'An e-fit?'

'A computer-made image of the killer,' he explained.

'So he did actually kill my father?' I said, somewhat sarcastically. 'The post-mortem results are in, are they?'

'Yes,' he said. 'According to the pathologist your father died from two stab wounds to his abdomen, one on each side of his navel. They were angled upwards, penetrating the diaphragm and puncturing both his lungs. It was a very professional job.' To my ears it sounded like the chief inspector almost admired the technique employed. There was certainly no sorrow in his voice that it had resulted in the loss of my parent. To him, I suppose, a murderous villain had got his just desserts after thirty-six years on the run.

'So what happens now?' I asked.

'About what?'

'My father,' I said. 'Can there be a funeral? And how about any family he may have in Australia? Have they been informed?'

'I understand the Melbourne police have been to his home address,' he said. 'They found no one there. It seems your father lived alone under the name of Alan Grady.'

'But he told me he had two daughters from a previous marriage,' I said. 'Has anyone told them?'

'Not that I'm aware of,' he said. His tone indicated that he didn't consider it in the least important. And he might have been right. According to my father, even he hadn't seen my sisters for fifteen years. They could be anywhere.

'How about the funeral?' I asked.

'That will be up to the coroner,' he said. 'The inquest will be opened on Monday. You should have received a summons to attend by now.'

I thought about the pile of unopened letters on my hall table. The opening of my mail, or rather the lack of it, was another of my failings. On a par with failing to eat properly, or at all.

'Why do they need to summons me?' I said.

'For identification purposes,' he said. 'You are the deceased's next of kin.'

So I was, I thought. How strange to be next of kin when, for all my life, I hadn't even known that I had any kin, other than my aged grandparents.

'But isn't it a bit soon to hold an inquest?' I said.

'It will only be opened for formal identification of the deceased and then it will be adjourned to a later date,' the chief inspector said. 'The coroner may issue a certificate for burial. But that will be up to him.'

Formal identification could be interesting, I thought. Talbot, Grady or Van Buren.

'As next of kin, is it my job to organize the funeral?' I asked.

'Up to you,' he said. 'It's usual but not compulsory.'

'Right,' I said. I looked at my watch. 'Is there anything else?'

'Not for now, Mr Talbot,' said the chief inspector. 'But don't go anywhere.'

'Is that an official request?' I asked.

'You know, there's something about you I don't like,' he said.

'Perhaps you just don't like bookmakers,' I said back.

'You are so right,' he said. 'But there's something else about you.' He jabbed his finger onto my chest.

I thought he was trying to intimidate me, or perhaps he was hoping to provoke me into saying something I would regret. So I simply smiled at him.

'I can't say I'm very fond of you either, Chief Inspector,' I said, staring him in the eye. 'But I don't suppose it will cloud the professional dealings between us, now will it?'

It certainly would, I thought. At least, it would on my side.

He didn't answer the question but turned on his heel and started to walk away. But he only went three paces before turning and coming back.

'Don't pick a fight with me, Mr Talbot,' he said, his face about six inches from mine. 'Because you'll lose.'

I decided that silence here was the best policy.

Eventually he turned again and walked off.

'Be careful, Mr Talbot,' the sergeant said to me in a more friendly tone. 'He doesn't like to be crossed.'

'He started it,' I said lamely in my defence.

'Just take the warning,' he said seriously.

'I will,' I said. 'Thank you, Sergeant.'

'And I'd also watch my back if I were you,' he said.

'Surely Chief Inspector Llewellyn is not that malicious?' I said jokingly.

'No, not quite,' he said with a smile. 'But I was really thinking about the man who killed your father. You were a witness to that, don't forget. I just wouldn't walk down any dark alleys alone at night, that's all. Witnesses to murders are an endangered species.' The smile had left his face. He was deadly serious.

'Thank you, Sergeant,' I said again. 'I'll take that warning too.'

He nodded, and set off to follow the chief inspector.

'Just a minute,' I called after him. 'Do you happen to know where my mother was murdered?'

He stopped and came back. 'Where?' he said.

'Yes,' I replied. 'Where did she die? And when?'

'Thirty-six years ago,' he said.

'Yes, but when exactly? What date? And where was she found?'

'I'll have a look,' he said. 'Can't promise anything, but I'll read the file.'

'Thanks,' I said.

He went off, hurrying to catch up with his boss, leaving me to wonder if my father's killer knew who I was, and how to find me.

'What was all that about?' asked Luca when I went back to our pitch.

'Tuesday,' I said.

'What exactly happened on Tuesday?' he asked.

'I was mugged,' I said, repeating my original story.

'Those two coppers have been here now to see you twice,' he said. 'Come on. Don't tell me it was just because someone mugged a bookie. What else?'

'Well,' I said. 'You know about the murder in the car park?'

'Yeah,' he replied. 'Of course.' Everyone was still talking about it.

'It seems the man who mugged me might have been the killer.'

'Oh,' he said. 'That's all right, then.' He seemed relieved.

'What do you mean, all right?' I cried, exasperated. 'He could have killed me too, you know.'

'Yeah,' he said. 'But he didn't.' He smiled. 'Betsy and I reckoned you must be in some sort of trouble with the law.'

'Oh, thanks,' I said sardonically. 'Such confidence you have in your provider.'

As predicted, the first two races, the Chesham and the Hardwicke Stakes, were each won by the favourite.

'That was fine by us,' said Luca into my ear after the second. 'We had that laid at better odds so, for a change, the favourite's done us a favour.'

'Well done,' I said back to him. 'Now for the fun and games.'

Betting on the Golden Jubilee Stakes was brisk with queues forming in front of me of eager punters wanting to hand over their money. As Luca had expected, Pulpit Reader was established as the market leader but at odds of four-to-one or better. The race was wide open and the market reflected it.

'Fifty on Pulpit,' said the man in front of me.

'Fifty on number five at fours,' I said to Luca, who pushed his keypad. I took the ticket from the printer and handed it to the man.

'What price number sixteen?' asked AJ, the next man in the queue, who was sporting today a rather traditional grey waistcoat under his expansive black jacket.

Our electronic board was not big enough to have all the runners displayed at once.

'Horse sixteen?' I said to Luca.

'Thirty-threes,' he said back.

'Tenner each way,' AJ said pushing a twenty-pound note towards me.

The ticket duly appeared from the printer.

And so it went on. Mostly smallish bets of ten or twenty pounds or so. A wager on the Golden Jubilee was more for entertainment than for making serious money.

We were still taking bets as the race started. A young woman in a black-and-white dress with a matching large-brimmed hat was my last customer, thrusting a ten-pound note my way even as the horses were passing the five-furlong pole. 'Ten pounds to win on horse number five, please,' she implored breathlessly from somewhere beneath her headgear. I took her money and issued the ticket.

'No more,' I said, but there were no more. Everyone was watching the race, most of them on one of the big-screen TVs set up opposite the grandstand.

The Golden Jubilee Stakes is the British leg of the Global Sprint Challenge and consequently it attracts horses from overseas. It was an American horse on this occasion that broke away from the pack in the final furlong to win by more than a length. The crowd were unusually hushed. Pulpit Reader, number five, could only finish fourth. The young woman in black and white had enjoyed less than a minute's run for her money, which would now remain firmly in my pocket.

People gamble for many reasons but it is always, ultimately, the thrill of the win that gives them the 'high' they crave. The professional gamblers, those few who can make their living from betting on the horses, would say that it is all about long-term returns, not short-term thrills, but even they would have to admit to having an extra burst of adrenalin running through their veins during a close finish involving one of their selections.

For most, gambling is for recreation rather than remuneration. It adds to their enjoyment of a day at the races. Some of my clients thought they'd had a really good day if they backed a couple of winners, even if their wagers on other losers had cost them more than their winnings. The delight of a win banished the memories of the losses.

Bookmakers, I suppose, would have to be placed in the 'professional gambler' category. Bookmaking is a business, and solid, regular returns rather than sharp peaks and troughs are the aim. Nevertheless, it still gave me a thrill to be able to keep the young woman's ten-pound note, especially when she had been so eager to place the bet even after the horses had started running. I suppose, to be honest, no one becomes a bookmaker unless they have at least a touch of Schadenfreude in them. After all, unlike for stockbrokers or investment portfolio managers, it was my clients' misfortune that made me richer.

Next up was the thirty-runner Wokingham Stakes and that was even more of a lottery than the Golden Jubilee.

The race was always like a cavalry charge, flat-out for three-quarters of a mile from the starting stalls along the straight to the winning post. It is also a handicap, which means that the better rated horses have to carry the most weight as determined by the handicapper, whose aim and dream it was that all the runners would finish in one huge dead heat. Wins by favourites have been rare, and rank outsiders have often claimed the prize.

Again betting was brisk with money spread fairly evenly on both the shorter-priced favourites and on the outsiders alike. Historically, there were very few pointers that helped the discerning punter in this race. Often, in sprints, one side of the track seems to produce more winners than the other, and the number of the starting stall a horse was drawn in could be a good indicator of its chances. However, over the years, the draw in the sprint races at Ascot hadn't typically proved to be much of a factor, with winners of the Wokingham Stakes coming from all across the course.

Nearly every punter has some system or another that they swear by, even if it's closing their eyes and sticking a pin into the list of runners in the racecard. Some will never back mares or fillies in races with colts on the all-weather surfaces, while others avoided short-priced favourites in handicaps. Some follow a particular jockey, or a given trainer with a proven record, and others will only trust their cash to horses that have run and been placed within the last seven days.

In general, those punters who do the best are the ones who are disciplined and who study the form. Disciplined in so far as they record everything, don't go mad on hunches, and don't panic when they have a losing streak, as they surely will.

The most successful are those who know about almost every horse in training. And they study the racing every day. They learn, over time, which horses run consistently to form and which do not. They discover which horses prefer right-handed tracks and which do better left-handed, which jumpers like long run-ins and which short, and whether they are more likely to win with uphill finishes or flat ones. They know if a horse runs above or below par on firm or soft ground, and also what weight suits a particular horse and whether to keep away from it in handicaps when it's rated too highly. They know where each horse is trained, if it runs badly after long journeys in a horsebox, and even if a horse tends to do better than its rivals in sunshine or the rain.

Too much information, some might say, but the discerning punter soon learns which pieces of the jigsaw are the crucial ones. Horse racing is not a science and there will always be surprises, but, over time, just like human athletes, good horses run well and bad horses don't.

Making a profit from gambling on horses involves identifying those occasions when the offered odds for a horse to win are better than the true probability of that outcome. So if the knowledgeable punter calculates that the chances of a horse winning a particular race are, say, one in two, and the odds offered by a bookmaker are better than evens, that is the time to bet.

In 1873 Joseph Jagger famously broke the bank at Monte Carlo by discovering and exploiting a bias in the casino's roulette wheel which made some numbers come up more often than others. However, these days, no one can seriously improve their chances of winning the National Lottery jackpot by simply studying how often the numbered balls have come out of the machines on prior occasions because so much effort goes into ensuring that the draw is completely random and unpredictable. But, in horse racing, if previous form was not a fair indicator of future performance then there would be no bookmakers, and probably no racing. Certainly there would not be British Thoroughbred racing as we know it, with over five million people per year attending race meetings and some seventeen thousand racehorses in training.

'Ten each way Burton Bank,' said a man in front of me.

'Ten pounds each way number two at seven-to-one,' I called to Luca over my shoulder.

I took the man's twenty-pound note and gave him the ticket in return. Ten pounds 'each way' meant, ten pounds on the horse to win, and ten on it to place, which in a handicap of over sixteen runners meant to finish in the first four.

The next person in the queue was the young woman in the black-and-white dress and matching wide-brimmed hat.

'Ten pounds each way on number eleven,' she said, tilting her head up so she could see me, and I could see her. She was gorgeous.

'Ten each way number eleven at sixteens,' I called to Luca.

The ticket appeared and I handed it over. 'Better luck this time,' I said to her.

She looked slightly taken aback that I had spoken to her, and she even blushed a little, her cheeks showing pink against her monochrome outfit. 'Thank you,' she said, taking the ticket and hurrying away. I watched her go.

'Do you take a forecast?' said the next man in line bringing my attention back to business.

'No,' I said. 'Win or each way only.'

He turned away. A forecast is a bet that predicts the first two finishers in a race. A straight forecast meant the first two in the correct order, and was known in the United States as an Exacta. There are lots of multiple bets from simple doubles or trebles when all selections have to win, to others with such strange names such as Trixie, Yankee, Canadian, Patent or Lucky 15, which contain multiple singles, doubles and trebles on three, four or five horses running in different races. We didn't accept any of them because it became too complicated, and too time consuming. We left those to the betting shops and the big boys. Luca was keener to take them than me, but our regular betting ring customers would go elsewhere if we kept them waiting longer than the next guy.

Betting became fast and furious as the race time approached. Everyone, it seemed, wanted to have a bet on the Wokingham. A probable long-odds winner was encouraging everyone to have a punt and the wad of notes in my hand grew steadily as the minutes ticked by to the start.

Burton Bank was just about holding his favouritism at seven-to-one, although there were two other horses whose prices had shortened to fifteen-to-two.

'Twenty pounds to win on Burton Bank,' said my next customer, a young man in morning dress.

'Twenty to win number two at sevens,' I said over my shoulder to Luca.

'Bloody hell,' he replied. 'The internet's gone down again.'

CHAPTER 8

'Phones as well?' I asked.

Luca was busy pushing buttons on his mobile.

He nodded. 'Same as before.'

The effect was startling. Suddenly there were men running everywhere with walkie-talkies in their hands and curly wires visible over their collars leading, I presumed, to inserts in their ears. They scanned the bookmakers' boards, on the lookout for sudden changes to the odds.

'Twenty pounds to win on Burton Bank,' repeated the young man in front of me, slightly irritated at the delay.

'Sorry,' I said to him. 'Twenty to win number two at sevens,' I repeated, turning to Luca. He looked at me and shrugged his shoulders then pressed the keys and out popped the ticket from the printer. I held it out to the young man, who snatched it away.

'A tenner each way number four,' said the next punter, a large man in a blue-striped shirt and red tie.

I glanced up at our prices board.

'Ten pounds each way number four at fifteen-to-one,' I said, and the ticket duly appeared.

Ten pounds each way wasn't going to be enough to significantly change the odds, I thought, not even on a relative outsider.

There was not much going on, although I could see some of the men with the earpieces moving down the lines of bookies making bets and keeping a close eye on the prices.

But no one tried to make any odds-changing bets with me and our board hardly altered in the five minutes or so before the race. But that didn't stop the chaps with the earpieces running up and down in front of me shouting at each other, both directly and through their walkie-talkies.

'What do you mean, it's busy?' one of them shouted into his two-way radio.

I couldn't hear the reply as it obviously played straight into his ear.

'Well get her out now,' he shouted. He turned to one of the others. 'There's a damn woman in the phone box making a call.'

It was almost funny.

Larry Porter clearly thought it was, and he stood full-square, laughing loudly.

'It's back,' said Luca just as the starting stalls opened and the cavalry charge began.

'What a surprise,' I said.

I watched the race unfold on one of the big-screen TVs. As was usually the case in the Wokingham, the thirty runners divided into two packs running close to the rails on either side of the course in the traditional commentator's nightmare.

The handicapper didn't quite get his dream of a multiple dead heat but still there was a pretty close blanket finish, with those running on the stand rail having a slight advantage.

'First number four,' announced the public address system. 'Second number eleven. Third number twenty-six. The fourth horse was number two.'

So Burton Bank, horse number two, had finished fourth. He had once again been made clear favourite with a starting price of five-to-one, so some of those bets made by the earpieces must have been to try to shorten his price. On Thursday, in the Gold Cup, Brent Crude, the favourite, had drifted badly when the internet went down so, I thought, the big boys' first instinct today must have been to back the favourite and drive down its price. It hadn't done them much good.

The winner had been returned at a starting price of fifteen-to-one. But there was nothing suspicious about that. The starting price of the winner of the Wokingham Stakes had regularly been at twenty-to-one or higher.

'What was all that about?' I said to Luca.

'Dunno,' he said. 'Nothing much seemed to happen.'

'No,' I said. 'But it was fun while it lasted.'

'Where did all those blokes come from?' he said. 'They must have been hiding in the stands somewhere.'

'It was a bit of overkill, if you ask me,' I said.

'They must have lost a packet last time.'

'I'll bet they didn't do so well this time either,' I said with a grin. 'And they don't like it.' I laughed.

'Serves them bloody right,' Luca said, laughing back at me.

It really did serve them right, I thought. The big boys had no sympathy for independent bookies as they tried to squeeze the life-blood out of us, so they couldn't expect much compassion in return when they got rolled over. In fact, the truth was, we absolutely loved it.

'Weighed in,' announced the public address.

The first in line to be paid out was the gorgeous young woman in black and white.

'Well done,' I said cheerfully, giving her fifty pounds for her ten-pound place bet on number eleven.

'Thank you,' she replied, blushing slightly again. 'My first win of the day.'

'Would you like to use it to make another bet?' I asked, pointing at the cash in her hand.

'Oh no,' she said in mocked shock. 'My boyfriend says I should always keep my winnings.'

'Very wise,' I said through gritted teeth.

Damn boyfriend!

The last two races on Royal Ascot Saturday have a distinct 'end of term' feel about them. The very last race of the day, the Queen Alexandra Stakes, is the longest flat race in the United Kingdom at more than two and a half miles, often attracting horses that normally run over the jumps. After the excitement of the Golden Jubilee and the Wokingham Stakes, which were both frantic six-furlong sprints, I always felt that the more sedate pace of the longer events was a slightly disappointing end to the meeting.

Betting was also light as punters drifted away, either to beat the race traffic, to have some tea and scones, or to sup a last glass of champagne in the bars. The betting ring was not exactly deserted but the men with the earpieces were now a fairly large proportion of those remaining. They wandered around aimlessly waiting for something untoward to happen.

It didn't.

The day fizzled out. The Queen went home to Windsor Castle, and Royal Ascot was over for another year.

Perhaps I wouldn't come back next year. Or maybe I would.

I spent most of Sunday with Sophie.

It was a lovely summer's day and we went for a walk in the hospital grounds. She had improved so much over the past five or six weeks and I was really hopeful that she would be able to come home very soon.

'Another couple of weeks,' the doctor had said to me when I arrived.

They were always saying 'another couple of weeks'. It was if they were afraid to make the decision to send her home just in case she had a relapse and then they would be blamed for discharging her too soon.

We walked around a small pond set beneath the overhanging branches of a great oak tree. The mental hospital had been created by transforming a minor stately home that had been bequeathed to the nation by someone in lieu of inheritance tax. The building had been greatly changed from its former glory but the grounds somehow remained rather grand, even though the formal flower beds had long ago been converted into simple lawn, more easily cut by tractor and gang-mower. The calm tranquillity of the gardens was meant to do the patients good, and the high-wire, supposedly escape-proof perimeter fence was out of sight, well screened behind trees. To be fair, the fence was there more to give the local residents a sense of security than to imprison the patients. Those cared for at this facility were placed in secure accommodation for their own safety, not because they posed a risk to others.

Broadmoor it was not.

'Did you have a good week at Ascot?' Sophie asked as we sat on a bench by the pond.

'Yes,' I said. 'A very good week.'

I still hadn't said anything to her about the events of the previous Tuesday, and maybe I never would.

'There was all sorts of excitement yesterday,' I said. 'Someone managed to turn both the internet and the mobile phones off. The big companies were having a fit.'

'I'm not surprised,' she said, smiling warmly at the thought. Sophie knew all about bookmaking. She had stood next to my grandfather and me as our assistant throughout our courtship and well into our marriage.

When Sophie smiled the sun still came out in my heart.

I took her hand in mine.

'Oh, Ned,' she sighed. 'I hate this existence. I hate being here. The other residents are all bonkers and I feel I don't fit in.' Tears welled up in her eyes. 'When can I come home?'

'Soon, my love, I promise,' I said. 'The doctors say just another couple of weeks.'

'They always say that,' she said with resignation.

'You don't want to go home too soon and then have to come back, now do you?' I said, squeezing her hand in mine.

'I never want to come back here,' she said bluntly. 'I'm absolutely determined, this time, not to become ill again.'

She had said it before, many times before. If being well was simply a matter of want and willpower, she would be fine for ever. Free choice had about as much chance of curing manic depression as a sheet of rice paper had at stopping a runaway train.

'I know,' I said calmly. 'I don't want you to have to come back here either.'

It was a major step forward in her recovery that she even recognized that she had been ill in the first place. For me, one of the most distressing things about her condition was that, when manically high or depressively deep, she couldn't appreciate that her bizarre, and occasionally outlandish, behaviour was in any way unusual.

'Come on,' I said, breaking the morbidity of the moment, 'let's go and have some lunch.'

We walked hand in hand back up the expansive lawn towards the house.

'I love you,' Sophie said.

'Good,' I said, slightly embarrassed.

'No, I mean it,' she said. 'Most husbands would have run away by now.'

Wow, I thought, she really is nearly better. For the time being, anyway.

'I haven't been much of a wife, have I?' she said.

'Nonsense,' I said. 'You've been the best wife I've ever had.'

She laughed. We laughed together.

'I will really try this time,' she said.

I knew she would. She really tried every time. But chemical imbalance in the brain couldn't be cured by trying alone.

'They have some new drugs now,' I said. 'We'll just have to see how they do.'

'I hate them,' she said. 'They make me feel sick.'

'I know, my love. But feeling sick for a bit is surely better than having to come back here.'

We walked in silence up across the terrace, the sound of our shoes on the gravel unnaturally loud in the still air.

'And they make me fat,' she said.

We made our way back into the building through the French doors of the patients' day room. What must have once been a spectacular salon with great works of art and crystal chandeliers was now a rather dull blue-vinyl-floored utilitarian open space. It was filled with functional but uninspiring National Heath Service furniture and lit by rows of fluorescent tubes hanging down on dusty chains from a superb ornamental plastered ceiling far above. Such sacrilege.

Sophie and I sat down at one of the small square tables, on chairs that were so uncomfortable they must have been designed by a retired torturer.

Overall, the staff were very good with the patients' families, encouraging us to spend as much time as possible at the hospital. There was even a guest suite for relatives to stay overnight, and Sophie and I were not the only family group sitting down to a Sunday lunch of roast beef and Yorkshire pudding in the day room. More comfortable chairs, I thought, would have helped.

'Please can I come home for next weekend?' she asked me.

'Darling, you know it's up to the doctors,' I said. 'I promise you I'll ask them later.'

We ate our meal mostly in silence.

The only topic Sophie wanted to talk about was going home, and I had just put the stoppers on that. But it was up to the doctors and not up to me. Patients in secure mental health accommodation could only be released back into the community on the say so of a consultant psychiatrist and by agreement of a relevant Care Programme Approach Review, involving someone called the Responsible Medical Officer as well as the appropriate Mental Health Care Coordinator. If they thought she needed two more weeks in the secure unit, then two more weeks it would be, however much I might want her home right now.

It was the drugs that were the problem.

Over the years, the doctors had tried electric shock treatment but, if anything, that had made things worse, so Sophie's only option was to take a daily cocktail of brightly coloured pills. Some of them were antipsychotic and others antidepressant, but they were all referred to as mood stabilizers. Whereas together they could usually prevent and treat Sophie's symptoms, they all had side effects of one sort or another. Not only did they make her feel nauseous, they also tended to reduce the activity of her thyroid gland while increasing her craving for carbo-hydrates. Hence, Sophie was right, they were inclined to make her fat, and that in turn was bad for her state of mind, especially for her depression.

But the most problematic thing about her condition was that, when the drugs made her feel free of any form of psychosis, she started to believe, wrongly, that she didn't need them any more. The pills, and their side effects, were then thought of as the problem rather than the solution and hence she stopped taking them, I think more by neglect than design, and then the whole wretched cycle started once more.

Some sufferers miss the manic 'highs' and so purposely stop taking their medication. The 'high' time for some can be very creative. There is a prevalent theory that Vincent van Gogh was a manic depressive and that during his manias he produced some of the greatest art that man has ever seen, while during his depressions he first cut off his own ear and then ultimately shot himself to death.

Many great writers and artists of the past have been referred to as 'troubled souls' long before their condition was seen as being a mental illness. Manic depression may have given the world more than it realizes. Nowadays, it has been relabelled as 'bipolar disorder' and appears to be almost fashionable amongst the young literati.

'Would you like some fruit salad and ice cream?' said one of the staff, taking our main-course plates.

'Yes, please,' I said. 'How about you, my love?'

'Yes,' she replied rather quietly. 'Lovely.'

'Are you all right?' I asked.

'Fine,' she said, but her eyes were distant.

The doctors were right, I thought. She might need at least another two weeks of their care to get the drug doses sorted out properly.

We finished our lunch and went up to her room. She regularly took a nap in the afternoons and I was hopeful that it had just been tiredness that had caused her to be somewhat vacant downstairs, and not the start of another inward-looking depressive episode.

The two of us sat down in armchairs in front of an old black-and-white war film on the television. Sophie drifted off to sleep while I read her newspaper, mostly the racing pages. Regular domesticity.

The inquest into the death of my father was opened and then adjourned on Monday morning at the coroner's court in Maidenhead.

The proceedings took precisely fourteen minutes.

Chief Inspector Llewellyn was called first and he informed

the coroner that a violent assault had occurred in the car park at Ascot racecourse on the sixteenth of June, the previous Tuesday, during the evening at approximately eighteen-twenty hours, which had resulted in the subsequent death of a man at Wexham Park hospital, Slough. The time of death had been recorded as nineteen thirty on the same day.

A written report from the post-mortem pathologist was read out stating that the primary cause of death was hypoxemic hypoxia, a lack of adequate oxygen supply to the organs of the body. The hypoxia had been brought on by pooling of blood in the lungs as a result of punctures to each side of the deceased's abdomen caused by a sharp-pointed bladed instrument approximately twelve centimetres, or five inches, in length, and a little more than two centimetres wide. The blade had been angled upwards during each strike and had, on both occasions, penetrated the diaphragm and ruptured a lung. The hypoxia had further resulted in acidosis of the blood plasma, which in turn had lead to cardiac arrest, cerebral ischemia and, ultimately, death.

Or, in laymen's terms, my father had died from being stabbed twice in his stomach with a knife. The wounds had caused his lungs to be full of blood rather than of air, so he had suffocated to death.

My father had, in fact, died due to a lack of oxygenated blood to his brain.

Just as my mother had. But for different reasons.

I was called by the coroner to give evidence of identification. The letter of summons had indeed been in the pile of mail I had opened on Saturday evening. Amongst other things, it spelt out the dire consequences of my failure to attend the court proceedings.

I was asked by the court usher to state my full name and address, and then to hold a Bible in my right hand. I read the Coroner's Court oath from a card. 'I swear by Almighty God that the evidence I shall give shall be the truth and nothing but the truth.'

'You are the deceased's son?' asked the coroner. He was a small balding man, the meagre amount of hair that he did retain being combed right over the top of his head. Throughout the proceedings, he had been writing copious notes in a spiral-bound notebook, and he now looked expectantly at me over a pair of half-moon glasses.

'Yes,' I said. I was standing in the witness box of the court.

'What was your father's full name?' he asked.

'Peter James Talbot,' I said.

'And his date of birth?'

I gave it. I knew every detail of my father's birth certificate as well as I knew my own. The coroner wrote it down in his notebook.

'And his last permanent address?' he asked, not looking up.

I pulled the photocopy of the driving licence from my pocket and consulted it. 'He lived at 312 Macpherson Street, Carlton North, a suburb of Melbourne, Australia,' I said.

'And when did you last see your father alive?' he asked.

'As he was lifted into the ambulance at Ascot racecourse,' I said.

He wrote furiously in his notebook.

'So you were present at the time of the assault?' he asked.

'Yes,' I said.

He wrote it down.

'Was that when your eye was injured?' he asked.

'Yes,' I said again.

The coroner seemed to glance over at Chief Inspector Llewel-lyn, who was sitting on a bench to his right.

'Are the police aware of your presence at the time of the assault?' the coroner asked me.

'Yes,' I said.

He nodded, as if he had done his bit for the investigation, and wrote something down in his notebook.

'Did you observe the body of the deceased after death at Wexham Park hospital?' he asked.

'Yes,' I said once more.

'Can you swear to the court – and I remind you, Mr Talbot, that you are under oath – that the body you observed at that time was that of your father?'

'I believe it was my father, yes,' I said.

The coroner stopped writing his notes and looked up at me.

'That doesn't sound very convincing, Mr Talbot,' he said.

'Until the day of his death,' I said, 'I hadn't seen my father, or even known of his existence, for the past thirty-six years.'

The coroner put down his pen.

'And how old are you, Mr Talbot?' he asked.

'Thirty-seven,' I said.

'Then how can you believe that the deceased was your father if you haven't seen him since you were one year old?'

'He told me so,' I said.

The coroner appeared amazed.

'And you took his word for it?' he asked.

'Yes, sir,' I replied. 'I did. We had been speaking about family matters for some time before the attack on us in the Ascot car park and I became convinced that, indeed, he was my father as he had claimed. In addition, I was informed by the police last Thursday that DNA analysis had confirmed the fact.'

'Ah,' he said. He turned towards Chief Inspector Llewellyn. 'Is this so, Chief Inspector?'

'Yes, sir,' he said, standing up. 'The DNA indicated that Mr Talbot and the deceased were very closely related. Almost certainly father and son.'

I briefly wondered why the police had not informed the coroner's office of the DNA results beforehand. It might have saved me from even attending.

The coroner wrote furiously for about a minute in his notebook before looking up at me. 'Thank you, Mr Talbot, that will be all.'

Nothing about Alan Charles Grady and, less surprisingly, nothing about Willem Van Buren. Identification of the deceased had been formally established as Peter James Talbot.

'May I arrange a funeral?' I asked the coroner.

He again turned towards the chief inspector. 'Do the police have any objection to an order being issued?'

Chief Inspector Llewellyn stood up. 'At this time, sir,' he said, 'we would prefer it if the body were to remain available for further post-mortem inspection.'

'And why is that?' the coroner asked him.

'We have reason to believe, sir, that the deceased may have been connected with other past crimes and we may wish to perform further DNA testing.'

'Do the necessary samples not already exist?' the coroner asked him.

'We may have the need to gather more,' said the chief inspector.

'Very well,' said the coroner. He turned back to me. 'Sorry,

Mr Talbot, I will not issue a burial order at this time. You may reapply to my office in one week's time.'

'Thank you, sir,' I said.

I looked at the chief inspector with renewed loathing. I was sure he had only objected to me organizing a funeral in order to irritate me.

'This inquest is adjourned,' said the coroner. 'Next case, please.'

Those of us only concerned with the death of the now formally identified Peter James Talbot stood up and filed out of the court. In addition to Chief Inspector Llewellyn, Sergeant Murray and myself, three other men and a young woman made their way ahead of me from the courtroom into the lobby. I was pleased to note that I couldn't see the shifty-eyed man from the car park and Sussex Gardens amongst them, not that I really expected him to be there. It would surely have been far too dangerous for him to appear as I might have recognized him and told the police.

However, I was rather concerned that one of these four strangers might have been sent by him to gather information so I rushed out to get a better look at them, and to see what they were doing.

One of the men and the young woman were standing with Chief Inspector Llewellyn and appeared to be asking him some questions, one with a notebook, the other with a hand-held recorder. Reporters, I thought. One of the other two men was chatting with Sergeant Murray, but I couldn't see the fourth anywhere in the lobby. I rushed out of the building but he had seemingly disappeared completely. I stood in the street turning round and round looking for him, but he'd gone.

I went back up the steps and into the building.

Both the reporters saw me at the same instant and hurried across.

'Do you know why your father was killed?' asked the young woman, beating the man to it by a short head.

'No,' I said. 'Do you?'

She ignored my question. 'Did you see the person who was responsible for his death?' she asked thrusting her recording device into my face.

'No,' I said.

'Would you recognize the killer again?' asked the man, forcing his way in front of me and elbowing the woman to the side.

'No,' I said, hoping that he would print the answer so the killer would read it.

'Did he do that to your eye?' the young woman asked, trying to push her way back in front of me.

'Yes,' I said. 'He kicked me. That's why I was unable to see the person responsible, or indeed anything else that happened.'

'But why was he killed?' implored the man.

'I have no idea,' I said. 'I hadn't seen my father for thirty-six years until the day he died.'

'Why not?' the young woman asked almost accusingly.

'He emigrated to Australia when I was one,' I said, 'and my mother and I didn't go with him.'

They suddenly seemed to lose interest in me. Maybe they could tell that I wasn't going to be much help to them.

What they really should have asked me was why my mother hadn't emigrated to Australia with my father. The answer was because she'd been murdered by him. Not that I'd have told them.

CHAPTER 9

Early on Tuesday morning I drove to south Devon and parked near a long line of multicoloured beach huts behind Preston Sands, in Paignton. I had left Kenilworth at four thirty to avoid any rush-hour traffic and had made it to what was described by the travel agents as the English Riviera in a little over three hours.

Ironically, I had driven right past Newton Abbot racecourse, where they were racing later that day. But I wasn't here for my work. Luca and Betsy had taken the equipment and would be standing at Newbury for the evening meeting. I hoped to be able to join them later.

I locked my old Volvo and went for a walk along the seafront.

It was still relatively early and Paignton was just coming to life with the deck-chair rental man putting out his blue-and-white striped stockpile in rows on the grass for the holidaymakers to come and sit on. There were a few morning dog-walkers about, one or two joggers, and a man with a metal detector digging on the sand.

It was a beautiful June summer day and, even at eight in the morning, the sun was already quite high in the sky to the east, its rays reflecting off the sea as millions of dancing sparkles. The temperature was rising and I was regretting not having worn a pair of shorts and flip-flops rather than my dark trousers and black leather shoes.

I thought back to the inquest the day before.

'South Devon,' Sergeant Murray had said to me quietly as we stood in the lobby of the courthouse.

'What?' I'd said.

'South Devon,' he'd repeated. 'That's where your mother was murdered. In Paignton, south Devon. Her body was found on the beach under Paignton pier.'

'Oh,' I'd said inadequately.

'On the fourth of August, 'seventy-three.'

'Right, thank you,' I'd replied.

'And don't tell the chief inspector I told you,' he'd said, keeping an eye on the door to the Gents through which his boss had disappeared.

'No,' I'd said. 'Of course I won't.'

He'd turned to move away from me.

'Did she have a child with her that was murdered as well?' I'd asked him. 'A baby?'

'Not according to the file I read,' he'd replied quickly before hurrying away from me as the Gents door had opened.

My grandmother had probably been confused, I thought.

I took off my shoes and socks, rolled up the legs of my trousers and walked on Paignton beach.

I wasn't really sure why I had come nearly two hundred miles in search of something that had happened nearly thirty-six years before. What did I think I would find, I wondered.

The previous evening I had used my computer to Google 'Paignton Murder' and had been surprised to find over twenty-two thousand hits on the web. Paignton must be a dangerous place, I'd thought, until I discovered that almost every reference was for Murder Mystery weekends or dinners at the local hotels. But there were, amongst all of those, reports of real murders by the seaside, though I could find nothing about the murder of a Patricia Jane Talbot in August 1973. The internet simply did not stretch back far enough.

So here I was walking along the beach as if simply being here would give me some insight into what had gone on in this place all that time ago, and why.

The tide was out, revealing a wide expanse of red sand, criss-crossed with multiple ridged patterns and grooves produced by the outgoing water. I strode purposefully southward towards Paignton pier, past the imposing grey sea wall of the Redcliffe Hotel, carrying my shoes and digging my bare toes into the sand. At one point, I stopped and looked behind me at the line of footprints I had created in the soft surface.

I couldn't remember when I had last left footprints on a seashore. My grandparents had taken me very occasionally to the sea when I had been small but we had never sat or walked on the beach. During the war my grandfather had been posted to North Africa and had spent two years fighting his way back and forth across the Egyptian desert. As a result, he had developed an aversion to any form of sand.

'Bloody stuff gets everywhere,' he used to say, so under no circumstances did we ever go near it. Once or twice he had been cajoled by my grandmother into sitting on the pebbles at Brighton while I had played in the water on day trips from our home in Surrey, but we had never holidayed at the seaside. In fact, thinking back, we had rarely holidayed anywhere. To my grandfather, going to the races every day was holiday enough, in spite of it being his job.

Paignton pier, like every other pier at seaside resorts around the country, had been built in the latter part of the nineteenth century to allow pleasure steamers to dock when the tide was out and the harbour was dry. Steamers that would disgorge their passengers to indulge in the new health fashion of the time, of bathing year-round in salt water. It was testament to the ability of the Victorian engineers that the majority of the piers still existed long past the time when most folk had decided that immersing themselves in the freezing sea did their health more harm than good.

But the seaside piers had survived because they had been adapted into centres of entertainment. Paignton pier was no exception and I could see that amusement arcades had been built over much of its length.

I stood on the beach in the shadow of the pier and speculated again about what had been done right here to my mother. I also wondered where I had been at the time and whether I had been with my parents here in Paignton on that fateful day. Had I been here before, in this very spot beneath the pier, as a fifteen-month-old toddler? Indeed, was I here when she'd died?

There was nothing much to see. I hadn't expected there to be. Perhaps I was foolish to have come and the image of where my mother had met her grisly end would haunt me for ever. But something in me had needed to visit this place.

I pulled my wallet out of my trouser pocket and extracted the creased picture of my parents taken at Blackpool. All my life I had looked at that picture and longed to be able to be with my father. It was his image that had dominated my existence rather than that of my mother. The grandparents who had raised me had been my father's family, not my mother's, and somehow my paternal loss had always been the greater for me.

Now I studied her image as if I hadn't really looked at it closely before. I stood there and cried for her loss and for the violent fate that had befallen my teenage mother in this place.

'You all right, boy?' said a voice behind me.

I turned round. A man with white hair and tanned skin, wearing a faded blue sweatshirt and baggy fawn shorts, was leaning on one of the pier supports.

'Fine,' I croaked, wiping tears from my eyes with the sleeve of my shirt.

'We could see you from my place,' said the man, pointing at a cream-painted refreshment hut standing close to the pier. 'We're setting up. Do you fancy a cuppa?'

'Yes, please,' I said. 'Thank you.'

'Come on, then,' he said. 'On the house.'

'Thank you,' I said again, and we walked together over to his hut.

'He's all right, Mum,' the man shouted as we approached. He turned to me. 'My missus thought you looked like you were going to do yourself in,' he said. 'You know. Wade out to sea and never come back.'

'Nothing like that,' I said, giving him a smile. 'I assure you.'

He handed me a large white cup of milky tea and took another for himself from the cheerful-looking little lady behind the counter.

'Sugar?' he asked.

'No, thanks,' I said, taking a welcome sip of the steaming brown liquid. 'It's a beautiful day.'

'We need it to last, though,' he said. 'July and August are our really busy times. That's when the families come. Mostly just a bunch of OAPs in June. Lots of pots of tea and the occasional ice cream, but very few burgers. We need the sun to shine all summer if we're going to survive.'

'Are you open all year round?' I asked.

'No chance,' he said. 'May to September if we're lucky. I'm usually a builder's labourer in the winter. If there's any work, that is. Not looking good this year with the economy going down the tubes. At least most folk aren't going abroad for their holidays, eh? Not with the pound so low. Too expensive.'

We stood together for a moment, silently drinking our tea.

'I must get on,' said the man. 'Can't stand here all day. I also run the pedalos and the wind surfers, and they won't get themselves out, now will they?'

'Can I give you a hand?' I asked.

He looked at my dark trousers and my white shirt.

'They'll clean,' I said to him.

He looked up at my face and smiled. 'Let's get on, then.'

'Ned Talbot,' I said, holding out my hand.

'Hugh Hanson,' he said, shaking it.

'Right then, Hugh,' I said. 'Where are these pedalos?'

I spent most of the next hour helping to pull pedal boats and wind surfers out of two great big steel ship's containers, lining them up on the beach ready for rent.

My trousers had a few oily marks on them from the pedal mechanisms and my white shirt had long ago lost its sharp creases by the time Hugh and I went back to the cream-painted hut for another cup of tea.

'Proper job,' he said, grinning broadly. 'Thank you.'

'Thank *you*,' I replied, grinning back. 'Best bereavement therapy I've ever known.'

'Bereavement?' he asked, suddenly serious.

'Yes,' I said. 'My mother.'

'I'm sorry,' he said. 'When did she die?'

'Thirty-six years ago,' I said.

He was slightly taken aback, which I suppose was fair enough.

'Long time to grieve.'

'Yes,' I agreed. 'But I only found out where she died yesterday.'

'Where?' He seemed surprised. 'Why does it matter where she died?'

'Because she died here,' I said. 'Just over there.' I pointed. 'Where I was standing on the beach.'

He looked over to where I had been, under the pier, then he turned back to me.

'Wasn't murdered, was she?' he asked me.

I stood there looking at him in stunned silence.

'Oh, I'm so sorry,' he said. 'I didn't think she'd been old enough to be anyone's mother.'

'She was eighteen,' I said. 'She would have been nineteen in the September.'

'I'm sorry,' he said again.

'How did you know?' I asked him.

'I didn't,' he said. 'But the murder of that girl was such big news around these parts. My father owned the business then, of course, but I was working for him. We were bigger then, with masses of boats for hire. Little motor boats with engines, you know, and those catamaran float things with paddles. That murder shut us down completely for a week, and the summer seasons took years to recover.'

I stood on the concrete walkway and looked again at the space beneath the pier.

'They never caught the man who done it, did they?' he said. 'That's what really did for us all. No one felt safe with a killer on the loose. People stopped coming to Paignton for years. Stupid. The killer was probably from up the line, anyway. After all, your mum wasn't local, was she?'

I shook my head. 'Were you here the day they found her?' I asked him.

'Certainly was,' he said. 'It was Father who saw her lying under the pier and went over to wake her up. Helluva mad, he was. Sleeping on the beach isn't allowed. We're always having things damaged by people who use our stuff for shelters. Anyway, he couldn't wake her up because she was dead. White, he went. I thought he was going to be sick. It was me as called the police. From a phone box that used to stand on that corner.' He pointed.

'Did she really look like she was asleep?' I asked.

'I presume so,' he said. 'I didn't see her close to.' He sounded frustrated. 'By the time I'd made the call some bloody do-gooder security man had set up a load of rope to keep people away.'

'Was she naked?' I asked.

'No,' he said. 'I don't think so.' He thought. 'It's a long time ago, but I think she had all her clothes on. Otherwise Father wouldn't have thought she was asleep. Would he?'

'Is your dad still alive?' I asked.

'No,' he said. 'The old boy died about ten years ago.'

Pity, I thought.

'Did anyone else see her before the rope went up?' I asked.

'A few other people,' he said. 'But I don't know who they were.'

I must have looked disappointed.

'There was masses about it in the local paper for days and days,' he said. 'They'll surely have copies of them in the local library. Those reporters would have found out if she wasn't properly dressed. They were here for ages. Television, too.'

I looked at my watch. It was already almost ten o'clock. The library must be open by now. 'Where is the library?' I asked.

'In Courtland Road,' he said. 'Not far. That direction,' he pointed.

'I might just go there later,' I said.

'Do you fancy a bacon and egg sandwich?' Hugh asked, changing the subject. 'I'm having one.'

'I'd love one,' I said.

We sat on chairs put out for the customers of the refreshment hut, and his wife brought each of us a fresh mug of tea and a huge sandwich with so much bacon and egg filling that it was falling out the sides. I ate mine with eager relish. I hadn't realized I was so hungry.

'How much do I owe you for that?' I asked, wiping my mouth on the back of my hand and drinking down the last of my tea.

'Don't be silly,' he said. 'You earned it.'

'Thanks, Hugh,' I said, and stood up. 'I hope the sun shines for you all summer.'

'Thanks,' he said. He, too, stood up and we shook hands. 'Are you sure you want to do this?'

'What?' I said.

'Find out more about your mother's death.'

'What do you mean?' I asked him.

'Sometimes it's better to leave sleeping dogs lie,' he said. 'You might find out something you don't like.'

How could anything be worse than finding out your own mother was murdered by your father, I thought.

'Thanks for the concern,' I said. 'I was only one when she died and I don't remember her at all. But I have a need in me to find out more. She made me who I am and I desperately want to learn more about her. At present, I know almost nothing. This is the only place to start.'

He nodded. 'Let me know if you need any help. You know where to find me.'

'Thanks,' I said, really meaning it.

I waved at his wife, who was still busily making prawn-filled baguettes and crab sandwiches behind the counter, and walked away.

'That way,' Hugh shouted after me pointing. He took half a dozen steps towards me. 'Go up Lower Polsham Road, under the railway, second left into Polsham Park and then Courtland Road is first on the right. The library is on the left, you can't miss it.'

'Thanks,' I said and walked in the direction he had pointed.

Paignton Library did indeed have a newspaper section but it only kept copies for the previous six weeks.

'You'll have to go to Torquay,' said a kindly lady behind the counter in hushed, librarian tones. 'They keep all the back issues of the local papers on microfiche.'

'Microfiche?' I said.

'Photographic sheets,' she said. 'The newspaper pages are photographed and made very small on the sheets. You need a special machine to see them. Saves us keeping mountains of the real papers.'

'And Torquay library definitely has them?' I asked.

'Oh yes,' she replied. 'They'll have all the back copies of the *Herald Express* and probably the *Western Morning News* as well.'

'Are they the local papers?' I asked her.

'The *Herald Express* is very local, just for Torbay, and the *Western* is for the whole of Devon and Cornwall.'

'Thank you,' I said, and departed back to my car.

I sat in a darkened room at Torquay library at one of the microfiche machines and read all there was in the *Herald Express* newspapers of August 1973 concerning the eighteen-year-old Patricia Talbot, found murdered under Paignton pier.

Just as Hugh Hanson had said, there had been masses about it for days and days. It had still been the front-page headline story some seven days after the discovery of the body. But in spite of all the column inches, there was very little actual detail, and no reports of progress with the investigation.

However, I did discover that she had not been found naked, as I had feared, and, in spite of some speculation in the reports, there appeared to have been no evidence of any sexual assault. The local police were quoted as confirming that she had been strangled and that she had been dead for several hours before she was discovered on the beach at seven twenty in the morning by a Mr Vincent Hanson.

Hugh's father, I presumed.

Most of the reports centred around the fear that an unsolved murder on the beach would have a detrimental effect on the local tourist industry that was already suffering badly from families going on cheap package holidays to Majorca instead of to the English seaside.

There was surprisingly little actual information about Patricia Talbot herself. No mention of whether she was on holiday in Paignton or had been working there. No report of any hotel where she had been staying, or even if she had been alone in the town or with her husband. Not a word about any fifteen-month-old son left motherless. Only once was my father even mentioned, and only then to report that he had nothing to say. There was no photograph of him. The actual quote – *'I have no comment to make at the moment,' said Mr Talbot outside Paignton police station* – had appeared in the paper three days after the discovery of the body.

So he hadn't run off immediately, I thought.

I had exhausted all the coverage in the *Herald Express*, so I went back to the reference library desk.

'Do you have the *Western Morning News*?' I asked a young member of the library staff.

'When for?' he said.

'August 1973,' I said.

'Sorry, we only have the *Morning News* back to 'seventy-four,' he said. 'You'd have to go to Exeter, or maybe to Plymouth, for any earlier than that.'

'Ah, well,' I said. 'Thanks anyway.' I began to turn away.

'But we have the *Paignton News* for 'seventy-three, if that's any good,' he said. 'They went out of business in 'seventy-six.'

The *Paignton News* had been a weekly publication, and the week of the murder it had reported nothing more than I had already read in the *Herald Express*. I almost left it at that, but something made me scan through the following week's edition, and there I found out what my grandmother had meant.

On the third page there was a brief account of an inquest at South Devon Coroner's Court that had been opened and adjourned into the sudden and violent death of one Patricia Jane Talbot, aged eighteen, of New Malden in Surrey.

According to the paper, the post-mortem report stated that the major cause of death had been asphyxiation due to constriction of the neck and that the hyoid bone had been fractured, which was consistent with a manual strangulation.

The piece concluded by stating that the deceased had been found to be pregnant at the time of her death, with a female foetus estimated at between eighteen and twenty weeks' gestation.

Indeed, he had murdered her baby.

He had murdered my sister.

Chapter 10

I didn't get to Newbury for the evening racing. Instead I went straight home to Kenilworth.

I was angry.

In fact, I was absolutely livid.

How could my father have come to Ascot, just one week previously, and been so normal and so natural, even so agreeable, when he held the knowledge that he had murdered my mother together with her unborn child?

It was despicable, and I hated him for it.

Why had he come back from Australia and turned my life upside down?

Had he come because of the glass-grain RFIDs and the money? Surely it hadn't been just to see me?

I lay awake for ages tossing and turning, trying to sort it all out, but all I came up with were more and more questions, and no answers.

Whose money was it in his rucksack?

Was the money connected to the RFIDs and the black-box programmer?

Was he killed because he hadn't handed over the money, or

was it the black box and the glass grains that were so important?

And what exactly were they for?

Every punter has a story of how they think a crooked trainer or owner has run the wrong horse in a race. How a 'ringer' has been brought in to win when the expected horse would have had no chance. Unexpected winners have always made some people suspicious that foul play has been afoot and, in the distant past, before racing was a well-organized industry, rumours of ringers abounded and there must have been some truth to them.

But running a ringer has always been more difficult than most people believe, especially from a large well-established training stable, and not only because horse identification has become more sophisticated with the introduction of the RFID chips. Sure, a horse will be scanned by an official vet the first time it runs and randomly thereafter, and this, together with the detailed horse passport, makes it difficult to substitute one horse for another, but the real reason is that too many people would have to be 'in the know'.

There is an old Spanish proverb that runs: *A secret between two is God's secret, between three it is all men's.*

To run a horse as a ringer requires the inside knowledge of a good deal more than three men. The horse's groom, the horsebox driver, the travelling head lad and the jockey just for a start, in addition to the trainer and the owner.

It would be impossible to keep it a secret from any of them because they would simply recognize that the horse was not the right one. People who work every day with horses see them as individuals with different features and characteristics, rather than just as 'horses'. It has often been said that every great trainer needs to know his horses' characters better than he knows those of his own family. Lester Piggott was said to be able to recognize any horse he had ridden when it was walking away from him in a rain storm.

Just as everyone would realize pretty quickly, if not immediately, that a celebrity lookalike was not the real thing, so too would racing folk easily spot a ringer, unless it was far removed from its normal environment. And it was too much to expect that a secret conspiracy of even a handful of people would hold for very long.

So what real good were the rewritable identification RFIDs?

I finally went to sleep, still trying to work out the conundrum.

I was not sure what the noise was that woke me, but one moment I'd been fast asleep, the next I was fully conscious in the dark, knowing that something wasn't quite right.

I listened intently, lying perfectly still on my back and keeping my breathing very quiet and shallow.

As usual in the summer, I had left open one of my bedroom windows for ventilation. But I could hear nothing out of the ordinary from outside the house. Nothing except for the breeze, which rustled the leaves of the beech tree by the road, and the occasional hum of a distant car on Abbey Hill.

I had begun to think I must have been wrong when I plainly heard the sound again. It was muffled slightly by the closed bedroom door but I knew immediately what it was. Someone was downstairs, and he was opening the kitchen cabinets. The cabinet doors were held shut by little magnetic catches. The sound I had heard was the noise made when one of the catches was opened.

I lay there wondering what I should do.

Sergeant Murray had warned me that witnesses to murder were an endangered species, and now I began to wish I had taken his warning a bit more seriously.

Was the person downstairs intent on doing me harm or was he happy to go on exploring while leaving me to sleep?

The problem was that I didn't really imagine my intruder was searching through my kitchen cabinets for something with which to make himself a cup of tea or coffee. He would be after my father's rucksack and its hidden contents, and they were not downstairs in the kitchen but were deep in the recesses of my wardrobe, up here with me in my bedroom. It would only be a matter of time before he would have to come upstairs and then he surely would know that I must be awake.

I thought about making lots of noise, stamping my way down the stairs and demanding to know who was in my house in the hope that he might be frightened away. But then I remembered the two stab wounds that had killed my father. Was my visitor the shifty-eyed man from the Ascot car park, and did he have his twelve-centimetre-long blade with him ready to turn my guts into mincemeat as well?

Ever so quietly I stretched out my hand towards the telephone that sat on my bedside table, intending to call the police. I decided it was better to be still alive, even if it did mean I would have the difficult task of explaining why there was thirty thousand pounds' worth of someone else's cash in my wardrobe. Much better, I thought, than drowning in my own blood.

But there was no dialling tone when I lifted the receiver. My guest downstairs must have seen to that.

And, as always, I had left my mobile in the car.

What, I wondered, was plan C?

There was nothing to be gained from simply lying there in

bed waiting for him to come up and plunge his knife into my body. I was sure he wouldn't just go away when he failed to find what he had come for downstairs. Clearly, he would rather have found the booty and departed silently, leaving me blissfully asleep, or else he would have come up and dealt with me first. But I was under no illusion that he would give up before he had searched everywhere, whether or not I was wide awake or fast asleep, or very dead.

It wasn't that dying particularly frightened me. But I didn't really want to go yet, not when Sophie was making such good progress. And not now that I knew I had sisters to meet in Australia. And particularly not before I had discovered what this was all about. I had always felt rather sorry for soldiers who died in wars, not only because they were dead, but because they would never know who won, or if their sacrifice had been worth it.

Maybe I just wanted to die in my own time, not at someone else's wish and whim.

I looked around in the dim luminosity that filtered through the curtains from the ambient street-light glow outside. Sadly, my bedroom wasn't equipped with any form of handy weapon.

I gently levered myself out of bed and pulled on a pair of boxer shorts. I might not be able to prevent myself being killed, but I was determined that I would not be found in a state of total undress.

Perhaps I should just throw the money and the other things down the stairs and let my visitor take them away. Anything to stop him coming up to get them himself, with murder in mind.

I silently crossed the room to the wardrobe, but before I had a chance to open it I heard the third tread of the staircase creak. I had been meaning to fix that step for years but I couldn't be

149

bothered to lift all the carpet. I had become so obsessed with the creak that I missed it out, always taking two steps together at that point. The wear of the carpet there, or rather the lack of it, was even becoming noticeable against the others.

My visitor hadn't known about it and in the darkness he wouldn't have spotted the under-used carpet. But I knew that the step always creaked as weight was applied, and also creaked again as the weight was removed.

I stood absolutely stock still beside my wardrobe listening. I was holding my breath and I could begin to hear the blood rushing in my ears. There had definitely been only one creak. The intruder had stopped on the stairs in mid-climb and was, no doubt, listening for any movement from me as hard as I was from him.

I had to breathe.

I decided to snort through my nose like a pig. I snored loudly and then exhaled in a long rasping wheeze. I snored once more and, quite clearly, I heard the third step creak again as my nocturnal visitor removed his weight from it. I assumed he was still on the way up, not going back down. I snored a third time then grunted as if turning over in bed.

The wardrobe was behind my bedroom door.

I flattened myself against the wall and stared at the door handle, which was a brass lever with a small scroll on the end. My heart was thumping so hard in my chest that I was sure it must be audible out on the landing.

The handle began to depress and my heart almost went into palpitations. Slowly the door opened towards me.

Attack had to be the best form of defence.

When the door was about half-way open I threw myself against it with all the force I could muster, attempting to slam it shut again. But the door didn't fully close because my visitor's right arm was preventing it. I could clearly see his gloved hand and his wrist protruding into my bedroom. There was a gratifying groan from its owner each time I pushed against the door, repeatedly throwing my weight against the wood.

'You've broken my bloody arm!' he shouted.

Good, I thought. Pity I hadn't torn it off completely.

'What do you want?' I shouted back through the door, still refusing to ease up the pressure to release his arm.

'Sod off,' he shouted back. 'I'm going to kill you, you bastard.'

Not if I had any say in the matter, he wasn't.

I put my right foot down on the floor to stop the door from opening, leaned back and then threw my whole weight against it once more.

This time he didn't just groan, he screamed.

So I repeated it. He screamed again.

'What do you want?' I shouted again.

'I want to break your fucking neck,' he said back to me through the door, sounding very close indeed.

I pressed again, the door squeezing against his damaged arm.

'And what exactly are you looking for?' I said.

'The microcoder,' he said.

'What's that?'

'It's a microcoder,' he repeated unhelpfully.

'What does it look like?' I asked

'A flat black box with buttons on it,' he said. 'Give me the microcoder and I'll go away.'

'I don't think you're in a position to make demands,' I said, while still pushing hard on the door. 'What does this microcoder do?'

Instead of answering he threw his weight against his side of the door to try and open it but my foot was still preventing that. However, the wood bent sufficiently for him to extract his arm. The door slammed shut.

My advantage, it seemed, was over, but I couldn't hear him going down the stairs.

'What does the microcoder do?' I repeated, shouting through the door.

'Never you mind,' he said, still sounding very close. 'Just give it back.'

'I haven't got it,' I said.

'I think you have.'

'Is it yours?' I asked.

'Your father stole it,' he said. 'And I want it back.'

'Was that why you murdered him?' I asked.

'I didn't murder anyone,' he said. 'But I could murder you, you bastard. I'm in agony here.'

'Serves you right,' I said. 'You shouldn't come snooping round other people's houses uninvited.'

'It doesn't give you the right to break my arm,' he whined.

'I think you'll find it does,' I said. 'Now get out of my house and stay out.'

'Not without the microcoder,' he said.

'I told you, I haven't got it.'

'Yes, you bloody have,' he said with a degree of certainty. 'You must have it. Where else would it be?'

We didn't seem to be making any progress.

I hooked my left foot around Sophie's dressing-table chair and pulled it towards me. I then placed the back of the chair tight under the door handle. I should have done that the first time, I thought. There was absolutely no way I was going to open my bedroom door while he remained in my house, so there was equally no chance I was going to hand over what he had called the microcoder.

Stalemate ensued for the next fifteen minutes or so.

I was wondering what he was up to when he suddenly banged on the door making me jump.

'Are you still awake in there?' he asked.

'What do you think?' I replied.

'Yeah, well, sorry and all that,' he said quite casually. 'I'll be off now, then.' He said it as if he'd just been round for a drink or something and it was time to go home.

'Who are you?' I said.

'Never you mind,' he said again. 'But I didn't kill your father.'

I heard him go down the stairs and the third step, my new friend, creaked twice as he descended. Then I heard the front door being opened. Then it was slammed shut.

I went across to my bedroom window and looked down. The man had indeed left my house and I watched the top of his head as he walked across the car parking area and onto the road. He appeared to be cradling his right arm in his left and, at one point, he turned briefly to look up at me, as if intentionally showing me his face. I recognized him immediately. It wasn't the man with the close-set eyes who had stabbed my father in the Ascot car park – it was the elusive fourth stranger from his inquest.

I stood looking out of my bedroom window for some time in case he came back. I neither saw nor heard any car drive away and I was still very wary as I finally removed the chair from under the door handle and peeped out onto the landing.

I didn't yet know how he'd made it into my house in the first place. I didn't really relish going downstairs only to find him there once more, having simply gone round the block and back in through one of the rear windows that faced the garden.

The house was quiet, but that didn't mean he wasn't there.

I stood at the top of the stairs, straining to hear any sound from below, maybe a breath or a shuffle of feet. But there was nothing.

I crept silently down, avoiding step three, listening carefully and ready to run back up to my bedroom bolt-hole at the slightest noise. There was no one there. He really had gone away, and he'd not come back again. I turned on all the lights and went round closing the stable door now that the horse had bolted.

In truth, I'd made it far too easy for him. As well as the fanlight in my bedroom being open, so was the one in the living room and he had simply put his arm through it, opened the big window beneath and climbed in. He'd left some muddy footprints on the fawn carpet under the window. No doubt I should now call the police and they could take photos of the prints to try and match them to a specific shoe size and manufacturer.

Instead, I used my hand-held vacuum cleaner to clear up the mess.

The phone handset in the kitchen was off the hook. I picked it up and listened. Nothing. I replaced it on the cradle then lifted it again and pressed redial. The LED read-out just showed 0. A female computer-generated voice stated, '*The number you have dialled has not been recognized, please check and try again,*' and that phrase was repeated for about six times before it shut off completely, leaving the line dead.

Apart from the mud on the living-room floor, my nocturnal

visitor, the fourth stranger, had been meticulously tidy in his search. The kitchen cabinets were all open but hardly disturbed, as were the sideboard cupboards in the dining room. He had been trying to be quiet.

However, far from answering any of the questions surrounding my father, my intruder had simply created new ones; in particular, was he working together with Shifty Eyes or did they represent different interests?

After all, he had only asked for the microcoder. There had been no mention of the considerable cache of money that had been hidden with it.

But if the fourth stranger knew where I lived, as he clearly did, then surely so could anyone else. I had, perhaps carelessly, freely given out my home address at the inquest when the fourth stranger would have heard it. It would now also be in the official record. It wasn't much of a leap to realize that the information could be obtained by any member of the public who really wanted it. Perhaps I should be on the look-out for another unwelcome night-time guest, one with shifty eyes, in search of bundles of blue-plastic-wrapped cash.

CHAPTER 11

On Wednesday I went to Stratford races.

Whoever thought that jump racing in June was a good idea hadn't envisaged racing at Stratford after a prolonged drought, when the River Avon was so low that the racecourse watering system hadn't been able to keep up with the evaporation from the sun-baked earth. The ground for weeks had been as hard as concrete and very few trainers were willing to run their steeplechasers in such conditions.

The overnight declared runners for Stratford had been so few that it was hardly worth the journey, even though Stratford was the second nearest course to my home, Warwick being a few miles closer.

Add the fact that Mother Nature had decided that, on this day, the six-week drought would break with numerous thunderstorms moving north from France, and one could understand why the midweek race-day 'crowd' was not really worthy of the name.

Only four bookmakers had bothered to turn up to try and wring a few pounds out of the miserable rain-soaked gathering. Even Norman Joyner, who almost always came to Stratford, hadn't bothered. And most of the public who had come had the good sense to stay dry in the Tote betting hall under the grandstand, leaving us four bookies to huddle under our large umbrellas with the raindrops bouncing back off the tarmac. Royal Ascot in the sunshine it was not.

The first race was a two-mile novice hurdle. According to the morning papers there were five declared runners but one of them had been withdrawn. The reason given by the horse's trainer was that the rain had affected the going, but that was a joke. The ground was so dry it would have needed rain akin to the Noachian Deluge to make any noticeable difference.

The four remaining runners appeared on the course and went down to the two-mile start while a few hardy punters made a dash across the ring towards us to place a bet before hurrying back to the shelter of the grandstand.

'It's not much fun today,' said Luca in my ear.

'It was your idea,' I said, turning to him. 'I'd have been happy staying in bed on a day like this.'

After my disturbed night, staying in bed had seemed like an excellent plan, but Luca had called me twice during the morning to see if I was coming to Stratford that afternoon.

'You don't have to come,' he'd said in the second call. 'Betsy and I can cope on our own, if you want. We had a good night at Newbury without you.'

I had begun to feel I was being eased out of my own business and that made me even more determined to be here. But now, as another rivulet of rainwater cascaded off the umbrella and down my neck, I wasn't at all sure that it had been the right decision.

'We must be mad,' shouted Larry Porter, again our neighbouring bookie.

'Bonkers,' I agreed.

I thought it was funny how we use certain words. Here were Larry and I, in full control of our mental capacity, using terms like 'mad' and 'bonkers' to describe each other, while the likes of Sophie, and worse, institutionalized in mental health facilities were never, any longer, referred to in such terms, even in private. And the terms 'lunatic asylum' and 'loony bin' were now as archaic and taboo as 'spastic' and 'cripple'.

The betting business was so slow that Betsy had complained about the rain and taken herself off to the drier conditions of the bar, and I was beginning to wish I could join her.

'Whose stupid idea was it to come to Stratford?' I said to Luca.

'Would you have preferred Carlisle?' he said.

Kenilworth to Carlisle was more than two hundred miles while the distance from my house to Stratford-upon-Avon racecourse was less than twenty.

'No,' I said.

'Well, shut up, then,' said Luca with a grin. 'You've got a waterproof skin so what are you worrying about? As least it's not cold.'

'It's hardly hot,' I replied.

'No pleasing some people,' he said to the world in general. 'Why don't you just go home and leave Betsy and me to make you a living.'

'But Betsy's gone off in a strop,' I said.

'She's only in a strop because she wants to do your job, and she can't because you're doing it,' he said.

He said it with a smile but he meant it nevertheless.

It seemed I really was being eased out of my own business.

But I suppose it was better than losing Luca and Betsy to a new outfit.

'You mean it, don't you?' I said seriously.

'Absolutely,' he replied. 'We need to be more ambitious, more proactive, more ruthless.'

I wasn't sure whether the 'we' included me or not.

'In what way do you want to be more ruthless?' I asked him.

'All that stuff at Ascot last week has shown me that the big boys are not invincible,' he said. 'Someone gave them a bloody nose and good luck to them. Bookmaking should be all about what happens here.' He spread his arms wide. 'Well, not exactly here today, but you know what I mean. Bookmaking is about standing at a pitch on the course, not being stuck in some anonymous betting shop watching a computer screen.'

I was amazed. I thought it was the computer gambling that made Luca tick.

'But you love the internet,' I said.

'Yes, I do,' he said. 'But only as a tool for what happens here. The on-course bookies need to set the prices and they should not be driven by the exchanges. By rights, it should be the other way round. We should be prepared to alter our prices for our advantage not for those of anyone else.'

'You sound like you're at war,' I said with a laugh.

'We are,' he said seriously. 'And if we don't fight, we'll go under.'

I remembered back to the time when I had been assisting my grandfather for a couple of years or so. I'd had the same sort of discussion with him then. Bookmaking was an evolving science and new blood, like Luca, needed to be ever pushing the boundaries. As he had said, without it we'd go under.

As is so often the case with small fields, the four horses in the race finished in extended line astern, the favourite winning it at a canter by at least ten lengths. There was hardly a cheer from the measly crowd, and the winner returned to an almost deserted unsaddling enclosure.

As Luca had said, it wasn't much fun.

A man in a suit came striding across from beneath the grandstand just as the rain began to fall in a torrent. The man was holding an umbrella but it didn't appear to be keeping him very dry. Too much water was bouncing back from the ground. His feet must have been soaked by the time he stopped in front of me.

'What the hell's going on?' he demanded.

'What do you mean?' I asked him in all innocence.

'With the bloody prices?' he said loudly.

'What about the prices?' I asked him.

'How come that winner was returned at two-to-one when everyone knows it should have been odds-on?'

'Nothing to do with me,' I said, spreading my hands out wide.

'Don't get bloody clever with us,' the man said with menace, pointing his finger at me.

'And who is us, exactly?' I demanded, trying to disregard the implied threat.

He ignored me and went over to remonstrate with Larry Porter, who told him to go away and procreate, or words to that effect.

The man was far from pleased. 'I'm warning you two,' he said, pointing at both Larry and me. 'We won't stand for that.'

Larry shouted at him again to go away, using some pretty colourful language that made even me wince.

'What was all that about?' I said to Luca.

'Just trying to rustle up a bit more business,' he said.

'How?' I asked.

'I thought we might tempt a few more punters over here if we offered a better price on the favourite,' he said, grinning at me. 'That's all.'

I stood there looking at him.

'You silly bugger. We don't play games with these guys,' I said seriously. 'Their bite is far worse than their bark.'

'Don't be so boring,' he said.

'I mean it. They are powerful people, and they stamp on irritations.'

Was this what he meant by being at war?

The starting price was not set by a single bookmaker's prices. It was a sort of average, but was actually the mode of the offered prices rather than a true average. A mode is that value that occurs most frequently in a sample.

At Ascot last week the number of bookmakers was very high so a representative sample of, say, twelve bookmakers' prices were used. The twelve were chosen not quite randomly as they always included those bookies at the highest-traffic end of the betting ring. If in the sample of twelve, five of the bookmakers had the price of a certain horse as the race started at, say, three-to-one, then its starting price would be three-to-one, even if four of them had the price at seven-to-two, and the other three at four-to-one. Three-to-one was the mode because it was the price that occurred most frequently.

If there were two modes because, say in the above example, five bookies had the price at three-to-one, and five of them had it at seven-to-two, then the starting price was always taken as the higher of the two odds. So, in that case it would have been seven-to-two.

161

At Stratford on this particular wet Wednesday in June there were only four ring bookmakers so the sample included all of them, but it was still only four. Only two of them needed to offer higher prices than was 'true' for the starting price to be recorded as 'too high'.

So Luca could not have affected the price on his own.

'Was it Larry's idea or yours?' I asked him.

'What do you mean?' he said, all innocently.

'It needed two of you,' I said.

'You were there too,' he said, with a degree of accusation in his voice.

It was true. I was there, and it was my name on the board, or it was my surname at least. So I would carry the can, if a can indeed had to be carried. But I now realized how much I had subconsciously delegated to Luca and his computer.

'So was it Larry's idea?' I asked, knowing full well that Luca had brains far in excess of Larry Porter's, and that it was bound to have really been Luca's idea. But I wanted him to give me the option of not disposing with his services, to give him the chance to lie to me so that I could try and fool myself that he wouldn't try it again, maybe the next time I wasn't there.

Was that why he had been so keen for me to stay at home and leave things to him and Betsy? Was that really why Betsy was in such a strop, and had decided to absent herself from the scene of the crime?

I could almost hear the cogs whirling in his brain. He knew exactly what I had asked him and why. It wasn't that I truly wanted to know whose idea and plan it had been. What I was really asking him was whether he wanted to keep his job.

If he started out in business on his own he would have to purchase a number at a future pitch auction, which would require considerable outlay to obtain a decent spot in the ring. And he would most likely end up with a high number and hence a lowly choice of position. Those bookies with the best pitches took the most money and, in a recession, it was no time to move further down the pack.

From my own point of view, I had come to rely very heavily on Luca. His expertise with our computer and the internet gambling had been instrumental in keeping the name of Teddy Talbot in the higher echelons of bookmaking circles. We had been remarkably profitable over the last few years, and I was not naïve enough to think that it was solely down to me. It was all to do with the teamwork that Luca and I had perfected. Finding a new bookmaker's assistant wouldn't be easy, perhaps impossible to find one as good as Luca.

The trouble was, he knew it.

But, that said, I couldn't keep him on if I didn't trust him not to bring my business down, either in standing or in monetary terms. If my grandfather had taught me one thing it was that reputation was important. Most bookmakers are not held in great respect by the majority on the racecourse. Punters tend to think they are being forever robbed blind by the bookies, but I considered that I had always acted fairly and honourably towards the betting public, and also towards my fellow book- makers, something that had not gone unnoticed by my regu- lar customers. I wasn't about to see all that change, and Luca had to make his mind up if he could play by my rules. I may be sure that I needed him but he, in turn, was now deciding if he needed me.

'How about offering me a proper partnership?' he said with a smile.

I took that as a positive sign.

'I'll think about it,' I said.

'Don't take too long,' he said seriously, the smile having vanished.

Was he threatening me, I wondered, or simply warning me that he'd had offers from elsewhere?

Being a bookmaker's assistant was, for some, a self-employed business in itself. In our case, Luca was my full-time employee, but he could do equally well, and maybe better, offering his expert services freelance on a daily basis to the highest bidder. Over the past seven years, since my grandfather had died and I had taken on Luca, I had often engaged a professional book-maker's assistant for various days here and there, either when one of us was ill or away on holiday or, in my case, tending to the needs of my sick wife. I tried to use the same man each time but there were half a dozen or so who were all highly capable and in regular demand.

Maybe Luca was considering joining their ranks, or perhaps he'd had an offer from another bookmaker to become a partner.

I looked over at Larry Porter.

Surely not him, I thought. I had always considered that I was a better businessman than Larry, but maybe he thought the same about me.

'Hi, Larry,' I called over across the rain-swept deserted six feet between us. 'What price will you give me on the favourite in the next?'

'Piss off,' he shouted back. 'You self-righteous git.'

Charming, I thought. It might have been funny if it wasn't for the fact that he and Luca had put us all in jeopardy by so blatantly changing the prices.

Larry clearly wasn't enjoying his afternoon at the races. And he wasn't the only one.

The day progressed with, if anything, a deterioration in the weather. The individual thunderstorms had coalesced into a single expanse of dark menacing cloud stretching right across the sky, and the rain fell continuously straight downwards in the still air, while the humidity rose to an oppressive hundred per cent.

No doubt the gardeners of middle England were delighted by the downpour but the punters at Stratford plainly were not. We took just two bets on the big race of the day, if that was an appropriate way of describing it.

The three-mile steeplechase chase on rock-hard going had attracted a paltry field of just three, in pursuit of a prize put up by a well-known Midland building company. It was not the lovely summer's day that the firm's directors would have hoped for to entertain their clients when they had handed over their sponsorship cheque to the racecourse. Two small groups of their guests stood round under company-logoed umbrellas, watching the horses in the parade ring and trying unsuccessfully to look happy. Then they scuttled off back to their private box in the grandstand to dry off, and to sip another glass of bubbly.

In the betting ring there was noticeably more activity than for the first couple of races, though that was due not to an increase in the number of punters braving the conditions but to the fact that several 'suits' from the big outfits had turned up. They stood around getting wet, scrutinizing the prices on our boards more closely than a stamp collector studying a Penny Black.

Nothing untoward occurred, of course, but I caught a brief glimpse of Luca and Larry Porter having a secret smile at one another. Just how long, I thought, would it be before they couldn't resist trying it again?

The race itself could hardly be described as exciting. The short-priced favourite, the only decent horse of the three, jumped off in front at the start and led the other two round and round the course by an ever increasing margin, winning by a distance, almost at the trot. One of the remaining two slipped over at the last fence to leave the other to finish second but so far behind the winner that the stands had long before emptied.

To add insult to injury, the stewards decided to abandon the rest of the day's racing, citing the hazardous nature of the course. It seemed that the heavy rain, coming down as it had on the rock-hard ground, was causing the top surface of the grass to skid off the underlying dry compacted soil, making the going treacherous.

Personally, I thought the stewards had done everyone a favour and we gratefully packed up our stuff and made our way to the car parks.

'Are you still OK for Leicester tomorrow evening, without me?' I asked Luca.

'Yeah, sure,' he said. 'Looking forward to it.' He smiled at me. I stopped pulling the trolley. 'OK, OK,' he said. 'I know. No funny business. I promise.'

'Let's talk at the weekend,' I said.

'Fine,' he replied. 'I want to talk things through with Betsy anyway.'

Betsy had appeared from the bar and had helped us to pack away the last few things. I was never quite sure what was going on in her head, and that day she had been more obtuse than ever. She had said hardly a word to me since a brief 'hello' when they arrived.

We loaded the equipment in the boot of his car while Betsy

simply sat inside it in the passenger seat. She didn't say goodbye to me.

'Have a good day tomorrow,' said Luca. 'Good luck.'

'Thanks,' I said. 'I hope it all goes well.'

Sophie was due to have an assessment with a consultant psychiatrist from a different hospital. It was the final hurdle for her to pass in order to be able to come home. Just as there needed to be agreement between two psychiatrists for her to be sectioned in the first place, there was also a need for such agreement for her to be, as they put it, released back into the community.

The stress of an assessment was, paradoxically, bad for her condition, so I always tried to be on hand to provide her with reassurance and comfort between the sessions.

I wasn't at all sure whether it was a good idea to leave Luca and Betsy to go to Leicester together without me, and without the services of one of the freelance bookmaker's assistants. It was an evening meeting with the first race at twenty to seven. I supposed I might have been able to get there after spending the day at the hospital. Hemel Hempstead to Leicester was just a quick trip up the M1.

'Betsy and I will be fine,' Luca said, clearly reading the dilemma in my face. 'I promised, didn't I?'

I must have still looked doubtful.

'Look,' he said. 'We will be doing the best for the business in every respect. No point in fouling it all up if you're thinking of offering me a partnership, is there?' He smiled at me.

'OK,' I said. 'But . . .'

'Do you trust me or not?' he said, interrupting me.

'Yes, of course,' I said, hoping it was true.

'Then leave it,' he said seriously. 'I'll do tomorrow evening with Betsy, on our own. Like you said, we'll talk at the weekend.'

He then climbed into the car, next to Betsy, and drove away, with me standing there watching him and wondering if life could ever be the same again.

The rain had thankfully eased a little as we had packed up the stuff, but now it began again in earnest, drumming noisily on the roofs of the cars around me.

I threw my umbrella in the back of my car, jumped in the front and started the engine. I was about to drive away when the passenger door suddenly opened and a man in a blue gabardine mackintosh climbed in beside me.

'Can you give me a lift?' he asked.

I looked at him in amazement, but he just stared forward through the windscreen, ignoring me.

'Where to?' I said finally. 'The local police station?'

'I'd really rather not, if you don't mind,' said the man. 'Couldn't you just drive for a bit?'

'And what makes you think I'd want to do that?' I asked him icily.

He turned towards me. 'I thought you might want to talk.'

My audacious hitch-hiker was the fourth stranger from the inquest, my unwanted nocturnal visitor of the previous night, complete with fresh plaster cast on his right arm.

'OK,' I said. 'You talk and I'll listen.'

I put the car into gear.

CHAPTER 12

'Well?' I said. 'Talk to me.' I drove along the Stratford to Warwick road.

'Why didn't you call the police?' he said.

'How do you know I didn't?' I glanced across at him.

'I stayed to watch. No one came.'

'That doesn't mean I didn't call them.'

'I watched you through the window,' he said. 'You vacuumed up the mess I left, and no one does that if they've called the police.'

I felt uneasy at the thought of him being outside my home watching me. 'How long did you wait?' I asked him.

'Not long,' he said. 'My arm hurt too much.'

'Serves you right.'

'You broke my wrist.'

'Good.'

We sat in silence for a while.

'Who the hell are you, anyway?' I asked him.

'Just call me John,' he said.

'John who?'

'Just John.'

'And what do you want?' I asked him again.

'The microcoder,' he said. 'Like I told you last night.'

'What makes you think that I've got it?'

'Where else would it be?'

'It could be anywhere,' I said.

'You have it,' he said with finality.

'Even if I did have it, and I don't, what right do you think you have breaking into my house to look for it?'

'It seemed like a good idea at the time,' he said. 'And I didn't break in. You left a window open. You were just asking to be burgled.'

'So that's what you are, is it?' I said. 'A burglar.'

'Don't be stupid,' he said.

I looked across at him. 'I'm not the one with a broken arm.'

'OK,' he said. 'I agree. That wasn't so clever.'

Again I drove in silence.

'Where to, then?' I asked.

'To wherever the microcoder is.'

'I told you, I don't have it.'

'And I told you, I don't believe you.' He turned in his seat and looked at me. 'For a start, if you didn't know what I was talking about, then you would surely have telephoned the police last night. And secondly, we know it was you that retrieved your father's rucksack from the hotel in Paddington.'

'What rucksack?' I said, trying to keep my voice as level and calm as possible and wondering, once more, if this John fellow and Shifty Eyes were working together. He had said 'we'. Was I, after all, on my way to meet again the man with the twelve-centimetre knife?

'Oh, come on,' he said. 'We'd been looking for his luggage

too, you know. And I'd been looking for your father as well, for weeks. Ever since he stole the microcoder.'

'Who are *we*?' I asked.

He didn't answer. He just turned back, and looked out at the road.

'Why did you murder my father?' I said slowly.

'I didn't,' he said, still looking ahead.

'But you had it done,' I said.

'No.' He turned again to face me. 'That was not me.'

'Then who was it?' I asked him.

'I don't know,' he said.

'And you expect me to believe you?' I said. 'Perhaps we should go to the police station and you can then explain to them exactly who you are, and why you were in my house last night.'

'I'll deny it,' he said. 'You vacuumed up the evidence, remember.'

I pulled the Volvo into a lay-by, and stopped the engine. I turned to him.

'And what is it you really want?' I asked.

'The microcoder,' he said flatly. 'That's all.'

'And what exactly is this microcoder, anyway?' I said.

'An electronic device.'

'Yes, but what does it do?' I asked.

He sat silently for a moment or two, clearly debating with himself as to how much he should tell me.

'It writes coded information onto animal identification tags,' he said.

'RFIDs,' I said absent-mindedly.

'So you *do* know what it is,' he said, slapping his knee. 'So where the hell is it?'

171

Now it was my turn to sit silently debating with myself how much I was going to tell this 'Just call me John' mysterious stranger.

'Are you some sort of secret agent?' I asked.

He laughed. 'What makes you think that?'

'You seem pretty secretive,' I said. 'And you talk about "we" and "us" as if you were part of an organization.'

He again stared for a moment through the windscreen.

'Indirectly,' he said, 'I work for the Australian Racing Board.'

'Do they know you break into people's houses?'

'They would deny any knowledge of my existence.'

'You don't sound Australian.'

'I'm not,' he said. 'English to the core. Can't stand the Aussies, really; too bloody good at cricket, if you ask me.'

'So this, so-called microcoder is to do with Australian racing?'

'It's to do with all racing, everywhere.'

'But is there much racing in Australia?' I asked. 'I've heard of the Melbourne Cup, of course, but not much else.'

'There's a lot more racing in Australia than that,' he said. 'There are six times as many racecourses in Australia than here in Great Britain, and twice as many horses in training. It's big business.'

'Do they have licensed bookmakers?' I asked.

'Yes, plenty of them,' he said. 'But all off-course betting is through the TAB, their equivalent of the Tote.'

'Well, you live and learn.'

'And you must have heard of Phar Lap?' he said. 'Most famous racehorse that ever lived.'

'The name rings a bell.'

'Well, he was an Australian horse,' John said. 'Back in

the thirties. He won fourteen group races in a row one year, including the Melbourne Cup.'

'Oh,' I said.

'Yeah, but he was poisoned with arsenic during a visit to the United States. Some said the horse was killed on the orders of the Chicago mob to prevent him winning again, and costing them a packet in illegal bets.'

'Why are bookies always cast as the villains?' I asked.

'That's because you are,' he said, smiling at me. 'Now, where's my microcoder?'

'So it's yours, is it?' I asked.

'Yes,' he said.

'How can I be so sure? And why is it so important?'

'It just is,' he said. 'And I know you have it.'

'How?'

'I had a description of the man who collected your father's luggage from the hotel in Paddington, though I didn't know it was you, not until I saw you at the inquest.'

'Lots of people look like me,' I said.

'Stop playing games with me, Mr Talbot,' he said seriously. 'The lady at the Royal Sovereign Hotel described you absolutely perfectly, including your black eye, though how she didn't question your name as Dick Van Dyke, I'll never know.'

I couldn't help smiling, and he noticed.

'What on earth made you come up with that?' he said.

Perhaps he was unaware that my father had used the name Willem Van Buren when he'd checked in. The hotel lady had said he was called Van something, and Dick Van Dyke had been all I could come up with at the time.

'If you know so much, how come you took so long to find him – so long, in fact, that I found his luggage before you did?'

173

'Because he wasn't using his real name,' he said.

'And what is his real name?' I asked.

'You tell me,' he said. 'You formally identified him at the inquest two days ago. So it's now officially recorded by the coroner as Peter James Talbot. But is that right? Who, then, is Alan Charles Grady?'

And who, I also thought, was Willem Van Buren, of South Africa?

'Tell me what you know about my father,' I said to John.

'Why should I?' he said.

'Do you want your microcoder back or not?' I asked.

'You probably won't like it.'

I was sure of that, if what I knew already was any indication.

'Well, for a start, I knew him only as Alan Grady. The first time I heard the name Talbot was after he was dead. I had been keeping a tight eye on Mr Grady for some time. He was followed from Melbourne, but I lost him at Heathrow. I now think that he never came through immigration but took another international flight straight out. But I don't know where to.'

I thought about the e-ticket receipt I had found tucked into the Alan Grady passport in my father's rucksack. There had been no other flights listed there, other than his return to Australia.

'Was he using the name Grady?' I asked.

'I don't know that either,' he said. 'Unfortunately I don't have access to airline passenger lists.'

'An unofficial tail, then?' I said.

'Absolutely,' he said. 'As I told you, officially, I don't exist.'

I wished.

'For how long exactly have you been keeping a close eye on my father?' I asked him.

'For years,' he said. 'Must be twenty, at least. As far as I know, he's always been known to the racing authorities. He used to run an illegal back-street bookmaking business in Melbourne.'

'But I thought you said that bookmaking was legal in Australia.'

'Only on-course bookmakers are legal,' he said. 'Needless to say, our friend Mr Grady was not one of those.'

'But I am, remember,' I said to him.

'Oh yes, so you are.' He looked like he had stepped in something nasty.

'You're showing your prejudices. We're not all bad, you know.'

'Aren't you?' he said, laughing. 'Well, Alan Grady had been hovering around the edges of racing in Australia for as long as I've been working there. He was mostly very good at keeping one step ahead of the security service, just doing enough to keep himself out of court.'

I was surprisingly quite pleased that he was good at something. 'Only mostly?' I asked.

'He did get convicted a couple of times,' he said. 'Small stuff, really. He did one short stretch inside for obtaining money with menaces. Unpaid gambling debts. Then he got himself turned over by another illegal outfit, and ended up bankrupt.'

At least that bit of my father's story had been true, I thought.

'How come a man can go to prison and also be bankrupted and still no one realizes that he's not using his real name?'

'But Alan Grady was his real name,' he said. 'Passport, driving licence, bank accounts, even a genuine birth certificate all in the name of Grady. He was Alan Grady. As I said, I didn't hear the name Talbot until the day after he died, and that was only by chance from someone I had lunch with at Ascot last Wednesday. He told me about the murder in the car park.'

'But how did he get a genuine birth certificate in a false name?' I asked.

'There must have once been a real Alan Grady,' he said. 'Perhaps your father stole his identity. Perhaps the real Alan Grady died.'

Or he was murdered, I thought. Should I tell him, I wondered, about the Willem Van Buren passport? On balance, I thought not. Not yet.

'So tell me about this microcoder,' I said.

'Seems you know already.'

'I know it can be used to write numbers onto RFIDs,' I said. 'But so what? Why was it worth chasing my father half way round the world to get it back?'

'Fraud,' he said.

'Yeah, I assumed that, but what sort of fraud?'

'Making one horse appear to be another,' he said.

'But so what?' I said again. 'Everyone knows that running a ringer in a race needs a conspiracy. Too many people would surely recognize the animal, and someone will spill the beans.'

'Ah, yes,' he said. 'But you could easily sell a foal or a yearling as another, with no risk then of anyone recognizing it as the wrong horse. Especially if you sell it to England from Australia, or vice versa.'

'But surely horses are DNA tested for their parentage,' I said.

'They are,' he agreed. 'But they are only retested if they eventually go to stud. And the DNA testing takes a long time. Not like using a hand-held scanner on the ID chip, which is instant.'

'But even if you switch a bad horse for a good one, and then sell it,' I said, 'what would you do with the good one you've kept? You can't sell the same horse twice.'

'No, but you could put it into training under its new identity. It would still be a good horse, and could make a packet on the track. And, if it's so much better than people think it should be, it would win at long odds, at least to start with. Just make sure you don't breed from it. Geld it even, to be safe.'

'And the bad one you sold would just be seen as another expensive failure?' I said. 'And there are lots of those about.'

'Exactly,' he said.

Everyone in racing knew about Snaafi Dancer. Bought as a yearling in 1983 for a world record price in excess of six and a half million pounds, he ran too slow to ever make it to a racecourse, and then turned out to be infertile. And he was just one of a whole string of flops that had been sold for millions, and then earned not a penny of it back.

'I grant you, it's a long-term strategy,' he said. 'But one that's quite likely to be profitable. Obviously you wouldn't do it with a really mega-valuable yearling as there would be masses of checks made, but loads of horses go to the sales each year. And even the horses-in-training sales now attract huge prices, and for geldings too.'

'But I thought those ID chips were meant to be secure and unchangeable,' I said.

'So did we,' he said. 'But it seems we were wrong. The chip that's inserted in a horse's neck contains a number that is unique for that horse, and it is supposed to be read-only and permanent. But someone has discovered that a very intense localized magnetic field can wipe the number from the chip, just the same way those security tags stuck on CDs in shops are wiped over a magnetic pad to clear them.'

'And, don't tell me,' I said, 'the microcoder can write a new number in?'

'Well, not quite,' he said. 'The magnetic field has to be so strong that the chip's electronics are completely destroyed. But the microcoder can write a different number into a new chip, which is then inserted in the horse's neck and, hey presto, you instantly have a different horse.'

'But how about the horse's passport with all its whorls and such?' I said.

'That would be OK if people bothered,' he said. 'But too many people believe the technology without question. Like in tennis. All those arguments about whether the ball was in or out have disappeared, thanks to the computerized Hawk-Eye system. The players believe it absolutely, as does everyone else. If Hawk-Eye says it was out, then it was out. Same with this. If the ID chip says that the animal is Horse A, then it's Horse A, even if it's got all the whorls for Horse B. The authorities try to get people to check both, but they still tend to believe the ID chips. After all, it's the same authorities that insist on them being inserted, and then they tell people they're foolproof. Only now they find they're not.'

'Does everywhere use the same ones?' I said.

'Pretty much,' he said. 'Except the United States. They don't use chips at all, at least not yet, because they tattoo the inside of the horse's lip. But if a horse comes from the States to race in Australia or Europe, it has to be chipped first.'

'By whom?' I asked.

'A vet authorized by the racing board.'

'Seems to me that the system needs changing,' I said.

'We need that microcoder back,' he said in reply.

'What's to stop someone making another one?' I said.

'Nothing, I suppose,' he said. 'But our boffins say it's not that easy.'

'How about the man who made the first one? He could surely make another.'

'Ah,' he said. 'Therein lies a tale.'

'What tale?' I asked.

'A trigger-happy Victoria State policeman shot him as he was trying to resist arrest.'

'Dead?' I asked.

'As good as,' he said. 'Got a bullet in his brain. Totally gaga.'

What a waste, I thought. Smarter than the boffins, and now what? A vegetable.

'Someone else will work it out,' I said. 'Probably some fourteen-year-old in his school science lab.' Or Luca, I thought.

'It would have to be someone with both the knowledge and the intent,' he said.

'If there are any with the knowledge, then there will be some with the intent. Trust me, I'm a bookmaker.'

He laughed. 'You're probably right. But we have to try and do what we can to stay ahead of them.'

'How about the tattoos the Americans use?'

'They're tricky to do, and become difficult to read as the horse gets older,' he said. 'And they're not fraud-proof either. It has been known for some unscrupulous souls to try to vary the original tattoo.'

We had been sitting in the lay-by for quite a while and, as we talked, I had been trying to think of what to do. Why had he said nothing about the money? Did he, in fact, know that the money had also been in the rucksack? Was I going to give him the microcoder and the cash? Did I have any choice in the matter? If John, here, had a direct line to the Victoria State Police, then he probably did to Chief Inspector Llewellyn as well. But why then had he entered my house uninvited through a window in the middle of the night?

'Never mind the horses,' I said. 'Do you have any personal ID?'

'What, here?'

'Yes,' I said. 'How do I know you are who you say you are?'

'I told you,' he replied slightly uncomfortably. 'The Australian Racing Board would deny all knowledge of my existence.'

'And why is that, exactly?' I said.

'The very nature of my job means I have to work under cover. If I was a normal employee then my cover would be blown. There are bound to be some people within the organization who would pass on the information to the very people I am trying to investigate.'

'But John who?' I said.

'Smith,' he said with a straight face.

John Smith. Oh yeah, I thought, pull the other one. But John was probably not his real name either.

'So where exactly is my microcoder?' he said.

'I gave it to a friend.'

'You did what?' he exclaimed. 'Who?'

'A friend who's an electronic specialist,' I said. 'To try and see what it does.'

He went pale. 'Well, get it back, now,' he almost shouted.

'I can't,' I said. 'My friend has gone away on holiday for a week. To Greece.'

I didn't know why I was so reluctant to simply hand it over. I suppose I thought that this John would then just disappear, in which case I would never learn anything more about my father.

Maybe it was also because I didn't really trust him. Not enough to hand over my trump card to him, not just yet, anyway.

'Where does this friend live?' John asked.

'Why? Are you thinking of breaking into another house?' There was more than a hint of sarcasm in my tone.

He looked at me out of the corner of his eye. 'If I think it's necessary,' he said.

'It's somewhere in High Wycombe,' I said. 'I don't know exactly where. There are lots of houses in High Wycombe. Are you going to break into them all?'

'Oh, ha ha,' he said. 'When does this friend get back from holiday?'

'Sunday, I think,' I said.

'And what's his name?' he demanded.

'Her, actually,' I said. 'And what makes you think I would tell you her name, anyway? You must be joking. You'd go and break into her house.'

'Mr Talbot,' he said seriously, 'I don't think you really understand the trouble you might be in. I assure you, I'm not the only person looking for that microcoder. And some of them might not be so . . .' He stopped as if thinking.

'Honest?' I said. 'Don't make me laugh.'

'Patient,' he said. 'There are some very nasty people out there.'

Be very careful of everyone, my father had said. I certainly intended being very careful of Shifty Eyes and his twelve-centimetre knife. And, as far as I was concerned, that included being very careful of Mr John Smith, here, as well.

'You call breaking into people's houses being patient?' I said.

He sat there in silence for a second or two, staring ahead.

'Where can I drop you?' I said. 'I have things to do.'

'Here will do fine. A colleague of mine has been following us since we left the racecourse.' He twisted round in the seat.

I looked in the rear-view mirror. There was a dark blue Ford in the lay-by behind us, but it was some way off. I couldn't see the driver due to the reflection of the sky from the windscreen.

'Give me a call when your friend comes back from holiday,' he said, turning back and handing me a business card. I looked at it and rotated it in my hands. A mobile telephone number was printed across the centre of one side. There was no name, no company, and no address, just the telephone number. 'Call me,' he said. 'For your own good.'

He opened the passenger door and eased himself out of my car.

'Go now,' he ordered, closing the door.

He stood there, as if waiting for me to depart. I, meanwhile, felt decidedly annoyed to think that someone had been following me. In fact, I was downright angry about it.

I started the engine but, instead of engaging forward gear, I put the Volvo into reverse, and accelerated backwards down the lay-by towards the Ford.

I'm sure I would have rammed him if he hadn't suddenly pulled out into the road and shot away, narrowly avoiding a collision with both a truck and a car towing a caravan. I snatched the Volvo into forward gear and pulled out to give chase, but I had no chance. Both the truck and the caravan were between me and the Ford, and I could see it in the distance, speeding away. The twelve-year-old engine under my car's bonnet was reliable, but well past its prime and, even with its gas-guzzling 2.3 litres plus turbocharger, it was unable to generate enough horses for me to pass the slower vehicles.

Damn it, I thought. That wasn't very clever. My first ever

under-cover, secret-agent, James-Bond-style car chase and I'd got stuck behind a bloody caravan. 'M' would not have been amused.

I turned the car round at the next junction and went back to the lay-by.

Naturally, there was no sign of either a dark blue Ford, or of a certain Mr John Smith, or whatever his real name was.

CHAPTER 13

Sophie's assessment took all morning and went on into the afternoon. It mostly consisted of a case conference between the medical staff, discussing whether they all considered that Sophie was well enough to go home. It needed unanimity on their behalf. Any dissent was likely to prove decisive. A consultant psychiatrist from another hospital chaired the conference.

In addition there was an informal presentation by Sophie, where she was invited to explain to the psychiatrists why she thought she was ready to leave their care. Then they, in turn, were free to ask her questions in order to try and determine her state of mind.

This was not the first time Sophie had been forced to go through this type of assessment. Six times before, she had endured sitting quietly while others discussed her mental health and then passed judgement on her fitness or otherwise to be released from hospital. Only on four of those six occasions had she been successful, and it was far from guaranteed this time.

'And what about you, Mr Talbot?' asked the visiting psychiatrist in the session after lunch. 'Are you able to be at home to support your wife through the first few days?'

'Of course,' I said. 'I am always there to give my support.'

'Do you work from home?' he asked, looking up at me from his notes.

'No,' I said. 'But I intend being there when Sophie leaves hospital.'

'And what line of business are you in?' he asked.

I paused for a moment. I had once had a bookmaker colleague who always claimed he was an accountant, only adding that he was a 'turf' accountant if challenged.

'I'm a bookmaker,' I said.

'In a shop?' he said, without a pause.

'No,' I said. 'I'm an on-course bookie, mostly at the Midlands meetings.'

'Horses or dogs?' he asked.

'Horses,' I said. 'Although I have stood at dog racing in the past, but there's little profit in it these days.'

He raised his eyebrows. 'And why is that?'

'Not enough tracks,' I said. 'There used to be masses of them, but they keep closing for redevelopment. Too few tracks mean too few dogs. It all becomes far too predictable. And the public's appetite for dog racing has also changed. Nowadays they all sit in restaurants and bet from their dinner tables using the Tote.'

'You make it sound as if you don't like the Tote,' he said with a smile.

'I don't,' I said. 'The Tote can never lose its shirt. It always takes its cut before paying out the winning tickets. They can't get it wrong because they don't have to set the prices, while I have to use my knowledge and experience to keep myself in business.'

'I see,' he said slowly, clearly losing interest.

'But I will be at home whenever Sophie needs me,' I said.

I decided not to mention unwelcome night-time visitors, or men with twelve-centimetre knives.

'Thank you, Mr Talbot,' said the psychiatrist. 'I'm sure you will.'

His tone implied that he didn't really believe it. He looked down and wrote more notes.

'Excuse me,' I said. He looked up. 'I assure you that Sophie's well-being is far more important to me than my work. I desperately want her home. And I will do everything within my power to ensure she remains safe and unharmed. I love my wife.'

I had sat all day holding Sophie's hand, listening to these emotionally distant professionals discussing her most personal secrets in matter-of-fact detail, and now I quite surprised myself with the passion of my plea. But I did want Sophie home.

I realized that I wanted it very much indeed.

'Yes, Mr Talbot,' said the psychiatrist, 'I believe you do.' He smiled at Sophie, who went on holding my hand very tightly.

He went back to writing a few more notes before looking up.

'Mrs Talbot, Mr Talbot, thank you both for your time. As you know, we shall require further discussion between us before we make our final decision. Today is Thursday. We should have an answer for you by tomorrow or Saturday.' He looked around at the other medical staff as if enquiring whether any of them had anything more to say. They didn't.

'Thank you, then,' he said, rising to his feet, indicating that our time was up.

'Thank you,' said Sophie.

We stood up in turn and made our way out of the conference room.

'I thought that went quite well,' I said to her quietly.

'Did you?' she said.

'Yes,' I said, being upbeat. 'Didn't you?'

'I don't know. I didn't like that psychiatrist much.'

'He seemed OK to me,' I said. 'I'm sure it will be all right.'

We walked together side by side along the corridor towards her room.

'Do you really love me?' she said.

'Yes,' I said. 'Very much.'

She didn't stop walking. But she did start smiling.

I spent the evening at the hospital with Sophie watching the television. Neither of us spoke about the assessment or what conclusion the medics might come to. Neither did we make any plans for the coming weeks. Twice in the past we had been cruelly disappointed, having decided to go away together on holiday only to have the case conference rule against release.

Nowadays we told ourselves that discharge was an un-expected bonus to be celebrated but, deep down, we would still be devastated if they refused to allow her home this time. The new drug regime was working well and Sophie was becoming less tired from the side effects as her body became used to the medications.

But neither of us wanted to tempt fate by discussing the matter, so we sat quietly watching a string of situation comedies on a golden-oldies TV channel.

Was I, in fact, being sensible in wanting Sophie to come home with so many unresolved issues surrounding my father?

John Smith, or whoever he was, had gone on ad infinitum about his blessed microcoder but he hadn't once mentioned any money. I wondered again if he even knew about the cash. He certainly did if he was working with Shifty Eyes. But had it been

Shifty Eyes in the dark blue Ford? Or was there someone else? Maybe John really was from the Australian Racing Board and there was a whole team behind him.

And what was the money for?

Give me the money, Shifty Eyes had hissed at my father before he stabbed him. Had the money been due as payment? And for what? And why then had Shifty Eyes then killed my father when he was the only one who knew where it was?

I tried to remember every detail of the stabbing as my eyes watched yet another situation comedy about dysfunctional family life. They should film my family, I thought, except it wouldn't be a comedy.

The man had run up and kicked me in the face but he had then turned his attention solely to my father. It had clearly not been a robbery as I had first thought. Our attacker had taken no notice of me at all until I shouted for help and the party crowd had begun moving towards us.

I remembered my father telling the man to go to hell and kicking him in the groin. That had made Shifty Eyes very angry and he had retaliated by stabbing out with his knife. Perhaps he shouldn't have done. Maybe killing my father had been a big mistake. There were an awful lot of cheap hotels in London. I had been very lucky to have found the right one, and the more so because my father had registered using a name that was neither Talbot nor Grady. Without knowing that it was in Sussex Gardens, it would have been an impossible task.

'Shall we have some coffee?' Sophie asked, interrupting my thoughts.

'Yes,' I said. 'That would be lovely. Shall I call the nurse?'

'No,' she replied. 'Since last week they've let me go down the corridor to the little kitchen. I'll get it.'

'Do you need any help?' I asked her.

'Ned,' she replied, looking at me sideways, 'I can make coffee on my own. I'll be all right, you know. I won't slit my wrists or anything.' She smiled at me. My heart now did the same flip-flop that it had, all those years ago, when we had first met and she had smiled at me.

'Are you sure?' I said.

'Positive. They might let me use the kitchen, but even they aren't crazy enough to leave sharp knives lying around for us, the real crazies, to harm ourselves.' She laughed at her joke, and I laughed with her.

She had come a long way even during the last week and she truly did seem better than ever this time.

'I am trying very hard, you know,' she said more seriously. 'I haven't missed a single dose of these new drugs and I do honestly believe that they are helping. I feel really quite well now, and ready again for the world.'

I stood up and hugged her. There were tears in my eyes.

'Go and get the coffee,' I said.

She left the room and I wiped my eyes on my sleeve. Tears of happiness and hope, at last, after so many of despair and hopelessness.

I thought about staying over at the hospital in their guest suite, but if I wasn't confident enough to go home alone tonight, what chance did I have of taking Sophie there tomorrow.

However, I was still quite wary as I pulled my Volvo into the parking area in front of the dark house. I sat in the car for a few moments looking all around for anything out of the ordinary. Everything seemed fine.

I quickly locked the car and made it safely to my front door.

There were a few letters and bills on the mat but no threatening notes or demands.

Calm down, I told myself.

I tried to, but it didn't stop me going all round the house checking that the windows were fully closed and drawing the curtains in every room. I had been quite disturbed to think of Mr John Smith looking through the window at me as I had vacuumed up the mess in the drawing room. He wouldn't be spying on me again tonight. I made sure of that by not allowing the slightest chink of light to escape through the blinds in the kitchen.

I laid the booty from my father's rucksack out on the kitchen table as I had done the first night I'd found it, and sat there looking at it.

Why didn't I deliver the whole lot to Chief Inspector Llewellyn and let him sort it out? Wash my hands of the affair and get on with my life, which was complex enough without microcoders, forged RFIDs and shifty-eyed men with long, sharp knives?

A good part of me thought that was a great idea.

But it had disadvantages, too. For a start, there would be the difficult task of explaining to the chief inspector why I hadn't given him the stuff as soon as I had found it, or even given him the necessary information so that he could have found it himself. I didn't exactly think he would be very happy about that. He might, with good reason, charge me with obstructing the police, and then what protection would they afford me against a knifeman? None whatsoever.

Second, keeping hold of the microcoder and the money might

give me some leverage, provided I kept alive long enough to use it.

I picked up my father's mobile telephone and tried again to turn it on, but without success. It had Nokia written on the front. My mobile was a Samsung. I tried my charger but the connection was wrong, naturally. I took the SIM card out of my father's phone and put it in mine but I seemed unable to get any details of his numbers. If there was anything there, he had stored it in the phone's memory, not on the SIM.

I dug around in the bottom drawer of my desk where I always put spare or old chargers but nothing would fit.

I picked up the Alan Charles Grady passport and examined it. It had been issued nine months previously and appeared to me to be genuine, but I had no real idea of what an Australian passport should look like. I turned the pages and found a stamp from an immigration officer at Heathrow showing that he had not entered the United Kingdom until the day before he came to see me at Ascot. It was the only UK stamp in his passport but there was also one from Dublin airport dated the previous week. So he *had* flown straight out again from Heathrow after his arrival from Australia, just as John Smith had thought, and using the name Grady.

I wondered what he had been up to in Ireland for six days and I decided it was time to find out. I couldn't just sit and wait for Shifty Eyes to turn up demanding his money with a knife at my throat for encouragement. Or, worse still, at Sophie's throat.

The following morning, Friday, I was waiting outside the local mobile telephone shop for it to open at nine o'clock sharp.

I'd not slept well, mostly due to imagining that I could hear creaks on the stairs. I had firmly wedged Sophie's dressing-table chair under the bedroom door handle when I had retired and, of course, it had still been safely there in the morning.

At ten past nine the door was unlocked by a female shop assistant who looked about twelve. 'Yes, sir,' she said in a bored tone. 'Can I help you?'

'I need a charger for this phone,' I said, holding out my father's Nokia and refraining from asking if her mother was in.

'No problem,' she said, with a little more interest. 'Mains or in-car?'

'Mains,' I said.

She went over to a display and took one of the chargers.

'This should be the one,' she said. 'Anything else?'

'Could you just check that it's the right one?' I said.

'It will be,' she reiterated.

'Could you just open it to make sure?' I said. 'Please.'

She obviously thought I was mad but she took a large pair of scissors from a drawer beneath the desk and cut through the plastic wrap around the charger. She plugged it into a socket and took the phone from me.

'There,' she said. 'It's charging. You can see from the little lines moving on the side.'

I looked and indeed the display was no longer completely blank as before.

'Thank you,' I said. 'Can you turn it on?'

She pushed a button on the top. The screen lit up and then the phone played a five-note tune. She handed it back to me with it still connected by the cord to the charger.

The phone had the message *Please Enter Your Security Code* displayed on the screen.

'It's a long time since I used this phone,' I said to her, 'and I can't remember the security code. Can you bypass it for me?'

'No chance,' she said, sounding horrified at the suggestion. 'I'm not allowed to do that. How do I know it's your phone, anyway?'

'So theoretically you could bypass the security code,' I said, 'if you really wanted to?'

'I doubt it,' she said. 'But I expect Carl could.'

'Who's Carl?'

'He works out the back,' she said. 'He mends mobiles. He's very clever.'

She disappeared and returned with a young man who didn't strike me as the very clever type. He was wearing faded, torn and frayed blue jeans, a plain off-white T-shirt and a knitted brown hat that reminded me of a tea-cosy. Tufts of fair hair stuck out from under the hat in all directions and there was a further supply of wispy blond fluff sprouting on his chin.

'Can you unlock this phone?' I asked him.

He didn't say anything but took the phone from my hand and looked at it.

'What's the four-digit security code?' he asked.

'I don't know,' I said patiently. 'That's why I need it unlocked.'

'What's the phone's IMEI number?' he said.

'IMEI?'

'International Mobile Equipment Identity,' he said slowly, as if for a child.

'I have no idea,' I said.

'It's normally written inside the phone,' he said, taking off the back and removing the battery. 'Hello. This one's been removed. There should be a sticker just here.' He pointed. 'That's what people do with stolen phones,' he said, looking warily at me.

'How else can I get this IMEI?' I asked, ignoring his suspicions.

'You could input *#06# on the keypad once it's unlocked,' he said unhelpfully. 'Or it would have been printed on a sticker on the box when you bought it.'

I decided against telling him I hadn't bought the phone. It would only further his opinion that the phone was stolen, which, if past form was anything to go by, it probably was.

He put the battery back into the phone and turned it on. *Please Enter Your Security Code* appeared again on the display.

'Can't you do it without the IMEI number?' I asked.

'No, mate,' he said, handing back the phone. 'Can't help you without the IMEI or the security code. Not without wiping clean the whole phone memory. Do you want me to do that?'

'No,' I said quickly. It was the phone's memory I wanted most.

I paid the girl for the charger and took it and the phone back to my home in Station Road. I sat again at my kitchen table, thinking about what to do next.

I wondered what the security code might be.

I punched in 3105. My father's real birthday had been the thirty-first of May.

The display momentarily read *Incorrect Security Code* before returning to *Please Enter Your Security Code*.

I tried 0531 for the American way of writing dates, but with the same result.

I inserted the year of his birth. *Incorrect Security Code.*

194

Next I tried 1234. *Incorrect Security Code.*

I looked at the copy of his driving licence. I typed in 0312, his house number. *Incorrect Security Code.*

The licence showed Alan Grady's birthday as 15 March 1948. I tried 1503. *Incorrect Security Code.* I typed in 1948. *Incorrect Security Code.*

It could be anything. I wondered how many wrong chances I'd have before the whole phone locked up for ever. If it was based on his phone number, I reckon I had no chance.

I worked out there were ten thousand different combinations of four numbers. If I input one combination every ten seconds it could take me one hundred thousand seconds, assuming I made no mistakes. One hundred thousand seconds was ... I sat there trying to do the mental arithmetic ... one thousand six hundred and sixty-six and two thirds minutes, which was ... nearly twenty-eight hours. With no sleep or breaks. And that assumed the phone didn't lock up completely because I'd keyed in too many wrong attempts. There had to be a better way.

I took the phone and the charger with me and decided to go back and see Carl to see if he had any other ideas.

But I never got there.

I sat in the car outside the shop and stared at the phone in my hand. I couldn't quite believe it. It was unlocked. I had entered *my* birthday, 2504, just for a laugh, and suddenly there it was – *Correct Security Code.*

So he hadn't forgotten. There may, of course, have been other events in his life that happened on the twenty-fifth of April, but I would assume it was my birthday he had remembered.

The phone rang in my hand making me jump.

I answered it.

'This is voicemail,' a disembodied female voice said. 'Please enter your security code.'

Not again, I thought. I tried 2504.

'You have three new messages,' said the voice. 'Message one received at ten thirteen a.m. on the eighteenth of June.'

Two days after he died.

'Alan, this is Paddy, Paddy Murphy,' said a male voice with a strong Irish accent. 'Where are you? You were meant to call me yesterday.'

I assumed, therefore, that Paddy Murphy and Shifty Eyes were not one and the same person. Otherwise, he would have known why there had been no call.

Messages two and three were also from Paddy Murphy, each with an increasing degree of urgency, asking, then pleading, for Alan to call him back.

'The caller's number was plus 353 42 3842 . . . ,' said the disembodied voice when I pushed the right button. I wrote it down on the notepad I always kept in the glove box of the car. Plus 353 meant it was a Republic of Ireland number. Perhaps Paddy Murphy was the man my father had flown to Dublin to visit.

So all I had to do now was find a certain Paddy Murphy in Ireland. Easy, I thought. I suppose it must be marginally more straightforward than finding someone called Chang in China.

And I had Paddy's telephone number, which helped.

CHAPTER 14

The rest of the telephone was less useful than I had hoped.

Unlike most people, my father had not used his mobile as his phone book. There were no entries at all on either the phone memory or on the SIM card. No handy names of contacts who might or might not have made a microcoder, and who now lay in a Melbourne hospital with a bullet in his brain.

No convenient names for my sisters with their telephone numbers.

The only useful thing was a list in the calls register of the last ten numbers he had called and five that he had received. One of them in each of the lists was the +353 number of Paddy Murphy.

I made a written note of them all, just in case the phone decided to die completely, but I wasn't even sure if they were UK, Irish or Australian numbers, or anywhere else for that matter.

I looked at my watch. It was a quarter to ten in the morning in Kenilworth. It would be the same in Dublin. But I wondered what time that made it in Melbourne, Australia.

I used my father's phone to call Paddy Murphy.

'Hello,' said a very Irish-sounding voice with the emphasis on the long final 'o'.

'Is that Paddy Murphy?' I asked.

'Who wants to know?' said the voice rather cautiously. Was Paddy Murphy not his real name either?

'This is Alan Grady's son,' I said.

There was a long pause from the other end.

'Are you still there?' I asked eventually. He was. I could hear his breathing.

'And who might Alan Grady be?' he said.

'Don't play games with me, Mr Murphy. Call me back on this number if you want to talk.'

I hung up.

He called back immediately, the phone ringing before I had time to put it down.

'Yes?' I said.

'And what line of business might you be in?' he asked.

'Selling,' I said.

'Selling what, exactly?' he replied.

'Depends on what you want to buy,' I said.

'Now are you playing games with me this time, Mr Grady?' he said.

'Maybe.'

'Are you the Garda?' he asked suddenly.

'Garda?'

'The Garda,' he repeated. 'The police?'

'Why do you ask?' I said, realizing finally what he meant. 'Have you been up to no good?' But the line was dead. Paddy Murphy, or whoever, had already hung up.

Damn, I thought. That hadn't gone at all well. He was

possibly my only real lead to discover what was going on, and now he had done a runner. Perhaps he believed I'd been trying to trace the call. I wish I had. My father had flown into Dublin, but Mr Paddy Murphy, if that was his real name, could be anywhere in the more than thirty thousand square miles of the Republic of Ireland.

I sat for ten minutes waiting and hoping for him to call. He didn't.

So I tried him again, but he didn't answer. How, I wondered, did one find out where a certain telephone number was situated? If it was a mobile I might have no chance, but a land-line would have an area code. I decided to ask Luca. If anyone knew, he would.

In the afternoon I drove to Kempton Park for the evening racing. Luca had called to say he would meet me at the course as he and Betsy were spending the day somewhere in Surrey, visiting friends, or something.

I'd asked him how things had gone at Leicester on the Wednesday evening.

'Fine,' he'd said. 'Good crowd. Plenty of business.'

'Profitable?' I asked.

'Very,' he'd replied without explaining further.

Why did I worry so much? Would it be better or worse if Luca was my official business partner? Indeed, should I sell him the whole enterprise and be done with it? But what else could I do? I had to earn a living somehow.

I turned off the congested Friday-evening M25 and fought my way against the commuter traffic to Sunbury and Kempton Park racecourse.

Race traffic was starting to build up to add to the Friday-evening woes and I crawled the last two miles nose to tail with other cars before turning into the racecourse car park behind the stands. There was free parking in the centre of the course but, at Kempton, I usually parked at the far end of the members' car park near the railway station. It was nearly impossible to pull our equipment trolley across the new all-weather track to the grandstand from the free car park, but only after I'd paid the parking fee did I remember that Luca had all the stuff with him.

I pulled into a spot as indicated by one of the parking mar-shals, who were, as always, efficiently placing as many cars as possible in the limited space available. Another car drew in beside me.

I sat in the car and called the hospital again. I had tried them twice before leaving Kenilworth but there had been no news to report. Again they were sorry, they said, there was still no decision from the psychiatrists and it was now being assumed by the hospital staff that Sophie would be staying there until Monday at the earliest. She wouldn't be pleased.

I watched as a train pulled into the racecourse station and disgorged a mass of humanity that literally swarmed to the racecourse entrances. It was a beautiful summer's evening with a gentle cooling breeze and the good weather had brought out the crowds in droves. A good night for business, I concluded, and stepped out of the car.

'Are you Talbot?' said someone behind me. 'Teddy Talbot?'

I turned round. There were two men standing between the cars, both wearing short-sleeved white shirts, open at the neck, with black trousers: uniform of the heavy mob. The shirts did little to hide the substantial size of their biceps, nor the tattoos clearly visible on their forearms. Neither of them was Shifty Eyes, but that hardly made me feel any better.

'Yes,' I said gingerly. 'Can I help you?'

Instead of replying the nearest man stepped forward quickly and punched me hard in the stomach.

The blow drove the air from my lungs and I went down to the ground badly winded, unable to catch my breath.

'Oh, I say,' said the man from the neighbouring car, looking horrified as he removed a jacket and some binoculars from his boot.

'Shut up,' said the puncher, pointing sharply at him, 'or you'll get the same.'

The horrified man shut up immediately and moved rapidly away. I didn't blame him. I would have moved rapidly away too, if only I could have drawn some air into my lungs. I rather hoped he had gone for reinforcements in the shape of a policeman or two, but I wouldn't have bet on it.

'I have a message from my boss,' the puncher said, returning his attention to me. 'Don't mess again with the starting prices.' He kicked me in the midriff. 'Get it?' he said. 'No more Stratford.' He kicked again. 'Get it?' he repeated.

He kicked me once again for good measure and then the two of them turned and calmly walked away, leaving me lying on the tarmac with my knees drawn up to my chest and a severe ache in my abdomen.

I had been holding my stomach with my hands and I now looked at them with concern. There was no blood. The punch had been just that. There had been no knife. I was intact, at least on the outside.

Slowly my diaphragm recovered from its spasm and my breathing resumed with a rush, which greatly improved the situation. I drew my knees up under me and used the door handle of my Volvo to pull myself semi-upright.

'Are you all right?' asked the horrified man, appearing tentatively round the back of his car.

'I'm fine,' I said, not feeling it.

'What was all that about?' he asked.

'Nothing,' I said.

'It didn't look like nothing,' he said accusingly.

'Could you identify those men to the police?' I asked him.

'Er,' he hesitated. 'Not really.'

'No?' I said. 'Then nothing happened. OK?'

'I'm only trying to help,' he said, somewhat pained.

'Sorry,' I said. 'And thank you for your concern.' If I'd really been seriously hurt, life-threateningly hurt, he might just have saved my skin by coming back. 'I promise you I am very grateful. My name's Ned Talbot.' I held out my hand to him.

He hesitated again, not taking it. 'I don't want to get involved,' he said. 'I didn't like the look of those men.'

'So you did see what they looked like?' I said.

He was slightly flustered.

'It's OK,' I said. 'I understand completely. I won't be describing them to the police either.' One kicking was more than enough, I thought.

I leaned wearily against his car and felt sick, the skin of my face cold and clammy.

'Right,' he said, and he turned on his heel and walked briskly away.

He may not have wanted to get involved but I still noted down the registration of his car on my notepad. Just in case.

*

Luca and Betsy were both waiting for me at our pitch in front of the grandstand. By the time I had recovered sufficiently and made my way through to the betting ring, they had set up everything and they were sitting on our metal platform in the shade of our large yellow TRUST TEDDY TALBOT umbrella.

'Hello,' I said. 'Have any trouble?'

'No,' said Luca. 'Traffic was fairly light really from Richmond, for a Friday.'

'No problems in the car park?' I asked.

'No,' he said. 'But I forgot how bloody hard it is to get that trolley across from the centre of the course.'

'I've just been given a message,' I said to him.

'Where?' he asked.

'In the car park behind the stands,' I said.

'Who by?' he said.

'I don't know,' I said. 'Someone who's not very happy about what happened at Stratford on Wednesday.'

'What sort of message?' asked Luca with concern.

'Fists and steel toecaps,' I said.

'What!' He seemed genuinely distressed. 'Here? In the car park?'

I nodded.

'You're having me on?' he said, but he wasn't smiling.

'Sadly, I'm not,' I said. 'And I could show you my bruised solar plexus to prove it.'

'God,' he said, clearly upset. 'I'm so sorry.'

'Why are you sorry?' said Betsy. 'You didn't do it.'

'Shut up, Betsy,' said Luca sharply, clearly annoyed.

'Don't talk to me like that,' she whined at him.

'Then don't say such stupid things,' he said to her. He turned back to me. 'Ned, I'm really sorry. Are you OK?'

'I'll live,' I said, without much warmth. It would do no harm, I thought, for Luca to realize that his little games had consequences, some of which were decidedly unpleasant, and not just for him.

Betsy went off towards the grandstand in a huff and both Luca and I watched her go.

'Go after her, if you like,' I said to him.

He said nothing but shrugged his shoulders and stayed just where he was. It would appear, I reflected, that we would soon need another junior assistant. And I wouldn't be sorry. I decided I didn't really like Betsy much. Maybe it was because she wasn't very bright. She was certainly streets behind Luca, and perhaps he could see it too.

'How about Larry?' I said. 'Is he here this evening?'

'He should be,' said Luca.

'Really?' I said. Why, I wondered, did Luca know that Larry should be here?

He looked at me sideways. 'Yeah, well,' he said. 'I just know.' I looked at him in mock surprise. 'He told me last night. At Leicester, all right?' Luca was visibly flustered, and that was a rarity.

'Do you have his phone number?' I asked.

'Sure,' he said.

'Then call him,' I said. 'Warn him to watch his back. And his stomach.'

Luca pulled his mobile from his pocket and pushed the buttons.

'Larry,' he said. 'It's Luca.'

He listened for a moment.

'So where are you now?' he said.

He listened again for a moment.

'Right,' he said. 'I'll call you later.' He hung up and looked at me. 'Too late. He's in Ascot hospital having X-rays for suspected broken ribs.'

'So who were they?' I said.

'Who?' he asked.

'Who do you think?' I said. 'Mike Tyson and his chum?'

'How the hell would I know?' he said. 'I didn't see them.'

'Who did we upset so much?'

'All of them,' he said. 'The talk was of nothing else last night at Leicester. Some of the other bookies were openly delighted, and one or two even congratulated us.' He was smiling.

What bloody fools, I thought. And it was me that gets the 'message', not Luca, because it's my name on the board.

'I told you not to mess with the big outfits,' I said. 'At least, you shouldn't mess with them so openly and obviously. We need to be more subtle. And far more devious.' I smiled back at him.

He was confused. 'What do you mean?'

'I don't know yet,' I said. 'But if you think I am going to let them get away with beating me up in racecourse car parks, you have another thing coming.'

Luca smiled broadly. 'Right,' he said. 'Great.'

'But first we need to know which of the big outfits resorts to use of the heavy mob.'

The rest of the evening was quiet in comparison, with not a single bully-boy to be seen. Business was brisk with the largely young crowd eager to be tempted into the evils of gambling.

Many of them were actually there for the pop concert that was taking place in front of the grandstand after racing, rather than for any particular love of the sport. But that didn't deter them from having a flutter on the gee-gees first.

The evening was conducted in huge good humour, helped by a continuous flow of alcoholic beverages and a string of tight finishes. I was almost able to ignore the dull ache in my guts that refused to go away completely, in spite of me swallowing a couple of pain killers.

A young woman stood in front of me wearing tight blue jeans and a skimpy top that displayed a pleasing amount of sun-bronzed midriff.

'Remember me?' she said.

I looked up from her midriff to her face. 'At Ascot last week,' I said. 'Black-and-white hat. I didn't recognize you without your finery on.'

She laughed, and I laughed back. Then she blushed. I remembered that, too.

'Come on, Anna,' said a young man who was pulling at her arm. The damn boyfriend, I assumed.

He pulled her away with him and I watched them go. Fleetingly, she turned once and waved at me before disappearing into the throng. At least someone thought of their bookie as a human being.

'I don't think Betsy will be coming back,' said Luca over my shoulder. Perhaps he had also watched the young woman being pulled away by her boyfriend, and it had reminded him of his own perilous romantic position.

'Do you want to go and find her?' I asked him. 'I'll manage on my own for a while.'

'In your dreams,' he said, slapping me on the shoulder.

That was a good sign, I thought.

'Do you want to go anyway?' I said.

'Nah,' he said. 'She'll come back if she wants to. I'm not going to go running after her. To tell you the truth, I don't really care if she comes back or not.'

I cared. Luca was much more fun without her.

'Are you staying on after?' he said.

'If you mean, am I waiting to listen to the concert, then, no, I'm not.'

'Are you going straight home?' he asked.

'Why?' I had intended going to see Sophie if it wasn't too late.

'I was hoping for a lift. We came in Betsy's car and she's probably gone home now without me. We were going to stay for the concert, but I don't want to any more.' He paused. 'At least I've missed the little horrors at the electronics club.'

Was it really only a week since I had given the microcoder to Luca to take to the club? It seemed like a month.

'Sure,' I said. 'I'll give you a lift, but you might need to get the train the last bit. I was hoping to go and see Sophie if we're not too late.'

'Ned, it's fine,' he said. 'I'll get the train home from here. It's no problem.'

I tried to think of the stations on the line to High Wycombe.

'I could drop you at Beaconsfield,' I said. 'That's on my way.'

'No, it's not,' he said. 'And it would take you ages to get to the station. I'll go on the train from here. Honestly, it's no problem.'

'OK,' I said, somewhat relieved. I would be pushed to get to the hospital for the end of the news anyway.

The last race of the evening was a five-furlong sprint for two-year-old maidens. A maiden didn't imply the sex of the animal, there were male maidens too. A maiden was a horse that had yet to win a race. Many of these maidens had never even been on a racecourse before, let alone won a race on one. Only one horse in the field had good previous form, finishing second twice, on one occasion just a neck behind the blossoming two-year-old star of the year. Naturally the horse, East Imperial, was a short-priced favourite when the betting opened.

'Don't even think of disrupting the internet tonight,' I said seriously to Luca.

He didn't deny it, but stood there looking at me with his jaw hanging open.

'You'll catch flies like that,' I said.

He snapped his mouth shut.

'How did you know?' he said.

'It didn't take rocket science,' I said. But, in truth, I hadn't known for sure. It had been a guess. And, it seemed, the guess had been bang on target. 'You are a wizard at electronics. And you and Larry have been up to all sorts of stuff. It seemed an obvious connection. Who else was in on it?'

'Only one or two others,' he said. 'Norman Joyner was. He was the only other bookie. It's only a bit of fun.'

My stomach didn't think it was funny, and I bet Larry's ribs didn't either, not any more.

'So were you going to do it again here, tonight?' I asked him.

'That was the plan,' he said. 'But Larry has the kit with him and he didn't make it.'

We both knew why he hadn't.

'Was it this race?' I asked.

'Yeah, of course,' he said. 'Red-hot favourite and all that.'

'But why?' I said. 'Where's the gain? Are you betting on it elsewhere?'

'No,' he replied. 'That's the beauty of it. There's no trail for them to chase. No one does well out of it that has anything to do with us. It just produces a chance windfall for everyone who happens to back the favourite in a betting shop at the starting price. And there will be masses of those. It's a ruse to make the big outfits lose a bit and also to give them a fit that someone else is playing them at their own game.'

'But it cost you money for the bets in the ring at Ascot to change the odds,' I said. 'I saw the cash in my hand.' And I remembered clearly the man at Ascot who had bet a thousand pounds, two monkeys on a loser. The man in the open-neck white shirt and the fawn chinos.

'Not really,' he said. 'A friend of Larry's started the betting with a grand of readies. Then the same money went round and round, with Larry and me backing with Norman, and him doing the same with us. The odds changed all over the ring but not much cash actually changed hands with anyone else, and that which did was covered by a little wager on the favourite at home by Larry's wife.'

Very organized, I thought.

'Was that also what you were up to at Stratford?' I said.

'Yeah, sort of,' he said. 'But, I grant you, that was a bit silly. It was too obvious. We hadn't really planned to do anything there, so we didn't have the kit with us, but there were so few bookies, and the weather was so bloody awful, we decided, there and then, to have some fun just by changing the odds on the boards.'

'Well don't ever do it again,' I said. 'If you are seriously interested in a partnership in the business, there's no place for messing about with the prices. Not only would you quickly destroy our reputation, you could put our livelihoods in jeopardy. Do you understand?'

He looked like a scolded schoolboy. The truth was that he had not been malicious, just bored. He had thought of it all as a game, but I had the bruises to prove it wasn't.

'I mean it,' I said. 'Never again.'

'Oh, all right,' he said, clearly fed up, but accepting the inevitable.

East Imperial, the favourite, won the race easily and was returned at a starting price of eleven-to-ten on, which was about right.

Overall, Betsy apart, it had been a good night for us and Luca and I packed up our stuff in good spirits. Normally the betting on the last race can be a little sparse and the crowd usually disappears rapidly when it's over. However, on this occasion the crowd built during the evening, and more so after the last as everyone jostled for a good spot to watch and listen to the band. Consequently, we had an audience as we packed up the trolley, and we had to force our way through the masses round the grandstand and out to the car park behind.

'Tell me about the equipment you use,' I said to Luca as we pulled the trolley down towards my car.

'What equipment?' he said, all innocently.

'You know what I mean. The kit you use to take down the internet and the telephones.'

'The internet's easy,' he said, almost bragging. 'It's the phones that are more testing.'

'Tell me,' I said.

'You don't actually make the internet go down,' he said, 'you just make the access to it work very slowly. So slowly, in fact, that it takes for ever to do anything.'

'And how do you do that?' I asked him.

'I make the racecourse server extremely busy doing something else,' he said, smiling. 'I use our computer Wi-Fi connection to give it a virus that causes it to chase round and round making useless calculations of prime numbers. That uses up all its RAM, its random access memory, so leaves it no space to do what it should be doing. Then, when I want, I turn the virus programme off and, hey presto, the calculations stop and the internet access is back to its rightful speed.'

It sounded all too easy.

'And the phones?' I said.

'Simple in principle,' he said. 'Emit a mass of white noise, that's a random radio signal, at the right frequency. It simply overwhelms the weaker signals from the telephone transmitters. Smothers them completely. Not very subtle, but effective over a smallish area like the betting ring. It's basically the same system the army employs in Afghanistan to block mobile telephone transmissions being used to remotely set off bombs.'

'How on earth did you come up with that?' I said.

'I didn't.' He smiled. 'It was one of the delinquents at the electronics club. He was trying to make a device to block police radios so they wouldn't be able to catch him. I just borrowed it and tweaked the frequency a little.'

'But how big is it?' I asked him.

'Small enough to fit in Larry's boxes,' he said. 'And it's powered by a car battery, same as the odds boards.'

'How often have you used it?' I asked.

'Only the three times at Ascot,' he said. 'It was only finished last week. The first time, on Tuesday, was just a test to see if it worked. Thursday was the target, as you've worked out. Saturday was just for fun, to see what happened.'

'But on the Tuesday, surely we nearly came unstuck,' I said. 'You told me that we would have been off another grand if the favourite had won the last, because you couldn't use the internet to lay it.'

'Yeah, well, we took a lot of late bets, and Larry had the switch.'

'Luca, retire the kit now, before it gets you into real trouble, and before it costs us in profits.'

'Yes, Boss,' he said mockingly.

'I mean it.'

'I know,' he said more seriously.

'But keep it safe,' I said. 'Just in case.'

He looked at me questioningly, but I didn't answer. Instead, I started to lift the equipment into the back of my car. However, my stomach muscles had had enough for one day and they cramped up, doubling me over in pain.

'Are you all right?' said Luca, rather alarmed.

'I will be,' I croaked, trying to ease the cramp.

'Do you need a doctor?' he said, genuinely concerned.

'No,' I said, straightening up and stretching. 'I'll be fine in a minute.'

'Oh God, Ned,' Luca said. 'I didn't plan for this to happen.'

'Of course you didn't,' I said, stretching again. 'But, I told you, I'll be fine.'

The cramp finally eased and I smiled at him. His worried expression improved slightly, and he lifted the rest of our stuff into the car.

'Now, tell me,' I said, changing the subject, 'what do you know about Irish telephones?'

'Not much,' he said. 'Why?'

'I wondered if you knew if they have area codes so you could tell where a number was in the country.'

'All I know is that Irish mobiles start with 86 or 87 after the 353.'

So Paddy Murphy's number hadn't been a mobile.

'How about 42?' I asked him.

'I don't know,' he said. 'Ask the internet. Google it. If it's an area code, it'll be on the internet.'

'Thanks,' I said. 'I will.' Now why didn't I think of that?

'When are we going to have our little chat?' he asked.

'About what?' I said, knowing the answer but wanting him to be the one to raise the subject again.

'A partnership,' he said.

We were standing together behind my car at quarter to ten at night with fading light after a busy evening's work.

'Not now,' I said. 'I'm too tired, and too sore.'

'When, then?' he persisted.

'Tomorrow afternoon we're at Uttoxeter,' I said. 'Do you want to come to me first and I'll take you up?'

'Fine,' he said.

'We'll talk in the car on the way,' I said. 'Unless Betsy's with us.'

'I somehow doubt that,' he said.

'What about your flat?' I said.

'No probs. That's one hundred per cent mine. She can go home to her mother.' His tone implied that the relationship was indeed well and truly over.

'Right, then,' I said. 'I'll see you tomorrow. Be at my place by eleven.'

'Are you sure you're OK?' he said.

'Positive,' I replied. 'Now get on home before you miss the train.'

'OK,' he said. 'See you tomorrow. Bye.'

He strode off towards the railway station and I watched him go.

Was my life going to be with or without Luca? Would it be the same or different? Worse or better? Safer or more dangerous?

Time, and tomorrow, would tell.

CHAPTER 15

I made it to the hospital in time for the last fifteen minutes of the news.

Sophie seemed so pleased to see me and jumped up and threw her arms round my neck when I arrived.

'Oh, I'm so glad,' she cooed. 'I thought you must be not coming as it's so late.'

'There was a pop concert after racing,' I said. 'Masses of people, so it took a long while to pack up and get out.' But it had helped make the traffic lighter, I thought.

I sat down next to her and she held my hand as we watched the last few items and then the weather. Neither of us wanted to say anything about the results of the assessment. We were both afraid of pre-guessing the result, only to then be disappointed. But, from my perspective, Sophie was now as well as I had ever known her over the last ten years.

I realized that, for the first time in a long while, I was completely relaxed around her.

Even when she had been home in the past, I had been ultra careful not to do or say anything that might upset her. I had become the true expert at walking on eggshells.

But things seemed different this time. She seemed stronger emotionally. It was almost as if *she* had been helping *me* through the ordeal of the previous day's assessment, rather than the other way round. Perhaps it was time to discuss the possible outcome. Time to grasp the nettles of life, and never mind the stings.

'Still no news, then?' I said.

'No,' she replied. 'It's very frustrating. All the staff here can't understand it. They all think it's a foregone conclusion that I should go home.'

'So do I,' I said. 'Darling, you seem so much better now than for a very long time.'

She smiled at me with genuine happiness, and my heart went flip-flop once more.

'I know,' she said. 'I feel absolutely wonderful and these new drugs are great. Far fewer side effects than before. And I don't feel so bloated by them.'

Could I really hope that life's previous bumpy up-and-down rollercoaster was now going to run smooth and flat? It was far too soon to believe that, but at least the starting signs were good.

'Have a nice day at Uttoxeter tomorrow,' she said as I stood up to leave.

'I will,' I replied, giving her a kiss.

I debated in my mind whether to worry her about Luca. I really wanted her opinion, and I suppose she had a right to know if I was about to become a fifty per cent partner rather than a sole proprietor of the business.

'Luca Mandini wants a full partnership,' I said.

'Does he indeed?' she said. 'He's still very young.'

'He's twenty-seven,' I said. 'That's not so young. And he's good. Very good.'

'Do you think you'll you lose him if he doesn't get it?' she asked.

'Probably. He'll either start up on his own or go to someone who'll give him what he wants.'

'But can you afford it?' she asked.

'Yes, I think so,' I said. 'I would save on his salary and it wouldn't be a whole lot different, money wise. I already give him a sizable share of the profits. But it would mean I'd lose some of my independence. We've been doing very well lately, with him running the computer. I don't really know enough of that side of things. If Luca left, I suppose I could always employ another assistant who does, but . . .'

'But not as good?' she said.

'Probably not,' I said.

'Seems a no-brainer to me, then. Give him what he wants.'

'You really think so?'

'Sure,' she said. 'Can you afford not to? Luca won't be able to simply walk away if he's a partner, will he? But make sure you tie him down with a contract so it costs him to leave.'

Tie him down with a contract so he can neither leave the business, nor destroy it with dodgy dealings, I thought. I had decided against telling Sophie about internet outages, mobile phones that wouldn't work and fixing the starting prices. I also failed to mention fists and steel toecaps in the Kempton car park. There were still limits to what was prudent.

But I was glad I'd asked her about Luca. Crystal-clear business thinking had always been her forte, when she was well, that is, and her current advice seemed as sound as her present mental state.

'Thank you,' I said to her. 'I'll do just that.'

We kissed goodnight, a joyous, loving kiss.

On this occasion, she was not even fed up at me for leaving her behind. I think we both knew she would be coming home with me on Monday, and a couple more days or so wouldn't matter.

Dundalk, the internet told me. Paddy Murphy's telephone was in Dundalk. I further discovered that Dundalk was some fifty miles north of Dublin on the north-east coast of the Irish Republic, close to the mouth of the Castletown River, and not far from the border with Northern Ireland.

My computer also told me that Dundalk was the biggest town in Ireland that was not actually a city, with a population of about thirty thousand. Within the surrounding area, the 42 telephone area code, there were nearly half a million people. I could hardly turn up in Dundalk asking for someone called Paddy Murphy, now could I? If I did, it would probably be *me* they would be throwing in the loony bin.

I was sitting in my office after another undisturbed night in Station Road.

I remained highly concerned about Shifty Eyes. I was under no illusions that he would have given up in his search for the money. Consequently, I had once again slept with the chair from Sophie's dressing table wedged under the bedroom door handle. I had also left the cash in the cupboard beneath the stairs, just in case he turned up with his twelve-centimetre knife. Perhaps he could then have been cajoled into taking the money without also using my body for target practice.

I looked again at my father's telephone. I had tried Paddy Murphy's number a few more times late the previous evening, after I had returned from the hospital. I pushed the button once more and heard the familiar ringing tone.

'If you were the Garda you'd be here by now,' Paddy said, answering. 'So I'll assume you're not.'

'No,' I said. 'I'm not.'

'So who are you?' His Irish accent was stronger than ever.

'I told you,' I said. 'I'm Alan Grady's son.'

'He doesn't have a son,' he replied.

'Oh yes he does,' I said.

'You don't sound Australian.'

'I'm not,' I said. 'I was born before he went to Australia.'

There was a long pause at the other end.

'Are you still there?' I asked.

'Maybe,' he said. 'What do you want with me?'

'How well did you know my father?'

'What do you mean, did?' he asked.

'My father was murdered at Ascot races. In the car park. He was stabbed.'

There was nothing but silence from the other end.

'When?' he asked finally.

'A week ago last Tuesday.'

There was another long pause.

'Have they caught who did it?' he asked.

'Not yet,' I said.

'Any suspects?'

'I don't know,' I said. 'I don't think so.'

'Don't they have any leads at all?' he asked persistently. I thought he might be a little scared. Perhaps he had good reason.

'The murderer was a man in his mid- to late thirties. Slim build with shifty-looking eyes,' I said.

'How do you mean, shifty?' he said slowly.

'Slightly too close together for his face,' I said. 'Do you recognize the description?'

He hesitated too long. 'Could be anyone,' he said.

'But you know who,' I said. It was a statement, not a question.

'No,' he said. But I didn't believe him.

'Is this man likely to come after you?' I asked.

'Why should he?' he said, with a slightly nervous rattle to his voice.

'I don't know. But you do.'

'No,' he said again rapidly.

'Denying it won't stop it happening,' I said. 'Who is it?'

'Do you think I'm bloody mad or something?' he said. 'Even if I knew, I wouldn't be telling you, now, would I?'

'Why not?' I asked him.

'Do you think I'm bloody mad or something?' he said once again. 'Because he'd kill me too.'

'He might do that anyway,' I said.

It added to his discomfort.

'Blessed Mary, mother of Christ,' he said.

'Praying won't help you,' I said. 'But telling me or the police might. And why would this man want you dead anyway?'

He didn't reply.

'Have you stolen money from him?' I asked.

Still nothing.

'Or is it something to do with the microcoder?' I said.

'The what?' he said.

'The microcoder,' I repeated. 'A black box with buttons on it.'

'Oh, you mean the chipwriter,' he said.

'Yes,' I said. 'Who does it belong to?'

'That depends,' he said. 'I thought it was Alan's.'

'Wasn't it?' I said.

'I think now that he may have stolen it,' he said.

'From the man with the shifty eyes?' I asked.

'No,' he said with certainty. 'Not from him.'

'I thought you didn't know who he was?' I said.

'I don't,' he said, but without conviction. 'But the chipwriter definitely came from Australia. I know that.'

'And Shifty Eyes doesn't?' I said.

'You'll be a bloody sneaky little bastard,' he said. 'To be sure.'

That's as may be, I thought, but I still hadn't gathered much information from this Mr Paddy Murphy.

'Why did my father come to see you two weeks ago?' I asked him.

'Who says that he did?' he said.

'I do,' I replied. 'But why? And what's your real name?'

'Inquisitive, aren't you?' he said.

'Yes,' I replied. 'And if I don't get some answers from you pretty soon, I might just go and give your phone number to the policeman investigating my father's murder. Then you can sit and wait for your Garda to turn up on your doorstep.'

'You wouldn't be doing that now, would you?' he said.

'Try me.'

Another pause.

'What do you need to know?' he asked.

'What my father was doing in Ireland, for a start,' I said.

Pause.

'He was delivering something,' he said at last.

'What?' I demanded. 'And to whom?'

'To me,' he said.

'What was it he was delivering?'

'Just something I'd bought from him,' he said.

'What was it?' I asked him again.

There was another pause. This was taking an age, I thought.

'Something for a horse,' he said.

'An electronic identification tag?' I asked.

'Yes,' he said slowly without elaborating.

'And a horse passport?'

'Yes,' he said slowly again.

'A forged horse passport and ID tag?' I asked.

Another pause.

'Come on,' I said loudly with frustration. 'Tell me.'

'But why should I?' he said.

'Because with Shifty Eyes on the lookout, I may be the only friend you have, Mr Paddy Murphy, or whatever your real name is.'

'But why would he be after me?' he said.

'You tell me. You're the one who knows who he is.'

'I can't,' he wailed.

'Yes you can,' I said. 'And you must. Suppose he kills you too. You would want to know that he was then caught, wouldn't you?'

'But I don't know his real name,' he said.

There were so many people using false names it was becoming ridiculous. Even I had effectively told Paddy Murphy that my name was Grady.

'Well, what do you know?' I asked him.

It was like getting blood from a stone.

'I know he kills horses,' he said.

'What!' I exclaimed. 'How?'

'In all sorts of ways. I know he killed one by putting ping pong balls up its nostrils so it began to suffocate. Horses can't breathe through their mouths like we can, and it caused this particular horse to drop down dead from a heart attack.'

I shuddered at the thought.

'But he always kills them in a way which looks like it was an accident. For the insurance money.'

I did some quick thinking.

'So, you switch a bad horse for a good one,' I said, 'kill the bad one and claim the insurance money on the good one?'

'Exactly,' he said.

It was a much safer bet than selling the bad one and taking the chance that someone does a DNA check on their new purchase.

'What happens to the good horse?' I asked.

Now that he had started to tell me it came easier. He was almost bragging at the cleverness of the scheme.

'It goes into training under the name of the nag, the bad one,' he said. 'If we're lucky, we can also make a killing backing it when it first runs in poor company, and wins easily at long odds.'

It was clever, I thought. But risky too. Making a horse's death appear accidental wasn't easy and, surely, the insurance company would be suspicious.

'How about the insurers?' I said. 'Don't they check?'

'To be sure, they do,' he said. 'They even have a special investigator who researches all horse deaths on which someone has made a claim in order to determine that they are genuine accidents.'

'So how come you can get away with it?' I asked.

'The insurer's special investigator has his eyes set rather too close together.'

*

Much to my surprise, and his, Betsy was with Luca when they turned up at my house at ten to eleven.

'She just turned up at my place this morning as if nothing had happened,' Luca said to me while she was in the bathroom. 'I can't believe it. She hasn't said a word about it.'

Perhaps she wasn't so dumb after all. Luca was surely a catch worth pursuing. He, meanwhile, seemed quietly laid back about it. But I also thought he was secretly rather pleased.

The three of us set off for Uttoxeter just after eleven in my old Volvo with Luca sitting up front, as usual, and Betsy in the back. As always, she was soon listening to her iPod through her white headphones, resting her head against the window and dozing.

'I've thought about what you asked,' I said to Luca.

'And?' he said, unable to disguise his eagerness.

'I'm prepared to offer you a full partnership in the business under certain conditions.'

'What conditions?' he said warily.

'Nothing too onerous,' I said. 'The same conditions would apply to both partners.'

'What sort of conditions?' he asked again, using a tone of voice full of suspicion and disagreement.

'Hold on a minute,' I said. 'There's no need to get on your high horse. Look at it from my point of view. I'd be giving up half my business, and half the profit, remember, and for what? I need assurances on a number of things. You need to show your commitment to the business in the long term for a start. That means we need a contract that would tie both of us to the business for at least five years, with penalties on either side for early departure. After five years, you would have fully earned your partnership with no financial input needed from you. But we do need to agree that, within that five-year period, I have a casting vote when there is no agreement between us.'

'Agreement about what?' he asked.

'The way in which the business develops,' I said. 'I can see that you are eager to push the boundaries.' And go beyond them, I thought, but decided not to say so.

'Yes,' he said.

'Well, that has to be done by agreement. Now don't get me wrong. I'm not totally against change and I will look at any suggestion you make, but, for the next five years, I will have the final say about how we change, if we do.'

'How about after that?' he said.

'Well, after five years, as full partners, we would have an equal say in how the business was run. If we couldn't agree then the partnership would have to end, but I can't see that happening. We would have to both give and take a little.'

'But for the next five years it would be me that does the giving and you the taking?' he said.

'Well, if you put it like that, then, yes, I suppose so.'

'That doesn't seem much different from now,' he said, with resignation in his voice.

I was losing him.

'Yes, it is,' I said. 'You are asking for quite a lot here, Luca, and I'm prepared to hand over half of a highly profitable business to you, at no direct cost to yourself. You would stop being an employee on a salary and become entitled to half the profit instead. But you would also be liable for half the losses if things went wrong, and I am trying to ensure they don't. I believe in you, Luca, but I also believe you need guidance until you've had a little more experience. I could be asking you to buy a fifty-per-cent share in the business from me, but I'm not. I'm giving it to you for free, but over five years.'

He sat in silence, thinking.

'I honestly think it's a great deal,' I said. 'And you don't have to make a decision right now. Think about it. Talk it over with Betsy, and with your parents, if you like. We can go on just as we are for as long as you want. For ever, if that's what suits you.'

He remained sitting silently beside me, studying the road in front, for quite a long way.

'Can we call it Talbot and Mandini?' he said finally.

I wasn't sure that I would go that far.

Larry Porter was at Uttoxeter, feeling very sorry for himself, and while he was not literally spitting blood from his damaged ribs, he was still spreading hate and venom all around.

'Bloody bastards,' he said to me, and anyone else who would listen. 'Who do they think they are, beating up innocent people in racecourse car parks?'

I was the innocent one, I thought, not him.

'Calm down, Larry,' I said. 'You'll give yourself a stroke.'

'But aren't you angry as well?' he said.

'Of course I am. But I'm not going to just get mad – I'm going to get even.'

'Now you're talking,' he said.

'Who were they, anyway?'

'I don't know,' he said. 'Some bully-boys or other.'

Not too easy to get even, I thought, if we didn't actually know who had been responsible.

I have a message from my boss, one of the bully-boys had said. *Don't mess again with the starting prices.*

It was a fair bet, therefore, that the message had come from one of the big bookmaking firms. They were the only ones who would have suffered from Luca and Larry's little game at Stratford races. But which big firm? There were half a dozen or so who might be in the frame, but I would have been surprised if one or two of those had resorted to beating people up in racecourse car parks. Conversely, it was exactly the behaviour I would have expected from a couple of the others.

'I hear you've been talking to Luca,' Larry said. 'About our amusements.'

'Yes, I have,' I said sharply. 'Larry, you really should know better.'

'Yes,' he said. 'Perhaps I should, but I'm that fed up with being treated like an irritation by these big corporations. I refuse to be swatted like a fly and muscled out of my job. They are all now having their own pitches at the races as well, so they can manipulate the odds even further. It's not just us who should be angry; the betting public shouldn't stand for it either.'

'Oh, come on,' I said. 'You must be living in cloud-cuckoo land if you think the betting public are ever going to feel sorry for us.'

'Yeah,' he replied. 'I suppose you're right.'

Damn right, I was. My grandfather always used to say that bookmakers could expect about as much sympathy as house-breakers: both were trying to rob other people's belongings, only the bookmakers were doing it legally.

I didn't actually agree with my grandfather, as gambling surely involved free choice, but it was an opinion that I knew was held by many of those with whom we did daily business.

'So what are you going to do about it?' Larry demanded.

'About what?' I asked.

'Getting even.'

'I'm not sure yet. But first, I'm going to find out whose orders those thugs were working to. And, Larry,' I said, looking him straight in the eye, 'no more little games. Understand?'

'Why are you being so bloody self-righteous all of a sudden?' he said.

'Because I recognize when not to poke a hornets' nest with a stick. Let us wait and bide our time, and let's not get stung again in the meantime.'

'OK,' he said with resignation. 'I suppose so.'

Larry wasn't happy. He wanted to lash out at those who had hurt both his body and his pride. But lashing out at a great big grizzly bear would simply result in another claw-swipe to the head.

Getting even required far more cunning than that.

CHAPTER 16

Mr John Smith, or whoever, was waiting for me next to my car in the Uttoxeter racecourse car park at the end of the day.

'Don't you have anything better to do than hang around in racecourse car parks?' I asked him sarcastically.

'Tomorrow's Sunday,' he said, ignoring me.

'How very observant of you,' I replied.

'Don't you be funny with me,' he said. 'Your friend is back from holiday tomorrow and I want the microcoder.'

'I don't know what time she lands,' I said. 'I'll call you when I've heard from her.'

'Make sure you do,' he said threateningly.

'You should be nice to me,' I said, 'or you won't get it back at all.'

'Watch it,' he said with real menace.

'Are you threatening me?' I asked.

'You'd better believe it,' he said.

'Well, I must warn you, I don't respond well to threats.'

'Take my advice, Mr Talbot,' he said, 'respond to this one.'

Gone was the patient good humour of last Wednesday afternoon. Mr John Smith, I imagined, was under pressure to get results.

He suddenly turned and walked away across the car park. I tried to see where he went but I lost sight of him amongst the departing crowd, and I couldn't tell if it was the dark blue Ford from the lay-by that he climbed into.

'What was all that about?' asked Luca, who had been silently watching the exchange. Betsy had been standing next to him throughout and her eyes were now wide with surprise and inquisition.

'Nothing,' I said, and started to load the equipment into the car.

'It didn't look like nothing to us,' Luca said.

I looked him in the eye, and then shot a quick glance at Betsy, hoping Luca would get the message that I didn't want to discuss the matter within her hearing.

'Just who was that man?' said Betsy. 'He didn't seem very nice.'

'It was nothing,' I said again. 'He wants something I have and we have been negotiating about the price. That's all.'

Luca looked at me with disbelief showing all over his face but he, too, glanced briefly at Betsy, telling me that he did, indeed, understand not to discuss the matter further with her there. Betsy, meanwhile, had not got the same message.

'What?' she said.

'What, what?' I asked.

'What have you got that he wants?' she persisted.

'Nothing much,' I said. 'A type of television remote. Forget it.'

She looked like she was about to ask me another question

230

when Luca interrupted her thought process. 'Where do you want to go for dinner tonight, Betsy?' he said.

'What?' she said angrily, turning towards him.

'Where shall we go for dinner tonight?' he repeated.

'We're going to my mother's,' she said sharply.

'Oh, yes,' said Luca. 'I forgot.'

He winked at me as we climbed into the car. Luca was nobody's fool, he forgot nothing.

Within ten minutes I could see in the rear-view mirror that Betsy was again listening to her iPod, and dozing with her head against the window.

'Betsy, please could you pass me a tissue?' I asked fairly quietly.

She didn't move.

Luca began to turn round.

'Leave her,' I said to him.

'So was this TV remote thing that the man wanted that RFID writer you showed me?' Luca asked me quietly.

'Yes,' I said. 'He calls himself John Smith, but I very much doubt that's his real name. He also says he's working for the Australian Racing Board.'

'Why don't you just give it to him, then?' Luca said.

'I don't know,' I replied. 'For some reason I don't altogether trust him, so I made up a story about giving it to a friend who had then gone on holiday.'

'Nice one,' said Luca sarcastically. 'Where to?'

'Greece, I think,' I said. 'I can't really remember. I told him she was back on Sunday, that's tomorrow.'

'She?' he said, almost laughing. 'So where did the RFID writer come from in the first place?'

'I was given it,' I said.

'Who by?' he asked.

'A man from Australia.'

'Not John Smith?' he said.

'No. Another man from Australia.'

'Hence the Australian Racing Board's interest in it?'

'Exactly.'

'So who was this other man from Australia?' Luca asked persistently. I began to wish we had never started this.

'Just a man,' I said evasively.

'So a mystery man from Australia just gave you a device for writing RFIDs and now the Australian Racing Board wants it back?'

It sounded implausible even to me.

'Yes,' I said.

'But is it theirs?' he asked.

'I don't know.'

'Why don't you ask the mystery man who gave it to you?'

'I can't,' I said. 'He's gone away.'

'Back to Australia?'

'Not exactly,' I replied. Further than that, I thought.

'So are you going to give it to the man in the car park, this John Smith?' Luca asked.

'I might,' I said. 'What do you think I should do?'

'Well, it's not yours, is it? So why not give it to him? And I tend to think that, next time he comes asking, you might just get another dose of fists and steel toecaps if you refuse. He seemed quite determined.'

'Yes, you're probably right,' I said. 'But there's still something about him I don't like. And I feel that giving up the microcoder is like giving up my trump card.'

'Microcoder?' Luca said.

232

'That's what the man calls it. But I know my father called it a chipwriter.'

'Your father?' Luca said, surprised. 'I thought your father was dead.'

'He is,' I said, without further elaboration. I'd forgotten that I hadn't told Luca that the man murdered at Ascot had been my father. As far as Luca was concerned my father had always been dead, and he knew I had been raised from babyhood by my grandparents.

'So how come your father knew about this microcoder thing?' he asked.

'It's a long story,' I said, trying to close the discussion.

'It's a long journey,' he said.

'Yeah, well, not long enough.'

'So what's next?' said Luca.

'Days off tomorrow and Monday, then Towcester on Tuesday evening,' I said.

'No,' he said, irritated. 'I meant what's next with this microcoder thing?'

'How difficult would it be to make another one exactly the same?' I asked him.

'I don't know,' he said. 'As far as I remember, it's just a radio transmitter that concentrates the radio signal at a point where you would put the RFID. It didn't appear that sophisticated.'

'Could you make another one?' I asked.

'Well, I don't know about that,' he said slowly.

'I don't want you to,' I added quickly. 'I just wondered if you could.'

'Yeah, I reckon I might,' he said. 'Or if I couldn't, one of the little hooligans from the electronics club would probably be able to do it in no time. They are like bloody magic when it comes to electronics. One of them even made a device that fooled the authorities into thinking he was at home wearing his ankle tag when he was really out all night breaking into people's cars. He said it gave him the best alibi anyone could ever want. Even the coppers were impressed.'

'How did they find out?' I asked.

'Oh, these lads may be damn clever when it comes to electronics,' he said. 'But they can be pretty dense otherwise. The bloody idiot broke into an unmarked police car that was parked right outside the police station and everything he did was recorded on an in-car video camera.'

I laughed. 'Almost as bad as that bank robber recently who wrote his demand note on the back of a cheque from his own cheque book. It had his name printed on it.'

'It's a good job villains are stupid or we'd all be victims,' Luca said with a laugh.

'But they are not all stupid,' I said, becoming serious. 'Remember, we never hear about the clever ones, because they don't get caught.'

'Good point,' he said.

Talking about not getting caught reminded me of the stash of banknotes still hidden in the cupboard under my stairs. Who did they belong to? Were they meant to be payment for Shifty Eyes for killing horses? Or maybe they were his cut for approving the insurance claims after the horses were dead. Either way, I was pretty sure they weren't actually mine, even if I did have a sort of claim to inherit them after my father's death, for they had been in his luggage.

'So do you want a copy of this microcoder?' Luca said, bringing me back from my daydreams.

'No, not really,' I said. 'I just wondered why it was so important to get this particular one back if any half-witted juvenile delinquent could simply make another.'

'But they would have to have something to copy,' he said. 'And they would have to know the right frequency to set it at.'

'Is that difficult?' I asked.

'Not if you have the original,' he said. 'But much more difficult, maybe impossible, without it.'

'So if our Mr John Smith – or whatever his name is – is so keen to get his hands on the original, is it because he doesn't have access to another one?' I said. 'But you would have thought that the Australian Racing Board had access to whatever resources they needed. I think that's why I don't trust him. He doesn't ring quite true.'

'So does that mean you won't give it to him?' Luca asked.

'No,' I said slowly. 'But I might just ensure it doesn't work properly before I hand it over.'

'That might be dangerous,' said Luca, grinning.

'You think so?' I asked.

'Yeah, but why not? Live dangerously.'

Or not at all, I thought.

Sophie came home on Sunday and her younger sister, Alice, came to stay at our house in Station Road to help out.

'I don't need any help,' Sophie said.

But we both knew she did. The change from institutional life to being at home was a huge step. Not least because there would be no one there to call on for help, for a chat or for a word of encouragement, especially when I was away at the races.

Alice was just the person we needed. She was busy, efficient, loving and free. And I was very fond of her, but in small doses.

One week of busy domestic efficiency was enough for any man.

On Sunday morning Alice arrived, very early, of course, from her home in Surrey and tut-tutted about the state of the house, especially the cobwebs in the bathroom and the unmentionable leftovers in the deeper recesses of the refrigerator. In no time she had donned a pair of bright yellow rubber gloves and was transforming the place.

She wasn't in any way angry about my domestic short-comings, and she made no snide remarks about how men couldn't keep themselves tidy, let alone the house, but Alice sometimes had a way of making me feel totally inadequate, and this was one of those times.

When we left together in my Volvo for the hospital at noon, the house was sparkling and fresh, and I was grateful. It wasn't just that Alice wanted everything to be clean and neat for her sister's homecoming, which of course she did, it was that she, and I, knew that Sophie would otherwise feel pressured into doing the housework and that, in turn, would make her feel guilty about having been in hospital. That guilt could be enough to restart the whole sorry manic-depressive sequence all over again. Sophie's mania had always begun with obsessive cleaning of the house.

However, I was more confident that, this time, the drugs were doing their thing. But it was vitally important to make sure Sophie kept taking them. All too often in the past she would eventually begin to crave for the manic 'highs', flushing her medication down the lavatory, seemingly unconcerned and indifferent about the dire consequences, and the prospect of another extended period of hospitalization.

She was packed and ready when we arrived. Her room, which had become so familiar to me, was now bare of her possessions and back to its 'hospital ward' status. Jason, her favourite nurse, was there to wish her goodbye and to help take her bags down to my car outside the front door.

'Thank you,' she said to him, putting her arms round his neck and kissing him on the cheek. 'Thank you to all the staff.'

Jason looked embarrassed by this show of affection but he took it in good grace.

'I won't say it's been a pleasure,' he said to me. 'But Mrs Talbot has been a model patient.'

He stood by the door and waved as we drove down the driveway, through the high gates and out into the real world.

Mr John Smith, or whoever, was waiting outside our house when we arrived home about an hour later. As I parked the Volvo he climbed out of the dark blue Ford that I had last seen disappearing ahead of me from the lay-by near Stratford. He had not been sitting in the driver's seat so I assumed there must be another man with him, but again I couldn't see properly against the reflection from the windscreen.

Dammit, I thought. I really didn't want to have to start explaining to Sophie about microcoders, bundles of banknotes and murders in the Ascot racecourse car park.

The last thing we needed was for him to force his way through my front door and disrupt Sophie's longed-for return home, so I marched straight across the road to talk to him. He came forward to meet me.

'Is that your friend?' he asked, nodding towards the house.

I turned and saw Alice lifting Sophie's suitcase from the car. It must have appeared to Mr Smith that someone was arriving back from holiday.

'Yes,' I said, turning back to him.

'Where's the microcoder?' he demanded.

'In her baggage, I expect,' I said. 'You wait here and I'll go and get it for you.'

'I'll come with you.'

'No,' I said quickly. 'If you want me to hand it over, you will have to wait here.'

I turned to walk back across the road, and he began to follow.

'No,' I said again, this time more forcefully. 'Either you wait here for me to get it, or I will have to explain to my friend what you are doing here, and about how I broke your wrist in my house. And she works for the police.'

He stopped. 'You told me she was an electronics specialist,' he said.

Had I? I thought. I couldn't recall.

'She maintains police radios,' I said. The trouble with telling lies is that they get more complicated as time goes on, and more difficult to remember.

'OK,' he said. 'I'll wait here, but you have just two minutes. Understand?'

'Five,' I said. 'I'll bring it out in five.'

It wasn't just threats I didn't like. I didn't respond particularly well to orders either.

I didn't wait for him to reply but strode straight back across the road to follow Sophie and Alice through the front door. This time he didn't follow me.

'Who's that man?' asked Sophie, turning in the doorway and looking back.

'Just a bookmaking friend. He's come to collect something.'

'Aren't you going to ask him in?' she said.

'I did,' I replied, 'but he's in a hurry to get home. He said he'd wait while I fetched it.'

'What is it?' she said.

'Just a TV remote that Luca has been fixing.' I went to the cupboard under the stairs and took out the microcoder. 'This,' I said holding it up to her.

She lost interest. 'Fancy some tea?' she asked.

'Love some,' I said. 'I'll be back in a few minutes.'

Sophie went into the kitchen with Alice to put the kettle on, and I waited a while in the hall, studying my watch, until its hands had moved slowly round a full five minutes. I didn't want to give Mr Smith, or whoever he was, the pleasure of having me come running at his command.

He was still standing where I'd left him. I held out the microcoder to him and he took it.

'Thank you, Mr Talbot,' he said. 'And the chips?'

'You didn't ask for the chips,' I said.

'Well, I am now.'

'Wait here.'

I went back across the road, collected the little bag of glass grains from the cupboard, and went out to hand them to him. He studied the bag.

'Where are the rest of them?' he said.

'That's all I have,' I said. 'That's all there ever were.'

'There should be twelve of them.'

'And how many are there now?' I asked innocently.

'Eight.'

'Sorry, that's all I have,' I said.

He didn't seem very happy. 'Are you sure?' he demanded.

'Yes, I'm certain,' I said. 'If I had any more I'd give them to you. They're no good to me, are they?' That might be true, I thought, but it hadn't stopped me keeping a couple of them back; one complete chip and the one I had broken with the knife, just in case.

But there had definitely been only ten chips in the bag when I had found it in my father's rucksack. So, if there really had been twelve originally, two of them were indeed unaccounted for. Perhaps Paddy Murphy could enlighten me as to their whereabouts.

'It will have to do,' he said, as if to himself. Then he looked up at me. 'Mr Talbot, I won't say I've enjoyed our little business together' – he held up his still-plastered right wrist – 'but thank you nevertheless for returning the microcoder.'

He turned, walked over to the dark blue Ford, climbed in and was driven swiftly away by his unidentified chauffeur.

He might not still be thanking me, I thought, when he found out that his precious microcoder now wouldn't work.

I hadn't been lying when I told Sophie that Luca had fixed it. He'd fixed it good and proper, by scratching right through the minute connectors on the printed circuit boards using a Stanley knife.

Sophie's first night home was not quite an unbridled success, but nor was it a disaster either. In fact, far from it.

There was the expected little spat between the sisters when Alice refused point-blank to allow Sophie to help prepare our supper.

'It's my house,' Sophie complained to me. 'And she won't let me do anything in my own damn kitchen.'

'Let her do it,' I replied soothingly. 'You know that she means

240

well.' I stroked Sophie's hand and she slowly relaxed. 'Come and sit down. Enjoy having someone cook for you.'

'I've done enough of that over the past five months, thank you very much,' she said. However, she still came and sat next to me on the sofa to watch the television.

I knew why Alice was so determined to do it all, and why she was so worried. The memory of Sophie's manic cleaning in that kitchen was fresh in both our minds.

'It's good to be home,' Sophie said, snuggling into me.

'It's good to have you home, my darling.'

We cuddled closer together on the sofa while watching experts on antiques trying to appear interested about dusty old junk salvaged from people's attics, while the junk's owners tried to look surprised, and not too disappointed, by the meagreness of the valuations.

'It's ready,' said Alice, putting her head round the living-room door.

The three of us sat at the kitchen table eating grilled salmon fillets, with penne pasta and peas.

'That was lovely,' I said, laying down my knife and fork.

'Mmm,' said Sophie, agreeing. 'And much better than the hospital food. Thank you, darling Alice.' Sophie smiled at her sister, and winked at me. I positively beamed back at her.

My Sophie of old was back. But for how long? How I wished it was for ever.

Needless to say, Sophie was not allowed to help with the washing up either, which amused her no end. I couldn't remember a time when she had come home from a stay in hospital so aware, and with such an acute sense of humour.

But, coming home had tired her, and we all turned in early, me taking Sophie up to our bed almost as I had done on our wedding night, and to do again the same things that all newlywed couples do.

For the first time in almost a week, my mind being on other matters, I went to sleep without wedging Sophie's dressing-table chair under the bedroom door handle.

CHAPTER 17

The creak of someone walking over the third step brought me instantly from deep sleep to sharp awareness. It was already light. I lay there in bed holding my breath and trying hard to listen for any movement on the stairs. I turned my head and looked at the door. Sophie still slept soundly beside me.

How could I have put her in such danger? I thought. What a fool I was.

The door handle slowly depressed and the door began to open. I could feel my heart pounding in my chest. What was I to do?

'I made you some tea,' said Alice, coming into the room carrying a tray with two mugs of steaming liquid.

'Oh, Alice,' I said with such relief in my voice that I almost cried. 'Thank you.'

'It's a beautiful morning,' she said in a whisper, looking at Sophie.

'Yes,' I replied in the same manner. 'I'll leave her to sleep.'

Alice put the tray down on my bedside table and, with a wave, she departed. I heard step three creak twice, as usual, as she went down.

What was I doing? I thought.

Was it time to go to the police and hold my hands up to my failings, and ask for their help and protection?

It was all well and good for me to perform the James Bond secret-agent act when it was only my life and my future on the line. But what would Sophie do without me, especially now that she was home and getting better? Maybe her recovery wouldn't last for ever, but surely I had an obligation to her in the meantime?

Shifty Eyes was still out there somewhere, and he would surely still be searching for his money. I was actually quite surprised that he hadn't already found me. Mr John Smith had seemingly had no problem in turning up in my home in the dead of night. Perhaps it was not as easy as I thought to get records from a coroner's court. Or perhaps Shifty Eyes would have had to give his name to get them, and I suspected he might have been reluctant to do that. Maybe he still didn't know that I existed, but I thought it unlikely.

Thinking about the coroner's court reminded me that today was when I should call their office to see if an order had been signed to allow for my father's funeral to take place. I wondered if my sisters knew yet that their father was dead, or whether they even cared.

Sophie slept in until nine thirty while the mug of tea cooled to room temperature on her bedside table. I took her up a fresh one and sat on the bed with her as she drank it.

'What a wonderful night,' she said, stretching her arms high above her head. 'This bed is just so comfortable.' She snuggled down again under the covers.

'It's been a very lonely bed without you in it,' I said.

'Oh, Ned,' she said, stroking my leg. 'Let's really try and make it work this time. I'm so tired of all this.'

If only, I thought. We had said this all too often in the past. False hope had burned in our breasts on so many occasions, only to be dashed each time by seemingly unstoppable events.

'Yup,' I agreed, ruffling her hair. 'Let's really make it work this time.'

But first I had some unfinished business to deal with.

I left her to dress and titivate herself in front of her dressing-table mirror while I went downstairs to call the coroner's office.

'The Thames Valley Police are still apparently objecting to a burial order,' I was informed by one of the officials. 'You could try calling them and asking. It may be an oversight on their part.'

'Thank you,' I said. For nothing.

I called Thames Valley Police Headquarters and asked to be put through to Chief Inspector Llewellyn.

'Ah, Mr Talbot,' he said, coming on the line. 'The bookmaker.' His tone was instantly unfriendly.

'Yes, Chief Inspector,' I replied with far more levity. 'And just why, exactly, don't you like bookmakers?'

'My father was addicted to gambling,' he replied with surprising anger. 'That, and the demon drink, they stole my childhood.'

I was astonished that he'd told me. But it explained a lot.

'I'm sorry,' I said.

'If you were really sorry, you'd give it up,' he said.

'But that wouldn't make much difference now, would it?' I said, somewhat sarcastically. 'There are lots of other bookmakers.'

'One at a time,' he said. 'One at a time. All you bookmakers are scum.'

Again, I was surprised by the passion of his outburst, but I could tell that whatever I might say would make no difference to his firmly entrenched opinion. His usually analytical, problem-solving, keen detective's mind clearly couldn't appreciate the lack of logic in his thinking on the issue.

'Can I go ahead and bury my father?' I asked by way of changing the subject. 'The coroner's court says that the police still have an objection to the issuing of a burial order. What is the objection?'

'Er,' he said. 'I'll have to get back to you.'

I reckoned that he only needed more time in order to think up a new excuse.

'Good,' I said, and gave him my home telephone number. 'I will be in all day today and I want to get on and make the arrangements.'

'Right,' he said, almost as if he was distracted. 'And Mr Talbot?'

'Yes.'

'You still haven't provided us with an e-fit of the killer.'

'Do you still need it?' I asked.

'Yes, we do,' he said. 'There has been little or no progress with this case.'

Probably, I thought rather ungraciously, because the victim had been with a bookmaker. At the time, Chief Inspector Llewellyn had been convinced that I'd been the killer, but the numerous statements of the champagne revellers in the car park had all agreed that I hadn't. And, much to his annoyance, they couldn't all be wrong.

'I'd love to come in and do an e-fit,' I said. 'I would have

246

expected you to have chased me before this. It must surely be a bit late? Any potential witnesses who saw the killer will have forgotten him by now.'

'We already have some e-fits from the other witnesses in the Ascot car park but, to put it mildly, they are not very consistent. Anything you can add may be helpful.' But don't bank on it, his tone implied.

'Right,' I said eagerly. 'When and where?'

'Any Thames Valley police station will do, provided it has the right staff and an e-fit computer.'

'Which one would be the nearest to Kenilworth?' I asked.

'Banbury, probably,' he said. 'I'll find out and call you back.'

He did so about five minutes later.

'It's fixed for two this afternoon, at Banbury,' he said.

'Fine,' I said. 'I'll be there. And is there any news about the burial order?'

'I will inform the coroner that we have no further objection to the issue of such an order,' he said formally. Was it my imagination or was Chief Inspector Llewellyn warming slightly? 'But I still don't trust you, Mr Talbot.'

Yes, it must have been my imagination.

'I'm sorry about that, Chief Inspector,' I replied. But I suppose, if I were honest, I would have to admit that he had good reason not to fully trust me. I wondered if I should ask him about a certain Mr John Smith, but I decided it might complicate things and lead to rather more questions than I would be easily able to answer, so I didn't.

Next, I again used my father's mobile to call Paddy Murphy.

'Well, hello,' he said cheerfully, again with the emphasis on the final 'o'. 'I didn't think I'd heard the last of you.'

'What's the name of the man with his eyes too close together?' I asked, getting straight to the point.

'I don't have his real name,' said Paddy.

'What name do you have?'

'Kipper.'

'Kipper what?' I asked.

'Just Kipper,' he said. 'But it's only a nickname.'

'Have you ever met him?' I asked.

'I haven't rightly met him, but I believe I saw him once.'

'In Ireland?' I asked.

'Hell, no,' he said. 'In England. Your dad was that frightened of him. Said he was a strange fellow, bit of a loner.'

If my father was as frightened of this Kipper as Paddy made out, why had he kicked out at him and told him to go to hell in the Ascot car park?

'What else did my father say about him?' I asked.

'He thought he was being paid too much for what he did,' said Paddy. 'Moaned about it all the time, your dad did.'

'But how did he know how much this Kipper was being paid?' I asked.

'I don't rightly know. Something about him bringing his share over from Australia,' Paddy said. 'Your dad claimed that he should have been getting as much as Kipper, for delivering the merchandise, as he put it. Then he laughed and said they'd find out soon enough that they should have been paying him more.'

'Who were *they*?' I asked.

'Search me,' he said.

'And what did he mean by saying they would find out soon enough?'

'I don't know that either,' he said.

Paddy Murphy wasn't being very helpful. He was suddenly backtracking. Perhaps he was now regretting having told me anything. I wondered if what my father had said about them finding out soon enough was to do with him stealing the microcoder.

'You told me that this Kipper worked for an insurance company,' I said. 'Which one?'

'Well, to be sure, I don't rightly know,' he said.

'Is the company Irish?' I asked. 'Or English?'

'I don't know that either,' he said. 'All your father told me was that Kipper's job was as an investigator looking into horse deaths. Maybe I just assumed he was with an insurance company.'

That wasn't very helpful either.

However, he went on to tell me a few interesting things about the two missing counterfeit RFID chips that could turn out to be very helpful indeed, not least that a horse that had supposedly recently died from colic had, in fact, been switched using the fake RFIDs with a much less valuable animal, which had then been killed for a large insurance payout. And he indicated that the horse had been a winner at the Cheltenham Steeplechase Festival the previous March.

I remembered reading something only the other week in the *Racing Post* about a horse dying from colic.

'What was the horse's name?' I asked him.

'No, no,' he said. 'I've told you too much already.'

Indeed he had, but he had been boasting about his cleverness.

'Well, let me know if this Kipper fellow turns up at your door,' I said.

'Bejesus,' he bellowed. 'I don't want the likes of him here.'

'He's dangerous, so keep clear of him.'

'To be sure, I will,' said Paddy.

'Also let me know when you're next in England,' I said. 'Perhaps we can meet.'

'Well,' he said a little uncertainly, 'I'm not sure about that.'

'Who are you, anyway?' I asked. 'What is your real name?'

'Now, that would be telling,' he said with a laugh, and hung up.

Chief Inspector Llewellyn himself was at Banbury police station to meet me at two o'clock. He was accompanied, as always, by Sergeant Murray, with his notebook.

'Hello, Chief Inspector,' I said cheerfully as he appeared in the entrance lobby. 'For what do I deserve this honour?'

'For telling me lies, Mr Talbot,' he said without any humour. 'I don't like people telling me lies.'

Oh dear, I thought, he must know about my father's luggage. How was I going to get out of this one?

'What lies?' I said, trying to keep my voice even. 'I told you everything I know.'

'You told me that your father had given you nothing at Ascot,' he said.

'That's right, he didn't,' I protested.

'But I have reason to believe that he may have given you a black box like a television remote control.' He paused and I stood there looking at him, saying nothing. 'We understand from Australia that your father is thought to have stolen such a box. Now, quite by chance, one of my officers on the case helps with a club for young offenders in High Wycombe and he tells me he saw a similar black box there last week. This morning my officer called the person who had brought the black box to the club and, surprise, surprise, that person says that you gave it to him.'

Thanks, Luca, I thought. But he could probably have said nothing else.

'Oh, that thing,' I said.

'So you were lying,' he said almost triumphantly.

In fact, I hadn't been. I had been completely truthful. My father had not given the box to me at Ascot, I'd actually found it with his luggage in Paddington.

'I'd forgotten about it, that's all,' I said. 'I was carrying it for him amongst our equipment. I found it the following day when I was setting up.'

Now I *was* telling lies, but Sergeant Murray wrote them down nevertheless.

'You should have given the box to me immediately you found it,' he said.

'Sorry,' I replied. 'Is it important?'

He didn't answer my question. 'Where is it now?' he asked.

'I don't know,' I said. Technically, that was not a lie.

'But what did you do with it?' he persisted.

'I threw it away,' I said. 'It didn't seem to do anything. I thought it must have been a garage door opener or something. Perhaps from his home. It wasn't much use to me, so I just dumped it in the bin.'

'Which bin?' He was beginning to lose what little patience he had.

'At home, last weekend, in the house wheelie bin,' I said. 'But the men have been to empty it since then, so it's probably somewhere on a Warwickshire council tip by now.'

'Didn't you think it was odd that he would carry his garage door opener half way round the world?' the chief inspector asked.

'Not really,' I replied. 'He had just told me that he was my father, who I believed had died thirty-seven years ago when I was a baby. Now, I admit I thought that was odd.'

'Are you now telling me more lies?' he said.

'No, of course I'm not,' I said crossly. 'I've come here to help you with an e-fit. Don't you think I want you to catch my father's killer?'

'I'm not so sure that you do,' he said slowly. 'And, Mr Talbot, don't go away anywhere without telling us first.'

'Why not?' I asked him sharply. 'Am I under arrest or something?'

'Not yet, no,' he said. 'Not yet.'

Producing the police e-fit was easy. I had dreamed so much about Shifty Eyes that I had little trouble transferring the image in my head to a picture on a computer. The young e-fit technician, as he was called, was an expert.

'A little bit wider,' I said about the man's face.

The technician turned the wheel on his computer mouse with his right forefinger and the face in front of me squeezed in or stretched out until it was just right. His eyes were added, rather too close together for the width of the face, and then a nose, mouth, and ears, each in turn adjusted in height, width and thickness by the rotation of the mouse wheel. Finally, short straight fair hair was grown instantly and made to stand upright on the top of the head.

Shifty Eyes, or Kipper, as Paddy Murphy had called him,

looked out at me from the screen and it sent a shiver down my back.

'That's it,' I said.

'Great,' the technician replied, punching the 'save' button on his keyboard. 'The chief inspector will be delighted.'

I doubted that, I thought.

I wondered if my image was anything like any of those produced by the other witnesses. But I had an advantage over them, I'd not just seen him in the Ascot car park, I'd seen him again in Sussex Gardens, and without his hoodie and scarf.

By the time I arrived back at Station Road, peace had broken out between the sisters. Alice had conceded that Sophie would be allowed to enter her own kitchen to help with the dinner preparations and Sophie, in her turn, had agreed to allow Alice to do all the cleaning up after her. It seemed like an excellent deal to me, especially as all I had to do was eat it.

'We're having Thai green chicken curry and sticky rice,' said Sophie with a flourish. 'They never once served spicy food in the hospital and I'm desperate for some. Alice and I walked down to the shops while you were out.'

'Great,' I said, meaning it.

'Where did you go?' she asked.

'Banbury,' I said.

'What for?'

Quick, think!

'I went to see someone who has a new device which he wants us to buy to put on our computer, at the races.'

'Oh,' she said, uninterested. 'And did you buy it?'

'No,' I said. 'It wasn't much good, and it was too expensive.'

What was I doing? Lying to the police was one thing, but lying to Sophie was quite another. I didn't like it. And it would have to stop. This whole secret-agent circus had to stop, and soon. Just as soon as Shifty Eyes was arrested for my father's murder, and the police in the form of Chief Inspector Llewellyn got off my back.

I spent much of Tuesday morning sitting in my little office doing some research, both on the internet and using the two printed volumes most familiar to anyone in racing: the *Directory of the Turf* and *Horses in Training*.

I wasn't really sure what I was looking for.

First, I searched back through the on-line editions of the *Racing Post* until I found the piece I had read about a horse dying. The horse had been called Oriental Suite and, according to the newspaper, it had died as a result of complications arising from a bout of severe colic. Oriental Suite had won the Triumph Hurdle, a high-class hurdle race for four-year-old novices, going away from his rivals up the Cheltenham hill last March. He had been tipped to be a future Champion Hurdler. The obituary quoted the horse's owner as being distraught over the untimely death. Racing, he declared, had been cruelly robbed of a future mega-star.

If Paddy Murphy was right, and the horse had been switched and therefore wasn't actually dead, the real truth was not that racing had been cruelly robbed of a future star, but that an insurance company had been cruelly robbed of a reasonable-sized fortune.

I removed from the top drawer of my desk the photocopies of the horse passports I had found in my father's rucksack. One of them was for a bay horse with the name Oriental Suite. I looked up Oriental Suite on the *Racing Post* website. In his short life, he had won nearly two hundred thousand pounds in prize money. No wonder he'd been well insured.

But why would anyone want to effectively kill off his potential champion steeplechaser? Many owners spent their whole lives, and often most of their wealth, trying to find themselves a champion horse. Perhaps it was all down to cash-flow, or maybe the owner believed he could have his cake and eat it too – collect both a big insurance payout *and* still have the horse go on to be a champion under a different name.

'What are you up to?' Sophie asked, coming in and standing behind me, stroking my back.

'Just researching the runners for the coming week,' I said.

Bookmakers, as well as regular punters, needed to keep abreast of all the winners and losers if they were to make a living from other people's folly.

'Do you want a coffee?' Sophie asked. 'That is if Miss Ugly Sister down there will let me into my own kitchen.'

'Now, now, Cinders,' I said, laughing. 'If Alice was one of the Ugly Sisters, she wouldn't let you leave the kitchen, not keep you out of it.'

'I know you're right, dearest Buttons,' she sighed. 'But she's beginning to drive me nuts.'

We looked at each other in surprise, and then both burst out laughing at what Sophie had said. Did it prove she wasn't nuts any more?

'I'll have a word with her, if you like,' I said.

'No, no, don't do that,' she said. 'I know she means well, but she's so . . . intense. I feel I have to be so careful not to upset her, while she is trying so hard not to upset me.'

'Go and tell her that,' I said. 'She'll understand.'

'I'll try,' she said, and went out.

I went back to using the internet and did some more research, including, amongst other things, looking up the declared runners for the coming week. I also used it to try and look up anything about valuable horses that had recently died in unusual or mysterious circumstances. But there was precious little information to be found.

In spite of being strong and physically fit, Thoroughbred racehorses were actually quite delicate creatures and, sadly, many of them died unexpectedly from injury or disease. Such events, while often being disasters for the horse's owner and trainer, were unlikely to be newsworthy unless it was the death of a potential champion, such as Oriental Suite.

After twenty minutes or so I began to wonder whether or not my cup of coffee was coming, so I went down the stairs to find out. As always, I carefully avoided treading on step three.

Alice and Sophie were both in tears, sitting at one end of the kitchen table, hugging each other. My mug of coffee stood alone at the other end, getting cold. I said nothing but walked over, picked it up and drank down some of the lukewarm brown liquid.

'Oh,' said Sophie, dabbing her eyes with a tissue. 'I'm so sorry.' She was more laughing than crying. 'I forgot. Alice and I have been talking.'

'So I see,' I said, smiling at them both.

'We've been talking about Mum and Dad,' said Sophie. 'They want to come over and see us.'

I stopped smiling. I hadn't spoken to Sophie's parents in nearly ten years, and I had no wish to start doing so again now. They had been so hurtful towards me when Sophie had first fallen sick, accusing me of bringing on the mania by acts of cruelty towards the wife whom I adored. Her father even told me that Sophie's illness was God's punishment for me being a bookmaker.

I had walked out of their house on that day, and had never been back. And, as far as I was aware, they had never set foot in my house, and I had no intention of inviting them to do so now.

'You can go and see them if you really want to,' I said. 'But count me out.'

Sophie gave me a pained look.

I knew that Sophie had seen her parents at various times throughout the previous ten years but we never spoke about it. I knew only because she was always agitated after the visits, and I didn't like it. Once or twice those agitations had led on to full-blown mania, and the subsequent depression. And, on at least one occasion I was sure of, an argument between Sophie and her stubborn, ill-tempered and self-righteous father had resulted in her early return to hospital.

'You know it's not a good idea,' I said to her gently. 'It always ends in a row of one sort or another, and rows are not good for you.'

'It's different this time,' she said.

That is what she always said. Of course, I lived in the hope that it would be different this time but, inside, I had to assume it wouldn't be. I would be unable to endure the future disappointment if I placed too great an expectation on her present progress only for my optimism to be dashed.

I could hardly tell her not to see her own parents, and she would probably ignore me if I did. But I felt quite strongly about it. However, I didn't want her going secretly behind my back, knowingly against my wishes. And, most of all, I didn't want to argue with her.

257

What was I to say?

'What do you think Sophie should do, Alice?' I said, side-stepping the problem and placing it on another's shoulders.

'I know Mum is very keen to see her,' she said.

'Then why didn't she visit her in hospital?' I asked. But I knew the answer.

'The hospital is so upsetting for them both,' said Alice.

It hadn't been a barrel of laughs for the rest of us but we had still gone. The truth was, I thought, that neither of Sophie's parents could bear to admit that their precious elder daughter was mentally ill and, provided they didn't actually see her in an institution, they could go on fooling themselves that she was fine and well.

However, they didn't fool me or, indeed, Alice, who had been painstaking and diligent in visiting her sister almost every other day. Even her two brothers had visited Sophie at least twice during her recent five-month stay. But, of her parents, there had been not a sign.

'You must do what you think is best,' I said to Sophie. 'But I would prefer it if they didn't come here. So go and see them at their place, if you like. I won't come, but if you do go, I think it would be a good idea for you to go with Alice.'

'To dilute them, you mean,' Sophie said.

'Yes,' I said. 'And to try and prevent a row.'

'Fine by me,' said Alice. 'If Dad starts being a pain, I'll kick him.'

She and Sophie laughed, their heads close together in sisterly conspiracy.

She'd better take steel-toecapped boots, I thought.

CHAPTER 18

The first race at Towcester's late-June evening meeting started at 6 p.m. I have always liked to be set up at least an hour before the first, in order to capture the early punters, and also to give time for us to sort out any problems we might have with our equipment, in particular flat batteries and poor wireless internet signal. Consequently, I drove in through the racecourse entrance archway a little before five o'clock and parked in the shade of a large oak tree in the centre of the car park.

I have always enjoyed going to Towcester races, and not only because most of their meetings have no admission charge for the public, and hence none for the bookies. I also loved the parkland course set on the rolling countryside of the Easton Neston Estate, and their recent investments in new facilities that made it an attractive venue for both bookies and punters alike.

As the racecourse was approximately midway between our homes in Kenilworth and High Wycombe, Luca and I had agreed to meet there, travelling in our separate cars, so I unloaded everything myself and pulled it on our trolley into the racecourse enclosure.

The betting ring at Towcester was unusual in so far that it

was in the space between the grandstands, rather than in front of them as on many courses. This was due to the stands having been built very close to the track, which I suppose was sensible as it gave a much better view of the racing for the spectators.

Luca was already waiting for me as I pulled the trolley to our pitch.

'Where's Betsy?' I asked.

'She's not coming,' he said. 'In fact, I don't think she will be coming again, ever.'

'Oh?'

'She packed up yesterday and moved out of my flat,' he said.

'I'm sorry,' I said, not meaning it.

'I'm not,' he replied. 'Not really.' He paused. 'I suppose I'll miss her.' He paused again. 'I'll definitely miss her in bed. Wow, she was so good.' He smiled at me.

'Too much information, Luca,' I said, laughing. 'Far too much information.'

We set up the stuff in silence for a while.

'I suppose we'll need a new junior assistant now,' Luca said.

'Yes,' I said. 'Any ideas?'

'There's a lad at the electronics club who might be good.'

'I don't want any juvenile delinquents.'

'He's a good lad at heart,' said Luca. 'He just fell in with the wrong crowd.'

'Talking about the electronics club,' I said, 'did you tell the police about that microcoder thing?'

'Oh, yeah,' he said. 'Sorry about that.'

'I should think so, too. I was nearly arrested yesterday.'

'God! I'm sorry. I didn't even know Jim was a copper until after he'd asked.'

'Tell me about it,' I said.

'This chap, Jim, who also helps at the club, he called me up yesterday morning and asked about that black box device thing you gave me to look at. Jim had helped me to investigate it. He was the bloke who fixed it up to the oscilloscope. So he just casually, like, asks me where I got it from, and I told him that you gave it to me. I didn't think I was doing anything wrong to say so, but Jim then says his boss will be most interested. So I ask him who his boss is and he says some chief inspector or something.'

'You could have bloody warned me,' I said, fighting with the catch that held our board up.

'Sorry,' he said. 'Jim called right in the middle of my own domestic crisis. Betsy had just accused me, point-blank, of sleeping with her sister, Millie.'

I stopped what I was doing and looked at him in surprise. Perhaps I might forgive him for not remembering to tell me about PC Jim.

'And have you?' I asked, intrigued.

'That's none of your business,' he said, laughing. 'But no, not exactly.'

'And what the hell does that mean?' I said.

'I kissed her. Only once, mind. At her birthday party. You know, we went there from Ascot. But Betsy caught us.'

'Oh, come on,' I said. 'Everyone kisses the birthday girl at her own party.'

'Not with tongues,' he said. 'And not out in the garden, behind a bush.'

'Ah,' I replied. That explained a lot. Betsy had been cool towards Luca ever since that party, and now I knew why.

'So what are you going to do?' I asked him.

261

'Nothing,' he said. 'Leave things to settle for a while, I think. Then I'll see how the land lies.'

'She may not have you back,' I said.

'Back? Are you crazy? I just thought I'd let things calm down for a while before I asked Millie out.' He grinned at me and I wasn't sure whether he meant it, or if he was just trying to shock his new business partner. Knowing Luca, it was probably both.

It was a lovely summer's evening at the races with a large crowd, many of them eager to have a flutter on the horses, and most of them in summer casual dress of shorts and T-shirts. It was a far cry from the morning-dress formality of Royal Ascot, and much more fun. The bars were soon doing brisk business, helped by the unusually warm weather, and before long there was a party atmosphere all around the betting ring.

Luca and I worked continuously, taking bets and paying out winners without a break, one of the disadvantages of not having a junior assistant. But, busy as it was, it was still one of those times when being a bookmaker was a real joy.

No one really becomes a bookie unless they have a bit of the showman in them. I just loved standing on my platform shouting out the odds and bantering with the crowd.

'Come on, mate,' shouted one heavyweight punter at me. 'Call that fair to have Ellie's Mobile at only three-to-one?' He looked up at the name at the top of our board. 'How can we "Trust Teddy Talbot" when you only offer it at that price?'

'If you'll ride it, you can have it at tens,' I shouted back at him.

All his mates roared with laughter.

'He couldn't ride a bike,' one of them shouted.

'Not without bending it,' shouted another.

'Give me twenty on the nose,' said the heavyweight, thrusting a note in my direction.

'Twenty pounds to win, number two, and make it at four-to-one,' I said to Luca over my shoulder. 'Special favour.'

'Cheers,' said the man, surprised. 'You're a real gent.'

I didn't know about that but, if I couldn't repay a bit of initiative and colour, then I was in the wrong business.

Ellie's Mobile, the favourite, romped home to win by four lengths at a starting price of three-to-one, cheered with great gusto by the ten-strong band of well-oiled mates, who had stayed near our pitch to watch the race.

'Well done,' I said to the big chap, who was beaming from ear to ear.

'My God!' he said loudly to whoever would listen. 'I've actually got one over on a bookie.'

'That makes a change,' chipped in one of the others.

They all guffawed, and ordered more beer.

'Weighed in,' sounded the public address system.

I paid the big man his eighty pounds in winnings plus his twenty-pound stake.

'Cheers,' he said again, stuffing the cash into a pocket. 'I'll trust Teddy Talbot any day of the week.'

Giving him a better price had cost me twenty pounds. But the man and his nine friends more than repaid that amount in losing stakes in the remaining races. And they did so with smiles on their faces.

In fact, the whole evening was fun, with plenty of punters and a good mix of favourites and outsiders winning the races.

Our overround, the measure of our overall profit, hovered around nine per cent throughout, and both Luca and I were tired but happy as we packed up the equipment onto our little trolley after the last.

'Where are you parked?' I asked him.

'In the centre,' he said. 'And you?'

'Up there.' I pointed. 'Where are we the rest of the week?'

'Worcester tomorrow afternoon, Thursday evening and Friday afternoon at Warwick, then Leicester on Saturday,' Luca said. He always remembered what we had arranged better than I. We sat down about once every six weeks or so to plan the time ahead, and it was getting near to when we would have to do it again.

'Better put everything in my car, then,' I said.

'Yeah,' he replied. 'I'll give you a hand.'

We dragged the trolley up the hill to the car park near the main entrance where I had left my car. All around us were happy racegoers also making their way to their vehicles in the late-evening sunshine. One of the reasons why evening racing was so popular was that, even in southern England, the sun didn't set until well after nine o'clock for two whole months during midsummer.

'How about your young delinquent friend?' I asked, as we pulled on the trolley handle. 'Can he come with you sometime this week so I can meet him?'

'I'll find out,' Luca said. 'And he's not a delinquent. He's a nice boy or I wouldn't even suggest it.'

'OK, OK,' I said, smiling. 'Ask him if he'd like to come and watch us one day this week. What's his name?'

'Douglas,' he said. 'Douglas Masters.'

His name didn't sound like that of a juvenile delinquent, but who was I to know? Kipper didn't exactly sound like a killer's name either, but it was.

'Calls himself Douggie. Can I tell him there's a job?'

'Sure,' I said. 'But tell him it's like an interview. No promises.'

Two large men were leaning on the oak tree waiting for us beside my car. I knew them from a previous encounter. As before, they were dressed in short-sleeved white shirts and black trousers.

I stopped the trolley about ten yards from them.

'What the hell do you want?' I shouted across.

Luca looked at me in stunned amazement.

'Eh?' he said. He obviously hadn't seen them or, if he had, he hadn't realized they were waiting for us.

'Luca,' I said. 'These are the two gentlemen who delivered a message to me in the Kempton car park.'

'Oh,' he said. Oh, indeed.

I looked down at the men's feet. Large, steel-toecapped work boots, same as before.

'We have another message,' one of them said. He was the taller of the two, the same one who had spoken to me at Kempton. Not that the other one was short. They both were well over six foot. The sidekick made up for his slight lack of height by being a good few inches broader than his more wordy companion. And he just stood silently to one side, bunching his fists.

Surely I was not to be beaten up again, I thought. Not here at this wonderful parkland racecourse, not with all these people about.

'What message?' I said. There was still ten yards between

us and I reckoned that, if they made a move towards me, I would turn and run. A ten-yard start should be enough for me to reach the relative safety of a busy after-racing bar in the grandstand.

'Luca,' I said quietly to him, 'if they move, run for it. Run like the wind.'

The look on his face was priceless. I'm not sure he realized until that point that he was in any danger.

'My boss says he wants to talk to you,' the man said.

'You can tell your boss to bugger off,' I said.

'He wants to do some business,' the man went on.

'Still tell him to bugger off,' I said. 'I don't do business the same way he does.'

'He wants to buy you out,' he said, ignoring me.

I stood there looking at the man in complete surprise.

'What?' I said, not quite believing what I'd heard.

'He wants to buy your business,' the man said.

'He couldn't afford it,' I said.

'I don't think you understand,' said the man. 'My boss wants your business and he's prepared to pay for it.'

'No,' I almost shouted. 'I don't think *you* understand. My business is not for sale and, even if it was, I wouldn't sell it to your boss, whoever he might be, for all the tea in China. So go and tell your boss to get stuffed.'

The man flexed his muscles and began to get red in the face.

'My boss says that you can either sell it to him the easy way, or lose it to him the hard way.'

'And who exactly is your boss?' I shouted at him.

He didn't reply but advanced a stride towards me. My head start had just been reduced to nine yards.

'Stay there,' I shouted at him. He stopped. 'Who is your

boss?' I asked again. Again he ignored me. And he advanced another stride. Eight yards.

I was on the point of running when another voice came from behind me.

'Hello, Teddy Talbot. You all right?' I turned and breathed a huge sigh of relief. The big man from the betting ring was staggering up the car park towards me, together with his band of brothers. 'You in need of some help?' he said, only slightly slurring his words.

I turned back to the two bully-boys.

'That would be great,' I said. 'I think these two men are just leaving.'

I stared straight at them and, finally, they decided to give up and go. Luca and I stood surrounded by the cavalry and we watched as the two men walked across to a black BMW 4x4 and drove away through the archway and out onto the London Road. I made a mental note of the number plate.

'Were those boys troubling you?' asked my mate, the large guy.

'Some people will do anything to get their losses back from a bookie,' I said somewhat flippantly. 'But, thanks to you lot, they didn't manage it today.'

'You mean those two were trying to rob you,' said another of the group.

'They certainly were,' I said, but not quite in the way I'd made out.

'You should have said so. I'm a policeman.'

He produced his warrant card from his pocket and I read it: PC Nicholas Boucher, Northamptonshire Constabulary. Off duty, I presumed, in multicoloured tropical shirt, baggy shorts and flip-flops.

'I got their car registration,' I said.

'Good,' said PC Boucher. 'Now what exactly did they say to you? Did they demand their money back?'

'Well, no,' I said. 'They hadn't quite, and you guys turning up must have frightened them away before they had a chance to. And I'm only assuming that's what they wanted. It wouldn't have been the first time.'

'Oh,' he said, rather disappointed. His case was evaporating before his eyes. 'Not much I can do if they hadn't actually demanded any money from you. But did they threaten you?'

'They looked quite threatening to me,' I said.

'We can't exactly arrest people for just looking threatening, now can we?' he said ironically.

'No,' I said. 'I suppose I can see that. But I'd love to know who they were so I can watch out and avoid them in the future.'

'What was their vehicle registration?' he asked.

I gave it to him.

'No promises,' he said. 'It's against the rules really.'

He took his mobile phone from his pocket and called a number.

'Jack,' he said into the phone. 'Nick Boucher here. Can you do a vehicle check? Registration Victor-Kilo-Five-Five Zulu-November-Victor.' He waited for a while. 'Yes,' he said. Then he listened again. 'Thanks,' he said finally, and hung up.

'Sorry. That vehicle is registered to a company, not to an individual, so it won't really help you.'

'Which company?' I asked him.

'Something called HRF Holdings Limited,' he said. 'Ever heard of them?'

'No,' I said. I looked at Luca, who said nothing but shrugged his shoulders. 'Thanks, anyway.'

'Are you guys going to be all right from now on?' said PC

Boucher. 'I've got to get this bunch of drunks home. I'm the designated driver.'

'Yes,' I said. 'Thanks.'

'See you next time, Teddy,' said the big guy, staggering a little and giving me a wave. I watched his group lurch over to a white minibus and fall into it. The passengers all waved enthusiastically at me through the windows as poor, sober PC Boucher drove them away. I waved back at them, laughing.

'HRF Holdings,' said Luca. 'Do we know them?'

'Not by that name,' I said.

'What, then?' he asked.

'I believe HRF Holdings Limited is a parent company,' I said. 'And I think I know one of its children.'

It took me less than an hour to get home, including a few extra trips round the roundabouts to ensure that I wasn't being followed by a certain black BMW 4x4 containing a couple of heavies.

I couldn't see anyone following me but they wouldn't have actually needed to. I was sure that whoever their 'boss' might be, he would have been able to find out where I lived with ease if he'd wanted to. My name and address were on the electoral roll for a start, and I hadn't bothered to tick the box to keep that information secret.

Consequently, I drove up and down Station Road a couple of times to see if the BMW was parked up somewhere awaiting my arrival. There was no sign of it, but I couldn't check every street in Kenilworth.

I parked the car in the space in front of the house and made it safely, unchallenged, to my front door.

'Hello,' said Sophie, coming to meet me. 'Had a good time?'

'Very,' I said. 'I always like Towcester, especially the evening meetings.'

'Hiya,' said Alice, coming out of the kitchen with a glass of white wine in each hand. She gave one of them to Sophie with a smile. I wasn't sure that drinking alcohol was necessarily a good idea on top of her medication, but I wasn't going to say so. For now, it was far more important that the truce between the sisters was still holding firm.

They had been out in Alice's car when I had left for the races, and I thought they might have been to see their parents in spite of telling me that they were off to Leamington Spa for the shopping. However, there was no sign of the agitation that Sophie normally displayed after such a visit, so I wasn't certain. And I wasn't going to ask. We went into the kitchen.

'Have you had a good day?' I asked them.

'Lovely,' Sophie said, without elaborating.

'So what time did you get back?'

'About seven.'

'Have you eaten?' I looked at my watch; it was now past ten.

'We have,' said Sophie. 'But I've kept some for you. I know you're always hungry when you get home after an evening meeting.'

I suppose it was true, but it didn't mean I always had something to eat. During the past five months, I had more often than not had a stiff shot of Scotch and gone straight to bed.

'And we've been at the crisps and dip,' said Alice with a giggle.

And the white wine, I thought, though, to be fair, Sophie seemed pretty sober even if Alice was obviously quite tipsy.

'Do you know anything about a rucksack?' Sophie asked casually as she stood at the cooker reheating my supper.

'What?' I said sharply.

'A rucksack,' she said again. 'A man came here. Said he wanted to collect a rucksack. He said you knew about it.'

'What sort of rucksack?' I said, rather flustered.

'A black and red rucksack,' she said. 'The man told us you were looking after it for him. He was quite persistent, I can tell you. I don't think he liked it much when I told him I knew nothing about it.'

Oh God, I thought.

'So you didn't give it to him?' I asked her.

'No, of course not,' she said. 'I don't even know we have a black and red rucksack. Where is it?'

'In the cupboard under the stairs,' I said. 'Did the man try and get into the house?'

'No,' she said, slightly perturbed by the question. 'Why would he?'

'I just wondered, that's all,' I said. 'So tell me what happened.'

'I told him to go away and come back when you were at home.'

'We then locked the house up tight, opened a bottle, and waited for you to get back,' said Alice with a smile. They were both remarkably calm about the man's visit. Probably because they didn't realize the seriousness of the situation. But why would they?

'When was this?' I asked.

'Around eight o'clock,' Sophie said.

'Can you describe the man?' I said to both of them.

'He was rather creepy,' said Alice.

'In what way was he creepy?' I asked.

'Oh, I don't know,' she said. 'He just was. And he was wearing his hood up, and a scarf. Now, I reckon you've got to be up to no good to be doing that on a night as hot as this.'

'Could you see his eyes?' I asked. 'Were they set rather close together?'

'Yes,' said Alice, throwing a hand up in the air almost excitedly. 'That's it. That's exactly why I thought he was creepy.'

So it had definitely been Shifty Eyes, the man that Paddy Murphy had called Kipper. He had found me at last.

'What are we going to do?' Sophie asked loudly, suddenly becoming scared. 'I don't want him coming back here.' In spite of the warm evening, she shivered.

'It's all right, my love,' I said, putting a reassuring arm round her shoulders. 'I'm sure he won't come back tonight.'

The doorbell rang and we all jumped.

'How sure?' Sophie said, looking worried.

'Ignore it,' said Alice. 'Then he'll have to go away.'

We stood silently in the kitchen, listening.

The doorbell rang again and there were also some heavy thumps on the door.

'I know you're in there,' shouted a voice from outside. 'Open up.'

I went out of the kitchen into the hallway.

'Who is it?' I shouted through the wood of the front door.

'Mr Talbot,' said the voice. 'I think you may have something of mine, and I want it back.'

'What?' I asked.

'A rucksack,' he said. 'A black and red rucksack.'

'But the rucksack belonged to Alan Grady, not you,' I said quickly, without stopping to think first. Damn it, I thought.

Why hadn't I just denied any knowledge of any rucksack? He might then have gone away, but he wouldn't do so now.

'I'm calling the police,' said Sophie coming into the hallway. 'Do you hear me?' she shouted loudly with a tremor in her voice. 'I'm calling the police.'

'There'll be no need for the police,' said the man calmly through the door. 'Just give me the rucksack and I'll go away.'

'Give him the rucksack,' Sophie said to me imploringly, her panicky eyes as big as saucers. 'Please, Ned, just give him the damn rucksack.'

'OK, OK,' I said.

I went to the cupboard under the stairs and fetched it. It was still full of my father's things.

'Give it to him,' Sophie urged me again, her voice quivering with fear.

I lifted the rucksack and turned to go upstairs with it.

'Where the hell are you going?' Sophie almost screamed at me.

'If you think I'm opening the front door with him there, you must be . . .' I didn't finish the sentence. 'I'm going to throw it to him, out the window.'

I went up to our bedroom and opened the same window through which I had witnessed the departure of Mr John Smith from my house only one week previously.

The man was close to the door and I couldn't see him as he was standing under the overhanging porch.

'Here,' I shouted.

He moved back into my sight. He appeared just as I had seen him the first time in the car park at Ascot racecourse: blue jeans, charcoal hoodie, with a black scarf over the lower part of his face. I couldn't tell if he was wearing the same black army boots

273

he had used to split my eyebrow, and I wasn't about to go down there to find out. As before, all I could see were his eyes, set rather too close together for the width of his face.

I held the rucksack out through the open window at arm's length.

'What's your name?' I asked him.

'Drop the rucksack,' he said, ignoring my question. He didn't have a strong regional accent, at least not one I could notice.

'What's your name?' I repeated.

'Never you mind,' he said. 'Just give me the rucksack.'

'How did you find my house?' I asked him.

'A little birdie told me,' he said.

'Which little birdie?'

'Never you mind,' he said again. 'Just drop the rucksack.' He held up his arms ready to catch it.

'It's only full of Mr Grady's clothes,' I said. 'I've searched it. There's nothing else there.'

'Give it to me anyway,' he said.

'Who are you working for?' I asked.

'What?' he said.

'Who are you working for?' I repeated.

'No one,' he said. 'Now give me the bloody rucksack.'

'Who's John Smith?' I asked.

In spite of only being able to see his eyes I could still tell that there was no recognition of the name. He didn't know a Mr John Smith but, then, that wasn't his real name, now was it?

'Give me the bag,' he hissed at me in the same way as he'd hissed at my father at Ascot. 'And give it to me now, or I'll break your bloody door down.'

I opened my hand and dropped the rucksack. In spite of having his hands up, he failed to catch it before it hit the concrete path, but he quickly snatched it up and was off, jogging down Station Road in just the same manner as I had previously seen him do in Paddington, near Lancaster Gate tube station.

I wondered how he had found out where I lived. If he had obtained the information that I had given the coroner at the inquest, then why had it taken him so long to arrive at my door? I thought back to what I had done over the previous twenty-four hours. Perhaps his little birdie had been at Banbury police station yesterday, or somewhere else in the Thames Valley Police. That e-fit would have been sent right round the force and perhaps someone recognized the face, someone who was not completely honest, someone who had then told Kipper who had made it.

I would never know exactly how he had found me, and I hoped that this would be the last time I would see him but, somehow, I had my doubts.

He would certainly find that the microcoder and the glass-grain RFID chips were missing from the rucksack as Mr John Smith now had them. And I had also kept back the three house keys on their ring, and the passports, the two photocopied equine ones, and both of those with my father's picture in them.

However, if Paddy Murphy was to be believed, and there was absolutely no guarantee of that, then it would be the stash of money that the man would be more concerned about. If he knew where to look, Kipper would find the three blue-cling-film packages of banknotes back in their original hiding place under-neath the rucksack lining. But, if he inspected them more closely, he might spot that the packages had been opened and then carefully resealed using clear sticky tape. And, if he then counted the cash, he might also discover that he was two thousand pounds short from each package.

It had seemed a good idea at the time. But now I wasn't so sure.

'What the hell was all that about?' Sophie demanded when I went down the stairs.

She and Alice were standing in the hall looking up at me with concerned but expectant expressions on their faces.

'Just an impatient man who wanted something I had,' I said to them, trying to make light of the encounter.

'But he was horrible,' said Sophie. 'Why did you give it to him?'

'But it was you who told me to,' I said slightly exasperated.

'Whose rucksack was it, anyway?' she asked.

'It belongs to a man called Alan Grady,' I said. 'He gave it to me to keep safe.'

'Who's Alan Grady?' she asked.

'Just a man from Australia that I met at Royal Ascot.'

'He's not going to be very pleased with you for giving his rucksack away to someone else.'

She seemed to have completely forgotten the fear and panic that had gripped her when the man had been standing outside our front door.

'I don't think he'll mind too much,' I said, without elaborating further. I smiled at the two of them. 'Now, what's for supper?'

'He won't come back, will he?' Alice asked nervously as I ate my macaroni cheese, the three of us sitting round the kitchen table.

'I don't think so,' I said. 'He has what he came for.'

At least, he had most of it, I thought. But would he come back for the rest? There was no doubt that he now knew exactly where I lived and, even though I had been half expecting him to turn up, it was still rather a shock that he had.

After my supper I went up into my little office to log on to the internet while the girls took themselves off to bed.

HRF Holdings Ltd was indeed a parent company, and one of the businesses it owned I knew very well. Tony Bateman (Turf Accountants) Ltd, to give it its full title, was one of the big five high-street betting shop chains. Their shops were presently mostly confined to London and the south-east of England, but the business was expanding rapidly north and westwards.

I made a search of the Companies House WebCHeck service and downloaded the most recent annual report for Tony Bateman (Turf Accountants) Ltd and for HRF Holdings Ltd. They were both private limited companies and the report recorded the names of the directors and the company secretaries, as well as a list of the current shareholders of each entity.

Just as there is no longer an individual called William Hill in charge of the William Hill bookmaking company, there was no sign in the report of anyone actually called Tony Bateman either as a director or as a shareholder of Tony Bateman (Turf Accountants) Ltd. It must have been a name from the past, I thought, possibly the company founder or maybe an individual bookmaker who was, at some distant time, bought out by a bigger concern.

I did, however, recognize one name prominent amongst the list of both the directors and the shareholders of the company. Henry Richard Feldman was well known on British racecourses. Now in his late sixties, he had made his money in property development, specifically in the docklands of both London and

Liverpool, although there were reports that a recent fall in house prices had hit him hard. For the past twenty years or so he had been a prolific and successful racehorse owner, mostly of jumpers. He was also the sole shareholder of HRF Holdings Ltd.

But why did he, or more precisely, why did Tony Bateman (Turf Accountants) Ltd want to buy my business?

Ever since betting shops were made legal in Britain in 1961, the big firms had been expanding their domains by buying out the small independent bookies. But mostly it had been the individual town-centre betting shops they had been after. However, more recently, they had also been turning up in the betting rings on the tracks, using their influence to further control the on-course prices.

Now, it would seem, it was the turn of my business to be in their sights whether I liked it or not. Tony Bateman Ltd wasn't so much after me and Luca, or even our customers, they were after our lucrative pitch positions at the racecourses. And, it appeared, they were prepared to resort to threats and intimidation to get them.

Sophie was fast asleep when, well after midnight, I finally went along the landing to bed. As always, coming home from hospital had completely exhausted her.

I crept quietly into our bedroom and, last thing, with both shifty-eyed Kipper and the bully-boys from HRF Holdings still out there somewhere, I put Sophie's dressing-table chair under the door handle.

Just to be on the safe side.

CHAPTER 19

On Wednesday morning I made the arrangements for my father's funeral. What I really wanted was to have a cremation because I believed it gave greater closure. However, the coroner's office had other ideas.

'The police have withdrawn their objection to a burial,' said an official. 'But they said nothing about a cremation. And I haven't heard anything from the CPS.'

'The CPS?' I asked.

'Crown Prosecution Service,' he said.

I sighed. Why was everything so damn difficult?

'Will you please ask them all, then,' I said, 'if they have any objection to a cremation.'

'Can't you do that?' said the official.

'But you would have to be told by them not me, which would involve another call anyway,' I said. 'So why don't you just telephone them in the first place?'

'OK, I suppose so,' he said, clearly reluctant.

'Good,' I said briskly before he could think of another excuse, 'I'll call you back in fifteen minutes.'

While I waited, I used the internet to look up undertakers

close to Wexham Park hospital. There were loads of them. I'd never realized that dying was so popular in that part of Berkshire.

I'd also never realized how expensive dying could be. A basic, no frills funeral would cost about a thousand pounds and that didn't include the substantial price of a grave plot or the charge for the use of the crematorium. Add to that the cost of the necessary certificates, as well as a fee for someone to conduct the service, and it soon became a hefty sum indeed. To say nothing of the extras that could be incurred if I wanted an eco-friendly cardboard coffin or a choir. I began to wish I'd taken a bit more from the blue-cling-film-wrapped packages to cover the expenses.

What, I wondered, would have happened if I hadn't been here?

I called back to the official at the coroner's office.

'The police are happy, after all, that a cremation of Mr Talbot's remains can take place,' he said. 'And the CPS doesn't seem to be bothered at the moment because no one has been arrested yet for the crime.'

'Great,' I replied. I had discovered that the cost of a cremation was much less than that for a grave plot. 'Tell me,' I went on, 'who organizes and pays for a funeral of someone who turns up from abroad and dies in England without any family or friends?'

'The local Environmental Health Department would have to see to it,' he said.

'And they pay?' I asked.

'Yes,' he said. 'But they then try and recover the money from the family or from the deceased's estate. But that won't happen here because you are the next of kin and you're here, so you can pay for it.' He made it sound so easy.

'How about if I couldn't afford to?' I asked.

'You could apply to the Social Fund for help,' he said. 'But you'd have to be receiving some sort of state benefit to qualify.'

Somehow it didn't seem quite fair that my father had turned up out of the blue when I had thought he'd been dead for thirty-seven years, only for me to be saddled with his funeral expenses, especially when his death was due to someone else sticking him in the guts with a carving knife. But I could tell that it was going to be no good arguing about it. There wouldn't be a huge amount of sympathy for someone who had murdered his wife, even if he then himself had been the victim of a violent end. I would just have to shut up and pay up.

I called the first undertaker on the internet list.

'We could fit you in this coming Friday,' the man said. 'We've had a cancellation at Slough crem. It's a bit short notice, though.'

I amusingly wondered how an undertaker could have a cancellation for a cremation. Perhaps the deceased had miraculously returned to life.

'What time on Friday?' I asked.

'Three o'clock,' he said.

Friday was just two days away, but I didn't think that really mattered. It wasn't as if there would be anyone else coming. I wondered if I should try to contact his family in Australia, to ask if any of them would want to attend. But I didn't even know who to contact, and no one from there had been in touch with me during the past two weeks, either directly or through the coroner's court, and they had my address.

'Three on Friday will be fine,' I said.

'Right,' he said. 'Where is your father's body?'

Good question, I thought. 'I presume he's still at Wexham Park hospital,' I said. 'But I'm not sure. The coroner's office will know.'

I started to give him their number.

'Don't worry, we've got it,' he said. 'We'll fix everything.'

For a fee, no doubt, I thought rather ungraciously.

'Do I need to book someone to take the service?' I asked.

'We can also fix that, if you like, but you don't have to have anyone religious if you don't want to,' he said. 'Anyone can take the service. You can officiate yourself if you want to.'

'No,' I said. 'I think he would have wanted a vicar or something.'

I couldn't imagine why I thought that. Perhaps it was me who would rather have a clergyman. I wasn't a very religious person but I did think it would be slightly odd if I officiated at the service and, at the same time, I was the only mourner present. Better to have an expert, so to speak.

'Any special request for music or hymns?' he said.

'No,' I said. 'Whatever the vicar thinks is fit will be fine by me.' I didn't exactly say that just a couple of quick words and straight into the fiery furnace would be ideal, but I made it clear that all I wanted was a simple funeral. The minimum that was acceptable would do well, I told him. It wasn't as if I'd had a life-long affection for my father.

'Do you want any flowers placed on the coffin?' he asked.

'I think not,' I said. Historically, cut flowers were placed on and around coffins to provide a sweet scent to cover any other unwelcome aromas that might emanate from the decomposing corpse within. I assumed my father's body had been stored in appropriate refrigeration since his death, so flowers should be unnecessary.

'As it's such short notice,' the man said, 'could we have full payment up-front by credit card?'

'Is that usual?' I asked.

'Quite usual,' he assured me. 'Especially as the deceased was not resident in this country, with no estate to be probated by the courts.'

As it was the custom in Britain to cremate the coffin with the body, I could see that it would be rather difficult for the under-taker to take it back due to lack of payment once the event had occurred.

I gave him my credit card number and my address.

'Thank you, Mr Talbot,' he said. 'Of course, we will send you an itemized account after the day.'

'Thank you,' I said.

The business of life and death went on.

I thought that it must be difficult to be a good salesman in the undertaking trade. There had to be a line where selling a higher-class, and hence more expensive, coffin to a bereaved family became exploitation rather than acceptable good corpor-ate practice. Especially if the coffin was almost immediately to be incinerated to ashes in a crematorium at a temperature in excess of eight hundred and fifty degrees centigrade.

'Is there anything else I need to do?' I asked.

'The death will need to be registered with the registrar,' he said. 'But, if it's still subject to an inquest, that will have to wait until after the inquest is over. In the meantime, the coroner will issue a temporary death certificate, and you will have to sign Form A.'

'Form A?' I asked.

'Application for a cremation. It has to be signed by the executor or the next of kin. But you can do that just before the service. Everything else we need we'll get from the coroner.'

'Right,' I said. 'I'll see you on Friday afternoon.'

I sat in my office for a while wondering who I should tell. I expect the police would want to know, but was I required to inform them? And should I tell my grandmother that her son's funeral was on Friday? Perhaps not, I thought. It would be far less distressing for her if I didn't.

And how about Sophie?

We had never really discussed my parents as I'd never had any memories of either of them. She still thought they had both died in a car accident when I was a baby. Should I now explain to her that Alan Charles Grady, the man who had owned the black and red rucksack, the man who had been murdered in Ascot racecourse car park, had actually been Peter James Talbot, my father? Not dead for the past thirty-seven years as she had thought, but dead for just fifteen days? And did I tell her that my mother had also not died in a car crash, but had been strangled on the beach under the pier at Paignton? And did I further tell her that it had been my father who was responsible?

I decided that I would, in time, tell Sophie all about the events of the past two weeks, but not just yet. She had enough to deal with at the moment, having just come home from hospital. I certainly didn't want to upset the balance of her life, not while she was still adapting to her drug regime.

I decided I would go to my father's funeral alone.

*

Luca arrived at Station Road at noon, and he had a spiky-haired boy with him. Douglas Masters, I presumed. He looked about sixteen. He was wearing a red-checked shirt with rolled-up sleeves, fawn denim trousers that looked like they were about to fall down off his hips, and dirty white trainers over yellow socks.

'Hello,' I said cheerfully, holding out my hand.

'Hi,' he replied without any humour. He shook my hand, but warily, leaning right forward to grasp it.

'Is he old enough?' I asked Luca. Eighteen was the minimum age for working as a bookmaker, or as a bookmaker's assistant.

'I'm eighteen,' the boy assured me.

'I'm sorry to ask, but I'll have to see some ID,' I said.

He pulled a dog-eared driving licence from his pocket and held it out to me. According to the licence, he was indeed eighteen, and two months. The photo on it made him look about thirteen.

'OK, Douglas, thank you,' I said. 'And welcome.'

'Duggie,' he said. 'Or Doug. Not Douglas.'

'OK,' I repeated. 'Duggie it is.'

He nodded. 'How about you?' he asked.

'Call me Mr Talbot for now,' I said.

'And him?' he said, nodding at Luca.

'That's up to Mr Mandini,' I said.

'Luca will be fine,' Luca said.

He nodded once more. 'Just so I know,' he said.

I think it was fair to say that young Mr Masters was economical with his words, and his expressions. I raised my eyebrows at Luca in silent question.

'Duggie will be fine,' said Luca, sticking up for his young friend. 'I think he's just a little shy.'

'No, I'm not,' said Duggie with assurance, but no grace. 'I'm just careful. I don't know you.'

'Are you always careful with people you don't know?' I asked him. My dying father had told me to be careful of everyone.

'Yup,' he said, being ultra careful.

'Good,' I said over-exuberantly. 'That's exactly what's needed in bookmaking. You can't be too careful, because you never really know your customers, or what they might be up to.'

He looked at me, cocking his head to one side. 'Are you taking the mick?' he said slowly.

'Something like that,' I replied.

He smiled. It was a brief smile but a vast improvement while it lasted.

'That's all right, then,' he said.

'Come on, let's go,' I said with a smile, 'or we'll be late.'

The three of us loaded up into my Volvo with Luca sitting up front next to me and Duggie in the back. Sophie came to the door to wave as we set off for Worcester races.

'How's she doing?' Luca asked me, waving back at her.

'Fine,' I said, not really wanting to discuss things in front of Douglas, but the young man was very quick on the uptake.

'Is she ill?' he asked from behind me.

'She's fine at the moment, thank you,' I said, hoping to end the conversation at that point.

'Cancer is it?' he said.

'No,' I said.

'My mum had cancer,' he said. 'It killed her in the end.'

'I'm sorry,' I said.

'Yeah,' he said wistfully. 'Everyone's sorry. Doesn't bring her back though, does it?'

There was no answer to that, so we sat in silence for a while, and I warmed to the boy.

'Duggie,' I said, 'how well do you know the others in the electronics club?'

'I know some of them,' he said. 'Why?'

'Are you careful of them as well?' I asked. 'Or would you trust them?'

'Maybe I'd trust them not to grass to the cops,' he said. 'That's about all.'

'How many of them are there?'

'Dunno,' he said. 'Quite a lot.'

'There must be sixty of them, at least, if you count them all,' said Luca. 'But they're not all there on any one night. Most come out of choice these days, but some still don't come unless they are told to by the courts, and others disappear from time to time, you know, when they get sent off to young offenders' institutions.'

'So how many of those sixty would you actually trust, Duggie?' I asked.

'With what?' he replied.

'With some money,' I said. 'Say to go and buy something for me, or to place a bet.'

'Maybe half,' he said. 'The rest would just spend it on themselves. On drugs, mostly.'

Half of them would be enough, I thought.

'Would you know which are the ones to trust?' I asked him.

'Sure,' he said with confidence. 'The ones who are my mates.'

'What did you do, Duggie?' I asked, changing the subject. 'To be sent to the club?'

There was a long pause.

'Nicked cars,' he said finally.

'For money?' I asked.

'Nah,' he said. 'For fun.'

'Do you still nick cars?' I asked.

'No,' he said.

'Do you have any recorded convictions?' I asked.

There was another long silence from the back of the car.

'Duggie,' I said. 'I'm not asking so that I can judge you myself, but I need to know under the conditions of my bookmaking licence.'

Under the terms for the issuing of licences in the mammoth Gambling Act, 2005, prior convictions did not, in themselves, mean an individual was not a fit and proper person to hold a bookmaker's licence. Equally, they didn't preclude someone from working as a bookmaker's assistant. But I needed to know. Convictions for violence would be a no-no.

'Yes,' Duggie said.

'Just for nicking cars?' I asked.

Convictions for fraud were also not permitted.

'Yes,' he said reluctantly. 'But I never really done it. I was told to plead guilty.'

'Who by?' I asked.

'Our poncey lawyer,' he said. 'There was a group of us. We all got done for it. The lawyer said we would get a lesser sentence if we pleaded guilty. So I did.'

'But why, if you didn't do it?' I asked.

'I was in the car, wasn't I?' he said. 'But I didn't know it was nicked. The poncey lawyer said I would get done anyway, so I should plead guilty.'

I wasn't sure whether to believe him.

'Is that all?' I said. 'Only the once?'

'Yeah,' he said.

'OK,' I said.

I drove on in silence for a while.

'I won't nick your money, if that's what you're wondering,' Duggie said eventually.

I wasn't, but I might keep a close eye on him anyway.

The Wednesday racing at Worcester was quiet compared with the previous evening at Towcester. There were not really enough runners in each race and, in spite of the closeness of the racecourse to the city centre, not that many punters had actually turned up. Those who had seemed to have little cash with them to gamble and, overall, it was not very a very profitable afternoon for us and hardly covered the cost of the petrol to get there.

One of the plus points, however, had been Duggie. He had gradually opened up as the day progressed and had clearly enjoyed himself. The more responsibility I gave him to pay out the winning tickets, the more confident I became in his ability.

'Where are we on Monday?' I asked Luca as we packed up after the last.

'Nowhere,' he said. 'It's a day off.'

'Not any more,' I said. 'We're going to Bangor-on-Dee.'

'That's a long way for a small meeting.'

'Nevertheless, we're going,' I said. 'I've looked at the race entries. Tell Larry Porter he's going too. And tell him to bring the box of tricks.'

Luca stopped loading the trolley, stood up and looked at me.

'Right,' he said, smiling. 'I will.'

'And Luca,' I said. 'I need you to do something for me on Friday.'

'We're at Warwick on Friday,' he said.

'Not any more we're not,' I said. 'Friday is now a day off from racing. I want you to go and see some of your electronic club delinquents, the trustworthy ones, Duggie's friends. I need their help.'

I explained fully what I wanted him to do and his enthusiasm level went off the scale. I didn't mention to him, however, that I'd be spending Friday afternoon at my father's funeral in Slough Crematorium.

'Duggie here will help you,' I said as we loaded the equipment into the back of the Volvo. 'He seems to know them pretty well.'

Duggie smiled. 'Does that mean I've got the job?' he asked.

'You're on probation,' I said. 'Until Monday.'

He looked at me uncertainly.

'Not that sort of probation,' I said with a laugh.

We discussed our plans as I drove back round the M42 in the rush-hour traffic, and then on to my house in Kenilworth.

'Warwick tomorrow evening, then?' said Luca.

'Definitely,' I said. 'Do you want to come here first or go straight there?'

'We'll come here first,' Luca replied. 'First race is at six thirty. Here at five?'

'Five will be fine,' I said.

'I hope your wife will be all right, Mr Talbot,' Duggie said as he climbed into Luca's car.

'Thank you, Duggie,' I said.

He would do well, I thought.

You could have cut the air in the house with a knife, such was the tension between the sisters. The truce, it seemed, was over.

Sophie met me in the hallway tight-lipped, with angry-looking eyes. She nodded her head in the direction of the stairs at the same time as looking up. I understood immediately that she wanted me to go up. So I did. And she followed.

Safely in the privacy of our bedroom, she explained the problem, not that I couldn't have guessed.

'My bloody father,' she said explosively. 'Why can't he be more reasonable?'

It was a rhetorical question. I'd been asking myself the same thing since the day I'd first met him.

'What's he done now, my darling?' I said in my most calming of voices.

'Oh, nothing,' she said in frustration.

Whatever he'd said was obviously about me, and she'd suddenly decided against telling me, probably to avoid hurting my feelings.

'Come and sit down, my love,' I said, sitting on the side of the bed and patting the space next to me. She came over and sat down. I put my arm round her shoulders. 'Tell me,' I said.

'My father can be such a fool,' she said. She started to cry.

'Hey, come on,' I said, stroking her hair. 'Whatever he said can't be that bad.' She said nothing. So I went on. 'He probably told you that it was me who was the cause of all your problems and you'd be much better off leaving me to come home to live with him and your mother.'

She sat up straight and looked at me. 'How did you know?' she asked.

'Because it's what he always says. Ignore him. He's wrong.'

'I know he's wrong,' she said. 'I told him so. In fact, I told him that it was him who was the cause of my problems, not you.'

'I bet he didn't like that,' I said with a laugh.

'No,' she said, also laughing, 'he didn't.' She wiped her eyes with a tissue from the bedside table. 'He said that he'd cut me out of his will if I didn't "see sense", as he put it.'

'I suppose seeing sense meant divorcing a bookmaker,' I said.

'Yes,' she replied, half laughing and half crying. 'I told him he could stuff his will up his arse for all I cared.'

'Good girl,' I said, giving her a hug.

'Then bloody Alice puts her two-pennyworth in.' Sophie became angry. 'Starts bloody agreeing with the old fool. I gave her what for, I can tell you.'

'I thought Alice liked me?' I said.

'I think she does,' Sophie said. 'But she's so frightened of the old tyrant, she won't say anything against him.'

So much for Alice having steel-toecapped boots to kick him with, I thought. More like fluffy pink slippers.

'So now you're having a row with Alice as well?' I asked.

'It seems like it,' she said.

'I presume she's still here?'

'Down in the kitchen,' she replied. 'But she said she's going home just as soon as you got back.'

'Do you want her to?' I said.

'Yes,' she said. 'No.' She paused. 'I don't know what I want.'

'Let's go down and Alice and I can have a glass of wine,' I said. 'Everything always looks better after a glass of wine.'

'I'll have a small one too,' Sophie said.

'Great.'

We went downstairs and found Alice in the kitchen, as expected. And she was fuming.

She opened her mouth as if to say something.

'Don't,' I said quickly. 'Don't say anything you might later regret.'

She snapped her mouth shut.

'Good,' I said. 'Now let's all have a drink.'

I went over to the fridge and took out a bottle of white wine and poured three glasses. I then sat down at the kitchen table and, in turn, the two girls joined me.

'Good,' I said again. 'Now, we all know your father is an idiot.' Alice again opened her mouth to say something but I held up my hand to stop her. 'But he's not such an idiot that he can't set us all against one another.'

'But . . .' she started.

'Look,' I said, interrupting. 'You've probably both said some things today you shouldn't have. You both feel hurt. But it can stop here, right now, if you want it to. So have some wine and think for a minute.'

I lifted my glass in the manner of a toast, holding it aloft. Sophie picked up hers and did likewise. Slowly Alice did the same.

'Cheers,' I said. Alice and I drank a sizable mouthful, while Sophie took a small sip. 'Now,' I said, 'that's better. Are we friends again?'

Neither of the girls replied but both of them had another drink.

Finally, the tension was broken by Alice, who laughed.

'Have you ever thought about taking up diplomacy?' she said to me. 'I reckon you could make peace in the Middle East.'

'No chance,' I said. 'The Arabs don't drink.'

The three of us sat at the table giggling uncontrollably at my tasteless joke.

Peace, it seemed, had been re-established for the moment in Station Road, even if not quite in the Gaza Strip. I was glad. I really didn't want Alice going home before Monday.

CHAPTER 20

At three o'clock on Friday afternoon I sat alone in the chapel of Slough Crematorium as my father's bare coffin was carried past me by four men from the undertakers and placed on the curtain-skirted catafalque at the front.

A clergyman in a white surplice over a black cassock came in and stood behind the lectern.

'Are you the son?' he asked.

'Yes,' I replied.

'Are we waiting for anyone else?'

'No,' I said.

'Do you wish to say anything at any point?' he asked me.

'No,' I said again.

'Right, then. We'll get started.'

The door at the back of the chapel opened with a squeak. I turned round. Sergeant Murray came in and sat down two pews behind me. I nodded to him and he responded in the same manner. I turned back to the minister, who then began.

'I am the resurrection and the life, saith the Lord; he that believeth in me, though he were dead, yet shall he live; and whosoever liveth and believeth in me shall never die . . .'

The clergyman droned on, rushing through the funeral rite as laid down in the Book of Common Prayer.

I didn't really listen to the words.

Instead, I sat and stared at the simple wooden coffin and tried hard to remember what the man inside it looked like. I had seen him alive only briefly, for hardly more than an hour, yet his reappearance had dominated my life for the past two and a half weeks, in a way it hadn't done for the previous thirty-seven years.

It was difficult to describe my full feelings, but anger was uppermost amongst them. Anger that he had now gone for ever, and anger that he had been here at all.

Undeniably, he was my father. The DNA had proved that. But it didn't feel like he had anything to do with me. But he, and his actions, had certainly been integral to the direction of my life, to who I was and to what I would become.

I wished I'd had longer to talk with him on the day he'd died, and the time to talk to him again, even if it was to rant and rave at his conduct, or to gather answers to so many unanswered questions: Why did he kill my mother? Why did he run away? Why didn't he take me with him? How could he have deserted me for so long? And, in particular, why did he come back?

I thought about his daughters, my sisters, so far away in Australia, who probably didn't even know their father was dead. Should I say a prayer on their behalf?

The minister was nearing the end.

'In sure and certain hope of the resurrection to eternal life through our Lord Jesus Christ, we commend to Almighty God our brother Peter, and we commit his body to the elements, earth to earth, ashes to ashes, dust to dust. The Lord bless him, and keep him, and give him eternal peace. Amen.'

As he was saying the last few words, the minister pushed a button on the lectern and I watched intently as my father's coffin slowly disappeared from sight behind long red curtains that closed silently around it.

The whole funeral had taken precisely nine minutes. The cremation would take a little longer. And then that would be that. My father's earthly body would exist no more.

If only his influence could be so easily and quickly eliminated.

'Lovely service,' I said to the minister on my way out. 'Thank you.'

'My pleasure,' he said, shaking my hand.

Everyone always says it's been a lovely service at a funeral, I thought, even if it hadn't. It was neither the time nor the place to criticize, however bad things had been. In this case, the service had been functional. And that was enough.

'Thank you for coming,' I said to Sergeant Murray as we stood together outside afterwards.

'Chief Inspector Llewellyn apologizes for not being here himself,' he said.

'I hadn't expected him to come,' I said. I hadn't, in fact, expected anyone to be here, and especially not the chief inspector, and not least because I hadn't told a soul about the arrangements.

'The coroner's office let us know,' he said. I nodded. 'The police always try to go to murder victims' funerals if we can.'

'Just in case the killer turns up?' I asked.

'It has been known,' he said, smiling.

'No chance today,' I said. 'Not without being noticed, anyway.'

'No,' he said with a nervous laugh. 'Not much of a crowd to hide amongst at this one.'

'How are things on the detective front?' I said. 'Any suspects yet?'

'Only you,' he said, but he said it with another smile. 'My chief really doesn't like you, does he?'

'Don't worry about it,' I said. 'The feeling's mutual.'

'Yeah, I've noticed.'

'Has my e-fit been of any use?' I asked.

'Yes, as a matter of fact, it has,' he said. 'It's been shown to some of the other witnesses and they now generally tend to agree with you. So yours has now taken on the mantle as being the most accurate.'

I was pretty sure that shifty-eyed Kipper wouldn't have been best pleased by that.

'But I haven't seen it reproduced in any of the newspapers,' I said. 'Or on the television.'

'It's been in the *Bracknell and Ascot Times*, and in the *Windsor and Eton Express*,' he said. 'But no one has yet come forward to say they recognize him.'

'Perhaps it would have been better to have put it in the Melbourne papers,' I said. 'Or at least in the *Racing Post*.'

'Now that's a thought,' he said. 'Maybe I'll go and recommend it to the chief inspector.'

And, with that, the sergeant made his excuses and departed.

That just left me and the undertaker, who had been hovering to one side.

'Was everything in order, Mr Talbot?' he asked.

'Yes, thank you,' I said. 'It was fine.'

'Good,' he said. 'And what would you like done with the ashes?'

'What are the choices?' I asked.

'You can have them, if you want,' he said. 'They will be ready for collection tomorrow. We can collect them for you and hold them at our offices for you, if you like. We'll be coming here anyway. Funerals take place on Saturdays.'

'What's the alternative?' I asked.

'They can be scattered here, in the garden of remembrance, if you would prefer,' he said. 'That way you wouldn't need to provide for a container.'

'Container?' I asked.

'If you wanted to take the ashes away, you would have to provide or pay for a container. Perhaps a box, or an urn.'

'Oh,' I said. 'No. Just have them scattered here, then. I don't want them.'

'Right,' he said. 'That will be all, then. I'll send you an itemized receipt in due course.'

'Thank you,' I said. 'That will be fine.'

He nodded to me, it was almost a bow, and then he walked quickly across to his car and drove away. I wondered if undertakers laughed more at home than other people to make up for the solemnness of their work, or whether they are so conditioned to having a sad disposition that they have difficulty letting their hair down.

I was left standing alone in the crematorium car park with that strange feeling of having mislaid something but I wasn't quite sure what, like when you leave a shopping bag on the counter and get half-way home before realizing it.

Perhaps it was a childhood that I'd mislaid, with loving parents, family holidays and happy Christmases. But was it *my* childhood that I'd lost, or those of my non-existent children? I stood next to my car and wept.

A few early arrivals for the next funeral spilled out of their cars and made their sombre way over towards the chapel. None of them bothered me. Weeping in a crematorium car park was not only acceptable, it was expected.

Early on Saturday morning I went to see my grandmother. I told myself it had nothing to do with having been to my father's funeral the day before but, of course, it did. I desperately wanted to ask her some more questions.

Sophie had come to the front door to see me off, still in her dressing gown and slippers. As far as she was concerned I'd spent the previous afternoon at Warwick races. I would tell her the truth, I thought, eventually.

'Give her my love,' she'd said as I'd left.

'I will,' I had replied, but both of us knew that my grandmother almost certainly wouldn't remember who Sophie was. She might not even remember who I was either, but I was going early in the day to give her the best chance. My grandmother was at her most lucid when she was not tired and, very occasionally, she would actually telephone me around seven in the morning and sound almost normal. But each day varied, and the good days were getting fewer, shorter and less frequent. It was an ever-steepening downhill run towards full-blown dementia, with just occasional small plateaus of normality to break the journey. Part of me hoped that she wouldn't survive long enough to reach rock bottom.

'Hello, Nanna,' I said, going into her room.

She was sitting in her armchair looking out of the window and she turned towards me. I went over and gave her a kiss on the cheek.

'Hello, Ned,' she said. 'How lovely.'

Today was clearly a good day. She looked very smart in a dark skirt, a white blouse with a line of small yellow and pink embroidered flowers down the centre, and a lavender-coloured cardigan over it, open at the front. And she'd had her hair done since my last visit.

'You look beautiful,' I said, meaning it.

She smiled at me, full of understanding. How I wished it could last for ever.

I sat on the end of her bed next to her chair.

'How have you been?' I asked. 'I like your hair.'

'I'm fine,' she said. 'Julie will be here soon.'

'Who is Julie?' I asked.

'Julie,' she repeated. 'She'll be here soon.'

I decided not to ask again.

'Sophie sends her love,' I said. A small quizzical expression came into her eyes. 'You remember Sophie. She's my wife.'

'Oh, yes,' she said, but I wasn't sure she really knew.

There was a knock on the door and one of the nursing home staff put her head into the room. 'Everything OK?' she asked.

'Fine,' I said.

'Would you like some tea or coffee?'

'Coffee would be lovely,' I said. I turned to my grandmother. 'Nanna, would you like some coffee, or tea?'

'I don't drink tea,' she said.

'I'll bring her some anyway,' said the staff member with a smile. 'She always says she doesn't drink tea but she must have at least six or seven cups a day. Milk and sugar?'

'Yes, please,' I said. 'One sugar.'

The head withdrew and the door closed.

'I like Julie,' my grandmother said again.

'Was that Julie?' I asked, but Nanna didn't answer. She was looking again out of the window. I took her hand in mine and stroked it.

We sat silently for a while until the woman came back in with a tray and two cups.

'Are you Julie?' I asked her.

'No,' she said. 'I'm Laura. But we do have a Julie here and your grandmother calls all of us Julie. We don't mind. I'll answer to anything.' She laughed. 'Here you are, Mrs Talbot,' Laura said, putting the tray down on a table beside her armchair.

It was comforting for me to know that there were such caring people looking after my Nanna.

'Thank you,' I said.

'Just pull the alarm if you need anything,' Laura said, pointing at a red cord that hung down the wall alongside my grand-mother's bed. 'She should be all right for a while, but call if she needs the loo or anything. She can sometimes get quite urgent.'

'Thank you,' I said again. 'I will.'

I sat patiently drinking my coffee as my grandmother's tea slowly cooled.

'Here, Nanna,' I said, giving her the cup. 'Don't forget your tea.'

'I don't drink tea,' she said, but she still took the china cup in her thin, bony hands and drank from it. The tea was soon all gone, so I took the empty cup from her and put it back on the tray.

'Nanna,' I said. She went on looking out of the window. 'Nanna,' I repeated a little louder while also pulling on her arm. She slowly turned to face me.

'Nanna, can you tell me about my parents? Can you tell me about Peter and Tricia?' It didn't seem odd for me to call my parents by their names rather than as Mummy and Daddy. I'd never had a mummy and daddy, only a nanna and grandpa.

She looked up at my face but the sharpness of fifteen minutes previously had begun to fade. I feared I had missed my chance and that I was losing her. At the best of times, what I was asking would not have been easy for either of us. In her present state it might be impossible.

'Nanna,' I said again with some urgency, 'tell me about Peter and Tricia.'

'Peter and Tricia?' she said, some of the sharpness returning.

'Yes, Nanna. Peter, your son, and Tricia, his wife.'

'Such a dreadful thing,' she said, turning away from me and again looking out of the window.

'What was a dreadful thing?'

'What he did to her,' she said.

'What did he do to her?' I asked, pulling gently on her hand to keep her attention. She turned back slightly towards me.

'He killed her,' she said slowly. 'He murdered her.'

'Tricia?' I asked.

'Yes,' she said. She looked back up at my face. 'He murdered Tricia.'

'But why?' I asked. 'Why did he murder Tricia?'

'Because of the baby,' she said.

'What about the baby?' I pressed her. 'Why did he murder her because of the baby?' I wondered if he had killed her because the baby wasn't his.

My grandmother stared into my eyes. 'He killed the baby, too,' she said.

'Yes,' I said. 'Whose baby was it?'

'Tricia's baby,' she said.

'But was Peter the father?'

'Peter ran away,' she said.

'Yes, I know,' I said. 'Peter ran away because he killed Tricia. But was Peter the father of her baby?'

That quizzical look appeared again in her eyes.

'It wasn't Peter,' she said slowly. 'It was Teddy who murdered Tricia.'

I sat there staring at her, thinking that she must be confused.

'No,' I said. 'Surely it was Peter who murdered Tricia? That's why he ran away.'

'It was Teddy who murdered Tricia.' She said it again quite clearly. There was no confusion.

I sat there stunned. So it was not my father but my grand-father who was the murderer.

'But why?' I asked pitifully.

'Because of the baby,' she said, equally clearly. 'Your grand-father was the baby's father.'

Oh my God, I thought. My mother's unborn female child, who would have been my little sister, would also have been my aunt.

I stayed with my grandmother for another hour, trying to piece together the whole sorry story. Trying to pull accurate details out of her fuzzy memory was like trying to solve a Rubik's cube while blindfolded. Not only could I not see the puzzle, I didn't know when, or if, I'd solved it.

But, now that she had started to give up the secret that had burned within her for so long, she did so with a clarity of mind that I didn't realize she still possessed. I knew it was true that some patients with even advanced dementia could recall events of long ago, in spite of the total loss of their more recent memory, and also their inability to function properly day by day. So it was with my grandmother that morning, as the awful knowledge poured from her, almost in relief of at last being able to share her hitherto private horror. I learned more in that one hour about my parents and my early life than I had managed to extract from her at any time in the previous thirty-seven years. And I didn't like it.

I discovered that the five of us had lived together in my grandparents' house in Surrey, my mother having moved in there on the day of her marriage. It wasn't something that I had thought about before but, clearly, my grandmother hadn't considered the arrangement at all unusual.

However, if what Nanna told me was right, and if I correctly read between the lines of what she said, severe tensions had existed between my mother and father throughout their short marriage. There had also been considerable friction between my parents and my grandparents. It had obviously not been a happy family home.

I found out that it hadn't only been my mother and father who were staying in Paignton at the time of Tricia's death. Both my grandparents had been with them, and I had been there as well. It seemed that the holiday in Devon had been my father's idea, an attempt to make things better between them all, but it had actually made them much worse.

'Peter and Tricia argued all the time,' my grandmother said, placing her head to one side and closing her eyes. 'On and on they went. They physically fought more than once. Peter slapped her, and she scratched his face.'

Hence the traces of my father's skin and DNA under Tricia's fingernails, I thought. The DNA the police had found, and had wrongly believed was her killer's.

305

'Then she told him that her baby wasn't his,' Nanna said. 'She told him that it was your grandfather's baby. He went completely wild.'

'Peter went wild?' I asked.

'Yes,' she replied. 'But Teddy went wild as well because she threatened to tell everyone and to get it in the newspapers. She said he would lose his bookmaker's licence.'

I wasn't sure if that was actually true, but it would have been enough to frighten my grandfather.

'But was the baby Tricia was carrying really Grandpa's child?' I asked her.

'Yes,' she said, opening her eyes and looking at me again. 'I believe it was.'

'But are you certain?' I pressed her.

'Yes,' she said. 'I had suspected it even before she said anything. I'd been telling Teddy over and over for months that we would be better off without her around, but he wouldn't have it. He thought he was in love with her. Then, the morning after Tricia tells us that he's the father of the baby, he walks into the hotel where we were staying and tells me it's finished between them. Then he calmly tells me that he's strangled the little bitch.'

I stared at her, almost in disbelief.

'But why did my father run away if he hadn't killed her?'

'Because I told him to,' she said, quite matter-of-factly, as if it was the most common of things to do.

'But why?' I asked her.

'So that Teddy wouldn't get arrested for murder.'

'But why didn't you go to the police?'

'Because then we would have been ruined,' she said, as if it was obvious. 'What would I have lived on with your grandfather in jail?'

The faithful, practical, scheming wife, I thought. She had not only seen no need to go to the police and repeat what her husband had said about strangling his daughter-in-law, she had even sent away her only son in the full knowledge that he would be blamed for the killing, simply to protect her income.

Perhaps strangling the 'little bitch' had been her idea, too. Was that what she had meant Teddy to do by continually saying they would be better off without her around? Had my grandfather finally got the message?

And my father had gone to the other side of the world, banished for ever by his domineering mother in order to save her tyrannical husband from justice. No wonder he hadn't asked after her when he had spoken to me at Ascot.

'How about me?' I said with passion. 'Why didn't my father take me with him?'

'He wanted to,' she said. 'But I told him he couldn't. I said that I would look after the child. He tried to say that he would come back for you but I told him to go and start somewhere else, and forget that you ever existed. It was for the best.'

'Not for me,' I said with barely contained fury.

'Oh, yes. It was the best for all of us.' She said it with unshakeable conviction. 'And I decided that it was definitely the best for me.'

It was like a knife to my heart. How could this woman have sent my father out of my life like that? He had done nothing to deserve it. And how could she have then kept silent about it for so long? Just because she thought it was the best for her.

I had sat in the chapel of Slough Crematorium only the previous afternoon with my head bursting with anger. Now, I felt totally bereft. I had been cheated of my right to grieve properly for my father, and I further believed that I had been cheated out of my rightful life.

I stood up. I didn't want to hear any more. I looked down at her, this frail demented eighty-year-old woman whose decisions had destroyed so much.

She, and my grandfather, had together raised me from babyhood into adult life in a stable home, even if it had not been a particularly happy one for me. I had loved them, trusted them and believed what they had told me as being the truth, only for it now to emerge as a tangled web of lies and deception.

I walked to the door without turning back, and I went away.

I would never visit her again.

CHAPTER 21

I went straight from the nursing home to Leicester racecourse but, afterwards, I couldn't recall a single moment of the journey. My mind had been too preoccupied trying to come to terms with what I'd been told.

As I had so hoped, I was, after all, not the son of a murderer. But I was the grandson of one. I had stood alongside my grandfather on racecourses for all those years as his assistant, unaware of the dreadful secret he and my grandmother had concealed. Far from being the ones who had stepped in and cared for me in my time of need, they had been the very architects of my misery.

Automatically, as if on autopilot, I parked the Volvo and began to unload the equipment. I pulled out our odds board with TRUST TEDDY TALBOT emblazoned across the top. I stopped unloading and looked at it. I would have laughed if I didn't feel so much like crying. Trust Teddy Talbot to ruin your life.

Luca and Duggie were waiting for me as I pulled the equipment trolley into the betting ring.

'How did you get on yesterday?' I asked. 'With the delinquents?'

'Great,' said Luca. 'We're all set.'

'Do you think they will do it right?' I asked.

'Should do,' said Duggie. 'And they're not all delinquents.'

I smiled at him. I suppose I was pleased that he was standing up for his friends.

'And besides,' he said. 'I told them you were a mean bastard and would come looking for them in the night if they spent your money on drugs.'

I stared at him and he simply smiled back at me. I couldn't tell if he was kidding or not.

'Good,' I said finally. 'Let's hope the horses are not all withdrawn at the overnight declarations stage.'

'How about you?' Luca asked as we set up our pitch. 'Did you have a good day?'

'No,' I said without clarification.

'Not Sophie?' he asked with concern.

'No,' I said. 'Sophie's doing well. I was just dealing with some other family business. Don't worry about it.'

He looked at me with questioning eyes but I ignored him.

'I've decided that we are going to change our name,' I announced. 'From today, we shall be known as Talbot and Mandini.'

I smiled at Luca, and he smiled back.

'But we haven't done the partnership papers yet,' he said.

'I don't care,' I said. 'If you're still up for it, then so am I.'

'Sure,' he said with real pleasure showing on his face.

'How about Talbot, Mandini and Masters?' said Duggie, joining in the fun.

'Don't push your luck, young Douglas,' I said. 'You're still on probation, remember.'

'Only until Monday,' he said with a pained expression.

'That will be up to me,' I said. 'And to Luca,' I added quickly, remembering my new position as partner rather than sole owner.

'Can we just change our name without telling anyone?' Luca asked.

'I don't know,' I said. 'I'll find out. But the name Teddy Talbot is coming off our sign as from today.'

I hadn't realized the forcefulness with which I had spoken until Luca stood stock still, looking at me.

'My,' he said. 'That must have been some mighty emotive family business you were dealing with yesterday.'

I glared at him. I was not in the mood for explanations, so the three of us continued to set up in silence.

'I'd never been to the races before last Wednesday,' said Duggie when we had finished. 'It's wicked.'

'I'm glad you enjoy it,' I said, assuming that was what he meant.

'It all seems smaller than on the telly,' he said. 'You know, the horses seem smaller and everything's so much closer together.'

'But you've only been to the smaller meetings,' Luca said. 'It's not like this at Ascot or Cheltenham.'

'But the horses can't be any bigger,' Duggie said.

'No,' I said. 'But there are lots and lots more people.'

'When do we go there, then?' he said eagerly.

'Soon,' I said. 'But concentrate on today first.'

Leicester was a long, thin, undulating track with the public enclosures squeezed together at one end. As with many racecourses, the space in the centre doubled as a golf course. I had occasionally played a round of golf and these holes would have suited me well, I thought, as there were no large trees to get stuck behind. Large trees would have spoiled the view of the racing.

The betting ring was in front of the glass-fronted grandstand and there were several other bookies also setting up before the first race.

'Where's Larry?' I asked Luca, noting his absence from the neighbouring pitch.

'Nottingham,' he said.

'But he is all set for Monday?'

'Sure is,' said Luca with a grin. 'Norman Joyner's coming too.'

'Good,' I said. 'Do they know?'

'They think it's the same as last time, at Ascot,' he said.

'Good,' I said. 'It will be, as far as they are concerned.'

The Saturday crowd was beginning to build with cars queuing for the popular car-park-and-picnic enclosure alongside the running rail. Even the weather had cooperated with blue skies and only the occasional puffy white cloud. A glorious English summer's day at the races. What could be better than this?

I suppose six losing short-priced favourites would be good.

Just as I was starting to relax from my earlier anxiety, and was actually beginning to enjoy the day, my two non-friends from Kempton and Towcester turned up and stood in front of me. Once more, they were wearing their 'uniform' of short-sleeved white shirts and black trousers, plus the work boots. I was on my platform at the time, which gave me a height advantage, for a change. It also gave me some courage.

'I thought I told you boys to bugger off,' I said down to them.

'Our boss wants to talk to you,' said the spokesman of the two.

'Well, I don't want to talk to him,' I said. 'So, go away.'

I felt reasonably confident that they wouldn't start a physical assault just here, not with hundreds of witnesses about.

'He wants to make you an offer,' said the spokesman.

'Which part of "go away" didn't you understand?' I said to him.

They didn't move an inch but stood full square in front of me. It wasn't very good for my business.

'He wants to buy you out.' It was like a stuck record.

'Tell him to come and see me himself if he wants to talk,' I said, 'rather than sending a pair of his goons.'

Thoughts of poking hornets' nests with sticks floated into my head. And I'd been the one to warn Larry against doing it.

'You are to come with us,' the man said.

'You must be joking,' I said, almost with a laugh. 'I'm not going anywhere with you two. Now move out the bloody way. I've got a bookmaking business to run.'

They didn't move.

Luca and Duggie came and stood on the platform on either side of me and a staring match ensued, us three against them two. It was like a prelude to a gunfight at the OK Corral. But who was going to go for their guns first?

'Sod off,' said Duggie suddenly, breaking the silence. 'Why don't you two arseholes go and play with your balls somewhere else.'

They both turned their full attention to him, this young slip of a lad, who I still thought looked only about fourteen years old.

The talkative arsehole opened his mouth as if to say something.

'Save it,' said Duggie, beating him to the draw. 'Now, piss off.'

There was something about the boy's assured confidence in the face of physical threat that had even me a little scared. The two men in front of me definitely wavered.

'We'll be back,' the talkative one said.

But Duggie wasn't finished with them. 'The man here told you he wasn't coming with you to see your boss, so go away now, and stay away.' He sounded so reasonable. 'Go on, scram, and you can tell your boss it's no deal.'

The men looked at him like two big sheep under the gaze of a tiny Border collie puppy and then, slowly, they moved to the side and walked away.

Both Luca and I watched them go out of sight round the grandstand and then we turned to Duggie in astonishment. He was smiling.

'All brawn and no brain,' he said. 'Guys like them need orders to follow. Can't think for themselves.'

If I hadn't seen it myself, I wouldn't have believed it.

'My God, Duggie,' I said. 'You were brilliant. Where on earth did you learn to do that?'

'The streets of High Wycombe are not so friendly as some people would like to think,' he said. 'Friday and Saturday nights can be rough, I can tell you, bloody rough.'

'I think he just completed his probation,' Luca said.

'Damn right he did,' I said. 'Welcome to the firm.'

Duggie beamed. 'Just so long as you don't sell out to those guys.'

'No chance.' Luca and I said it together.

*

The rest of the day was tame by comparison to what had gone before. The six favourites didn't all lose but, nevertheless, our afternoon was both profitable and enjoyable, with Duggie warming to his new-found permanent status.

He was a natural showman with a quick wit and, as his confidence grew, he was a great success with the punters. He hardly stopped talking and bantering with them all afternoon. There was no doubt in my mind that we did far more business because of it. Some of our neighbouring bookies weren't too pleased, however, especially when Duggie would shout across at their potential customers that they could get a better deal from us, even if they couldn't.

But our neighbours were not our friends, they were our competition. In a way, I was quite pleased that Larry Porter had been at Nottingham. I didn't want to antagonize him before Monday. I needed his unwitting cooperation.

The two goons didn't reappear at our pitch but I was worried they might be waiting for us outside the racecourse gates, or in the car park, where there would be fewer witnesses for them to worry about. I didn't exactly relish another of their 'messages' being applied to my solar plexus.

'Where are you parked?' I asked Luca as we packed the equipment onto our trolley.

'Across the road in the free car park,' he said.

'Good, so am I. Let's keep together when we go, just in case we find we have unwelcome company.'

'Too bloody right,' he said.

'Wait for me, then,' said Duggie. 'I'm just going for a pee.'

He ran off towards the Gents, leaving Luca and me standing beside the trolley.

'Any movement on the Sister Millie front?' I asked, unable to contain my curiosity any longer.

He smiled broadly. 'Negotiations are continuing,' he said. 'But, as yet, there has been no breakthrough. She wants to, but she thinks Betsy will murder her if she does. And she's probably right. But it certainly makes life interesting.'

'Just don't let her meet Duggie,' I said, 'or you'll have no chance.'

He pulled a face at me. 'Yes, all right, Grandpa,' he said. It was only meant as a joke but it brought back, in a wave, all that I had been trying to banish from my consciousness.

The tears welled in my eyes and I turned away from him, embarrassed by such a show of emotion.

'God,' he said. 'I'm sorry.'

'I'm fine,' I said, not feeling it, and also not turning back.

'Anything you want to talk about?'

'No,' I replied.

Duggie appeared from the Gents to save me from further inquisition.

'OK, then,' Duggie said cheerfully, 'let's go get 'em.'

I'm glad he's so keen, I thought. I would much rather let 'em go without us.

As it was, much to Duggie's obvious disappointment, my fears were unfounded. There was no sign of the goons outside the racecourse entrance and none in the car park either. Perhaps they had received further instruction from their mystery boss. However, I would still keep a wary eye open for a black BMW 4x4 on my way home.

I didn't believe that I had seen the last of them.

*

On Sunday, Luca and I had planned to be at Market Rasen races in Lincolnshire but we decided that, with the two goons still on the prowl, and with our plans for Monday, it was prudent to lie low for a day. To say nothing of shifty-eyed Kipper, who might still be lurking in some car park with his twelve-centimetre knife, looking for his missing money.

Anyway, it suited me to spend a day with Sophie, especially as Alice was departing back to her home in Surrey. Sadly, she was not going permanently, but just to do some washing and to gather some different clothes.

'How about your job?' I asked her over breakfast.

I knew that she had taken a week's holiday from her position as a local radio producer in Guildford, but her week was up.

'A few days more won't worry them,' she said.

I made no fuss, even though I didn't consider that her continued presence was really necessary. Maybe I could stand it for a few days more. But I was beginning to yearn for the time when Sophie had been in hospital, when I didn't have to make the bed every morning, or put my dirty coffee cup immediately in the dishwasher; when I could walk around the house in my underwear, and lie down flat on the sofa to watch football on the television; and when I could leave the seat up on the lavatory, and burp and fart whenever I wanted to. In five months, I had become quite used to living on my own.

It wasn't that I didn't want Sophie at home. Of course I did, and I loved it. I just wasn't so sure about her sister being here too. Alice was becoming not so much a domestic goddess, more of a domestic nightmare.

'How long is she coming back for?' I asked Sophie, as we waved Alice away.

'Just a little bit longer, I think,' she replied. 'Alice likes to feel that she's in charge, and she thinks I still need a little more of her care. To be honest, though, I would be quite happy if she didn't come back tonight.'

So would I, I thought. But Alice's presence had at least made me feel a little better as Sophie had not been alone in the house when I'd been at work. I think Sophie herself felt the same way, and she had not objected much when Alice had announced her intention to come back.

We closed the front door and went back into the kitchen.

'I can't believe I've been home a week already,' she said. 'It seems like only yesterday I left the hospital.'

I thought it felt like a month, but I didn't say so.

I went up to my office while Sophie pottered around in the kitchen, relishing being able to do things without Alice constantly offering help, and advice.

I logged onto the *Racing Post* website and checked the declarations for Bangor-on-Dee races for Monday. It was good news. The short-priced favourite in the two-mile hurdle race for maidens was still running. As were the others I wanted.

Sophie came into my office with a cup of coffee for me.

'Thank you, my darling,' I said.

She stood behind me, stroking my shoulders and playing with my hair.

'What are you doing?' she asked.

'Just checking the runners for tomorrow,' I said.

'Can I come with you to the races?' she said.

'Of course,' I said, pleased. 'We're going to Bangor tomorrow. It's quite a long way, but you can come if you like. We're at Southwell for the evening meeting on Tuesday, and then the July Festival at Newmarket on Wednesday, Thursday and Friday.'

'Are you staying in Newmarket?' she asked with slight concern.

'No chance,' I said. 'Not at the prices the hotels charge during July week. The bloodstock sales are on too, don't forget. The town is bursting with people. I'll come home each night.'

She was relieved. 'Good,' she said. 'Maybe I'll come to Southwell on Tuesday if the weather's nice. I find there are too many people at Newmarket.'

'That would be lovely,' I said, meaning it. I shut down my computer. 'Why don't we go out to lunch?'

'What, now?' she said.

'Yes. Right now.'

'Great idea.' She smiled.

We went to the pub in the village of Avon Dassett, where their speciality was sixty-four different ways to have a pie. Sophie and I, however, opted not to go for a pie but for the Sunday roast lamb, which was delicious.

After lunch I drove the few miles to the Burton Dassett Hills Country Park, where I stopped the car on a ridge with a view all the way to Coventry and beyond.

And there we sat in the car while I told Sophie about my father.

I had lain awake for much of the night going over and over in my mind the secrets I had gleaned from my grandmother, and weighing up whether I should tell Sophie anything just yet. It was true that she had been very well during her first week home from hospital and hadn't once accused me of drinking or being drunk, which, I knew from experience, was always the first sign that things weren't quite right.

I had watched her carefully every morning to check that she swallowed her medication, but I was also painfully aware of how easily in the past her behaviour had begun to change for the worse at times of stress or anxiety, and I desperately didn't want to cause her either of them unnecessarily.

However, there was a real need in me for her to know the truth. I realized that I was bottling up my pain, and my anger. I feared they would overwhelm me and cause an explosion in *my* head, the outcome of which in the long run might be more damaging both to Sophie and to me. I needed, perhaps selfishly, to share the knowledge in order to talk it through and ease the burden. Maybe I should have sought out one of the hospital psychiatrists to give *me* some therapy and treatment, but Sophie was the one I really wanted to provide me with the help I needed.

I started by telling her about my father's sudden appearance at Ascot and the shock of finding that he hadn't died in a car crash all those years ago as we had thought.

'That's great,' she said. 'You always wanted a father.'

But then I told her about him being stabbed in the racecourse car park, and about him dying at the hospital. She was upset and deeply saddened, mostly on my behalf.

'But why was he stabbed?' she asked.

'I think it was a robbery that went wrong,' I said.

I considered that it was still prudent not to mention anything about microcoders, false passports or blue-plastic-wrapped bundles of cash. Best also, I thought, not to refer to my father's black and red rucksack discovered by me in a seedy hotel in Paddington, and subsequently collected from our home by his murderer.

'But *you* could have been killed,' she said, clearly shocked.

'I would have given the thief the money,' I said. 'But my father told him to go to hell, and kicked him in the balls. I think that's why he was stabbed.'

She was a little reassured, but not much.

'But why didn't you tell me about it straight away?' she implored.

'I didn't want to upset you just before the assessment,' I said in my defence. And she could see the sense in that. 'But that's not all, my love. Far from it.'

I told her about my mother and the fact that she hadn't died in a car accident either. As gently as I could, I told her about Paignton pier and how my mother had been found murdered on the beach beneath it.

'Oh, Ned,' she said, choking back the tears.

'I was only a toddler,' I said, trying to comfort her. 'I have no memory of any of it. In fact, I don't remember a single thing about my mother.' And, of course, Sophie had never known her.

'How did you find out?' she asked.

'The police told me,' I said. 'They did a DNA check on my father. It seems that everyone at the time thought he'd been responsible, and that's why he ran away, and also why Nanna and Grandpa made up the story of the car crash.'

'How dreadful for them,' she said.

'Yes, but it wasn't actually that simple,' I said.

I went on to tell her about my mother's pregnancy and,

eventually and carefully, I told her the whole story about the baby being my grandfather's child and how it had been he who had strangled my mother to prevent anyone from finding out.

She went very silent for some time as I held her hand across the car handbrake.

'But why, then, did your father go away?' she asked finally.

'He was told to,' I said.

'Who by?'

Sophie had once loved my grandparents as if they had been her own. Now I laid bare the awful story that my grandmother, our darling Nanna, had orchestrated the whole affair. She certainly had been responsible for me having had no father to grow up with, and quite likely had been instrumental in my mother's demise as well.

Sophie just couldn't believe it.

'Are you absolutely sure?' she asked.

I nodded. 'I found out most of it yesterday,' I said. 'When I went to see her.'

'Did she tell you all this?' Sophie asked with a degree of scepticism.

'Yes,' I said.

'But how? She's losing her marbles. Most days she can't remember what she had for breakfast.'

'She was quite lucid when I spoke with her yesterday,' I said. 'Surprisingly so, in fact. She couldn't really remember who you were, but there was nothing much wrong with her memory of the events of thirty-six years ago.'

'Was she sorry?' Sophie asked.

'No, not really,' I said. 'I think that's what I found the hardest to bear.'

We sat together silently in the car for some while.

All around us were happy families: mums and dads with their children, running up and down the hills, chasing their dogs and flying their kites in the wind. All the things that normal people do on Sunday afternoons.

The horrors were only inside the car, and in our minds.

CHAPTER 22

On Monday morning, I picked up Luca and Duggie early from the Hilton Hotel car park at junction 15 on the M40 motorway and the three of us set off for Bangor-on-Dee races with happy hearts, but with mischief in mind.

The bruises on my abdomen, inflicted by fists and steel toe-caps at Kempton Park races, had finally begun to fade but the fire of revenge still burned bright in my belly. I had told Larry Porter that I would get even with the bastard who had ordered the beatings, and today was going to be my day.

'Did you check with Larry?' I said to Luca. 'Has he got the stuff?'

'Relax,' Luca said to me. 'Don't worry. Larry will be there in good time.'

'Did you speak to any of your friends?' I asked Duggie. 'To remind them.'

'All OK,' he replied. 'As Luca said, relax, everything is fine.'

I hoped he was right.

We arrived at the racecourse early and I parked in one of the free car parks. I went to pay the fee at the bookmaker's badge entrance while Luca and Duggie unloaded the equipment and pulled it through to the betting ring.

'Where's the bloody grandstand?' said Duggie, looking round.

I laughed. 'There isn't one.'

'You're having me on,' he said.

'No,' I said. 'There really isn't a grandstand at Bangor.'

'How do the punters see the racing, then?' he asked.

'It's a natural grandstand,' I said. 'The people stand on the hill to watch the racing.' The ground fell away down towards the track, giving ample room for a good view of the horses.

'I've seen it all now,' he said.

'No, you haven't,' I said. 'In southern Spain they race along a beach with the crowd wearing swimming trunks and sitting under sun umbrellas. It's proper racing with starting stalls, betting, the lot. It even gets TV coverage.'

'And, in St Moritz, in Switzerland,' Luca said, 'every year they race on a frozen lake. I've seen it. It's amazing. But there are no swimming trunks, though, more like fur coats; it's midwinter.'

'They race on snow in Russia, too,' I said. 'And back in the eighteen hundreds they used to have racing right along the frozen Moscow River – actually on the ice.'

'Then why do they cancel racing here whenever it snows?' Duggie asked.

'Good question,' I said. 'Obviously the wrong kind of snow.'

We giggled. But it was nervous laughter.

We set up our pitch and Luca commented favourably on the new name on our board. I had spent the previous evening painting over the TRUST TEDDY TALBOT slogan and had replaced it with, it had to be said, some pretty poorly painted white letters saying simply TALBOT AND MANDINI.

'I'll have to change the wording on our tickets as well,' Luca said. 'I'll do it now.'

He set to work while I went to the Gents. The nerves were clearly beginning to get to me.

'There's a public pay-phone on the wall round there,' I said when I went back. I pointed down the side of the building between the seafood bar and the gentlemen's lavatories.

'I'll have to be making a call to my granny, then, at the appropriate time,' said Luca, smiling.

'No way,' I said. 'I'll need you here, on the pitch.'

'What's the problem?' Duggie said.

'I don't want anyone being able to use the public pay-phone when the mobiles stop working,' I said.

'That's easy,' said Duggie. 'I'll go and fix it.' And off he went before I had a chance to stop him.

He was back in a couple of minutes.

'All done,' he said. 'No one's going to use that phone today.'

Luca and I looked at each other.

'What did you do?' I asked Duggie.

'What do you think?' he said. 'I broke it. Then I went into the office and complained that the phone wouldn't work. They've put an OUT OF ORDER sign on it now.'

I laughed. 'Well done.'

'Yeah,' he said. 'But they offered me the use of the secretary's phone instead, if it were urgent, like.'

'Ah,' I said. I didn't want anyone using the secretary's phone either.

'It's simple,' said Duggie. 'I got the secretary's phone number, so I get a mate to call it at the right time and then not hang up.

It will tie up the line so no one can call in or out on it. In fact I'll get a few of my mates to all call, just in case they have more than one line on that number. That'll tie them all up.'

'But won't your mates' numbers show up on caller ID?' I said. 'I don't want them traced.'

'So I'll get my mates to withhold their numbers, or they can call from the phone boxes in Wycombe,' he said. 'It's dead easy.'

'OK,' I said. 'Fix it.'

Larry Porter arrived and began to set up his pitch alongside ours.

'Have you got the equipment?' I asked him.

'Yes. All set,' Larry said. 'Bill's coming separately, later.'

Bill, I assumed, was the man I had seen at Ascot in the white shirt and fawn chinos who had placed the 'two monkeys' bet with me when the internet and phones had gone down just before the Gold Cup.

The maiden hurdle was the fifth race of the afternoon and I became more and more nervous as the clock ticked round to four thirty, race time. Monday afternoon racing anywhere was always quiet and today was no exception. But the lack of activity in the betting ring did nothing to help settle the butterflies in my stomach.

In all, the bookmaker turnout was reasonable. I counted sixteen of us in the main betting ring and there were a few others over near the course, all of us chasing the meagre pickings from the sparse Monday crowd. But, other than Larry and Norman, I didn't recognize any of the other bookies as we were at the northern extent of our usual patch, and I wouldn't normally be standing at Bangor.

At long last, it was nearing the maiden hurdle race time.

The horses were in the saddling boxes and the punters were beginning to make their selections. There were nineteen runners, with Pool House the fairly short-priced favourite at six-to-four. The horse had raced three times previously and finished second on the last two occasions. And today it was being ridden by the many-times champion jockey who had made the journey from Lambourn especially to ride this one horse, so he, for one, expected it to win. And all the newspapers agreed with him.

With the horses in the parade ring, and with precisely six minutes to go before the scheduled start time, I nodded imperceptibly to Larry, who pushed his out-of-sight switch to turn on the phone jammer. At the same time I nudged Luca, who activated his virus on the racecourse internet server, effectively putting it out of action and isolating the racecourse from the outside world.

I thought of the thirty juvenile delinquents and hoped that they were all poised to place their bets.

A man in a white shirt and fawn chinos suddenly appeared in front of me. Bill, I assumed.

'Grand on number four,' he said, thrusting a wad of banknotes towards me.

Number four was the second favourite.

'Grand on number four at three-to-one,' I said loudly over my shoulder.

'Offer at eleven-to-four,' Luca said equally loudly.

'OK,' said the man. I gave him the TALBOT AND MANDINI printed ticket and the price changed on our board.

'Give me a monkey on four at threes,' Luca bellowed at Larry Porter.

'You can have it at five-to-two,' Larry shouted back.

'OK,' said Luca, who then turned the other way towards Norman Joyner. 'Give me a monkey on number four,' he shouted even louder.

'Fine,' shouted Norman back. 'At nine-to-four.'

Within less than a minute the price of horse number four was tumbling all over the betting ring and, as a result, the price of Pool House, the favourite, was tending to drift longer.

The panic from the boys from the big outfits wasn't as dramatic as it had been at Ascot but it was fairly impressive, nonetheless. They rushed around trying desperately to get their phones to work, but without success. I saw one of them rush off to use the pay-phone but he was soon back with a frustrated look on his face.

But they had all clearly been well briefed after the incident at Ascot. They clearly knew that the price of the hot favourite had, on that occasion, lengthened during the time when the internet and phones were down. They would also know that, when the favourite then won, they all got hit badly because all the bets in the high street betting shops were paid out on the starting price, and that had been artificially made too high.

Consequently, the big-firm boys, those with the cash in their pockets, now took it upon themselves, in the absence of orders from their head offices, to back the favourite heavily, to bring its price down again to six-to-four.

There was almost panic to get their money on with the ring bookies before the start. I took a number of big bets and, reluctantly, we brought the price of Pool House down from seven-to-four, first to thirteen-to-eight, then to six-to-four, and finally to eleven-to-eight before the off. The horse had actually started at shorter odds than it would have if we had done nothing.

The race began and Larry switched off his phone-jamming device, while Luca cured the internet server of his virus.

'That didn't bloody work, did it?' said Larry angrily. 'Now if the favourite goes on and wins, I stand to lose a packet.'

But the favourite didn't win.

A complete rank outsider called Cricket Hero beat it by two lengths, and was returned at the surprisingly long starting price of a hundred-to-one and without a single cheer from the watching crowd. We hadn't taken a single bet on the horse so, from the paying-out point of view, it was a very satisfactory result and went some way to make up for our lack of business in the previous races.

'Hold the fort a minute,' I said to Luca.

I went over to watch Cricket Hero being led into the winner's unsaddling enclosure. There was a distinct lack of enthusiastic applause from those who had turned up to see the horses come in, but there would have been very few amongst them, if any, who would have backed it. The horse's connections, however, were absolutely delighted and beaming from ear to ear as their horse circled round and round, steaming gently from under its rug. I looked in the racecard to see what they had down as the name of the trainer. Miles Carpenter, it said, from Ireland.

I leaned on the rail close by to the person I assumed was Mr Carpenter. He was smiling like the cat that got the cream.

'Well done, Mr Carpenter,' I called to him.

He turned and took a stride towards me. 'Thanks,' he said in a thick Irish accent.

'Nice horse,' I said, nodding at the bay, but the truth was it didn't look that good. Compared to the other horses whose well-groomed rumps had shone in the summer sunshine, the winner's coat had been allowed to grow rather long and, in places, it was matted and dull. His tail was a jumble of knots and his hooves were not nicely blackened like most racehorses' are when they run. In fact, the horse looked like an old nag. That's partly why his price had been so high. No one wants to bet on a horse that doesn't look good in the parade ring. Generally speaking, horses that don't look very well don't run very well either.

But appearances can be deceptive.

'Yes,' he replied with a big smile, coming a step closer. 'I think he's going to be a champion.'

I spoke directly to him, quietly but quite clearly. 'Oriental Suite, I assume.'

The smile instantly disappeared from his face.

'And you,' I went on, 'must be Paddy Murphy.'

'And who the fuck are you?' he said explosively, coming right up to me and thrusting his face into mine.

'Just a friend,' I said, backing away and smiling.

'What do you want?' he snarled.

'Nothing,' I said. I turned away leaving him dumbstruck behind me.

He had already given me what I wanted. Confirmation that Oriental Suite was, indeed, now called Cricket Hero. Not that I had really needed it.

I assumed that the real Cricket Hero was dead. Switched with Oriental Suite using the Australian fake RFIDs and then killed for a large insurance payout.

To be honest, Cricket Hero's death had not been a great loss to racing. I had looked him up on the *Racing Post* website. He had run a total of eight times, always in bad company, and had finished last or second-to-last on every occasion. His official rating had been so low as to be almost off the bottom of the scale. But that would all change now.

The horse now running as Cricket Hero was actually Oriental Suite and one thing was absolutely certain. Oriental Suite should never have started any race at odds of one-hundred-to-one, let alone a low-quality maiden hurdle at Bangor-on-Dee on a quiet Monday afternoon in July.

I thought about the two photocopied horse passports I had found in the secret compartment of my father's rucksack. One of them had been in the name of Oriental Suite. But the other had belonged to a horse called Cricket Hero, and I had been struck by the similarities in the markings and hair whorls of the two horses as recorded on the diagrams.

And I had been looking out for the name Cricket Hero to appear in race entries ever since.

'You call that getting even?' Larry Porter said loudly to me as I made my way back to our pitch.

'Keep your voice down, you fool,' I said to him.

'But it didn't bloody work, did it?' he said at only slightly lower volume.

'I can't make the favourite win every time, now can I?' I said.

'Bloody good job it didn't,' he said. 'Norman and I took so much money on it in those last minutes we would have been well out of pocket, I can tell you.'

Norman Joyner stood next to Larry, nodding vigorously.

'But you aren't,' I said, smiling. 'So what are you worried about? You both ended up in profit on the race, didn't you?'

'No thanks to you,' Larry said, still grumbling.

'I reckon we'd better not try it again,' said Norman.

'Fine,' I said. That would suit me very well.

'Those big firms must be laughing all the way to the bank,' he went on.

'But they lost the money they piled on with us near the off,' I said.

'Peanuts, mate, peanuts. They will still keep all the money the mugs put on that favourite in their betting shops.'

True, I thought. But I knew of one firm that wouldn't be laughing.

Tony Bateman (Turf Accountants) Ltd, the high street betting shop subsidiary of HRF Holdings Ltd, employers of the two bully-boys with their steel toecaps, would be far from laughing all the way to their bank.

There were more than fifty Tony Bateman betting shops in the chain, scattered throughout London and the south-east of England. I had looked up all their addresses on the internet.

If all had gone according to plan, at precisely five minutes before the due time of the race, and therefore exactly one minute after we had isolated the racecourse, thirty members of Duggie and Luca's electronics club, the juvenile delinquents from High Wycombe, had each gone into a different Tony Bateman betting shop and placed a two-hundred-pound bet to win. The bets had not been placed on the hot favourite but on the outsider Cricket Hero, payable at the starting price.

Even now, I hoped, each of the thirty would be collecting twenty thousand pounds in winnings, that was six hundred thousand pounds in total. And all the bets had been financed by the six thousand pounds worth of cash that shifty-eyed

Kipper would have found he was short from the blue-cling-film-wrapped packages hidden beneath the lining in my father's black and red rucksack.

The deal with the juvenile delinquents had been easy. Luca and Duggie had handed over two hundred pounds in cash to each of them together with an address of one of the Tony Bateman betting shops. They were given strict instructions. Go to the shop whose address they had been given and make the bet at exactly four twenty-five, two hundred pounds to win on Cricket Hero. If the horse lost then they were simply to walk away, curse their luck, and otherwise keep quiet. If it won, then they were to try and collect the winnings, and a quarter of it would be theirs to keep. Luca and Duggie would take the other three-quarters from them that night. I hoped that all thirty of them would have kept to the bargain, even though I was pretty sure that a few might have simply pocketed the two hundred quid and hoped that the horse lost.

But enough of them would have placed the bets and a single two-hundred-pound bet, even on a hundred-to-one longshot, should not have raised too many suspicions at each separate betting shop. If the head office had managed in time to notice that six thousand pounds had swiftly gone onto such a rank outsider, they would have been powerless to do anything about the starting price. Larry's mobile phone jammer and Luca's internet server virus had seen to that, helped along by Duggie's little expertise with the telephone land lines.

'They may not pay out,' Luca said. Bookmakers, particularly the big chains, had a nasty habit of not paying out on bets if they thought someone had been up to a fiddle. Not that we had, of course. We had simply piggy-backed on someone else's fiddle.

'Maybe not immediately,' I said. 'But I think they will in the end. It really wouldn't be sensible for them to upset so many of High Wycombe's finest juvenile delinquents, now would it?'

He laughed.

And I knew something that he didn't.

The owner of Oriental Suite, the same owner who had been quoted in the *Racing Post* as being distraught over the death of his horse and the man who had pocketed the large insurance payout, was none other than a Mr Henry Richard Feldman, director and shareholder of Tony Bateman (Turf Accountants) Ltd and sole shareholder of HRF Holdings Ltd. The very same man who had sent his bully-boys to give me a 'message' at Kempton Park racecourse with their fists and steel toecaps.

Getting even had, indeed, required considerable cunning.

And almost the best part of the whole scheme was that Larry Porter and Norman Joyner firmly believed that it hadn't worked. They went on grumbling about it for the rest of the day.

I was certain that Mr Feldman would eventually see sense and pay out on all the bets, just as I was sure that he would, in the end, decide not to pursue his plans to take over my business. Both would be the price for my silence. And he would know that a letter had been lodged with my solicitors to be handed to the British Horseracing Authority in the event of my sudden or suspicious death.

Just to be on the safe side.

CHAPTER 23

Luca, Duggie and I could hardly contain ourselves as we packed up the equipment after the last race. Larry had been so frightened by the prospect of his heavy losses that he gave the electronic phone jammer back to Luca and swore to me that he would never try anything like that again. I bit my lip hard so that I wouldn't smile.

We loaded the stuff in my Volvo and I drove back south towards Warwickshire, Luca next to me as usual, with Duggie behind him.

'The look on Larry's face when that race started was priceless,' said Luca, laughing. 'He was in a complete panic.'

'Norman didn't look too happy either,' I said, joining in the hilarity.

'I heard one of those suits saying that he knew something was up when he couldn't get a line on the secretary's phone,' said Duggie.

'Thanks to you,' I said, looking at him in the rear-view mirror. 'Well done.' He beamed.

I drove in silence for a while. We were all enjoying wallowing in the success of it all.

'What are you going to do with all that money?' Duggie asked eventually.

'Well,' I said. 'I thought of donating it to charity. Perhaps the Injured Jockeys Fund.'

'Good idea,' said Luca very seriously. 'It's a very good cause.'

I went on driving.

'But then I thought it would be more fun if we had it,' I said.

We all burst into laughter.

'Much better idea,' said Duggie, banging the back of the front seats in his excitement.

We discussed the money for the next twenty minutes.

Provided Tony Bateman paid it all out, and assuming that all the thirty bets had actually been placed, and at the hundred-to-one starting price, then the total winnings would be six hundred thousand pounds. A quarter of that would go to the thirty delinquents at a rate of five thousand pounds each. Luca, Duggie and I decided that we would split half the total, three hundred thousand, jointly between us, with the other quarter going anonymously and jointly to the two charities, the Injured Jockeys Fund and Racing Welfare, just to ease our consciences.

'Can we do this every week?' asked Duggie. 'Biggest pay cheque I've ever had, I can tell you.'

'Better than that,' I said. 'Gambling winnings are tax free in the UK.'

We all laughed again.

I had decided that splitting the money equally amongst the three of us was the only way. Duggie's help with the delinquents had been crucial, and his little intervention with the bully-boys at Leicester had made me grateful that he was on my side and not theirs. I wanted to keep it that way.

We were still all in high spirits when I finally turned into the

Hilton Hotel car park at junction 15 on the M40, where Luca had left his car.

'Do they let you park here for free?' I asked him.

'I didn't ask,' he said.

'But how do you get out?' There was a barrier down at the car park exit.

'Duggie and I will go in for a celebration drink,' he said. 'I'll get a token from the barman.'

'Don't get breathalysed,' I said.

'I won't,' he said in farewell. He and Duggie gave me a wave as I turned the car in the hotel entrance and drove away. I thought it was a good job you couldn't lose your licence for having euphoria-induced adrenalin in your bloodstream. I would be well over the limit.

My mobile rang as I negotiated the turn out onto the main road.

The phone was in its hands-free car cradle and the number of the caller was shown across the green rectangular display at the top. It was Sophie's mobile number.

I pushed the button. 'Hello, my darling,' I said cheerfully into the microphone that was situated next to the sun visor. 'I've just dropped Luca and Duggie at the Hilton, and I'll be home in about ten minutes.'

But it wasn't Sophie's voice that came back at me out of the speaker.

'Hello, Mr Talbot,' said a man's voice. A chill ran right down my spine and I nearly drove straight into an oncoming lorry. 'You still have something of mine,' he said. 'So now I have something of yours.'

I became cold and clammy all over.

'Let me speak to my wife,' I said.

There was a slight pause, then Sophie came on the line. 'Ned, Ned,' she screamed. She sounded very frightened, and there was a quiver in her voice. 'Help me.'

'It's all right, Sophie,' I said, trying to calm her. 'Everything will be all right.'

But she wasn't there any more and the man came back on the line. 'Do as I say, Mr Talbot, and she won't get hurt.' The tone of his voice was really quite normal but there was real menace in his meaning.

Not only did I fear for Sophie's safety, I feared more for her state of mind.

'What do you want?' I asked him.

'I want the rest of the items that were in that rucksack,' he said. 'I want the chips, the chipwriter, and the rest of the money.'

That confirmed to me that the man was shifty-eyed Kipper. I had feared that I'd not seen the last of him, or of his twelve-centimetre knife, and my fears had clearly been well founded.

'I haven't got the items with me,' I said.

'Go and get them, then,' he said, just as if he was telling off a miscreant schoolboy who had forgotten his books.

'Where are you?' I asked.

'Never you mind,' he said. 'And don't hang up. Keep on the line. If you hang up I will hurt your wife. Do you understand?'

'Yes,' I said.

'Good. Now, where are my things?'

What was I to say? Telling him that I had given the RFID chips and the microcoder/chipwriter to Mr John Smith was unlikely to help get Sophie released unharmed. As for the money, it was still spread amongst the juvenile delinquents. True, I had the take from the afternoon's racing at Bangor-on-Dee in my pocket, but it certainly didn't run to six thousand pounds after such a slow day. Perhaps, at best, there might be half of that.

'They're at my house,' I said.

'Where in your house? I couldn't find them.'

I didn't like the sound of that.

I thought quickly.

'In the cupboard under the stairs,' I said. 'In an old paint tin.'

There was a pause.

'Go and get them,' he said. 'Now. But don't hang up the phone. Where are you now?'

'On the Warwick by-pass,' I said.

'Go to your house, but keep talking to me. If you hang up, I will kill your wife.'

It was the first time he had used the word kill, and a fresh wave of fear swept over me. God knows how Sophie was feeling if she'd heard it.

'All right, all right, I won't hang up,' I said quickly. 'Now, let me talk to my wife again.'

There was another pause.

'Ned,' she cried down the phone. 'What the hell's going on?'

'Sophie,' I said. 'It will be all right, my love. I promise. I'll get the things he wants and he will let you go. Stay calm.'

'I will stay calm, Mr Talbot,' shifty-eyed Kipper said, obviously taking the phone back. 'Just get my things and we can all stay calm. But do not hang up the phone.'

'What happens if I lose mobile signal?' I said.

'You had just better hope you don't,' he replied.

I realized why he didn't want me to hang up. As long as I was on the line to him, I couldn't call the police.

'OK,' I said. 'I'm turning off the A46 into Kenilworth.'

There was no reply.

'Where shall I bring them?' I asked.

'Just get them first,' he said. 'Then I'll tell you what to do.'

I made the few turns in Kenilworth and drew up outside my house alongside Alice's car, which stood alone in the parking area. Where, I wondered, was Alice?

I looked at my watch. It was ten minutes to eight, and I was hungry. I hadn't eaten anything since a single slice of toast for breakfast, some twelve hours ago. But hunger was something I could easily endure.

'I've arrived at my house,' I said into the microphone.

'Good,' he said. 'Go in and fetch the stuff. Take your mobile phone with you, and don't hang up.'

'It might hang up automatically when I take it out of the hands-free system.'

'You had better hope it doesn't,' he replied. 'If you hang up the phone, I'll kill your wife.'

'But it hangs up on its own when I take it out,' I pleaded. 'It's done it before.'

'Take it out now,' he said.

I lifted the phone out of its cradle and, of course, it immediately hung up. Oh God, I thought, now what do I do? Do I call back or what?

Before I had a chance to decide the phone rang in my hand.

'Hello, yes,' I shouted into it. 'I'm here.'

Please let it be him, I prayed, and not my bloody voicemail.

'Good,' said Kipper. My heart rate went down by at least half. I would never have thought that I would be relieved to hear his voice.

'OK,' I said. 'I'm getting out of the car and going in.'

The front door was open about two inches, and I began to fear that he might actually be inside the house waiting for me.

341

'Are you in my house?' I asked him.

There was no reply.

'I need to know if you are in my house,' I said again.

Once more, there was no reply.

'Stop playing games with me.' I spoke firmly into the phone. 'I am not going through my front door until you tell me where you are.'

'Do as you are told,' he replied. 'I'm in charge here, not you. Now, go into your house and get my things.'

'No, I will not,' I said, my heart rate climbing again. 'I will not go through my front door only for you to plunge your knife into me the same way you did to my father at Ascot.'

There was a long pause from his end.

'Are you still there?' I asked eventually.

'I'm here,' he said. 'How come your name is Talbot and not Grady?'

I suddenly realized he hadn't known that the man he knew as Alan Grady, the man he had murdered in the Ascot car park, had been my father.

'My father's name was really Talbot, not Grady,' I said.

'Ah,' he said. 'Now that might account for why I have been unable to find out about him.'

He obviously hadn't traced me through the inquest records because he hadn't known which records to look at. But he must have known that my father was dead, I thought. The stabbing had been an expert job.

'Are you in my house?' I repeated into the phone.

'If I was in your house I would have gone to the paint tin and taken what is mine by now.'

Did I believe him? But did I have any choice but to go in anyway?

I pushed the front door open wide with my foot until it turned on its hinges as far as it would go, almost flat against the wall. There was not enough space for him to be hiding behind it.

'Have you got them yet?' he asked, making me jump.

'No,' I replied.

I stepped into the hall. I could hear nothing. I walked quickly down the hall past the cupboard under the stairs and into the kitchen. Everything from the kitchen cabinets was strewn across the floor. I stepped carefully through the mess to the house telephone, but there would be no using that to call the police. The wire had been cut right through. I went through into the living room and found the same things had been done to both the phone and the cupboards in there. I had no doubt that the third extension, the one in the bedroom upstairs, would have suffered the same fate, but I still started up the stairs to check. Step three creaked as I stepped on it.

I thought I could hear a slight banging.

I stopped to listen.

The faint knocking sound came again, but I wasn't sure of exactly where from.

'Have you got the stuff?' Kipper said to me through the phone.

'No,' I said. 'I'm having a pee.'

'Hurry up.'

I put the phone down to my side, and listened once more.

I could definitely hear someone knocking. It was below me.

I rushed back down the stairs and opened the cupboard beneath them.

Alice lay there on her side curled round the vacuum cleaner and with her arms tied behind her back. She was banging her tied-up feet on the floor. A tea towel gag had been wrapped

343

around her face so I pulled it down, and she immediately spat out a dirty dishcloth that was in her mouth.

'Ugh,' she said, and was promptly sick on the floor.

'You bastard,' I said into the phone.

Kipper laughed. 'Ah, you've found my little surprise.' He sounded pleased with himself.

I went back into the kitchen, fetched a pair of scissors and cut through the plastic garden ties that had secured Alice's wrists and ankles. She sat on the hall floor, rubbing where the plastic had dug into her flesh. I put a finger up to my mouth in the universal 'be quiet' gesture and pointed at the phone.

'Phone the bloody police,' she shouted, ignoring me.

'I wouldn't do that if I were you,' said shifty-eyed Kipper through the phone. 'Not if you want to see your wife again.'

'Alice, I can't,' I said.

'Why the bloody hell not?' she demanded.

'He's got Sophie,' I said. 'And he's on the other end of this phone.'

'Tell him he's a fucking piece of shit,' she said with passion, continuing to rub her wrists. I was quite taken aback by her vulgarity. Alice had always been so prim and proper, at least in my hearing.

Kipper had obviously heard what she had said because he laughed again. 'Tell her she should be happy to be alive.'

I didn't bother.

'Now get my things,' he said, 'and go back to your car.'

What was I to do? I had to make him think that I still had them or he would hurt or kill Sophie. And I needed to set up a swap, I thought. That would be a good start but, so far, I hadn't actually worked out how to.

344

But first I needed something to swap for Sophie. I took a canvas shopping bag off the hook on the back of the kitchen door and started putting things into it. First, the wad of bank-notes, the takings from Bangor races, came out of my trouser pocket and into the bag. Next, I took a clear polythene sandwich bag and put ten grains of rice in it from Sophie's rice jar. Finally, the instruction booklet for the kitchen television, together with the TV remote control, went into the shopping bag as well.

Alice stood in the kitchen doorway, watching me with wide eyes. 'What are you doing?' she said. 'Call the police.'

I again put my finger to my mouth and this time she under-stood. I also held up the cut phone wire and she nodded.

'OK, I've got it all,' I said into the phone.

'Go and get into the car and drive back onto the A46 towards the M40.'

'OK,' I said.

I put my hand over the microphone and spoke to Alice. 'I've got to go and give this to the man.' I held up the shopping bag. 'I'll come back here with Sophie. Are you OK?'

She nodded again slightly but I noticed tears on her face. She was clearly very shocked. It's not every day you get tied up and left in a cupboard under the stairs with a dirty dishcloth rammed into your mouth. Thank goodness.

I stroked her shoulders in reassurance and then went back out to my Volvo with the shopping bag.

'OK,' I said into the phone. 'I'm back in the car. I'm going to put the phone back in the hands-free cradle, but it may hang up again.'

'Leave it, then,' he said. 'Keep it in your hand.'

I reversed out onto Station Road and retraced my path to the A46.

'OK,' I said, holding the phone to my ear. 'I'm now on the A46 going towards the M40.'

I didn't get stopped for illegal use of a hand-held mobile phone. There's never a policeman about when you want one.

'Leave the A46 and take the A425 towards Warwick,' he said. 'Take the third turning on the right, Budbrooke Road. Follow it round to the right. Go to the very end of the road.'

'OK,' I said to him. I still wasn't sure what I would do when I got there.

I took the A425 and then slowly turned into Budbrooke Road. It was an industrial estate sandwiched between a canal and a railway line. Large characterless modern blocks built of seamed metal stood on either side of the road. No doubt, during the working day this area was busy with people and traffic, but at eight fifteen on a Monday evening it was completely deserted.

I drove slowly down to the very end of the road and stopped between two of the big soulless buildings. I turned the car round so I was looking back up the road, but my Volvo was the only car about and I began to wonder if I was in the right place.

'Are you here?' I asked.

'I'm here,' he said.

'Where?'

'Shut up and wait.'

I wondered if he was waiting to see if I'd been followed. I sat there for what seemed like ages but it was probably only a couple of minutes. I looked all around. If he was watching me, I couldn't tell where from.

'OK,' he said finally through the phone. 'Open the car door, put the things out on the ground and drive away.'

'What about my wife?' I asked.

'When I am satisfied that I have everything, I will let her go.'

'No way,' I said. 'If you want your things, you will have to let her go now.'

'Do as you are told,' he said again.

'No,' I said. 'If you want this stuff then you will have to come here now and swap it for my wife.'

'An exchange?' he asked.

'Yes,' I said. 'An exchange.'

He laughed. 'Mr Talbot, this is not a spy movie. Leave the things on the ground and go.'

'No, I will not,' I said again firmly. 'I want my wife back now.'

He didn't answer and I began to fear that he had gone. But then a small silver hatchback moved slowly down the road and stopped, facing me, about thirty yards away.

The driver's door opened and Kipper stood up next to the car. He lifted the phone to his ear.

'Where's my stuff?' he said.

I opened the door to the Volvo and stood out next to it. I, too, lifted a phone to my ear.

'Where's my wife?' I said.

He reached down into the car and pulled her up from the back seat. She stood up next to him. I could see that her hands were behind her back, presumably tied, and there was what looked like a pillowcase over her head.

'Take that off her head,' I said into the phone.

He pulled the pillowcase away and Sophie blinked in the bright summer evening sunshine. He held her in front of him with his right arm over her shoulder. And he had his twelve-centimetre-long knife resting against her neck.

'Where's my stuff?' he asked again through the telephone.

I could feel my heart pumping in my chest. I put my hand

into the Volvo, picked up the canvas shopping bag and held it up.

'Show me,' he said.

I pulled the wad of banknotes out of the bag. I held it up above my head and waved it at him. Most of the notes were tenners and twenties, but he wouldn't be able to see from his distance that they weren't all fifties, or even Australian hundred-dollar bills.

'Show me the chipwriter,' he said.

With a dry mouth, I put the money back in the bag and carefully picked up the television remote control. I held it up with the back of it facing towards him. From where he was standing, I hoped that it would appear to be a black box of approximately the right size and shape. I held my breath for a few seconds and then, equally carefully, I put the remote back in the bag.

'And the chips?' he asked.

I held up the sandwich bag with the grains of rice in it. I could hardly tell them apart from the real RFID chips, and I was the one holding them. He would have had no chance of doing so from thirty yards away. I put them back in the shopping bag as well.

'And here are the horse passports,' I said holding up and waving the TV instruction booklet around so that he couldn't see it too clearly. 'Now release my wife.'

'Go over there and put the bag on the ground.' He pointed towards the building to my right, his left.

I put the TV instruction booklet back in the bag and walked about fifteen or twenty steps over to where he had pointed. I put the bag down on the ground and stood next to it. I was still twenty yards or so from where he stood holding Sophie, the knife at her neck glinting in the sunlight.

'Now go back to your car,' he said through the phone, even though I could hear him plainly without it.

'Let my wife walk away from you,' I said to him. 'When she starts walking, I will walk away from the bag.'

'Mr Talbot, you really have been watching too many spy films,' he said with a laugh.

It may have amused him to think that we were taking part in a spy movie but I didn't feel at all like laughing. Not with my humble TV remote control acting the part of an electronic microcoder/chipwriter, and a bag of simple rice grains appearing as some programmable RFIDs. And certainly not when my wife's life might depend on them remembering their lines.

'Let my wife go,' I said firmly to him, 'and then these are yours.' I pointed down at the shopping bag.

The recovery of the items must have become an obsession with him. He looked over longingly at the bag. He removed the knife from Sophie's throat and gently pushed her away from him towards my car. I let her go a few strides, just enough to be out of his reach, and then I started moving slowly backwards towards the Volvo, watching Kipper intently for any sudden movements.

He walked around the front of his car, and started towards the bag.

Sophie was now about half way to my car, but she wasn't going anywhere near fast enough for my liking. Her face showed the relief at being away from Kipper's grasp, but she clearly didn't fully realize the ongoing danger of the situation.

It would have been nice to have had the time to allow Sophie to climb gently into the passenger seat, but Kipper was almost at the bag, and a single glance would enlighten him instantly that my kitchen television remote control was not the microcoder/chipwriter he was expecting.

'Sophie, run,' I shouted at her urgently. At the same time I sprinted for the Volvo and opened the rear door. Sophie ran towards me. I took a couple of strides forward, grabbed her, and literally threw her across the back seat. I slammed the back door and was in the car almost before Kipper realized he'd been fooled. I tossed my phone over onto the passenger seat as I slammed the driver's door shut and locked it.

The first part of the scheme had gone exactly to plan. Now all I had to do was get Sophie and me safely away. I started the engine, threw the car into gear, and shot past Kipper's silver hatchback with my back wheels spinning on the loose surface.

I could see him shouting something at me but I couldn't hear what it was, and I didn't care. He ran over to his car and, all too soon, the silver hatchback appeared large in my rear-view mirror as I waited at the junction with the Birmingham Road for a gap in the traffic. He came right up behind me at speed and rammed the Volvo forward, right out into the path of a speeding white van.

I closed my eyes and waited for the crash, but somehow the van driver managed to avoid the collision by swerving round me with a squeal of his tyres and a blast of his horn. It didn't seem to me that he had braked one little bit as he sped away towards the A46 roundabout.

Sophie was lying full-length across the back seat where I had thrown her, still with a black plastic tie binding her hands behind her back. 'Ned, what's happening?' Her voice was remarkably calm and collected for someone who has just had a knife at their throat. Where, I thought, was the expected panic?

The answer was that the panic was up here in front, with me.

CHAPTER 24

I suppose if one had to be involved in an impromptu stock-car race along the highways and byways of Warwickshire, an old Volvo 940 2.3 litre turbocharged estate might actually be one's car of choice. In their prime, they hadn't been nicknamed 'The Volvo Tank' for nothing.

At the A46 junction I debated with myself which way to go. Kipper in his silver hatchback was right up against my tailgate and I could feel the Volvo lurch every time he hit me. If I went down towards the M40 I would have to deal with the traffic lights on the motorway junction. Equally, if I went straight on the A425 towards Birmingham, there were traffic lights within a few hundred yards. So I decided to turn right onto the A46 back towards Kenilworth and Coventry.

I swept onto the roundabout so fast that my mobile phone slid off the passenger seat and down the gap between it and the door. Sod it, I thought. I'd wanted to call the police with that, but I would have had to stop the car to retrieve the phone from down there. And, at the moment, stopping was completely out of the question.

Kipper kept darting back and forth around the rear of the

Volvo like an annoying insect. Twice he gave me such a big nudge that I feared I would lose control completely, and my car was still fishtailing badly as it sped down the slip road and onto the A46 dual carriageway.

In spite of being thrown around by the constant lurching of the car, Sophie had managed to get herself into a fairly upright position on the back seat. I smiled at her in the rear-view mirror. She looked back at me with wide frightened eyes.

'Can you untie me?' she asked.

'Not just at the moment, darling. I need both hands to drive.'

The car lurched as it was struck again by the hatchback. Sophie lay back down on the seat.

Fortunately, the A46 was quite empty at that time of the evening and I was able to put my foot down. The Volvo speedometer climbed to well over ninety miles per hour, but still I couldn't get away from Kipper's car, which seemed to be stuck to me like a limpet. Twice he tried to get alongside but both times I swerved to cut him off, forcing him back. The road was only two lanes wide each way at this point but I knew that it went to three after the next junction. Keeping him back then would not be so easy.

What I needed was a police car but, of course, there wasn't one to be seen.

Our two cars raced along the road together towards the junction. At the very last moment I jerked the steering wheel to the left and went across the white painted road hatching and up the slip road, hoping that Kipper wouldn't be able to make the turning. Sadly, he was able to follow, slowing only momentarily to cross the grass verge, which sent up a shower of earth and stones.

I shot up the slip road to the roundabout at the top of the

rise. I hoped that nothing was coming round it for I wasn't about to slow down. My tyres squealed in objection as I took the first exit along the country road towards the village of Leek Wooton. It was single carriageway, so I now had to cope with the oncoming traffic as well as trying to keep Kipper behind me.

I thought the best plan was to drive to the nearest police station and park right outside the door. Surely, even shifty-eyed Kipper wouldn't be crazy enough to try anything there. The only police station that I knew well was in Kenilworth because I'd had to go there a couple of times to show them my driving documents. But I also knew it was a very small office, and that it didn't operate round the clock. Would it still be open at this time of the evening? I assumed there also must be a police station in Warwick, and I was aware there was a large one in Leamington Spa, but I didn't know exactly where, and I wasn't about to ask a bystander for directions.

Kenilworth would have to do, I thought. Even if the police station was shut, it might still be enough to put Kipper off.

I tore down the road towards Leek Wooton with the silver hatchback seemingly glued to the back of the Volvo. At one point he tried to overtake me so I pulled right into the middle of the road, swerving back to my side only at the last second to avoid an oncoming truck whose driver was leaning heavily on his horn.

At the new roundabout outside the entrance to the Warwick-shire Golf Club I had to slow down slightly in order to make it round. Kipper in the hatchback, however, went the wrong way round the circle to try and get an advantage and he almost made it as we emerged side by side. But he was now on the wrong side of the road. I squeezed him over yet further until his offside wheels were almost on the grass but still he wouldn't give up.

I looked across at him, and I swear he was laughing at me. Finally, an oncoming car forced him to brake and fall in once more behind me.

I ignored the thirty-miles-per-hour signs at the entrance to the village, hoping desperately that a child didn't step out into my path. At more than double the speed limit, I would have had no chance to stop in time.

I realized that I didn't even have my seat belt on, so I reached up behind me for it and clicked its buckle into the lock at my side. But Sophie had no chance of doing the same.

'Darling, please lie down on the floor behind the seats,' I said firmly. 'Get as low as you can and brace yourself with your feet. Just in case we have an accident.' I glanced over to her and tried to give her a reassuring smile.

'When will all this stop?' she cried.

'We're on our way to the police station right now,' I said. 'It will stop there.'

But it didn't. Because we never reached the police station.

Beyond the village of Leek Wooton, the road to Kenilworth is straight, flat and narrow, but only about a mile in length before it reaches the outskirts of the town.

I worried briefly about how I would deal with the many road junctions ahead, but for now it was as much as I could do to keep my car straight and on the tarmac surface as the silver hatchback continually thumped into the back. Why couldn't he lose control or terminally damage his car?

So far we had not encountered much other traffic but our luck ran out as we left the village. A line of four cars was following a slow-moving builder's lorry that was piled high with sand. I could see a van coming the opposite way, but it was still some distance off. I swung out and overtook all four cars and the lorry as if they were going backwards, with my hand firmly on the horn to stop anyone else pulling out. Kipper tried to come through behind me but he ran out of room and had to brake hard and dive in behind the lorry in order to miss the oncoming van.

Suddenly, I was away from him. But not for long, and not by much, and I watched in the mirror as he quickly swept past the lorry and set off in pursuit.

I looked ahead in absolute horror. In the distance, there were some road works with a set of temporary traffic lights, and I could see a line of waiting vehicles.

I was doing about eighty miles an hour and the road works were beginning to loom large. I glanced in the mirror and, even at this speed, the silver hatchback was gaining on me fast. Again, I looked ahead. Traffic was coming the other way, headed by a huge articulated lorry, and there were trees lining both sides of the road.

I made a quick decision.

'Sophie, my darling,' I shouted. 'Brace yourself against the seats as hard as you can.'

With about four hundred yards still to go to the temporary traffic lights, I took my right foot off the accelerator and stood hard on the brake.

My old Volvo 940 estate weighed a little over one and a half tons but, in spite of their age, the brakes were in excellent working order. With a small amount of shuddering from the anti-lock system, the car pulled up in a much shorter space than that shown as the stopping distance for eighty miles per hour in the Highway Code. I wouldn't have been surprised if the tyres had actually dug grooves in the road surface, so quickly did the car come to a halt.

Kipper hadn't a hope of stopping in time. For a start, he had been going faster than I, and he'd still been accelerating in his attempt to catch me.

I looked up into the rear-view mirror. The Volvo had almost stopped completely before Kipper realized what I'd done. White smoke poured from his tyres as all four wheels of the hatchback locked up, but by then it was far too late.

I had hoped that he might have hit a tree, or the oncoming truck, but his locked front wheels meant he couldn't steer, and he came thundering on, straight towards the back of the Volvo. I watched him coming ever closer almost as if it was happening in slow motion and, in the last moments before the impact, I flicked off my car's ignition, pulled the seat belt tight, clasped my hands firmly together in my lap and put my head back against the headrest. All the while shouting at Sophie. 'Brace! Brace!'

There was a tremendous bang as the vehicles collided. I don't know how quickly he was still travelling but it was fast enough to throw the Volvo violently forward and sideways onto the grass verge, in spite of me still having my foot pressed down hard on the brake pedal. At the same time, the air bag in front of me inflated with another bang and a cloud of white gas.

Then there was another huge thump from somewhere behind me. Something else had collided, but not with us, the Volvo hadn't moved again.

'Sophie, Sophie,' I shouted urgently, fighting to undo my seat belt and turning round in my seat. 'Are you all right?'

'Yes, Ned, I'm fine,' she said, almost calmly, from the back. 'Is it over?'

357

'Yes, my darling, it's over.'

But I didn't know that for certain. I couldn't even see the silver hatchback from where I was, let alone know the state of its occupant.

'Can you please untie me, then?' she asked. 'I'm bloody hurting.' She still sounded remarkably unfazed by the whole affair.

The driver's door wouldn't open and I began to be a bit panicky as I could smell petrol. The last thing I wanted was to be trapped inside a burning car.

I pushed and shoved but the door wouldn't budge, jammed shut by the collision. The windows were electrically operated but I didn't fancy turning on the car ignition with flammable fuel all over the place. I struggled over the centre armrest into the passenger seat and, thankfully, the passenger door opened easily. I scrambled out of the car onto the verge.

'You all right, mate?' shouted someone from behind me.

'Yes, fine,' I said, turning round. 'How about him?' I pointed at the crumpled mess that had been the silver hatchback, which was now some ten yards or so behind the Volvo.

'Doesn't look too good, I'm afraid,' he said. 'I've called the ambulance, and the police.'

I looked around. The road was completely blocked and the traffic queues were beginning to build up in both directions. People were spilling out of their vehicles to come and have a closer look at the crash. I didn't really care.

I tugged frantically at the nearside back door of the car but it wouldn't open, so I went back in through the front and knelt on the passenger seat looking over.

Sophie was curled up on the floor, still with her hands tied together with the plastic garden tie. I needed some scissors, or a knife to free her. I thought fleetingly about the knife Kipper had with him, but I decided it wouldn't be such a good idea to go and fetch it, not just now. I needed to get Sophie loose as soon as possible, and before anyone came snooping around asking why I had a tied-up woman in the back of my car.

I knew that there was a pair of scissors somewhere amongst our bookmaking equipment. We often used gaffer tape to fix the odds board to the umbrella pole when it was windy, and we always needed scissors to cut it.

I looked towards the back of the estate. Our equipment boxes, which had been neatly stowed at Bangor, were now all in a jumble. The collision had completely buckled the big top-hinged back door of the Volvo but, amazingly, the back window was still intact. I slithered on my stomach over the top of the passenger seat, and then over the back seat into the luggage space. I found the scissors in the second box I tried.

I soon had Sophie cut loose and safely out of the car. I sat her down on the grass verge and told her to wait.

'Please don't leave me, Ned,' she wailed.

I looked lovingly at my battered, sore and frightened wife. 'There's absolutely no chance of that,' I said, kissing the top of her head. 'I'll be back in a moment.'

The road was rapidly filling with people from their cars as I walked round behind my Volvo to inspect the damage. It was pretty bad, with the rear off-side corner of the car completely staved in. The back wheel on that side was at the wrong angle, and the tyre was burst, and I could see petrol still dripping out onto the road from the ruptured fuel tank. But it was not half as bad as the near-total destruction of the silver hatchback.

It seemed that Kipper's car had collided not only with my Volvo Tank, but then also with the oncoming traffic, the first impact having bounced the hatchback onto the wrong side of the road and straight into the path of the huge truck. The driver was wandering amongst the crowd in a bit of a daze. 'I had no chance,' he kept saying to everyone. 'That car came straight across the road. I had no chance.'

Nor had shifty-eyed Kipper. The truck had ploughed straight into the driver's door of the hatchback, mangling the whole of the vehicle almost beyond recognition. A couple of men were leaning in through the broken windows trying to help him. And, in the distance, I could hear the sirens coming closer.

Another James-Bond-style car chase was over and, this time, I thought, 'M' might have been fairly proud of me. I was only shaken, not stirred.

But I suddenly felt quite ill. This was reality, not a spy movie.

Sophie and I sat side by side on the grass verge for quite some time while a team of firemen, police and ambulance staff did their best to remove Kipper from the twisted wreckage of his car.

It seemed remarkable that he was still alive, but apparently it was only just. The efforts of the emergency crews were trying to keep him that way.

I rather wished that they wouldn't bother.

Sophie and I had been assessed by a paramedic as being physically unharmed before being wrapped in red ambulance blankets and asked to wait.

We waited.

After a while, a bright yellow and black helicopter landed in the cornfield alongside the road and soon a doctor in a bright orange flying suit came over and asked us if we were both OK.

'Yes,' we said in unison. He went over to join the team working on the hatchback.

Sophie took my hand. 'We are OK, aren't we, Ned?' she said.

'Yes,' I said with certainty. 'We are definitely OK.'

Epilogue

Six months later Sophie and I went to Australia to look for my sisters while Luca, my new, fully documented, legal business partner, and his young full-time assistant, Douglas Masters, carried on our flourishing business at home without me.

'Don't hurry back,' Luca had said the day before I left. 'Duggie and I will do just fine. And Millie will help us when she can.' Millie, it seemed, had moved in with Luca, and she hadn't yet been murdered for doing so by her sister, Betsy.

Since that glorious Monday in July at Bangor-on-Dee races, I had discovered renewed energy and enthusiasm for my work. Bookmaking had become fun again, not least because Sophie had often stood with me, paying out winning tickets and bantering with the crowds as she'd never done before. She had clearly been taking lessons from Duggie.

It had actually been Sophie's idea to go to Australia, but I'd jumped at it.

Understandably, she had had one or two problems after the events involving Kipper and the car crash. At the time I'd been amazed at her calmness but, according to the psychiatrists, this had been due to her brain bottling up the stress and literally switching off some of her emotions. Only afterwards did the fear and the panic manifest themselves with a physical reaction. I had found her four days later in the middle of the night lying awake in our bed, shaking uncontrollably and soaked in sweat. It had been a very frightening experience for us both and she had been returned immediately by ambulance to the hospital in Hemel Hempstead for further treatment.

Fortunately, the panic attack had been short-lived and she was soon able to return home, but not before yet another full assessment of her condition. Since then she had been doing really well with only a couple of minor setbacks. On one occasion, when she had a particularly nasty cold, some of her cough medicine had reacted badly to the anti-depressants and she'd had a bit of a wobble. I had come home, stone-cold sober, from the races and she accused me of being drunk. That was always the first sign to arrive, and the last to leave. I had sat up all that night waiting for the expected decline into full mania, but in the morning she had been fine. The new drugs really were working, and both of us had begun to hope, and to make plans for a future.

Slowly, over the months, I had recounted to her the complete story of those three weeks in late June and early July. I told her the full details of my father's murder, about finding his rucksack and its hidden contents. I told her about Mr John Smith and the microcoder, about finding him in our house, and breaking his wrist. I even told her about Luca and Larry's little games with the phones and internet at Ascot, and how I had extracted revenge for the attack on me at Kempton by the big-firm bully-boys.

Once or twice she told me off for not having contacted the police straight away, and she was, justifiably, really quite cross that I had placed myself, and her, in such danger from a known murderer.

I had tried to explain to her that I didn't like the policeman in charge of the case but she, quite rightly, had said that personalities shouldn't have made any difference. But of course they did. Chief Inspector Llewellyn's poor opinion of bookmakers in general, and of me in particular, had clouded his judgement in the same way that my antipathy towards him had clouded mine. Even when it was all over, he had still been reluctant to admit that I'd had nothing to do with my father's murder.

I had been to see him the day following the car crash, at the Thames Valley Police Headquarters near Oxford. He'd told me that the driver of the silver hatchback, known to me as Kipper but now properly identified as a Mr Mervyn Williams, had indeed survived, but he was still in a critical condition, and had been transferred to the specialist head-injury unit at Frenchay hospital in Bristol. Apparently, according to the police who had attended the scene, he hadn't been wearing his seat belt at the time of the accident.

'It wasn't an accident,' I'd said flatly. 'The man was trying to shunt me off the road at the time, and I was just lucky that the truck hit him and not me.' I had decided against telling the chief inspector about me making an emergency stop in order to precipitate the crash in the first place.

'But why?' he had asked me.

'Because I think he's the man who murdered my father. I presumed that he was trying to do the same to me, to eliminate me as a witness.'

'What makes you think it's the man who murdered your father?' he'd asked.

'I think I recognized him at one point, when he tried to pass me.'

'How very interesting,' the chief inspector had said, and he'd lifted the telephone on his desk.

Mervyn Williams, I discovered at a second meeting with the chief inspector just a week later, was a qualified veterinary surgeon, originally from Chepstow in South Wales, but he had been living in Newbury for the past ten years as some sort of veterinary investigator for the RSPCA. A police search of his house had uncovered a red-and-black rucksack, still with an airline baggage tag attached with GRADY printed on it. Results were eagerly awaited for a DNA test of blood spots discovered on the sleeve of a charcoal grey hoodie from Mr Williams's wardrobe and consistent with my description of the Ascot attacker's clothes. And a further search of the mangled remains of his silver hatchback had also uncovered a kitchen knife of the correct proportions to have inflicted the fatal wounds to my father's abdomen.

I chose not to ask the chief inspector if I they had also found the remote control to my kitchen television, although I could really have done with it back.

'So what happens now?' I'd asked instead.

'That depends on if, and how well, Mr Williams recovers,' the chief inspector had said. 'He's been formally arrested on suspicion of murder but the doctors are saying he has massive brain damage, so he'll probably never be fit to plead, even if he survives.'

'What does that mean?' I'd asked.

'If he's unfit to plead, there would be no criminal trial as such. But there would be what is called a trial of the facts, when the evidence is placed before a jury and they would effectively decide if he had done it, or not. But, of course, there would be no actual declaration of guilt or innocence, and no sentence.'

'So what would then happen to Mervyn Williams?'

'If he's unfit to plead, he'd technically be a free man, but if he recovers enough so that he becomes fit, he could still be tried for murder. There doesn't seem to be much doubt that he was the man responsible, and the DNA should prove it. Your e-fit was remarkably accurate considering you only saw him for a second or two in the Ascot car park, and with his hood up too.'

I hadn't enlightened him that the fleeting glimpse in the Ascot car park hadn't been, in fact, the only occasion I'd seen the man.

The chief inspector had shown me a photograph of Mr Mervyn Williams that the police had taken from his home. I'd looked once more at the man I had known only as shifty-eyed Kipper, with his eyes set rather too close together for the shape of his face, the man I'd last seen laughing at me as he'd tried to overtake on the road to Leek Wooton.

'So is that it?' I'd said.

'For the moment,' the chief inspector had replied cautiously. 'But I still have a niggling feeling you haven't told me the whole truth.'

He was, I supposed, quite a good detective really.

Thanks to the nearly six-hundred-thousand-pound generosity of Mr Henry Richard Feldman, Sophie and I travelled upstairs, in Club Class, from London to Sydney on a British Airways jumbo jet, sipping vintage champagne for most of the way.

It had taken a little while for Tony Bateman (Turf Accountants) Ltd to pay out on the juvenile delinquents' bets, but they had been persuaded by HRF Holdings Ltd, their parent company, to see sense in the end.

Only two of the thirty had failed to make the bet, instead pocketing the two-hundred-pound stake. They were now ruing their mistake to the tune of four thousand, eight hundred smackers, as well as the well-earned derision of the other twenty-eight.

Duggie and Luca had given some of their own winnings to refit the electronics club with new equipment, and I'd spent a couple of thousand of mine on some more comfortable dining chairs for the mental hospital grand salon.

Just in case.

The source of all our riches, the horse Oriental Suite, now running as Cricket Hero, had raced twice more since Bangor-on-Dee, winning easily on both occasions, but at starting prices far shorter than our hundred-to-one bonanza of July. His trainer, Miles Carpenter, also known to me as Mr Paddy Murphy, had stated in a television interview that he hoped the horse would win at the Cheltenham Steeplechase Festival the following March.

However, according to reports in the *Racing Post* in early December, Cricket Hero had suffered a massive heart attack at home on the gallops and had dropped down, stone dead. 'Just one of those things,' the paper had said. 'Sadly, it happens all too often in racing.'

I, meanwhile, wondered if it had actually been that particular horse which had died, if ping pong balls had been involved, and whether or not he'd been insured for a small fortune.

Sophie and I landed in Sydney at six in the morning on a glorious January southern-hemisphere summer's day, just as the sun began to peep over the horizon to the east. I had a wonderful view of the city as we approached from the north with the still-dark Sydney Harbour Bridge spanning a ribbon of early light reflected from the water beneath.

I was so excited.

I had always wanted to go to Australia, even before I had discovered that my father had been living there. Somehow, to me, it still represented the new frontier of man's occupation of the planet, although I am sure the Aboriginal people would have viewed things somewhat differently.

All the way from England on the aeroplane I had read my guidebooks and, by the time we arrived in Sydney, I'd become a bit of an expert on all things Australian.

The very first sighting by a European of what is now Australia didn't take place until 1606, by which time William Shakespeare was writing and performing his plays in London, and Christopher Columbus had known about the Americas for more than a hundred years. The very first settlers, together with the first convicts, didn't arrive to set up a penal colony in Botany Bay for almost another two centuries, and some twelve years after the United States had declared its independence from Britain.

By European standards, Australia is vast, and still rather empty. The land area is nearly twice that of the whole of the European Union, while the population is less than a twentieth. If spread out evenly, only seven Australians would live in each square mile of their country, whereas more than a thousand would occupy the same space in England.

But, according to my guidebooks, the Australians are not spread out evenly, with nine out of ten of them living in the major coastal cities. Meanwhile, much of the interior is barren uninhabited desert with such original names as 'The Great

Sandy Desert' and 'The Little Sandy Desert'. However, there is also tropical rainforest covering a great swathe of the state of Queensland in the north-east.

In fact, I was astounded by the diversity of physical geography that exists within a single country. But I supposed I shouldn't have been. Australia stretches from almost the equator in the north, to half way to Antarctica in the south, and is as far across from east to west as the distance from New York to Los Angeles.

How was I ever going to find my sisters in such a huge country?

Sophie and I had planned to spend the first few days in Sydney, getting over jet lag and doing the things all tourists do.

Courtesy of Tony Bateman, we stayed in a magnificent five-star hotel overlooking the busy harbour. I could have happily sat by the window in our room watching the yellow and green harbour ferries shuttling in and out of the wharfs on Circular Quay, but Sophie was keen for us to walk everywhere, and see everything.

First, we climbed the steps to the Opera House and marvelled at the shell-like arches of its iconic roof. Then we trekked round the Botanical Gardens and rested on Mrs Macquarie's Chair, a seat carved out of the natural rock by the convicts in 1816. The seat has a panoramic view of Sydney Harbour and, the story goes, Mrs Macquarie, the governor's wife, would sit there for hours on end, longing to be aboard one of the ships leaving for England, and home.

After three days of dawn-to-dusk tourism, including climbing to the very top of the Harbour Bridge, Sophie and I were exhausted, and our sore feet were grateful for the short breather as we flew the hour or so to Melbourne.

Before we'd left England, I had used the internet to engage a private detective to help in the search for my sisters, and he was waiting for us at Melbourne airport.

'Lachlan Harris?' I asked a young man holding up a TALBOT sign at the baggage claim.

'Sure am,' he said. 'But call me Lachie.' He was short, about thirty, with a well-bronzed face and spiky fairish hair, with highlights.

'Ned Talbot,' I said, shaking his hand. 'And this is my wife Sophie.'

'G'day,' he said in typical Australian fashion. He shook her hand too. 'Good to meet you both.'

'Any news?' I asked, eager to hear immediately. I had purposely not called him from Sydney, although, at times, I had been quite desperate to do so.

'Yes,' he said. 'As a matter of fact I have some good news for you. But let's get out of the airport first. I'm taking you to see your father's house.' And, with that, he picked up our suitcases and turned for the exit. We followed, but I was rather frustrated by his lack of explanation.

'All in good time,' he said when we were in his car, leaving the airport.

'But what's the news?' I asked him again.

'I've found the two daughters of Mr Alan Grady,' he said.

'My sisters,' I said, all excited like a young child on Christmas morning.

'Yes,' he said. 'As you say, your sisters.' He didn't go on.

'And?' I asked eagerly. 'When can I meet them?'

'There's a slight problem,' he said.

'What problem?'

'They don't believe you're their brother.'

'What?' I cried. It wasn't something that I had even considered. 'Why not?'

'They say they have documentary evidence that shows their father, Alan Charles Grady, was born in Melbourne in March 1948. I've checked with the State of Victoria records office,' Lachie said. 'Alan Charles Grady was indeed born in the Royal Melbourne hospital on 15 March 1948. I have a copy of his birth certificate.' He removed a folded sheet of paper from his jacket pocket and handed it over.

Mr John Smith, or whoever he was, had told me in my car near Stratford that my father's 'Alan Grady' birth certificate had been genuine, but I hadn't really believed him.

'It must be a fake,' I said. 'Or else my father must have stolen the identity of the real Alan Grady.'

'I've checked in the register of deaths,' Lachie said. 'No one called Alan Charles Grady who had that birthday has been recorded as dying.'

'Perhaps he died somewhere else, not in Australia,' I said. 'Maybe on the ship where my father worked.'

I looked at the birth certificate. Both of Alan Grady's parents were named, together with their addresses and occupations.

'How about these parents shown on the certificate?' I asked.

'Both dead,' said Lachie. 'I checked. It seems they both died in the swine flu epidemic that struck Melbourne in 1976. They were quite old by then, in their seventies. You know, they were elderly parents even when their son was born.'

'Did they have any other children?' I asked him.

'None that I could find.'

'So where does that leave me?' I asked, somewhat deflated.

'I didn't say the Grady daughters wouldn't meet you,' he said. 'Simply that they don't accept that you are their brother.'

'Oh,' I said. 'That's all right, then. I'll just have to convince them.'

Lachie Harris drove Sophie and me to Macpherson Street, in Carlton North, and pulled up outside number 312.

It was the middle property of a terrace row of single-storey houses, all with verandas and elaborate wrought-iron railings.

'Victorian,' Lachie said. 'That's Victorian by era rather than by the state we're in.' He laughed at his little joke. 'These types of properties are known as Boom Homes as they were built during the boom time of the nineteenth century. After the gold rush of the 1850s.'

'They're very pretty,' Sophie said. 'But they must be dark inside.'

The houses were long and thin from front to back and, as terrace homes, they had no windows down the sides.

'Can we see?' I asked. 'I've got the keys.' I showed him the ring and the three keys that had been in my father's rucksack.

'Ah,' said Lachie apologetically. 'I'm afraid we can't.'

'Why?' I asked. 'I am his son.'

'His daughters have taken out an injunction to prevent you entering the property.'

'They've done what!' I was astounded.

'Sorry,' said Lachie. 'These types of property are worth quite a lot these days, and the Grady daughters tend to believe that you are only here because you are after their inheritance.'

I sat there with my mouth open.

'I don't want money,' I said, exasperated. 'I want family.'

'Nevertheless,' Lachie went on. 'This whole business is going to be a legal can of worms. Alan Grady left a will and, as we all know, where there's a will there's a disgruntled relative.' He laughed again.

'But if there's a will then what's the problem?' I said. 'Surely he would have left everything to his daughters anyway.'

'The will is in the name of Alan Charles Grady,' Lachie said, 'and, according to the registry here, he's not dead. You, meanwhile, claim that the man who owned this house was your father, a Peter James Talbot, now deceased, but it doesn't say that on the property deeds.'

Now it was me who laughed. Absolutely nothing about my father was as it appeared.

'Can't we just go and have a quick peep inside?' I said. 'No one would ever know.'

'I'm afraid we can't,' he said. 'Those keys might work in the door locks but they won't be any good for the padlocks the court has had applied as well.'

'Oh,' I said, peering closely at the house, but it was too dark behind all the lacy ironwork to see the front door properly.

The earlier excitement of my arrival in Australia had evaporated completely. I felt dejected and lost. 'So what's next?' I asked miserably.

'Well, let's look on the bright side,' he said. 'The Grady girls have agreed to meet you and I have set up the meeting for tomorrow. It's Australia Day and we are going to the races.'

'Horseracing?' I asked.

'Yes, of course,' he said. 'I've arranged for us to meet them at Hanging Rock races tomorrow afternoon.'

'Are they married?' I asked, eager for knowledge. 'Do they have children?'

'Not married,' Lachie said. 'Can't say about children, but I don't think so.'

'Didn't some schoolgirls once go missing at Hanging Rock?' Sophie said. 'During a picnic.'

'That was in a film,' said Lachie. 'But it wasn't a true story.'

'What are their names?' I asked.

'What, the girls in the film?' Lachie said.

'No, silly, the Grady daughters.'

'Patricia and Shannon. Patricia's the elder. She's twenty-nine. Shannon is two years younger.'

I was absolutely astounded. My much maligned, but innocent, father had apparently named his first Australian daughter after his murdered English wife.

Lachie picked up Sophie and me from our hotel at eleven o'clock the following morning and drove us the hour and a half north-west from the city to Hanging Rock races.

'It's been a dry summer,' said Lachie as he drove past mile after mile of scorched brown farmland. 'There's a serious bushfire risk at the moment. I'm quite surprised they're even racing at Hanging Rock. They ran out of water last year and had to transfer the races to another course at Kyneton.'

'Why exactly are we meeting my sisters up here?' I asked.

'They live up this way.' It seemed like a good reason.

'How many meetings do they have a year?' I asked him.

'At Hanging Rock?'

I nodded.

'They race only two days. New Year's Day and Australia Day. It's country racing. Quite small. It's not like Flemington.'

Flemington was where the Melbourne Cup was held each November.

Hanging Rock racecourse was, indeed, no Flemington, nor a Royal Ascot either. But it was lively and bustling with people on their Australia Day out. Most of the buildings were temporary hospitality marquees and, as at Bangor-on-Dee, there was no grandstand other than a natural bank from which to watch the racing.

The racecourse was within the Hanging Rock Recreational Reserve and was dominated, as its name might suggest, by the hanging and other rocks of a five-hundred-foot-high volcanic outcrop behind the enclosures. Unlike Leicester racecourse, this one did have trees in the middle. Lots of them. Eucalyptus gum trees that would at times obscure the horses on the far side from the crowd.

And from the stewards, I thought.

Overall, it was a delightful setting, with great elm trees providing shade for the punters as they gathered round the bookmakers like the proverbial bees around the honey-pot. Gambling was gambling, the same on both sides of the globe.

Lachie had obviously spun some yarn to the Hanging Rock Racing Club because we were met at the entrance by a small delegation.

'Welcome to Hanging Rock races,' said Anthony, the club chairman, shaking my hand. 'Always a pleasure to welcome a fellow racing enthusiast from England.'

'Thank you,' I said, shaking his hand back, and feeling like a bit of a fraud.

And they had laid on lunch for the three of us in one of the marquees.

'What on earth did you tell them?' I said to Lachie in a quiet moment.

'I told them that you ran one of the biggest bookmaking firms in the UK and were looking to possibly expand over here.' He smiled broadly. 'It got us a free lunch, didn't it?'

'But how about my sisters?' I said.

'They'll be along later,' he said. 'I couldn't get them the free lunch as well, now could I?'

The lunch itself was excellent and would have easily rivalled anything served at Royal Ascot. There was even a country-and-western band appropriately called, in this land of poisonous snakes, the 'Original Snakeskins', who wandered amongst the marquees making music and entertaining the happy crowd.

We were at a table laid for ten that included the club dignitaries as well as the chairman, who was seated on the far side of Sophie. I, meanwhile, had been placed next to an official from the Australian Racing Board who, I discovered during the meal, was the head of their security service.

'I wouldn't have thought there was enough skulduggery going on at Hanging Rock to warrant the presence of the head honcho,' I said, smiling at him.

'I hope you're right,' he said. 'But I have a holiday home just down the road in Woodend. So this is my local course. And I'm not working today. I'm here simply to enjoy myself.' He took a swig of his beer.

'Busman's holiday?' I said.

'Exactly.'

We ate in silence for a while.

'Do you have any undercover staff in the security service?' I asked him quietly, while the others at the table were deep in conversation. 'Any secret investigators?'

'A few,' he said, draining his beer glass, and purposely not giving me any details.

'How about an Englishman?' I asked. 'Someone called John Smith?'

It was his turn to smile at me. 'Now, Mr Talbot, there are lots of Englishmen called John Smith.'

'This particular one was principally interested in something he called a microcoder.'

The smile disappeared from his face, but only for an instant.

'Anyone for another beer?' he said suddenly, standing up from the table holding his empty glass.

'Lovely idea,' I said, also standing up.

We walked together down to the bar at the end of the marquee, leaving the others at the table.

'What do you know about a microcoder?' he asked me intently. The busman's holiday was over. This was now a work day after all.

'That it is used to write fake RFID identification chips.'

'Oh, God,' he said, clearly disturbed. 'Do you know where it is?'

'Not any more,' I said. 'I did have it in England, but I gave it to this Mr John Smith.'

I could tell that the head of Australian racing security wasn't at all pleased to hear that. Not one little bit. 'For God's sake, why did you give it to him?'

'Because he told me he worked for *you*,' I said in my defence. 'But he also told me you'd deny it.'

'I do deny it,' said the security man. 'If he's the person I think he is, then he did use to work for us. At least, we thought he did, but about a year ago we began to suspect that he'd been abusing his position by investigating only those people who wouldn't pay him handsomely to overlook things. There probably wouldn't have been enough hard evidence to win a court case, but we fired him nevertheless, and we also banned him from all Australian racecourses. We've since discovered that he was involved in a group that was switching horses using fake ID chips. Horses were being killed.'

'For the insurance money?' I asked.

'Yes,' he said, surprised that I knew. 'Some illegal off-course bookmakers were also involved in the scam.'

I decided that it would not really be a good time to tell him that my father had been one of those illegal bookmakers.

'We feared he was up to the same tricks back in the UK,' the security man said. 'And now you've just confirmed it.'

'What's his real name?' I asked.

He was clearly reluctant to tell me. His very occupation was one of investigation and secrecy, and he was plainly much more accustomed to gathering information than releasing it. 'We're still investigating the affair here, and we are trying desperately to recover the device before it's used again.'

'I wouldn't bother if I were you,' I said.

'Why on earth not?' he demanded somewhat crossly.

'The microcoder doesn't work any more.' I smiled at him and thought back to how Luca had taken his Stanley knife to the printed circuit boards. 'I made some significant and incurable alterations to its circuitry before I gave it away.'

'But why?' he asked.

'Because I didn't altogether trust Mr John Smith.'

The head of Australian racing security thought for a moment and then smiled back at me. 'I think you mean, you didn't altogether trust Mr Ivan Feldman.'

'Ivan Feldman,' I repeated slowly, almost to myself. So that was Mr John Smith's real name. 'I wonder if he's any relation to Henry Richard Feldman of HRF Holdings Ltd.'

I decided that he probably was. A son, maybe.

My sisters were to join us in the marquee for afternoon tea, and Lachie went away after lunch to collect them. Presently, I saw him waiting in the doorway. Most of the official party had left by this time, gone off to do other things like watch the races, make presentations to the winners, or chase the kangaroos away from the finishing straight.

I waved Lachie in and he was followed closely by two young women, both of them with brown hair and high cheekbones, just like me.

I didn't need to convince them that I was their brother. They both knew instantly that it was true. The three of us looked so much alike. Introductions weren't necessary. We simply hugged one another and cried.

Finally, I managed to introduce them to Sophie, who was also in tears.

'Ned has always wanted sisters,' she said to them, wiping her eyes.

I was simply too overcome with emotion to say anything.

Sophie turned to me. 'And they're going to be aunties as well,' she said, crying huge tears of joy. 'Because I'm pregnant.'